RISE OF THE THRALL LORD

PROTECTORS OF
PEN WICK

BOOK TWO

F.P. SPIRIT

Copyright @ 2021 F. P. Spirit
Cover Art by Jackson Tjota
Cover Design by Amalia Chitulescu
Interior Design by Designs by Shannon
Edited by Sandra Nguyen
ISBN 978-1-7364377-2-8

Thanks to Tim for creating the world of Thac, and to Daniel, Eric, Jeff, John, Mark, and Matt for their roles in bringing the characters to life. Also, thanks to the rest of my friends and family who gave their time and support in the creation of this book.

BOOKS BY F.P. SPIRIT

The Heroes of Ravenford

Ruins on Stone Hill

Serpent Cult

Dark Monolith

Princess of Lanfor

The Baron's Heart

Rise of the Thrall Lord

City of Tears

Protectors of Penwick

TABLE OF CONTENTS

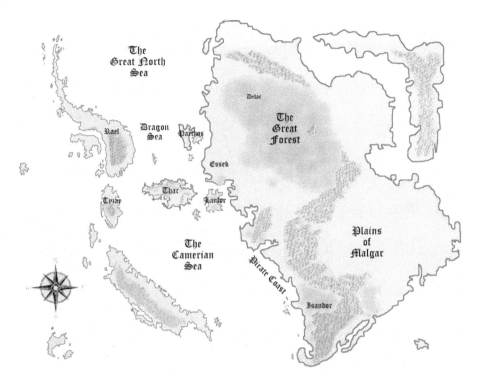

Penwick has suffered three invasions in the last one hundred and fifty years. The first to invade the city were the armies of the Golem Master during the time of the Thrall Wars. The second invaders were the Parthians, who occupied Penwick during the War of Ash. The last invasion occurred only twenty years ago when the Clans of the Coast, led by the Warlord Eboneye, raided the city. During each occupation, the invaders seemed to be seeking some hidden treasure in, or around, Penwick. Many such legends exist, the city itself having been built upon older cities of unknown origin. To this day, whatever they were searching for remains a secret along with Penwick's mysterious past...

- Lady Lara Stealle, High Wizard of Penwick

1
WELCOME TO PENWICK

This huge group had just teleported into the very heart of Penwick!

It was late morning in the Lord's Square, and the sun had nearly reached its zenith in the pale blue skies overhead. The heat
emanating from the golden orb beat down on the white cob-
blestones of the wide plaza and the reddish-brown rooftops
of the large halls that encircled it. To the east, beyond a high
wall of gray stone, the bright summer rays glinted off the tall alabaster spires of Avernos Keep.

The sights, sounds, and smells of city life assailed the senses of
the small group that popped into its midst from out of nowhere.
Numerous folks bustled about, intermingled with riders and horse-
drawn carriages. The aroma of various foods wafted across the expansive square from numerous carts set up around its edges. A cacophony of voices, hoofbeats, whistles, and other noises surrounded
them on all sides.

Lloyd Stealle drank in the familiar sight with a combination of surprise and relief. It had only been a few months since he left home, but it felt more like years. So much had happened in that short amount of time that he was not the same green youth who had left this bustling city behind.

Case in point—he and his friends had just wrested the Marsh Tower, and the powerful crystal held therein, from an army of undead. It had been no small feat, but an even greater task now lay before them. A second tower and its crystal had fallen to a horde of demons, and they needed to be stopped before their numbers swelled into a full-blown invasion of Thac.

Lloyd felt a delicate touch on his arm. He turned to see a pair of electric-blue eyes staring up at him. "Are we in Penwick?"

Andrella Avernos was a striking young woman with a keen intelligence and the wit to match. The daughter of former Baron and Baroness of Ravenford, Andrella also happened to be Lloyd's newly promised fiancée.

Lloyd felt suddenly foolish. He should have realized the others wouldn't necessarily recognize the city. A sheepish grin spread across his lips, his free hand going to the back of his neck. "Well, yeah."

"It would appear Elistra doesn't quite know her own strength," a familiar voice murmured behind them. Lloyd glanced over Andrella's head toward a tall elf in pale purple robes. Glolindir wore a bemused expression, though Lloyd could see a trace of pain in his eyes.

Glo's love, the psychic Elistra, had used the incredible power of the tower crystal to teleport them here. Unfortunately, Elistra had stayed behind to master the crystal—a necessary precaution if they were to keep that tower from also falling into the demons' hands.

Seth folded his arms across his chest, the halfling's tone practically dripping with sarcasm. "So, are we just going to stand here all day, or what?"

"Well, since we're here, we might as well try and talk to the Penwick Council, to see if we can get their support," Aksel surmised, the little gnome cleric as pragmatic as ever.

"From what I've heard, I don't think that's going to be all that easy, even if Lloyd's parents are members," Elladan chimed in, a half-smile adorning the elven bard's handsome face.

Lloyd let out a heavy sigh. Elladan was not wrong. Murky politics divided the governing body of Penwick. Even though the Baron had final say, he was not a strong leader. Thus the smooth-tongued words of those who opposed Lloyd's parents tended to sway his opinion.

"Speaking of your mother and father, when do I get to meet them?" Lloyd peered down to see Andrella gazing up at him expectantly.

"Um, now?" Lloyd responded after a moment, sounding perhaps a bit more surprised than he intended.

"Well then, let's go!" Bubbling with enthusiasm, Andrella ignored his momentary lapse. She laced her arm through his and started off across the plaza, only to stop short when confronted with the crowd that had formed around them.

Lloyd followed the crowd's gaze back toward the group that had teleported here with them. His eyes swept over Glo, Aksel, Elladan, Donatello, Cyclone, Kara, Ves, Ruka, Sir Renardo, and Sir Stolay, until they finally settled on the large dragon, Calipherous.

Lloyd slapped himself on the forehead. Of course they were drawing a crowd. This huge group had just teleported into the very heart of Penwick! The city had magical wards in place to protect against such things, but Elistra's use of the tower crystal must have overpowered them.

Well, as my mother would say, first things first, Lloyd thought to himself. Calipherous' sizable horned head stuck out like a sore thumb above the others. Warm coppery scales covered most of his body, speckled here and there with small spots of teal blue. The large bat-like wings that sprang from his back remained folded close to his muscular body, tapering down almost to the tip of his long, sinuous tail.

Unlike the dragon sisters, Ves and Ruka, Cal had never learned to shapeshift into human form. Ves, being the sensible one of her sisters, approached the copper dragon and placed a gentle hand on his snout. "Cal, maybe you should meet us at the temple?"

The Temple of the Ralnai lay on the other side of the Penderbun River, just past Castle Avernos. The huge walled-in complex would be the perfect place for a large dragon to avoid the crowds.

"Yes, I believe you are right," Cal rumbled in his deep voice. Without another word he spread his wings. The graceful wedge-shaped appendages stretched to a width greater than Cal himself. The crowd backed away as those wings began to slowly beat, stirring up the dust from the square around them.

The large dragon rose about a dozen yards into the air, then deftly swiveled toward the east. With a single great beat of his wings, he took off like a shot toward the keep and then past it.

Whew, Lloyd let out a sigh of relief. That was one problem solved. Now they needed to extricate themselves from this crowd before the town guards arrived. Lloyd would explain the situation to his mother and she would square things away with the city.

A wan smile crossed Lloyd's lips as he yelled to his friends over the din, "We should probably get going! Follow me and I'll take you to an inn where you all can get some rooms!"

"Sounds good to me," Kara exclaimed, the tall lady warrior wiping the dust off her dark armor. "I could use a good hot bath."

Lloyd half expected a flirtatious remark from Donnie, but the sandy-haired elf remained uncharacteristically silent. He had been in a dark mood since their last battle, where he had been forced to kill their old friend Alana. She had been turned into a vampire, leaving him little choice. Though they were all saddened by the tragic event, Donnie had taken it extra hard.

Lloyd exhaled a deep breath. They'd all been through so much already and the gods only knew what the future held for them. A sudden squeeze of his arm brought Lloyd's attention back to Andrella. The bright smile that lit up her face warmed him to his very soul.

Feeling invigorated, Lloyd began pushing his way through the crowd. "This way, everyone."

Vestiralana ta Yatharia Greymantle had never felt fear before—well, at least not for herself. She had always been willing to do anything and risk everything for those she loved.

Ves had not been scared by the petty little Princess of Lanfor's attempts at mind control. Nor had she been afraid to face Theraxia, the huge red dragon who could have snapped her in half. She hadn't even batted an eye at battling the undead dragon that couldn't be killed.

Yet now she knew there were things worse than death. What Theramon had done to her frightened Ves to her very core. Even now, despite the ejection of his dark seed, she still felt as if a shadow hung over her soul.

Mired in thought, the young lady dragon followed along, absently twisting the ends of her long golden hair as Lloyd led them through the streets of Penwick. She barely noticed as they passed the tall white towers of Avernos Keep. She paid little heed as they crossed the arched stone bridge over the wide, azure waters of the Penderbun River. She hardly blinked at the stark grey tower that rose above the Hault School of Magic and Wizardry.

None of these sights phased Ves until the golden-capped spires of the Temple of the Ralnai came into view. The temple itself was set back into a wide complex surrounded by a tall outer wall.

As soon as Ves saw the temple grounds, she halted in her tracks.

"What are you stopping for?" a gruff voice sounded behind her.

Cyclone stood with his arms folded, staring impatiently at her. She had initially been leery of this rugged human—after all, he hunted her kind. Nevertheless, he had proven to be a valiant, if unlikely, ally. In fact, Cyclone had put his own life on the line in their bitter struggle with an undead dragon.

"My apologies," Ves responded, politely moving out of his way.

Ruka stepped out of the line with her. "What's wrong, Ves?"

Ves looked over the young teen as she debated how to answer. Even with her sandy hair and emerald green eyes, one could easily see the resemblance between them. Yet their temperaments were vastly different. Where Ves did her best to be calm and diplomatic, Ruka seemed to revel in being irritable and sarcastic.

The young lady wanted so desperately to talk to someone, but she couldn't bring herself to burden her sister. Aside from their differences, Ves was the oldest and thus responsible for both of her sisters. She had to be strong; she couldn't show weakness in front of either one of them. "Nothing. I... was just wondering if Thea would be at the temple."

Thea Stealle was a Priestess of Arenor, the Ralnain God of Light. She had been the one to discover the dark seed implanted within Ves. All things considered, she might be the best person for Ves to confide in.

"My sister lives in the rectory these days. You'll most likely find her there or in the temple."

Ves gazed toward the front of the line to see Lloyd peering at her. The rest of the companions had stopped behind him and were now staring her way. Ves wrung her hands together, suddenly feeling quite self-conscious. "Please don't wait on my account. I'm going to stop here at the temple for a while."

"I think I'll join you," Aksel chimed in.

"Us, as well," the holy knights Stolay and Renardo agreed.

Ves hadn't expected any company on this side journey of hers. Now that she had made up her mind, she wanted to talk to Thea alone. Still, she couldn't be rude to these people who had been so good to her and her family.

A wan smile crossed Ves' lips. "That would be nice."

Lloyd gave them directions to the inn, then started off with the others in tow. Ruka lagged behind, eyeing her sister intently. "Are you sure you're okay?"

"I'm fine," Ves lied. "Now go."

Ruka eyed her a moment more, then shrugged and headed off after the others.

While Ves had been talking to the others, Aksel and the knights had already started toward the entrance to the temple grounds. What she hadn't expected to see was Cyclone leaning against the outer wall, his muscular arms folded across his chest.

The hunter stared at her with those keen blue eyes as if he could see into her very soul. "Sure you are."

Ves was taken aback. This human never showed emotions other than anger. What could he possibly know about how she felt? "What makes you say that?"

"Hmph," Cyclone huffed. "I ain't blind."

Ves arched an eyebrow. Perhaps she had misjudged this human. Maybe there was more depth to him than people gave him credit for.

After a moments debate, she decided to let her guard down just a bit. "I need to be stronger."

"Why?" Cyclone asked brusquely.

The question was so simple that it caught Ves off guard. She struggled with how to answer this exceedingly direct human when he surprised her yet again.

"Let me guess. It has to do with that Theramon creep."

"Yes." Ves nodded, her eyes dropping to the ground. She felt so ashamed, but she couldn't seem to shake this feeling of dread that hung over her.

"Tsk," Cyclone clicked his tongue. "Ain't nothing to be embarrassed about. That jerk's unnatural."

Something about the hunter's words made Ves feel better. He was right; this Theramon wasn't normal. She lifted her gaze, the trace of a smile spreading across her lips. "Perhaps you're right."

"I usually am." Cyclone laughed as he pushed off the wall. He now stood very close to her.

Strangely, Ves found she didn't mind. This human was different from the rest. "So what do you suggest?"

Cyclone shrugged. "We could train together."

Ves mulled over the idea. The hunter was strong. He also exhibited dragon-like qualities at times—bronze dragon, specifically, just like her and her sisters. *Perhaps it could work.*

She met his gaze evenly. "I accept."

"Good," Cyclone agreed. "I'll search for a place outside of town where we can train away from prying eyes." He strode away without another word.

Ves felt oddly better as she watched him go. Something about his self-assuredness resonated with her. She wanted to be more like that.

Ves let out a deep sigh, then strode up to the temple gate and into the grounds beyond.

Althea Kitren Stealle felt at peace for the first time in a very long time. Her life had changed dramatically after the tragedy on Thorn Isle. Thea had lost all her childhood friends, as well as her innocence, but in turn found Arenor. Joining the clergy, she threw herself into the study of the divine.

The road had not been an easy one, but Thea was no stranger to hard work. Furthermore, her studies in the art of the spiritblade had opened her awareness to life beyond the veil. Thus, in four short but demanding years, Thea earned the coveted title of Auric Priestess. Having just recently passed the tests, she now devoted much of her time to contemplation in the Chapel of Arenor.

Situated behind the Temple of the Ralnai, the chapel was easily the size of a small-town temple. A life-sized statue of Arenor stood in the alcove above the main altar. Two vestibules opened up on either side, the one opposite from Thea dedicated to Phobas, the original God of Light. The one in which Thea currently prayed was dedicated to Arenor in his earlier role as the Hand of Light.

As Thea knelt before the small altar, communing with the light about her new standing and responsibilities, she heard someone whisper her name.

"Thea."

Just a few feet behind her stood Vestiralana Greymantle. Garbed in a shimmering silk bronze dress, the young lady waited for her with a quiet poise that belied the terrible deed that had recently been forced upon her.

Her prayers all but forgotten, Thea sprang up and grasped each of the young lady's hands. Despite the long, golden-blonde hair and blue-green eyes, the resemblance between Ves and Ruka caught her off guard. A sudden chill went up Thea's spine as a vivid flashback of the events on Thorn Isle played through her mind.

"I'm sorry. I didn't mean to startle you." Ves sounded mortified.

Mentally chiding herself, Thea forced the vision away and gave the young lady the warmest smile she could muster. "That's alright. I'm glad to see you. How are you feeling?"

"It's gone," Ves murmured in a voice so soft that Thea could barely hear her.

"Gone?" Thea repeated, not sure she had heard correctly.

Using her spirit vision, Thea peered beyond the veil and into the next plane. Though enveloped by a huge aura, Thea could indeed find no trace of the dark seedling that had been implanted in the midst of Ves' energetic body. Pulling her vision back, however, she did note a darkness hanging just at the edges of the young lady's aura.

Sweeping her gaze around the small chamber, Thea noted they were alone. She pulled Ves down into the nearest pew and said in a hushed tone, "Tell me everything."

Thea listened with rapt attention to Ves' explanation. The Empress had used the tower crystal to create a dark version of Ves. In doing so, she had unintentionally pulled the seed out of her. In the end, Ves had slain her dark doppelganger.

"I suppose I should feel better," Ves paused a moment as mixed emotions played across her face, "but I still feel violated." That last word was said so softly that again Thea could barely hear it.

Thea's heart went out to this brave young woman. She herself had nearly been violated four years ago on Thorn Isle. It had been a horrific experience, one she barely escaped. Despite that, she couldn't imagine what to say to help this tortured soul. So she prayed.

The answer came to her immediately as clear as if Arenor were standing right next to her. *This is what you trained for, Thea—to help souls in need just like this.*

It was exactly the phrase she needed to hear. With a silent *thank you,* she resumed her discussion with Ves, hoping to help the tormented woman lift the darkness that hung over her soul.

Andrella Avernos felt mixed emotions as she waited in the foyer of the Lucky Heroes Inn. She hadn't realized what a sheltered life she'd led back in Ravenford. Andrella had experienced so many new things in the short time since she left, both terrible and wonderful.

Andrella felt horrible for Donnie, having to slay his former love Alana like that. She couldn't begin to imagine what he was going through. Andrella was also worried for Ves. What Theramon had done to her was unforgivable. She fervently hoped that Ves found whatever answers she sought at the Temple of the Ralnai.

Still, despite her concerns, Andrella could not help but feel excited. She was engaged, after all, and about to meet Lloyd's parents.

Yet beneath her excitement lurked more than just a touch of nerves. *What if his parents don't like me?*

The young lady looked anxiously over her outfit, a golden-laced scarlet dress with matching bodice and boots. Known as a *Regalia of the Phoenix*, the magical artifact boosted her fire spells and granted her immunity to fire. Although quite handy for adventuring, it wasn't exactly what she imagined herself wearing to meet Lloyd's parents.

Lifting her gaze, Andrella spied Lloyd at the front desk congenially chatting up the innkeeper. A warm smile spread across her lips, her anxiousness momentarily forgotten. His tousled brown hair, youthful face, and well-muscled physique presented an extremely attractive package. Moreover, though a dynamo on the battlefield, he was actually quite the gentleman.

Andrella found this all very appealing – even more so that he appeared to be growing out of his shell. He had all the markings of being a fine ruler someday, someone she could trust to govern by her side.

"Copper piece for your thoughts?"

Roused from her musings, Andrella found Glo standing beside her. The young lady gave him a feeble smile. "Not sure they're worth that. Just daydreaming is all."

Glo matched her expression. "I know the feeling. I'm afraid I'll be doing a lot of that until I can see Elistra again."

A keen wave of sympathy washed over the young lady. Circumstances and misguided intentions had separated the couple once before. Glo and Elistra had just managed to patch things up when events forced them apart again.

Andrella placed a tentative hand on Glo's arm. "I think it would do you good to concentrate on something else." A sudden idea struck her. "I know, why don't you come with us?"

Glo arched a single eyebrow at her. "Come with you to meet Lloyd's parents? Wouldn't I just be in the way?"

Before she could answer, Lloyd came striding across the room toward them. "Well everyone's got a room now. Are you ready to go?"

Andrella nudged her head toward Glo. "Will you please tell him that it's okay if he comes with us?"

A frown crossed Lloyd's brow, but his eyes lit up as he peered at Glo. "Oh yes, of course. My mom would love to meet a fellow wizard, especially one who's seen all the things that you have."

Glo eyed his friend with skepticism. "Are you certain?"

Andrella squeezed Glo's arm. "I insist."

Glo gazed from her to Lloyd and back again, then shrugged. "Very well."

The three of them started toward the door when Andrella remembered her dress. She grabbed her skirt and exclaimed, "Oh no. I can't meet your parents looking like this!"

Lloyd placed a strong arm around her shoulders. "What are you talking about? You look beautiful."

Andrella almost melted then and there. She touched his face ever so gently. "You are definitely getting better at this," she peered back down at her dress, "but honestly, it's my first time seeing your parents. I need to make a good impression."

"I think I can help with that," Glo interrupted them.

Andrella narrowed an eye at the wizard. "You can? How?"

In answer, Glo traced his hands through the air in a vaguely familiar pattern. She felt a slight amount of mana build up until he released it with two soft words. *"Mutare speciem."*

Andrella felt the magic encircle her and watched with fascination as her clothes changed appearance. When the spell finished, she found herself garbed in the same fine emerald gown she had worn when she first met Lloyd and the others.

Andrella looked herself over from every angle she could manage. When she was done, she gave the wizard a grateful smile. "This will do very nicely."

The corner of Glo's mouth lifted ever so slightly. "Glad you like it."

Lloyd wore a puzzled expression. "What happened to her phoenix dress?"

Andrella exchanged a glance with Glo and laughed. "Oh, I'm still wearing it. Glo just changed its appearance is all."

Lloyd cocked his head to one side. "Oh, I get it. It's like a disguise spell, but you only used it on her clothes."

Glo touched the side of his nose with his finger. "Exactly."

Grinning from ear to ear, Andrella laced her arms through Lloyd's and Glo's. "Very well then. Let's get going."

The trio marched off together down the road and toward the gate that led out of the city.

2
LUNCH WITH THE IN-LAWS

"Let me guess—she's up in her lab."

So what's your home like?" Andrella asked, her voice tinged with just a touch of nervousness.

Lloyd shrugged. "It's a typical ranch. There's the main house, a couple of barns…"

Glolindir half-listened to the conversation as the trio rode up the coast. The lush green trees of a small forest paralleled the road along the one side, while the steep drop-off of a tall cliff ran along the other. The sound of crashing waves drifted up from far below, the azure waters of the sea stretching out to meet the horizon.

Given the choice, Glo would have preferred to walk, basking in the sun and the beauty of nature along the way. Unfortunately, Lloyd's home lay two miles up the road, and Andrella refused to accumulate "road dust" on the way. Thankfully, a stable sat just outside the city gates and they were able to hire out some horses for the day.

Andrella let out a low whistle as Lloyd finished describing his home. "That's a typical ranch? It sounds more like an estate." Her expression turned wistful. "It must have been fun growing up there."

Lloyd rubbed the back of his neck. "Sort of. I mean, it was at times, but it's a lot of work keeping a ranch running. Not that we did it all ourselves—my parents employ a ton of ranch hands. Once I started training with my dad, though, I had almost no time to myself."

Glo attempted to follow the conversation, but try as he might, his thoughts continued to wander elsewhere. Their success at the Marsh Tower in the City of Tears had come at a cost. The deaths of Alana and Sir Craven had been a blow to them all, but Glo couldn't even begin to imagine what Donnie was going through. He wondered if his friend would ever be the same.

Furthermore, Ves didn't seem right. Glo thought being rid of Theramon's influence would have made her whole again. Yet, he could still see a trace of darkness hanging over her just beyond plain sight.

Andrella's brow knit into a frown. "I thought you liked being a spiritblade?"

Lloyd gave her a sheepish smile. "Oh, I do, but trust me, it can be exhausting."

Andrella's eyes danced with amusement as her lips formed into a wry smile. "Most things are that are worth it."

Lloyd's choking roused Glo from his somber thoughts. The young man's cheeks had turned a bright shade of scarlet.

"Sorry." Andrella giggled, her entire face lit with mirth. She reached over, their eyes meeting as she grabbed her fiancé by the hand.

Glo could almost feel the electricity pass between the two. It immediately made him think of Elistra.

Parting from the seeress again had been extremely difficult for the young elf. Their recent reconciliation had healed a part of him that he didn't even realize was broken. Yet now it felt as if a piece of him had been ripped away.

Still, Elistra had not made the choice lightly. The very survival of Arinthar hung in the balance. Glo only recently discovered just how much his immortal love had sacrificed for their world. He had promised her that from then they would be in this together. Thus he supported her decision and even offered to stay with her at the tower in the marshes. Unfortunately, Elistra had seen a different path for him, one equally as critical to their success.

"There it is!"

Lloyd's excited cry stirred Glo from his solemn musings. They had reached a summit in the road. Spread out below them lay an immense plot of fenced-in land.

"Oh my," Andrella's breath caught in her throat. "That has to be at least ten times the area of Ravenford Keep."

Lloyd grinned back at her. "It's pretty big for around here, but I've heard there are much bigger ranches on the mainland."

Andrella exchanged a knowing glance with Glo. Lloyd didn't have a vain bone in his body. He never let compliments go to his head, always pointing out someone or something better than himself.

"Well I, for one, can't wait to see it," Andrella assured her unassuming fiancé.

The three of them spurred on their horses and trotted down the road toward the Stealle estate. The road split at the bottom of the rise, one branch continuing up the coast while the other headed directly for Lloyd's home. They followed the latter, eventually coming to a tall, framed gate that spanned their path. Across the top beam hung a sign that read, *Chateau De Stealle.*

Lloyd wore a wistful expression as they rode through the open gate. "Home sweet home."

Glo empathized with his friend. Nearly half a year had passed since the young elf left home. Sometimes Glo wished he could go back, if only for a brief visit. Cairthrellon, however, lay halfway across Thac, and much still needed to be done here in the outside world.

The main buildings of the Stealle estate stood far back from the gate. The trio set forth, barely making it half the distance when another rider trotted out to meet them.

A lean, muscular man sat tall in the saddle of a beautiful brown and white paint. The rider wore a bright scarlet uniform indicative of the armed forces of Penwick.

"Father!" Lloyd cried in excitement, spurring his horse forward.

Glo could not help but smile at his friend's reaction. The young man had no qualms about showing his emotions. Glo traded a mirthful glance with Andrella before the two of them followed suit.

Reaching his father first, Lloyd reined his mount in and practically leapt from his saddle. Lloyd's father did the same, the two men rushing into a fierce embrace.

Kratos Stealle stood even in height with his towering son. The resemblance between the two was uncanny, but where Lloyd had brown hair, Kratos' was jet black. Though still youthful in appearance, Glo noted a trace of grey in the older man's temples.

Kratos grabbed Lloyd by the shoulders, his eyes narrowing as he looked his son over. "Lloyd, my boy, you've grown. Not in height, mind you," a subtle laugh escaped his lips, "but I can definitely see a change in you."

An embarrassed smile spread across Lloyd's face. "Well, a lot has happened since I left."

Kratos pressed his lips together and nodded. "So I've heard."

As Glo and Andrella dismounted, the elder Stealle shifted his attention to them. "And these are a couple of your new companions, I trust?"

Lloyd nudged his head toward Glo. "This is my friend Glolindir, Father. He is a wizard from the lost city of Cairthrellon."

Glo found Lloyd's choice of the term 'lost' quite amusing. The city was actually hidden away behind magical barriers from the rest of the world. Still, he wasn't the type to correct his friend.

"Well met," Glo said, extending his hand to Lloyd's father. He immediately regretted it. Kratos' grip was as vicelike as Lloyd's.

Thankfully, Kratos failed to notice his discomfort, instead appearing impressed. "An elven wizard from Cairthrellon? My wife is definitely going to want to meet you."

"And who is this ravishing young lady?" Kratos said, turning his attention to Andrella.

Lloyd took Andrella by the hand and presented her to Kratos. "This is the Lady Andrella Avernos, Father," he paused for an instant before adding, "my fiancée."

Caught off guard, Kratos was rendered momentarily speechless.

Andrella, ever the diplomat, filled the void in the conversation with a perfect curtsey. "It is a pleasure to meet you, sir."

Kratos' face exploded into a wide grin. "Sir will just not do. You may call me Father, my dear." He stepped forward and embraced the young lady.

Andrella practically melted in his arms. "Thank you... Father."

Kratos stepped back and beamed at the couple. "My, my, our little Lloyd is engaged. Just wait until your mother finds out."

The elder Stealle abruptly slapped himself on the forehead. "Where are my manners! Please follow me back to the house. Lara will want to meet you both, and while we're at it you can join us for lunch."

"That would be very nice, Father," Andrella responded politely.

"We do have a lot to tell you," Lloyd added.

They all remounted and followed Kratos back to their ranch home.

Andrella felt as if there were butterflies in her stomach. She had been somewhat apprehensive to meet Lloyd's dad, the celebrated Hero of Penwick, Admiral of the Penwick Navy, founder of the Stealle Academy of the Sword, and a member of the city council. Kratos, however, turned out to be absolutely charming. Now came the hard part, though—meeting Lloyd's mom.

Lara Stealle was no less accomplished than her husband. She not only held the title of High Wizard of Penwick, but had formed the Hault School of Magic and Wizardry, and also sat on the city council. Andrella worried that someone like Lara would want an accomplished spouse for her son, yet Andrella had no such achievements to her name.

The Chateau de Stealle did little to calm her nerves. A sprawling u-shaped grey stone structure, the center section of the main house stood three stories tall. A pair of short towers rose on either side of the front entrance, with a steep-dormered roof that swept upward from the first floor. A two-story wing jutted out on either side of the main house, forming a small courtyard out front. While certainly not the size of Ravenford Keep, it appeared to be a very luxurious estate.

The inside of the house proved equally impressive. The entrance opened into a large foyer with a vaulted ceiling and a rich marble-tiled floor. A circular stairwell rose up along one wall to an open hallway on the second floor.

Kratos led them across the house to an expansive room with a deep mahogany-grained décor. Multiple couches and chairs lay spread across the room. Some faced a huge open hearth, while others sat opposite a bank of windowed doors with a breathtaking view of the surrounding lands.

Kratos bade them to make themselves comfortable. "If you don't mind waiting here, I'll go get Lara."

The corner of Lloyd's mouth lifted slightly. "Let me guess—she's up in her lab."

Kratos responded with an ironic smile to match his son's. "Where else would she be?"

Unable to stop fidgeting, Andrella went to peer out the back doors. A lush carpet of green grass spread out in all directions. Groves of tall trees stood interspersed throughout the landscape. A range of purple mountains rose off in the distance against a background of deep blue sky.

Andrella breathed a deep sigh. *It really is beautiful here.*

A pair of strong arms wrapped themselves around her waist. She peered over her shoulder to see Lloyd grinning down at her. "This used to be my favorite place to sit when I was a kid."

Andrella tapped him on the chin with her finger. "Somehow I can't imagine young Lloyd ever sitting."

"Touché," Lloyd responded with a laugh.

Andrella's nerves had just begun to settle when a new voice called out from behind them. "Lloyd!"

Andrella whirled around to see a woman in fine royal blue robes standing in the doorway. While the top of her head barely reached to her husband's nose, Lara Stealle nonetheless presented an imposing figure. Time had not detracted a bit from this woman's beauty. Her skin showed a rose-colored complexion with just the hint of freckles.

Long, straight light-brown hair draped down over her shoulders, and her piercing blue eyes sparkled with a keen intelligence.

Andrella felt quite self-conscious as Lloyd rushed across the room to greet her. The two of them briefly embraced, then Lara laced her arm through Lloyd's. They crossed over to Andrella, stopping a few feet from the now absolutely nervous young lady.

Lara held her gaze for a moment, although to Andrella it felt more like an eternity. She was certain those piercing blue eyes would see through to the fraud she was underneath—a totally vapid young woman with no true substance to speak of.

Finally, a warm smile spread across Lara's lips. "Lloyd, who is this absolutely stunning young lady?"

Lloyd grinned as he took Andrella by the hand. "Mom, I'd like you to meet my fiancée, the Lady Andrella Avernos."

"Pleased to meet you…"

Before Andrella cold finish, Lara stepped forward and embraced her wholeheartedly. "Welcome to the family, my dear."

All the nervousness Andrella had previously felt melted away in that moment. Lara laced her arm through hers and leveled a stare at her husband and son. "It will be so nice to have another daughter in this house full of men."

Almost as if choreographed, both father and son peered at the ground. An embarrassed smile crossed their faces as they rubbed the back of their necks in unison.

Andrella did her best to suppress a laugh. *Like father, like son.*

"And who is this fine young elf?" Lara's attention quickly shifted.

In her anxious state, Andrella had nearly forgotten about Glo. The tall elf had also drifted across the room and stood at one of the back doors.

A now thoroughly embarrassed Lloyd swiftly introduced their elven friend.

"*Elen sila lumenn omentilmo,*" Lara addressed Glo in a formal voice.

Andrella immediately recognized the language as elvish. Though not certain of the full meaning, she caught the words *star*, *shine*, and *meeting*.

Apparently impressed, Glo responded in an equally formal tone. "*Saesa omentien lle.*"

Andrella knew that one. It meant a *pleasure meeting you.*

Lara pressed her lips together. "So you are from the lost city of Cairthrellon? I will definitely need to pick your brain, young sir."

Glo gave her a slight smile and a nod. "It would be my pleasure, Lady Stealle."

Without warning, a grumbling sound emanated from Lloyd's abdomen. Lara peered at her son and laughed gaily. "I see some things never change."

She patted Andrella on the arm. "Come on, my dear. We better feed these gentlemen before they starve to death."

Glolindir found himself absolutely mesmerized by the natural splendor of the Stealle estate. While not set in the midst of a forest like his home, the surrounding grasslands and intermittent groves held a beauty all their own.

Kratos and Lara also proved to be quite interesting. Though both had larger-than-life reputations, neither came across as pretentious. On the contrary, they seemed quite friendly and down to earth. Glo supposed he shouldn't have been surprised considering Lloyd's good nature and tendency to treat everyone as equals.

Kratos leaned close to Glo as they followed Lara into the kitchen. "I'd like to thank you for watching out for our Lloyd. I have to admit, we were a bit worried when he headed out all on his own."

A soft chuckle escaped Glo's lips. "To be honest, Lloyd watched after us as much as we did him."

"As it should be with all good friends." Kratos nodded approvingly.

The kitchen at Chateau de Stealle proved to be as impressive as the rest of the house. Foremost, it was quite large. Long counters and tall cabinets spanned the walls around a huge cooking hearth. A wide oak-topped island sat in the middle of the area with a number of tall chairs lined up on one side. Across the room stood a large oval oak table with seating for six.

Bright sunlight filtered through a wide window and another windowed door. All in all, the kitchen had a very homey feel.

Lara bade the men to sit down while she and Andrella prepared lunch. Glo immediately noted how uncomfortable the young lady appeared. Truth be told, in all their time on the road, Glo had never seen Andrella cook.

Kratos must have read his mind. He whispered under his breath, "Not to worry. Lara is not exactly a cook, either."

Lloyd placed a hand to the side of his mouth and added in a hushed voice, "It's usually a crap-shoot with mom. When Pallas or Thea are home, they won't let her anywhere near the kitchen."

At that same moment, Lara dumped something into a cooking pot hanging in the hearth. Whatever it was, the pot responded with a loud *poof.*

"Behave yourself," Lara scolded the lifeless pot with a wag of her finger.

Glo did his very best to suppress a laugh.

"Speaking of Pallas, where is he?" Lloyd asked his father.

"He's filling in for me as temporary head of the fleet," Kratos explained. "When Hightower warned us about those Dunwynn ships headed south, we sent some ships of our own up to Colossus Point—just in case they decided to cross the treaty line."

Glo winced at the mention of the Dunwynn ships. They had not gone further south, but instead turned upriver and ended up at the docks in Vermoorden. The companions had rushed there prepared for a fight, but managed to resolve things through a combination of diplomacy and intimidation.

"The Duke is greedy," Lloyd agreed, "but I don't think he'd cross the line and start an all-out war with Penwick."

"Perhaps this union between you and Andrella can further curb his expansionist tendencies," Kratos noted with an ironic smile.

Lloyd folded his arms and scoffed. "I'm not holding my breath."

Kratos cast a quick glance at Andrella, but the young lady seemed quite preoccupied wrestling with a knife and a bunch of carrots. "Hightower also kept us apprised of the events surrounding Gryswold and Gracelynn."

Lloyd sat back in his seat and grimaced. "Yeah, things were a bit touch-and-go there for a while."

Kratos placed a reassuring hand on his son's shoulder. "What counts is that you saved them both. Honestly, your mother and I couldn't be prouder."

Lloyd's face reddened with embarrassment. "Thanks, Dad," he mumbled.

Despite one or two more kitchen mishaps, Lara and Andrella served up a hearty stew. They all adjourned to the kitchen table, where Andrella filled up everyone's bowl. Glo noted a mild burning smell, but ate it anyway, gulping down the overdone pieces. When offered seconds, however, he held up his hand. "That was really quite—filling."

Kratos, his expression neutral, managed a covert wink in Glo's direction. Lloyd, on the other hand, accepted both seconds and thirds. Glo finally understood where the young man had developed his cast-iron stomach.

During lunch, the trio recapped their efforts in the City of Tears. They also related all they knew about the towers and the impending demon invasion.

Lara gently tapped her chin, her brow deeply furrowed. "So there are six of these towers still standing, each housing one of these powerful cruex crystals?"

"Yes." Glo gave her a solemn nod. "The seventh tower is said to have sunk with the Isle of Namlon."

Lara chewed on her lower lip. "And these crystals are fueled by the power of living souls?"

"That's what we were told," Lloyd affirmed with thinly veiled anger.

"That's barbaric!" Kratos exclaimed, slamming his hands down on the table.

Lara clucked her tongue at her husband. "Now Kratos, the Naradon Empire was not exactly known for its gentle approach to conquest."

"But the emperor's letters to the empress did seem to indicate he had a change of heart in the end," Andrella countered hopefully.

Lara pressed her lips together and slowly nodded. "Perhaps. Perhaps he even had a hand in the destruction of the seventh tower— which would explain why we're all still alive today."

Kratos rose and began to pace around the kitchen. "That won't last if these demons spread to the rest of the towers."

Lara got up as well and went over to him. She placed a hand on his arm to stop him from pacing. "This Elistra appears to have the one tower protected for now."

She peered over at Glo. "Isn't that right?"

"Indeed," Glo agreed with a heavy sigh.

Lara let go of Kratos and strode over to the door. Her expression grew thoughtful as she peered out the paned glass into the distance. "And I'd have to imagine these other towers have safeguards in place or they'd have already been taken."

Glo exchanged a subtle nod with Andrella, who in turn answered for them. "We believe so. However, the demons are using their tower and its crystal to grow their numbers..."

"...and once their forces are great enough, you fear they'll attack the other towers," Kratos finished for her.

"Yes," Andrella affirmed with a grim nod.

"Which is why we need to know more about them," Glo quickly added. "Is there really a tunnel network connecting the towers, and if so, what is this purple worm the empress seemed to be so afraid of?"

Lloyd stood and placed his hands firmly on the table. "It's also why we need to talk to the city council. We need to work fast if we're going to find weapons that can stop the demons."

Lara wheeled around to face them, her chin firm with resolve. "The Hault School has the most in-depth library this side of Palt"— she swept her gaze from Glo to Andrella—"but you have to be a member."

"Mom..." Lloyd began with clear exasperation.

She cut him or with a wry smile before he could finish. "...which is luckily something I can offer you, being Head Mistress of the school."

Glo and Andrella exchanged a grateful glance before replying in unison, "Thank you, Lady Stealle."

"As for the council, there is a meeting tonight," Kratos addressed Lloyd's point. "I'm certain we can get you in, but I'm not sure how willing they will be to help."

Lloyd looked down and shook his head as he slammed his fist into his other hand. "I know, but we have to at least try."

Lara and Kratos exchanged an approving glance. Lloyd had definitely grown in his understanding of politics.

Lara strode back to the table and swept her eyes over the trio. "I think this calls for a bit of prep work. Perhaps we should meet with your entire group and fill you in on what you are up against."

"I think that's a wonderful idea!" Andrella exclaimed.

Kratos steepled his hands together. "I have some business to attend to at the academy first. If you can inform your companions, we'll meet them at the inn where you're staying afterwards."

Lloyd cast a curious glance at Kratos. "What business, Father?"

Kratos sighed. "Nothing out of the ordinary. Just another young blade who wants to test their mettle against the original 'Protector of Penwick.'" The elder Stealle suddenly raised a brow. "I have an idea, Lloyd. Why don't you fill in for me? That way I can see what you've learned these last few months."

Lloyd beamed with pride. "I'd be honored, Father."

Andrella clasped her hands together. "Can I come as well?"

Kratos smiled at the young lady's enthusiasm. "Certainly, my dear."

"I'd be interested as well, if you don't mind," Glo added, curious to see this academy he'd heard so much about.

Kratos reached out and clasped the elf on his shoulder. "Absolutely. Any friend of Lloyd's is always welcome at the academy."

Glo felt truly touched by the gesture. In fact, the support these two seemed willing to offer was just shy of amazing. Glo found himself suddenly envious of Lloyd. While his own mother had always been supportive, his father had been the exact opposite.

After helping clean up the kitchen, the travelers gathered their things and reconvened in the foyer. Just before they left, Lara pulled Andrella aside.

"I'd like you to come back and stay with us as long as you're in town, dear."

The offer caught Andrella by surprise. "I—couldn't possibly impose like that."

"Now don't be silly," Lara insisted. "You can have one of the guest rooms in the east wing."

Andrella's face lit up with a radiant smile. "How could I possibly resist such a generous offer? Thank you, Lady Stealle…"

Lara placed a finger over Andrella's lips before she could say another word. "That's Mom, dear."

"Mom," Andrella corrected herself. She threw her arms around the older woman, both positively glowing as they embraced like mother and daughter.

3
AURIC PRIESTESS

Such priests and priestesses carried the light of Arenor inside them

The Temple of the Ralnai proved to be equally impressive on the inside. Nearly three dozen rows of seating spanned the long aisle that led to the altar. Tall, ornate, golden columns stretched upward at regular intervals to the vaulted ceiling in shades of blue that curved overhead. Two more levels rose up on either side, with further seating that reached back to the outer walls. Midday light filtered in through a myriad of tall, arched stained-glass windows, each in turn depicting one or more of the Ralnain gods in all their glory.

The altar stood on a raised semi-circular dais, surrounded on both sides with seating for clergy and choir members. A short, intricately carved railing traced the edges of the entire platform. Another aisle circled around the back of the dais, the entrance to a half-dozen small chapels radiating out from it. Inset into the wall above each chapel stood a life-sized statue of a Ralnai god.

Directly behind the altar, on a level higher than all the others, stood a statue of Arenor, the God of Light. A doorway opened just beneath the holy effigy, leading to the main chapel.

Despite having practically grown up in the Temple of the Soldenar back in Caprizon, Aksel had never seen such a vast and extravagant place of worship. Even so, there was no denying the feeling of divine power that saturated the space between these expansive walls.

Unable to resist, Aksel visited each of the smaller chapels in turn. Each one held a few rows of seats facing a portrait of a Ralnain god. An array of colored candles lay spread just beneath each portrait. Aksel lit a candle in each, then sat and communed with the Ralnai in the name of the Soldenar. Once done, he passed beneath the statue of Arenor and entered into the main chapel.

There the little cleric paused. Before him lay an area the size of a typical town temple. About a dozen rows of seating stretched before him, leading to a wide alcove. In that alcove stood an altar with another life-sized statue of Arenor above it.

Off to one side, Aksel spied a shrine dedicated to the Phobas. The original God of Light "disappeared" nearly six thousand years ago, around the end of the Third Demon War. Strangely enough, none of his followers lost faith or their divine power. Still, when Arenor rose to take his place, Phobas was slowly forgotten by the masses.

"Cleric Aksel?"

The young gnome whirled about to find Ves staring intently down at him. At just over five feet, she nonetheless towered over his diminutive frame.

Beside Ves stood a woman in pristine white robes, perhaps a full head taller than the lady dragon. The woman had an almost angelic air about her, her porcelain skin with a trace of freckles only adding to that impression. Her pale blue eyes danced with amusement as she noted the reverence on Aksel's face. "It is rather impressive, isn't it?"

Ves cleared her throat and gestured toward her new companion. "Aksel, I'd like you to meet Thea Stealle, Lloyd's sister. Thea, this is Aksel Alabaster from the city of Caprizon."

Thea pressed her hands together in front of her chest and executed a slight bow. "Well met, fellow cleric."

As she did so, Aksel's attention was drawn to the symbol embla-
zoned on her chest—a golden hand surrounded by a circle with six
rays spreading outward. The little cleric bowed in kind. "Well met,
good priestess."

That symbol identified Thea as an Auric Priestess of Arenor, a
special devotee to the God of Light. Such priests and priestesses carried the light of Arenor inside them and could expend that power to
defend against the darkness. Thus, while they made excellent healers,
they were also scourges of evil, especially the undead.

Thea straightened herself, her eyes still dancing as she brushed
the ends of her long, wavy black hair off her shoulders. "I see that
you are well-versed in theology. I can also tell from your robes that
you are a disciple of the Soldenar."

Aksel pressed his lips together, his brow rising. "I can see that
you are also well-versed. I've not met many outside of Caprizon who
are familiar with gnomish deities."

Thea's cheeks grew rosy. "Well, I believe it's important to study
the gods and goddesses of all the pantheons, be it elvish, gnomish,
human, or otherwise."

Aksel was truly impressed. Thea seemed to be as equally open-
minded as her brother. "Now I know for certain that you're Lloyd's
sister."

An ironic laugh escaped Thea's lips. "Ah yes. Well, we both suffer
from many years of Stealle indoctrination."

It was Aksel's turn to laugh. "I think this world could use a bit
more of that."

The little cleric had taken an immediate liking to this woman. Not
only was she intelligent and fair-minded, but she also had a wry sense
of humor.

"Speaking of Lloyd," Thea artfully redirected the subject, "I just
received a message from my mother. My father and brother are headed over to the academy and would like us to meet them there."

"Any idea why?" Aksel asked, his curiosity piqued.

A thin smirk graced Thea's lips. "Apparently, someone challenged
my father and Lloyd is standing in for him."

Aksel arched a single eyebrow. Lloyd standing in for his father?
That I have to see.

"You two go ahead," Ves urged them in a soft voice. "I'm going to stay here and pray for a bit longer."

Aksel noticed a slight pallor to Ves' normally well-tanned skin. Despite having thrown off Theramon's influence, she still didn't seem quite right.

Thea apparently noticed as well. She placed a hand on Ves' shoulder. "I think that's a good idea."

Aksel and Thea exchanged a wordless glance as they left their troubled friend behind. Aksel prayed that Ves could find the solace she so sorely needed somewhere within the vast walls of the temple.

Elladan Narmolanya swiftly settled into his room at the Lucky Heroes. The elven bard had traveled all over central Thac, including the great capital city of Lymerdia. Thus, the quick change in surroundings and the busy streets of Penwick hardly fazed him.

On the contrary, Elladan was far more worried about Donnie. The slight elf had been unusually quiet since the death of Alana. The two had been so close that Elladan couldn't even to begin to imagine the pain his friend was going through. Still, in all the time he had known him, Donnie had never been one to talk about his feelings. Instead, he was far more likely to soothe his problems with women and drink.

Yet this time was different. Donnie had withdrawn into himself. Elladan couldn't even get the normally gregarious elf to join him for lunch in the common room. In fact, everyone seemed preoccupied except for Seth.

Aksel and Ves had stopped at the temple. Glo had gone with Lloyd and Andrella. Cyclone and Xellos went to investigate the countryside. Kara left to message her order.

Even Ruka had declined to join them. The teen seemed more edgy than usual, since her attempt to comfort Donnie resulted in him pushing her away.

Not long after lunch, Elladan received word to meet Glo at the Stealle Academy. Someone had challenged Lloyd's father, and Lloyd was going to fight in his stead. That news roused even Donnie from his self-imposed confinement. A short while later, Elladan, Donnie, Ruka, and Seth all stood outside the school.

Ruka let out a low whistle. "Get a load of this place."

"Overcompensating much?" Seth added with a derisive snort.

These two tended to pick everything apart, but this time Elladan had to agree. The huge brownstone building that housed the Stealle Academy of the Sword took up an entire city block. Mostly a single-story structure, a tall clock tower rose high above the front entrance. A wide flight of stone stairs climbed from street level to a pair of iron-bound doors.

Glo stared down at them from the open doorway with an arched eyebrow. "Trouble finding the place?"

This time Ruka responded with a loud snort. "Finding it wasn't exactly the problem."

"The problem is that this building goes on and on forever," Seth finished for her, stretching his arms as wide as they would go.

"That's because it's more than just a glorified training hall," an unfamiliar voice stated behind them.

Aksel ascended the steps toward them with a tall woman in cleric's robes by his side. The bard's gaze was immediately drawn to the soft curve of her heart-shaped face and the glint of mirth in her pale blue eyes.

"Really? What else is there?" Elladan drawled with his most charming smile.

The woman's hands went to her hips as she met his gaze with an impish stare. "There are classrooms, workshops, meditation rooms, a good-sized library…"

"What do they study—needlepoint of the sword?" Donnie interrupted her with a boyish grin and a pretend parry with his fingers.

Elladan barely held back a groan.

Seth, on the other hand, had no such compunction. "I think I liked it better when he was sulking."

Seth had a point. As worried as Elladan had been about Donnie, he found it annoying that all it took was a pretty face to rouse him from his misery.

The woman regarded Donnie with thinly veiled amusement.

"Actually, they study many subjects at the academy, including history, spirituality, tactics, weaponry…"

"And just how do you know all this?" Donnie interrupted her once more with yet another toothy smile.

"That's Thea, Lloyd's sister, you dolt," Ruka declared with a scathing stare at the incorrigible flirt.

"Lloyd's sister?" Donnie's cheeks reddened with embarrassment. Totally flustered, he stammered awkwardly, "Um—well then—I guess that explains it."

Thea placed a hand over her mouth to stifle a laugh, then shifted her attention to the dragon teen. "Ruka, I see you haven't changed a bit."

Ruka seemed strangely reluctant to respond, her gaze shifting to the ground. "Thea. How are you?"

"I'm doing wonderful, thank you," Thea stated with clear conviction. Before Ruka could respond, Thea climbed up next to her and wrapped her arms around the teen.

Ruka stood there frozen for a moment or two, then finally raised her arms and patted Thea half-heartedly on the back. "That's—good."

"So how do you two know each other?" Glo asked curiously.

Both women gazed at him blankly before replying in unison, "Long story."

Their response practically screamed of a fascinating tale to the bard's ear, but it was quite obviously a touchy subject. Elladan decided to divert the conversation to save them further embarrassment. "So, Aksel, how did you and Thea meet?"

Aksel, astute as ever, immediately picked up on the change of subject. "Ves introduced us. Thea is an accomplished cleric—an Auric Priestess of Arenor, in fact."

Elladan cocked his head to one side and eyed Thea with growing respect. "A Priestess of Arenor? Doesn't that mean you can use your light both for healing and as a weapon?"

Thea pressed her lips together and nodded appreciatively. "I see you know a bit about ecclesiastics."

Elladan gave her a half-smile and shrugged. "A bit."

Their eyes locked for a brief moment before Glo interrupted

them. "But you also know a lot about the academy. If I remember right, Lloyd said you studied here before your accident—"

Ruka, still next to Thea, cut him off as she began to cough violently.

Elladan silently shook his head. Glo's sheltered upbringing had left the elf with a definite lack of social skills.

Meanwhile, Ruka had practically turned a shade of gray. Thea peered down at the teen and grabbed her firmly by the hand. "Yes, I studied here until the incident, but it changed my life for the better. Now I can use my spiritual abilities as more than just a weapon."

Ruka stopped choking and met Thea's gaze with a wide-eyed stare. "So—you're happy?"

A broad smile crossed Thea's lips, her entire face practically glowing. "Absolutely."

Elladan found himself entranced by this amazing woman. It felt as if his entire world had grown just a little bit brighter from meeting her.

"Are you alright?"

Donnie's question broke Elladan out of his trance. He glanced uncertainly at the slight elf, not sure if that had been directed at him. Donnie, however, was staring at Ruka.

Ruka waved him off with one hand while rubbing her face with the other. "I'm fine. Something just flew in my eye."

"Ahem," Aksel covered the awkward moment by formally introducing Thea to the others.

When he got to Elladan, the bard executed a deep bow. "Elladan Narmolanya, at your service."

"Pleased to meet you, Elladan," Thea responded with a sparkle in her eye.

Once everyone had been introduced, Glo suggested they go inside. Thea fell in next to Elladan and walked silently beside him.

A trace of guilt suddenly washed over the bard. *This is Lloyd's sister. How would he feel if something were to happen between us?*

For the first time in a very long time, the bard found himself tongue-tied. Reaching for anything to say, the words tumbled from his mouth before he could stop them. "You know, I'm a student of history myself. I love history—especially war history—battles and tactics."

Smooth Elladan, real smooth, he chastised himself mentally.

Somehow, Thea didn't appear to mind. She peered at him with seeming interest in his lame attempt at banter. "Really? So you've studied music, history, war tactics, and theology? That's quite the repertoire."

Feeling like he had dodged an arrow, Elladan played it cool. "What can I say? I have an unquenchable thirst for knowledge."

A light laugh escaped Thea's lips; it was almost lyrical in nature. "Well then, maybe we should get together sometime and compare notes."

Elladan's heart practically skipped a beat. Thea had said that rather offhandedly, and she wasn't even facing his way. Still, he couldn't stop himself from beaming.

"I'd like that," he responded in a soft tone, all of his previous misgivings washed away.

4
STEALLE ACADEMY OF THE SWORD

*Yellow flames danced up and down her blades with
small sparks of blue mixed in*

L et's see what you've got." Kratos' voice echoed off the walls within the huge training hall of the Stealle Academy. The empty space had been designed to accommodate the numerous cadets of Penwick forces who passed through its halls each year.

Banners hung along the wall, displaying heralds of both the city and the House of Stealle. Numerous racks of practice weapons lined the hall on all sides. Lines had been painted across the wooden floor, designating appropriate areas for sparring.

Squaring off with a pair of practice swords, Lloyd grinned back at his father with more bravado than he actually felt. "I've learned a thing or two since I've been away."

The young man had bittersweet memories of this place. Mastering the art of the spiritblade had not come easily to Lloyd, especially when compared to his siblings. Both had proved to be prodigies—Pallas agile and keen-minded, and Thea with her uncanny grasp of the spiritual.

Lloyd had been clumsy at first, a fact his brother never let him forget. Further, try as he might, the young man had a great deal of trouble quieting his mind. He had to work twice as hard and longer than most, but in the end Lloyd finally earned the right to be called a spiritblade.

"Show him that thing you do where you disappear and reappear behind your opponent!" Andrella cried from her nearby seat with obvious pride.

Lloyd's cheeks grew warm as the blood rose to them. Andrella thought the world of him, but she had no idea how inexperienced he was compared to his father.

"Hm, so you've managed to master the teleport technique." Kratos eyed him intently, most likely trying to gauge his growth via his aura. That was another ability which Lloyd had yet to grasp.

Lloyd shrugged, still feeling inadequate. "I kind of had to."

"Necessity"—Kratos suddenly lunged at him—"is the best teacher."

Lloyd felt surprised as he slid out of the way. In the past, he would never have seen that coming. Is Dad purposely moving slower?

Lloyd attempted to counter his father, but instead got caught in a counter-parry. Dummy. You should have expected that.

Pushing his blade aside, Kratos slid through Lloyd's guard, straight for his torso. Still, he seemed to be moving slower than usual. Lloyd instinctively parried with his other blade and successfully back-pedaled into a defensive stance.

Kratos drew back as well and gave him an approving nod. "Not bad. Not bad at all."

"I agree. You've gotten faster, little brother," a familiar voice sounded from the entryway.

Lloyd glanced over to see his friends enter the room. In their midst stood his sister, Thea. Their practice bout all but forgotten, Lloyd rushed over to greet her. Sweeping her upward into the air, Lloyd thought to himself that she had grown lighter.

"Whoa!" Thea cried as he hoisted her up and spun her about. "I think you've also put on some muscle."

"He is quite strong," Andrella noted as Lloyd gently put his sister down.

Landing gracefully, Thea faced the young lady. "And you must be Andrella." She stepped forward and pulled Andrella into a warm embrace. "Welcome to the family."

Andrella's expression was one of pure joy. "I've always wanted a sister."

Thea pulled back, a wry smile on her lips. "I'm not exactly the 'play dress up' type, but I do have a friend who does, who's like a sister."

Andrella's eyes danced with glee. "Well then, I can't wait to meet her."

The next few minutes were spent introducing the rest of the companions to Lloyd's father. Once they were done, Donnie reminded them why they had gathered there in the first place. "So where's this upstart we heard about?"

"I'm right here," a voice echoed from the entryway.

All heads turned in that direction.

A slim woman with a tan complexion leaned against one of the door jambs, the frilly white arms of her shoulderless blouse folded across her chest. Deep brown eyes stared out at them from beneath a bright red bandana, her long, light brown hair spilling over the one side. A pair of curved swords hung from the dual belts strapped across the woman's waist.

Kratos moved to the front of the group. "And to whom do we have the pleasure of speaking?"

The woman pushed away from the door jamb. She moved with a lithe, catlike grace as she strode up to meet him. Stopping about an arm's length away, the top of her head barely reached Kratos' nose. Still, she met his eyes with a confident stare, the difference in height not seeming to bother her in the slightest.

"My name is Solais"—she hesitated a brief moment—"Onueva." She looked Kratos up and down. "And I suppose you are the 'great' Kratos Stealle?"

A thin smile crossed Krato's lips. "I don't know about 'great,' but I am indeed Kratos Stealle."

The corner of Solais' mouth twisted upward. "Either way, I am here to challenge you to a duel"—she stood back and rested her hands on her sword hilts—"whenever you are ready."

Lloyd studied this woman intently. Her current stance, the way she moved, and the positioning of the blades at her sides, all suggested she was an experienced fighter.

Thea edged her way next to him and whispered in his ear, "Watch yourself. This one has a powerful aura."

Kratos hesitated, most likely gauging the woman for himself, then responded to her challenge. "I'm afraid I can't do that."

Solais cocked her head to one side and narrowed her eyes at him. "I've heard many stories of the great Kratos Stealle. None of them suggested that he was 'chicken.'"

The slur on his father irritated Lloyd. He nearly took a step forward, but Thea placed a restraining hand on his arm.

Kratos responded with a closemouthed laugh. "It's not that, young lady. It's merely that you are not ready for someone of my level."

A momentary trace of anger washed over Solais' face, but it disappeared equally fast. She shifted from one foot to another and pushed her thumbs into her belt. "Well, isn't that convenient. So what do you suggest? Should I meditate on a mountain top for a year or two first?"

"I could tell her a couple of places to go," Seth murmured off to one side.

Lloyd had to stifle a snort. Leave it to Seth.

If Solais heard his comment, she ignored it. Her gaze remained firmly fixed on Kratos.

Kratos took in a deep breath. "I don't think that will be necessary." He stepped aside and motioned to Lloyd. "This is my son. If you can best him first, then I shall give your challenge serious consideration."

Lloyd squared his shoulders as Solais' gaze fell upon him. The intensity in her eyes caused the space in the center of his brow to tingle. Thea was right, this woman does have power.

After looking him over, Solais breathed a reluctant sigh. "Very well, but none of this practice-weapon crap."

"Fine by me," Lloyd responded to her challenge.

As he went to get his blades, Thea smacked him on the arm and hissed, "I thought I told you to watch yourself."

Lloyd halted in his tracks. Despite her ire, he could clearly see the look of concern in her eyes.

Ever since Lloyd could remember, Thea had been looking after him. Between their parents' constant responsibilities and Pallas joining the navy, it had fallen on her shoulders to raise her younger brother. Up until now, Lloyd had thought of his sister as being far older, but in reality she was only two years his senior.

Lloyd suddenly realized how difficult it must have been for Thea to raise him. In truth, that responsibility should never have been thrust upon her.

The young man reached out and placed a sympathetic hand on Thea's shoulder. "I'm not a kid anymore, sis. Plus," he added with a wink, "she's not the only one with power."

Thea held his gaze for a few moments, then let out a long sigh. "You're right. You're an adult now and I shouldn't tell you what to do."

Lloyd felt a sudden tug on his other arm and met Andrella's stern gaze. "But I certainly can."

The young man sighed at thought of having to explain himself a second time. Yet as he opened his mouth to speak, Andrella put a finger to his lips.

"I understand. Just be careful," she told him in a soft voice, then stood upon her toes and kissed him briefly.

"If you're done over there, lover-boy, let's get this party started already," Solais called out from the nearest sparring square.

Lloyd arched an eyebrow at her, but Seth cut him off before he could respond. "Aw, does somebody needs a hug?"

Solais leveled a gaze at the halfling that could melt steel. "Watch it, shorty, or you'll be next."

Not intimidated in the slightest, Seth folded his arms across his chest and clicked his tongue. "Tsk. You'll be lucky to last that long."

Solais glared at him for a moment longer, but then a thin smile crept across her face. "I like you. You've got guts."

Lloyd appreciated Seth's support, though he hadn't quite expected it. More often than not, he'd been on the receiving end of the halfling's sharp tongue.

The young warrior hurried to grab his blades before anything else happened. Luckily, everyone simmered down and took seats along the wall.

Moments later, Lloyd joined his opponent out in the sparring square. The two of them spread out about ten feet apart. Solais drew her blades and fell into a fighting stance.

Lloyd eyed her curiously as he did the same. He had never quite seen a stance like that before—one blade held before her and the other almost above her head. To the untrained eye, her flank appeared wide open, but Lloyd had enough experience to know that wasn't quite true. In fact, strange as it appeared, he could find no clear opening in her stance.

Kratos walked up between them, holding out his favored weapon—a long-bladed, two-handed katana. He glanced first at Solais, then at Lloyd. Finally, he stepped back, swiped his blade downward, and uttered the word, "Begin."

Solais didn't waste any time. She rushed in, her twin blades flickering almost faster than the eye could see. She slashed at him from odd angles that seemed nearly inhuman in nature.

Thankfully, Lloyd wasn't wholly dependent on his vision. He sensed her moves as she made them, staving off her lightning-fast attacks. Furthermore, though somewhat unorthodox, he recognized elements of her style. It was almost as if she had spiritblade training.

Circling each other, the pair engaged in a few swift exchanges, the clash of their swords echoing across the hall. Slowly adjusting to her rhythm, Lloyd began to test her defenses.

After a few more quick exchanges, Lloyd finally broke her guard. The tip of his blade caught Solais across the left arm, cutting through her frilly sleeve and leaving a red gash across her skin.

Cheers went up amongst his friends, but died as Solais immediately retaliated. She flicked her blade almost faster than he could follow, slicing across the back of his hand.

Lloyd swiftly back-pedaled and examined the stinging wound. She had neatly cut through his leather glove and into the skin beneath. Any deeper and it might have cut a tendon, making it impossible for him to grasp his sword.

Lloyd looked up at Solais and grinned. "You're good."

Solais peered up from her own wound and gave him a begrudging nod. "You're not so bad yourself—for a pampered noble."

Lloyd shrugged, ignoring the verbal jab. "Guess it's time to get serious."

The young warrior stilled his mind and reached down inside to the very core of his being. There in the midst of the darkness shone a white-hot star—the spark of life that was his inner spirit. Focusing his intent, he touched it.

The energy rushed up and outward into his limbs. It flowed through his hands and into his blades, where it burst forth into red-hot flames.

The corner of Solais' mouth upturned slightly as she eyed the crackling fire that engulfed his blades. "Oh, so it's going to be that kind of fight? Maybe this won't be so boring after all."

The young woman slowed her breath and a low hum came from her throat. Lloyd could feel the energy rising within her. He watched with fascination as her swords, too, lit on fire. Yellow flames danced up and down her blades, with small sparks of blue mixed in.

"Those are electrical arcs," Ruka commented from the sidelines.

"Is she some kind of spirit blade?" Andrella asked in a hushed voice.

"Similar, but not exact," Thea answered, her tone laced with concern.

Lloyd supposed he should be worried as well, but the young man couldn't quite suppress his excitement. He met his opponent's eyes, and though she would not admit it out loud, realized that she shared his enthusiasm.

The duo clashed once again in another barrage of swift exchanges. Blades flashed in all directions, leaving trails of fire behind them. Fiery sparks flew this way and that, yet neither seemed able to gain an advantage.

After the sixth clash, Lloyd decided to try something else. He took a few steps backward and once again stilled his mind. This time as he reached inside, the world around him slowed to a standstill.

When he touched his spirit, the energy burst forth, surging through every corner of his being. His entire body vibrated with power, then all at once, the world shifted around him. It moved past in a frantic blur, then suddenly stopped.

Lloyd now stood directly behind Solais. Yet before he even had a chance to move, she lashed out backward and caught him in the gut with her boot. Somehow she had anticipated his move and knew just where to strike!

Stunned by the unexpected turn of events, Lloyd found himself again on the defensive. Solais was on him, her blades flickering so fast that he could barely hold them off. Abruptly she broke through his guard, the tip of her sword mere inches from his throat.

"Lloyd!" he heard Andrella cry from the sidelines.

Instead of cutting him, however, Solais held her blade at his neck. Lloyd could smell the ozone from the sparks that danced across her blade.

Solais stared at him with a keen intensity, as if she were trying to read his mind. Lloyd met her gaze unflinchingly. He had been stupid, thinking he could win a battle with flashy moves against this level of opponent. She had neatly anticipated and countered his teleport technique. At this point, he deserved whatever scar she decided to give him.

Solais held his gaze for a moment or two, then surprisingly pulled back. "It would be like kicking a puppy," she mumbled under her breath.

Lloyd stepped back and let out the breath he'd been holding. The fight was over. Solais had clearly won. Andrella came running to his side and threw her arms around him. "Are you alright?"

Lloyd grinned sheepishly, his hand going to the back of his neck. "Yeah, I'm fine. Just my pride wounded, is all."

"I told you to watch yourself with this one," Thea admonished him. She stood there with her arms folded, wearing that look of disappointment he saw so often as a child.

Lloyd responded with a heavy sigh. "You were right about Solais. I should have listened to you."

Thea raised an eyebrow. "That's it? No excuses?" She pressed her lips together and gave him a begrudging smile. "You really have grown."

In the meantime, Solais approached their father. "So, have I earned the right to fight you?"

Kratos appraised her for a few moments, then gave her a curt nod. "You have"—a wide smirk crossed her face—"but it will have to wait. Right now we have some city business to attend to."

Solais' face fell for a moment, but she quickly recovered, sheathing her blades with a shrug. "Fine. I can wait…"

"…to get your ass kicked." Seth snorted from the sidelines.

Solais fixed the halfling with a hard stare. "Oh, and what makes you so sure of that, half-pint?"

Ignoring the jab, Seth smirked. "You and Lloyd were evenly matched. He might have beat you if he hadn't been so careless."

Solais folded her arms across her chest. "Oh really?"

A wicked grin crossed Seth's lips. "Just calling it like I see it."

Lloyd stared at Seth with disbelief. He was not used to the halfling standing up for him. Still, he had not missed Seth's point about his own carelessness. If he hadn't tried that stunt, perhaps he might have had a chance after all. Either way, this was a lesson he would not soon forget.

Solais held Seth's gaze for a few more seconds, then shrugged and spun on her heel. "Whatever," she called over her shoulder as she slowly sauntered out of the hall.

Donnie hadn't quite been himself since what he had been forced to do at the Marsh Tower. Any woman he'd had feelings for inexplicably met an untimely demise, or worse. Xira had been the first, then Miranda, and now Alana.

There was no doubt about it—when it came to relationships, Donnie was cursed. It was the singular reason he had pushed Ruka away. Though he liked to complain about it, she wasn't relatively that much younger than him. Truth be told, he couldn't abide it if something were to happen to her because of him.

So Donnie had kept mostly to himself these last couple of days. Still, the invitation to see a spiritblade battle had piqued his interest. On top of that, things had gotten extremely interesting when this Solais showed up, exhibiting similar talents.

The young woman had left the academy hall just moments ago. Lloyd's father stood there staring after her, deep creases furrowing the blade master's brow.

"Well, that was odd," Kratos muttered under his breath.

Lloyd's sister, Thea, strode up next to him, her eyes also following the receding Solais. "She definitely channels energy like a spiritblade."

Kratos gave his daughter an absent nod. "True, but that stance she took—I've only seen it once before."

"When was that?" Lloyd asked, drawing up next to his father and sister.

Kratos faced the two of them, his expression grim. "When I fought Eboneye."

Eboneye, the pirate warlord who had performed the impossible feat of uniting all thirteen Clans of the Coast. The same pirate who shortly thereafter led the pirate clans on a full-scaled invasion of Penwick. According to legend, it had been Kratos who faced Eboneye to end the invasion. Apparently that legend was true.

Lloyd peered at his father incredulously. "Are you saying that Solais is a pirate?"

"Or a Shin Tauri," Donnie said before Kratos could respond. He normally didn't like to speak of things that dredged up his past, but in this case he felt it was warranted.

As he expected, all eyes in the hall fell upon him.

Kratos narrowed his gaze at the slight elf. "Go on."

Donnie took a moment to weigh his response. There were some things he didn't want to talk about—memories that were just too painful. "I might have spent some time along the mainland coast. While I was there, I may have run into a Shin Tauri or two."

"You mean the legendary warriors from Isandor?" Lloyd asked with growing excitement.

Donnie pressed his lips together and nodded. "From what I've seen, Shin Tauri can channel energy just like you spirit blades."

Kratos appeared quite intrigued. "A warrior who mixes Shin Tauri techniques with a fighting stance of the pirates of the coast. Very interesting."

Donnie thought so as well. In all his years with the pirates, they and the Shin Tauri had been mortal enemies. He wondered what could have happened to bring the two sides together.

"Yeah, real fascinating, but don't we have bigger fish to fry?" Seth interjected.

Kratos eyed the halfling with more than a trace of amusement. "Quite right, Master Seth. I'll go get Lara. We'll meet you all at the Lucky Heroes in an hour."

As the group broke up, someone wrapped an arm around Donnie's shoulders. He turned to see Elladan peering at him with a half-smile. "So, you spent time on the pirate coast?"

Donnie grimaced. This is exactly what he wanted to avoid. "A bit."

"You must have stories," Elladan urged, the bard's eyes bright with anticipation.

Donnie felt suddenly cornered. Searching for a way to get out of it, his gaze fixed on Thea as she walked up to join them. "Maybe some other time? We're in a huge new city, and I know how much you love to shop. Maybe the good Priestess Stealle here can show you around?"

Thea pressed her lips into an inverted smile and nodded. "I do know a few places where you can get a good bargain."

Elladan's eyes lit up at the word 'bargain.' He gave Thea one of his most charming smiles and offered her his arm. "Well then, lead the way."

Donnie let out a huge sigh as the pair marched off together. He had managed to dodge another arrow.

"Not sure how the Stealles are gonna feel about that."

Donnie followed Seth's gaze as he stared after Elladan and Thea, the pair still arm in arm. They did seem rather cozy. The slight elf swept his eyes around the room, but Kratos had already left and Lloyd was busy with Andrella.

With no one else taking notice, Donnie merely shrugged. "I'm sure Elladan will be on his best behavior."

Seth snorted. "Heh. That's what I'm afraid of."

5
DARK TREASURES

They were searching for something called the crystal key

Thea had not led an easy life. Perhaps it looked that way to those who envied her family, but for her, life had always been a series of trials. She had learned at an early age not to depend on her mother—not that she held a grudge against her, mind you. No one could ever stay mad at Lara Stealle, one of the most selfless, giving individuals in all of Thac. When not performing her wizarding or council duties, Lara would be somewhere about the city, helping with community projects or social programs.

Thus, Thea had modeled herself after her mother. By the time she passed the toddler stage, she had already begun to look after her baby brother, Lloyd. Thea also fiercely admired her handsome and dashing father. She initially took up the art of the spiritblade to be closer to him, but soon found that she was quite good at it. Her deeply spiritual side made her a formidable student of the blade.

The road Thea traveled now was not an easy one, but it had its rewards. Still, every so often, she found herself missing the old days.

"So where are we headed first?" Elladan asked as they descended the steps from the Stealle Academy.

Thea cast a sidelong glance at the handsome elf and shrugged. "That depends on what you're looking for."

Elladan stopped at the base of the stairs and ticked off a list of items on his fingers. "Cooking utensils, seasonings, rations, armor, weapons"—he paused and flashed her a knowing smile—"Lloyd loves new weapons."

A soft chuckle escaped Thea's lips. "He certainly does."

A sudden flash of intuition washed over her. She pursed her lips together and narrowed an eye at the flamboyant elf. "You watch out for him, don't you?"

Elladan's eyes lowered and his cheeks reddened slightly. "Guilty as charged."

There was something so genuine about his reaction that Thea felt a sudden warmth well up inside of her. As charming as Elladan had been since they met, she found his concern for her baby brother far more alluring than anything else he could have said or done.

Elladan raised his eyes to meet hers, his hands waving about as he attempted to cover his embarrassment. "I mean—he's the nicest of guys—and he also has lots of potential. Since we've been traveling together, I've tried to teach him a thing or two about tactics and diplomacy."

Both Thea's eyebrows shot up in disbelief. "My brother? Lloyd? Are you sure we're talking about the same person?"

Elladan laughed, his tone rich and lyrical. "He's got his rough edges, for sure, but you'd be surprised at how he's learned to handle himself." He paused and winked. "If you don't believe me, just ask Andrella."

Thea's brows knit together as she puzzled over this enlightening information. She had been quite worried about Lloyd when he left, yet it seemed he had fared better than she ever imagined.

Thea reached out and placed a hand on Elladan's arm. "Thank you. It's good to know he has someone else looking out for him."

Elladan gently patted her hand. "Honestly, it's been my pleasure."

Thea met his blue-eyed gaze and felt something stir deep within her. This Elladan was not at all what she expected. Considering his good looks, she assumed he'd be stuck-up. He seemed anything but, however.

They held each other's stare for a few moments before she remembered herself. She pulled her hand away and turned on her heel to hide her embarrassment. "Well then, we should probably get shopping before our hour is up."

"Lead the way," Elladan urged as he fell in step beside her.

Thea had never met someone who liked to haggle as much as Elladan. He was good at it, too. She had taken him down to the south market, where they could hit a number of shops at once. In the short time they had together, they covered nearly a half-dozen stores. In each one, Elladan searched out the best items and bargained the owners down to outrageously good prices.

Their bags full, she led them north, back toward the Lucky Heroes Inn. They had just exited the marketplace when he brought up the one subject she had hoped to avoid altogether.

Elladan cast her a furtive glance. "This may be none of my business, but what exactly is the story behind how you and Ruka met?"

Thea abruptly froze in her tracks, a myriad of emotions welling up inside of her. Though she tried to suppress it, Elladan must have caught a hint of her inner turmoil.

"Never mind. Forget I asked." Elladan held a hand up in front of him, his face gone gray with anguish.

Without realizing it, Thea's spiritual senses kicked in. Piercing the veil, she observed the energy around him that emanated from his spirit. Aside from a couple of dark spots, which could easily be attributed to the harsh effects of the material world, his aura was basically pure.

Wrenching her vision back to the third plane, she gave him a wan smile. "No, that's alright."

She started walking again, slower this time, her voice strained as she spoke. "It was four years ago. My friends and I had been search-ing in and around the city for any sign of Eboneye's treasure."

Elladan tilted his head to one side and raised a dark eyebrow at her. "Eboneye's treasure?"

Thea leaned in closer, the tension starting to drain from her shoulders as she whispered conspiratorially to him. "The pirate clans occupied Penwick for close to three months, far longer than it would take to merely loot the city."

A stray wind blew across the streets as they turned the corner. El-ladan slicked back his thick mop of jet-black hair as comprehension dawned on his brow. "So they were looking for something."

"Exactly," Thea confirmed, a touch of the old excitement stirring in her gut. "They were searching for something called the Crystal Key, and in the process amassed every jewel and gem they could find in the city."

Elladan pursed his lips together, his mind whirring as he drew to the next obvious conclusion. "A city this size? That's a lot of gemstones."

This Elladan was sharp—she liked that. "About the same time we found out where they had stashed them, this strange girl showed up in town asking about Eboneye."

"Ruka?" Elladan hazarded a guess.

"Ruka," Thea confirmed with a sly nod. She paused a moment as they passed through a crowd, then continued as they reached the foot of the Lord's Bridge. "She ended up joining us on that ill-fated journey to Thorn Isle."

As Thea uttered that name, the revery she'd been experiencing suddenly vanished. This was the part that haunted her in her night-mares. Her eyes shifted away, looking out over the crystal-blue waters of the Penderbun River as it passed beneath them.

After a half-minute of silence, she felt a gentle hand on her arm. "It's totally fine if you want to stop there."

Thea let out a short sigh. She had started the story, and she wasn't some milksop who blanched at the first sign of discomfort. She re-sumed the tale as they left the bridge and turned up the road toward her mother's school.

"Let's just say that instead of some legendary treasure, we ran afoul of real pirates on that isle." Thea paused a moment, a lump forming in her throat. "It didn't end well for any of us..."

Thea mentally berated herself for the umpteenth time. She had been so stupid—so naïve. They had all paid the ultimate price for it—Dom, Vic, Lynn, Alys.

She suddenly felt a warm hand engulf hers. Normally she wouldn't entertain such advances, but from the look on his face, she realized it was meant as a form of comfort.

Steeling her nerves, Thea forced herself to finish the rest of the story. "We woke up later that evening in the Temple of the Ralnai. All of us had been raised, the fee paid by some mysterious benefactor."

She paused a moment, forcing back the moisture that had begun to form in the corners of her eyes. "It wasn't until later that I found out it had been Ruka. That day was the last time I saw her—until now."

Elladan squeezed her hand, his voice soft. "How could you know? You were just a kid."

Thea gave him a grateful smile as she slowly pulled her hand away. "Maybe, but it's a lesson I'll never forget.

"Anyway, we're here," she added as they turned the last corner just before the northeast city gate. The Lucky Heroes Inn sat two buildings down the street from where they stood.

"Aren't you going to join us?" Elladan asked, the look of disappointment on his face painfully obvious.

Thea considered it for a moment, but she was feeling a bit too emotional right now. She needed to meditate and recenter herself first. She gave him an apologetic smile. "I'm sorry, but I'm afraid I need to get back to the temple. I'm sure I'll see you again soon."

"I look forward to it," he said with a charming grin. Elladan took her hand, bowed, and kissed it.

Thea felt hard-pressed to keep her cheeks from turning red. She stood there for a few moments as he strode away down the crowded city street, then mentally chided herself.

Now, don't let yourself go falling for some handsome elf—no matter how charming or understanding he may seem. With that last thought, she spun on her heel and marched back down the street toward the temple grounds.

6
SEEKING COUNCIL

So what you're saying is they're a bunch of self-serving morons

Seth Korzair felt tired to the bone. Growing up among crooks and thieves, he had never been able to let his guard down. Things hadn't improved much after meeting Aksel, Glo, and Lloyd. Their desire to help others kept them all constantly on the move. While Seth didn't mind looking out for his friends, he really just wanted to settle down in one place.

Fat chance of that happening, though, with this demon invasion hanging over their heads. If they didn't stop them, there would be no place left to live in Arinthar. Heck, there wouldn't be anyone *left* to live anywhere.

Still, the idea of meeting with the Penwick Council left Seth less than thrilled. If there was one thing he hated more than being dragged all over Thac, it was politics. Rulers and governing bodies rarely did what was best for their people. Motivated by greed and self-interest, they stole from them, like any thief. Worse, they conned people by telling them taking their money was in their own best interest.

Seth breathed a weary sigh. *I'm getting too old for this. When this is all over, I'm definitely settling down.*

Aksel had procured them a private room in the back of the Lucky Heroes. The companions, along with Kara, Ruka, and Xellos, had already gathered there before Lloyd's parents arrived.

The moment Lara Stealle walked in the room, she cast a spell to block scrying. She then sat down, folded her hands on the table in front of her, and gazed purposefully around the room. "Now we can talk."

Seth was pleasantly surprised. *A wizard with some common sense for a change.*

Lloyd started with the niceties of introducing everyone. As soon as he finished, Lara got straight down to business.

"We managed to get you on the schedule for this evening." She sat back and drummed her fingers against the tabletop. "The real question is, what exactly do you expect from the council?"

Direct and to the point. Seth was really starting to like this woman.

Glo arched an eyebrow at Lara's query. He clasped his hands together in front of him and stared at her intently. "I thought we already discussed this. The demons and the towers pose a serious threat to all Arinthar, and speed is of the essence in stopping them."

Lara steepled her hands together and rested her chin on them, her facial expression speaking volumes as to her own distaste for politics. "True, but the rest of the towers would not be viewed as an immediate threat to Penwick. While Kratos and I understand the gravity of the situation, I'm afraid many of the other council members would not see it that way."

Typical, short-sighted diplomats, Seth thought, her answer not surprising him in the slightest.

It obviously frustrated Glo, though. He sat back in his seat, exasperation written across his face as he gazed at Elladan.

Not missing a beat, Elladan mouthed the words, *I told you so,* before addressing Lara. "Just to be clear ma'am, we're not expecting any troops from Penwick. We just want to continue borrowing one of your airships is all."

Lara pursed her lips together, her brow furrowing as she considered his words. She paused a moment, then peered questioningly at her husband. Kratos responded with a silent nod, sat up taller in his seat, and took up the conversation.

"Again, Lara and I do recognize this, but you need to understand what is going to drive the council's decision. Right now we only have the two airships, and they were only lent to you because of the undead menace encroaching on our neighboring towns. With that threat gone, the council will be loath to relinquish them again."

Unable to suppress it any longer, Seth let out a derisive snort. "So what you're saying is they're a bunch of self-serving morons."

Lara and Kratos looked at each other, then burst out laughing. Flush from amusement, Lara fanned herself as she responded to his candid observation. "Oh my, Master Seth—we heard you were rather blunt, but you certainly don't disappoint."

"That's Seth for you," Lloyd affirmed, a grin splitting his face from one ear to the other. He paused, his smile quickly fading. "Look, I know I'm no expert at politics, but shouldn't it at least count for something that we stopped the 'undead menace'?"

Kratos locked eyes with his son, the amusement draining from his face as well. "In truth, it will count with those of the council who are not 'self-serving,' as Master Seth so accurately put it. Another thing in your favor is that neither ship got damaged in battle—though one question was raised."

"And what was that?" Andrella asked, sliding closer to Lloyd's side.

Kratos got up out of his seat and began to pace around the room. "Well, according to our latest reports, the Cloud Hammer should be returning here in the next two days. Yet, it appears that the Remington will be a bit longer—something about dropping off snipers?"

"I can explain that," Aksel said, rising from his seat and straightening his robes.

Kratos stopped his pacing and gestured toward the little cleric. "Please, by all means."

"Our friends Martan and Kalyn hail from Deepwood, "Aksel explained. "They went with the Remington to recruit a troop of Deepwood Snipers before meeting us outside the marshes."

"I see." Kratos pressed his lips together and nodded his understanding. "So once they drop these snipers off, they'll be headed back here?"

"The Remington will," Aksel confirmed with absolute candor, "though our friends won't be on it. They have some unfinished business to take care of in Deepwood first."

Aksel didn't expound further, which was probably just as well. If Seth guessed right, Kalyn probably wanted to clear Martan of the murder charge that hung over his head. Martan had been blamed for the death of his foster father. Yet instead of standing trial, he ran, urged on by Kalyn's idiot brothers.

Appearing satisfied with Aksel's explanation, Kratos sat back down again and exhaled a long breath. "Very well, that leaves us with just one more question. The council received a report that the Princess of Lanfor took off for this 'Demon Tower' on her airship with two platoons of Dunwynn troops aboard."

"That's like spitting against the wind," Kara stated brusquely.

Seth could see the anger seething in the angel warrior's eyes. He couldn't really blame her. Kara had descended to their world to fight in the third Demon War—nearly seven thousand years ago by Seth's reckoning. So, she'd been putting up with crap like this for longer than any of them, with the possible exception of Elistra—Miss Immortal, herself.

Kara rose to her feet, her impatience mounting as she spoke. "That place was crawling with demons when we escaped, and that was nearly a week and a half ago. With the tower crystal, they might have twice as many demons there by now. Anya would be a fool to try and engage them, even with her airship and all those dragons." She emphasized that last point by banging her fist onto the table.

Seth barely suppressed a snort this time. "Are you kidding? The name Anya practically rhymes with crazy."

Kara's face contorted into a wicked grin. "Is she truly that insane?"

Donnie grabbed Kara by the arm and urged her to sit back down. "Sadly, yes, she is that insane, but there's no way to stop her now."

A warrior himself, Kratos' face mirrored his complete understanding of Kara's frustrations. "It's alright. Thank you for your honest assessment."

Somewhat mollified, Kara responded with a curt nod.

Kratos shared a brief glance with his wife and once again some silent communication took place between the two. Lara then rolled up her long-hanging sleeves and swept her gaze around the room.

"Okay, so we've established that you are hoping to continue to use of one of our airships. We also know that there are those on the council who will oppose your request. Now, let's talk about who those folks are and how we might get them to come around."

Upon hearing that, Seth rolled his eyes to the heavens. The last thing he needed to hear was how to mollify these council jerks. He pulled his hood up over his head, slid down in his seat, and folded his arms, silent wishing he was anywhere else but here at the moment.

In the past, Lloyd's eyes glazed over whenever his parents talked about politics. It had never been one of his favorite subjects.

Lloyd preferred straightforward battles with a weapon in hand. The backstabbing that took place in the political arena went against everything he had been taught to believe in. More than not, he'd hear his parents vent their frustrations after a council meeting. Lloyd did not envy them in the slightest.

This time, however, was different. The very fate of the world might ride on getting the council's support.

Lara rose from her seat and traced a pattern through the air. *"Temporaria illusion."*

As the words left her lips, an image appeared above the center of the table of a portly, beady-eyed, balding man with a thick reddish-brown mustache. Everyone at the table sat forward for a better look as she proceeded to describe the council members and their affiliations.

"This is Caverinus Avernos, the current Baron of Penwick, the head of the city council, and Gryswold's eldest brother," Lara said with a pointed look at Andrella. "He is very insecure and therefore easily influenced. Many on the council take advantage of that singular weakness."

Lloyd had heard that Gryswold did not leave Penwick on the best of terms with his brother. That was not surprising, considering the difference in temperament between the two. Still, Lloyd worried that the Baron's dislike for Gryswold would carry forward to his niece. "Mom, I'm not sure Andrella's relationship to the Baron will do us much good."

A look of keen satisfaction spread across Lara's face. "Yes, Lloyd, I'm glad to see you thinking that through. However, Andrella's standing as the sole heir to the Dunwynn throne would definitely carry weight with him."

Lloyd felt a squeeze on his arm. He peered down to see Andrella grinning up at him. She leaned in close and whispered in his ear, "See, you're getting the hang of this."

Lloyd blushed and rubbed the back of his neck. He wasn't so sure about that, but he was glad she thought so.

Lara waved her hands again and another image appeared slightly below and to the right of the Baron. The man portrayed had a regal air about him. He appeared slightly younger than the Baron, but had a full head of auburn hair with a neatly cropped beard and mustache.

"This is Aillinn Avernos, the Baron's younger brother and the Lord of the West Marches." As Lara pointed from one picture to the other, a dotted line appeared in the air, linking the two. "However, where Caverinus is weak-willed, Aillinn is anything but that."

"Also unlike his brother, he actually cares about the people of Penwick," Kratos added with just a trace of bitterness.

Lara cast a sympathetic look at her husband, then nodded in agreement. "We are of a like mind in that respect, and thus Aillinn's interests typically align with ours. Therefore, he would most likely support your cause."

Lloyd had met Aillinn once or twice. Thinking back, the man was a lot like Gryswold, although perhaps not as rough around the edges.

Lara motioned with her hands once again and another figure appeared below and to the right of Aillinn. This image portrayed a rather young woman, but with a stern expression that made her appear far older than her years. Garbed in red and silver armor, her honey-blonde hair was cropped just below the chin. "Carenna High-tower is Lord Hightower's granddaughter and the current Protector of Penwick. Considering her lineage and position, she tends to put the safety of our citizens first."

"She's also one heck of a warrior," Kratos noted with obvious admiration.

Lloyd remembered crossing swords with Carenna a few times throughout his studies. She had whooped him solidly at each encounter. She could even hold her own against his father.

Lara motioned with her finger again, this time drawing a solid line through the air between Aillinn and Carenna. "As a seasoned spiritblade, Carenna would recognize the danger presented by the demons. So we can most likely count her on our side."

Lara stopped talking at that point, clasped her hands together, inverted them, and stretched her arms out in front of her. Lloyd winced at the popping noises that came from her fingers as she did so. He hated it when she did that.

"Ah, that's better," Lara declared with obvious satisfaction. "Now, where were we?" She pursed her lips together, her entire mouth shifting to one side as she mulled over the diagram floating above the tabletop.

Lloyd loved his mother dearly. She was one of the smartest people he had ever met. Still, there were times when she could be totally absentminded.

"The opposition, dear," Kratos reminded her with a gentle smile.

Lara's eyes lit up, her entire face brightening. "Ah, yes, the opposition."

Her long-hanging sleeves having slipped back down, Lara rolled them up and once again waved her hands through the air. The visage of an austere-looking gentleman with craggy features appeared on the opposite side of the illusion from Aillinn. The man had long salt and pepper hair, with a closed cropped beard and mustache to match. "Alburg Dunamal is a well-to-do merchant and the city's Master of Coin. He also leads the other faction within the council."

Elladan leaned in closer and peered intently at the image of Alburg. As a student of diplomacy, he had done his best to teach Lloyd a thing or two over these last few months. "So is this Alburg the one we have to convince?"

Lara's face scrunched into a grimace. "Not exactly."

She paused a moment, as if searching for the words. "Basically, Alburg stands against anything that costs Penwick money, resources, or that garners our support."

She gestured toward Kratos. "We assume he views us as some sort of competition to his political aspirations."

Lloyd knew that to be only partially true. What his mother left out was the personal grudge Alburg had against them for the death of his daughter, Alys. Even though she had been resurrected, Alburg still held it against their family.

"So there's no real reasoning with him, then," Elladan attempted to clarify.

This time Kratos answered, his face plagued with mixed emotions. "No, not really."

Lara grabbed her husband's hand and squeezed it. Kratos gave her a wan smile in return, before she pressed on.

The next image Lara produced appeared next to Alburg. It portrayed a pale man with a hawkish face and an expression that practically exuded arrogance. The long black hair that framed his features made him look almost vampirish. "Kennig Lisink is the Lord of the Keltins. He is a rich nobleman who maintains his fortune by shipping Keltin Ale and other products all over Thac."

She paused a moment as she traced a solid line between Alburg and Kennig. "Since he is highly dependent on merchant ships, Lisink tends to align himself with Alburg most of the time."

"So another self-serving jerk," Seth commented from underneath his hood.

Lara chuckled with amusement. "True—and not one that can be reasoned with, either, unless the demon incursion interrupts his shipments."

"I think we can safely assume that by then it will be too late," Aksel said candidly.

"Agreed," Lara replied, with a deferential nod to the little cleric.

She hesitated a moment, wringing her hands together nervously before creating the next image. The illusion that appeared below Lisink portrayed a man with wavy blonde hair and scruffy facial features. Beneath the stubble, he bore a striking resemblance to Lara. "And now we come to my dear brother, Argus Hault, the Lord of the Penwick Army. One might think our interests would naturally align, but that is not always the case."

Lloyd could clearly see the sadness in his mother's eyes. Personally, he was not a fan of Uncle Argus. The man was unreasonably jealous of his father and the attention that went to the navy. What Argus didn't seem to realize was the fault lay also with Alburg. Dunamal wanted a strong fleet to help protect his merchant ships.

Lara breathed a regretful sigh as she drew a dotted line from Alburg to Argus. "Argus and I do not see eye-to-eye on many topics. Yet, since the airships are not within his domain, he might not necessarily side against us."

"Pardon me, ma'am," Elladan drawled, "but that doesn't sound exactly encouraging."

"No, unfortunately it is not." Lara did her best to smile, but gave up and shrugged instead.

The next image she drew appeared just below Alburg. This one portrayed another young but grim-faced woman. Garbed in the red-and-brown outfit of the town guard, her long brown hair covered most of her features as if she were trying to hide her youth.

Lara took in a deep breath. "Finally, we come to the last member of the council. Taliana Gailgre is the Lady of the Watch. Her primary concern is policing the city gates, walls, and streets."

Andrella leaned in and peered closely at the young woman's image, her expression thoughtful. "Is she someone who could be possibly swayed?"

Lara pressed her lips together and bobbed her head from side to side. "It's possible."

She motioned in the air and two dotted lines appeared: one connecting Taliana to Alburg, and the other going from her to Carenna. "Taliana works closely with Carenna, and up to a few months ago seemed to follow her lead. However, recently, her council votes have been more in line with Alburg."

"Bribery." The word floated out from under Seth's hood. "Or blackmail," he swiftly amended.

"We've had both possibilities checked into," Kratos admitted, "though nothing conclusive has been found so far."

"Either way," Lara pressed on, "if Taliana recognizes the dangers posed by the demons, she might be swayed to support our side."

Andrella sat back and folded her arms across her chest. "Again, that doesn't sound too promising."

"Unfortunately, I can't disagree," Lara said as she waved her hands twice more. An image of both herself and Kratos appeared in the floating diagram next to Aillinn. Two solid lines traced through the air from Aillinn to Lara and Kratos.

"And there you have it," Lara declared as she plopped herself back down into the empty chair.

Silence fell over the room as they all looked over the floating diagram. About a half minute went by before Elladan stood and rubbed his hands together.

"From everything you've told us, we're most likely looking at a stalemate between the two factions within the council." He swiped his finger down the center of the illusion between Alburg and Aillinn.

Lara sighed and hung her head. "Yes—that tends to happen a lot."

Elladan eyed Lara and Kratos with his typical half-smile. "Then perhaps it's best to just target our argument directly at the Baron."

Kratos and Lara shared a glance, the former responding with a grim nod. "That's exactly what Alburg does. He plays on Caverinus' fears and often sways him to his side."

"Interesting," Elladan murmured, his eyes glimmering as he continued with his train of thought. "You also implied that Andrella's position might impress him."

"I did," Lara agreed, turning to pointedly stare at the young lady, "and it might, if she's up for the challenge."

Andrella looked over the floating diagram once more, then squared her shoulders and met Lara's gaze evenly. "I would be more than honored to represent our cause in front of the council"—she cast a quick glance toward Aksel—"with your approval, of course."

Aksel stared back at her, his expression impassive. "I think the Stealles know the council best. I'm fine with following their recommendations."

"Very good," Lara replied, with another nod to Aksel.

She waved her hand once more and the entire floating image faded away. Lara then swept her eyes around the table. "There's just one more thing"—she said, her eyes shifting subtly to one side as she spoke—"something that could work in our favor."

Lloyd knew his mother well enough to know she was about to drop a fireball on them. "Alright, Mom, what is it?"

Knowing she had been caught, a weak smile crossed Lara's lips. "Well, rumor has it that Dunwynn bought five airships, so the council wants to negotiate for more. If they get them, then they might be more inclined to relinquish one for your use."

The implications of what she just said had barely registered with Lloyd when Glo leapt to his feet. "Are you saying that Theramon is going to be at the council meeting?"

Theramon had been the one going around Thac selling airships to different parties. He had sold them to Penwick, Dunwynn, and had even been in talks with the Wizard's Council out of Lymerdia.

"Yes," Lara answered Glo's question simply.

At that point, Ruka exploded. "Why, that no good son of a— "

"Ruka!" Donnie placed a hand on her shoulder and tried rather unsuccessfully to calm her down.

Ruka practically shoved him away while continuing her tirade. "I'm going to rip his entrails out and feed them back to him. Then I'll rip him limb from limb and have him healed so I can do it all over again!"

While the others tried to calm her down, Lloyd explained to his parents what Theramon had done to the Greymantle sisters. As it turned out, they already knew about Ves, but had no idea about the kidnapping of their younger sister, Maya. As soon as Lloyd told them about it, their expressions grew grim.

"Enough," Lara spat out the word with a force that boomed across the room.

Ruka immediately halted her tirade and met Lara's gaze with a defiant glare.

Lara spoke each word that followed with a measured tone as hard as steel. "As much as it pains me to say this, we cannot directly confront Theramon in front of the council."

Ruka open her mouth to object, but Lara held up her hand in a silencing gesture. "However, once he has left the council chambers, all bets are off. He will either return your sister immediately, or face not just your wrath, but ours as well." She grabbed Kratos by the arm and the two of them stood there, their faces reflecting their deadly resolve.

Upon hearing that, Ruka's anger abated somewhat. She folded her arms across her chest and fixed them with a hard stare. "That I have to see."

"No, you don't," Donnie said in a firm voice, positioning himself directly in front of her.

Ruka's eyes flashed amber as they fixed on the slight elf. The roll of thunder could be heard somewhere off in the distance. "Oh yeah? Who's going to stop me?"

"I am," Donnie replied, his voice softening and filled with emotion, "because I care."

Ruka glared up at him, her hands going to her hips. "Yeah? Well you've got a funny way of showing it."

The sting of her words caused Donnie to visibly flinch. He grimaced, but then tentatively reached out and grasped her shoulders. His voice dropped to barely above a whisper. "That's because I don't want to see you get hurt."

Ruka suddenly seemed at a loss for words. Her anger completely dissipated, her eyes widened as her cheeks reddened. "You don't?"

"No, I don't," Donnie said softly, his voice filled with emotion.

Nearly everyone in the room was moved by Donnie's admission with the exception of Seth, and surprisingly, Lloyd's mother. Lara pulled Lloyd to one side and whispered in his ear, "He does know it's dangerous to toy with a dragon's emotions, doesn't he?"

Lloyd shrugged and whispered back, "Honestly, I don't know if he does, Mom."

Either way, Donnie convinced Ruka to stay with him back here at the inn. As a further precaution, they planned to send Xellos over to the temple to watch over Ves. As a final safeguard, Glo cast a telepathic mind link between himself, Donnie, Xellos, Aksel, and Seth.

With it nearly being time for the council to meet, Lara and Kratos went on ahead. As the rest of them prepared to follow, Lloyd's concern for Andrella grew. The very fate of their world might now rest squarely on her shoulders.

Lloyd drew her off into the empty hallway, pulled her close, and looked her gravely in the eyes. "Are you sure you're ready for this?"

Andrella gave him a winsome smile and tenderly brushed the hair from his brow. "I appreciate your concern, my love, but this is what I've been trained to do since I was a little girl. Trust me, I've dealt with pompous, self-serving nobles from Dunwynn to Orlon and beyond."

Lloyd was about to object further when she stood up on her toes, wrapped her arms around his neck, and kissed him soundly. His head swam from the warmth of her lips and the intoxicating smell of her perfume. His worries swiftly faded away, all but forgotten in a wave of passion.

7
DUCHESS TO BE

Wouldn't it be best to let Dunwynn throw their resources at it?

Castle Avernos dwarfed the keep in Ravenford where Andrella grew up. Thick walls surrounded the grounds, topped
with stone battlements. A tall tower stood at each corner
where the walls met, and two gates with thick wrought-iron
portcullises provided the only access to the grounds—one
on the town side and the other from the river below.

The keep itself rose four stories high, but reached five and even
seven levels at the tallest towers. A light alabaster stone comprised
most of the building. Numerous windows dotted each floor, some
opening to wide enclosed balconies.

The throne room proved to be just as grand, with its ornate red
columns, immense golden chandelier, and ten-step white marble
staircase that led up to the level of the throne. A huge shield hung
behind the throne depicting the heraldic of Penwick—a golden lion
above two crossed swords on a split background of red and black.

Two guards flanked a side door that led to the council chambers. The companions waited just outside for their turn to be called in to see them.

Lloyd seemed particularly pensive, pacing back and forth around the room. "What's taking them so long?"

"It's politics—they'll drone on forever." The words came from beneath Seth's hood. Upon their arrival, the halfling resumed his position from their pre-meeting—slid down in a chair, hood pulled over his head, and arms folded across his chest.

Elladan stood and grabbed Lloyd by the arm as he passed. "Seth's right, you know. You keep this up and all you'll do is wear a path in the Baron's nice marble floor."

Lloyd stopped, his face reddening with embarrassment. "Yeah, I guess you're right." The young man glanced over at Andrella with an apologetic smile.

Andrella forced herself to smile back, but in truth she felt nearly as nervous as Lloyd. Her worries didn't stem from a lack of training, though. As she previously confided to Lloyd, diplomacy had been ingrained into her at a very young age. Nor did her anxiety come from a lack of experience.

Andrella had achieved a variety of diplomatic successes over these last few months. She had temporarily overseen the entire town of Vermoorden and had diffused a takeover by Dunwynn troops. She had gotten her Uncle Kelvick to listen to reason about the demons. She had even held her own against the erratic Princess of Lanfor.

Still, this time felt different. Appropriating that airship was a key part of their strategy to stop the coming demon invasion, and it was up to her to convince the council.

She placed a hand over her fluttering stomach. *Am I truly up to the task?*

At that moment, the door to the council room opened. Lara stood in the entryway, her expression solemn and her voice officious. "The council will see you now."

Get it together, girl, Andrella silently chastised herself. Straightening to her full height of five feet, seven inches, she marched forward in as dignified a manner as she could muster.

"Thank you, Lady Stealle," she said in a courtly voice as she entered into the room beyond.

The size of the council chamber took Andrella by surprise. A large, ornate mahogany table formed the centerpiece of the room. Eight equally ornate chairs lined either side of the table, but they paled in comparison to the end chair with its high back, depicting the heraldic of Penwick. Her Uncle Caverinus, the Baron of Penwick, currently occupied that chair.

Andrella recognized the other council members from the illusionary images Lara had conjured. Her Uncle Aillinn sat on the Baron's right, with Kratos next to him, then Lara, and finally Carenna Hightower. On the Baron's left sat Alburg Dunamal, followed by Argus Hault, Kennig Lisink, and Taliana Gailgre.

Andrella instinctively knew that the members were seated in 'pecking' order. Further, they had split across the table by affiliations.

The chair at the other end from the Baron appeared less ornate than the rest. Though its occupant had his back to her, Andrella immediately recognized that golden-blonde hair and those garish gold robes.

Theramon. The last time they met, the psychic immortal had been possessing Maya's body. Still, his chilling presence was unmistakable.

Theramon appeared to be just finishing his sales pitch to the council. "…and that is why I would be willing to offer you the same deal I have given to the Duke of Dunwynn…"

"Hi." A soft, child-like voice diverted Andrella's attention away from the proceedings.

A number of high-back benches lined the walls around the chamber. On the one directly opposite the council sat a little girl with golden-blonde hair in a white dress with a bright blue bow.

Maya! Andrella's heart practically leapt into her throat. She nearly ran to the kidnapped girl's side, but a firm hand restrained her.

"Don't," Glo whispered in her ear. "That may not be Maya."

Andrella froze in place. Glo was right. Theramon had fooled them before. After what he had tried to do to Ves, there was no telling if that was actually Maya. Andrella forced herself to smile.

The little girl held up a porcelain doll that had been seated in her lap and peered at Aksel with a hopeful smile. "Do you want to play?"

The girl sounded so forlorn that Andrella thought her heart would break. She was certain Aksel felt the same, but somehow he managed to keep his voice steady.

"Not right now. Maybe after our meeting?"

The little girl's blue eyes lit up, dimples forming at the corners of her mouth. "Okay," she said with the innocent certainty of a child, then went back to playing with her doll.

Andrella gulped. If that wasn't Maya, then it was an incredible likeness.

Across the room, the conversation had stopped. Theramon turned in his chair, his violet-shaded eyes fixed on the companions. "Ah, so we meet again."

Andrella put on her best diplomatic face. "Theramon, you look different than the last time we saw you."

The immortal rose from his chair with the hint of a smile and gestured toward his sparkling robes. "It must be the outfit."

Andrella found his dark attempt at humor less than amusing.

Theramon turned to face the council. "Ladies, gentlemen, I'm sure we can continue this conversation at a later time."

"But…" Dunamal began to object.

Theramon cut him off with a gesture. "Ah, my dear Alburg, our business can wait. These folks have far more pressing matters to discuss."

Theramon walked away from the table before anything more could be said. Lloyd and Lara flanked Andrella on either side as he passed, but he merely gave them an insincere smile before seating himself next to Maya.

Lara ushered the companions forward, directing Andrella to the open seat and the rest of them to the side benches. Interestingly enough, Seth was not among them. Andrella secretly envied the halfling for cleverly ducking out of the meeting.

Lara next made introductions all around, pointedly presenting Andrella as the heir to the Dunwynn throne. When she had finished, Aillinn came over and warmly embraced Andrella.

"My dearest niece, it is so good to finally meet you. I trust your father is well?"

Andrella felt an immediate affection for this goodhearted man. "Yes, Uncle Aillinn. He is quite well, thanks to the timely intervention of my fiancé and friends." She ended with a gesture toward her companions.

"Well then, I see we are already indebted to this fine group," Aillinn said loudly, with a pointed look at the Baron.

Caverinus appeared quite uncomfortable at being put on the spot. He awkwardly adjusted himself in his seat and cleared his throat. "Yes, yes. You are quite right, Aillinn."

The Baron fixed his beady eyes on Andrella, his tone sounding less than sincere. "Welcome, niece. I hope you find your stay here in Penwick far more enjoyable than those cold 'northern' cities."

Andrella responded with a genteel smile. "Thank you, uncle. So far I have been made to feel quite at home. With a bit more encouragement, I might be convinced to make this fair city of yours my permanent place of residence."

Caverinus practically beamed at her words. "That is quite excellent news." He peered at Lara and Kratos. "I don't know what the two of you have been saying to her, but whatever it is, I highly approve."

A look of barely suppressed amusement danced across Lara's face. "Oh, I'm fairly certain the credit for that belongs all to our son." She gestured toward Lloyd.

Still swelling with pride, Caverinus followed her gaze. "Indeed, young Stealle. You have done Penwick proud."

"In more ways than one, from the reports I hear," Aillinn added, taking advantage of the Baron's sudden good mood. "I understand that this business with the undead tower went well?"

"Yes, sir." Lloyd shot out of his seat and answered emphatically.

"Please then, give us your report," Aillinn urged.

Lloyd gave a brief account of what had transpired in the City of Tears. His explanation painted a vivid picture of the power the Empress wielded, due to the tower and its crystal. He ended with the demons' attempt to take the tower once she had fallen.

After Lloyd finished, Aillinn again addressed the Baron. "And thus the second thing we are indebted to this group for, Caverinus."

Following Aillinn's lead once again, the Baron addressed his appreciation to Lloyd. "Indeed. Well done, young man."

So far, their meeting with the council had gone smoothly. Uncle Aillinn turned out to be a masterful politician, specifically when it came to influencing his brother. Lara and Kratos appeared equally satisfied with the proceedings.

On the other side of the table, Alburg seemed less than thrilled. He gestured impatiently at Aillinn. "Yes, yes, good job and all, but can we move this along? We do have pressing matters at hand."

The Baron once again adjusted himself in his seat. "Yes, quite right, Alburg." He folded his hands on the table in front of him and peered across its length directly at Andrella. "I do believe you had a request for us?"

Andrella immediately discerned Alburg's ploy. He had lost control of these proceedings and was attempting to recoup by trivializing their concerns. She had seen this done before and knew exactly how to handle it.

Andrella met the Baron's gaze with a refined smile. "Yes, uncle, in fact I do. However, with no disrespect to Master Dunamal," she directed a deferential nod toward Alburg, "I do believe it's important to understand the gravity of the situation with respect to these demons and towers."

She finished by sweeping her gaze around the entire table. When her eyes met with Carenna's, the warrior pulled a parchment from the pile in front of her and raised it for all to see.

"I have my grandfather's report on that right here. I'm afraid we haven't had a chance to review it as of yet, though," she explained with an apologetic look toward Andrella.

This was going better than Andrella had anticipated. She gestured toward the papers in Carenna's hand. "Would you be so kind as to read it out loud," she glanced at the Baron, "with your permission of course, uncle."

Caverinus sat back in his chair and waved impatiently at Carenna. "Go ahead."

Carenna stood and read the report aloud. It contained a summary of the companions' meeting with Lord Hightower three days prior. The report emphasized the growth of the demon army and the potential catastrophe were they to acquire a second tower.

Andrella quietly gauged the room as Carenna read. The Baron's expression grew more and more nervous. Aillinn, Kratos, and Lara appeared openly concerned. On the other side of the table, Alburg's expression soured. Lisink seemed wrapped in his own thoughts. Argus fidgeted uneasily in his seat. Taliana seemed torn, her face impassive though her eyes betrayed her growing anxiety.

Silence pervaded the room once Carenna finished. Even Alburg seemed momentarily at a loss for words.

Andrella swept her eyes around the council table, taking the opportunity to hammer her point home. "So as you can see, time is of the essence."

Her bold statement prompted an immediate response from Argus. His eyes narrowed as he spoke in the tone one took when schooling a young child. "Young lady, if you're looking for forces to march on this Demon Tower, we simply cannot afford them. The Penwick army isn't quite the size of the navy."

Argus paused and cast a spurious glance at Kratos. "We are stretched thin as it is, dealing with the remnants of this undead incursion."

Kratos slammed his hand on the table, meeting Argus' gaze with a hard stare. "It would have been far worse if this group had not already dealt with the tower in the marshes. Penwick could have been flanked from the north and the south."

Argus' cheeks reddened with anger. He sputtered as he struggled to respond, but Alburg silenced him with a curt gesture.

A smug smile crossed Alburg's face as he replied instead. "Ah, yes, Kratos, you bring up an excellent point. This second tower is closer to the northern region. Wouldn't it be best to let Dunwynn throw their resources at it?" He ended with a pointed look at the Baron.

Caverinus immediately picked up on his lead. "Yes, yes, quite right, Alburg. Didn't we have a report on that the other day?"

"We did," Carenna answered his query. She swiftly recounted a report on Dunwynn troops that had flown off for the tower with the Princess of Lanfor.

When she finished, Alburg slammed both his hands down on the table in triumph. "Well, there you have it. Problem solved."

Kratos had forewarned them about this tact the council might take. Andrella had prepared a rebuttal in her mind, but Kara beat her to it.

"It won't be enough," the angelic warrior stated emphatically from her seat on the bench behind Alburg.

Alburg glanced over his shoulder with a scornful expression. "Really? And why is that?"

Kara rose from her seat and paced around the chamber as she recounted a bloody tale of destruction from the Third Demon War. Her descriptions were both graphic and terrifying. When she was done, even Taliana had turned pale.

Only Alburg remained stubbornly unconvinced. He waved a dismissive hand through the air. "Those are bard tales at best, and bards do tend to have a flair for the dramatic."

Elladan, seated next to Kara, looked as if he was going to protest. Andrella, however, beat him to it. "I'm afraid to say, Master Dunamal, but you are wrong on that point. Kara is a Thul Dunin, an angel of the host. What you have just heard is a firsthand account of events that unfolded nearly six millennia ago."

For the first time since they had entered the chambers, Alburg appeared unsure of himself. He cast another glance at Kara, a single eyebrow raised.

Argus, however, doggedly returned to his original argument. "Even if that is true, the point is still moot. We cannot afford the resources for an assault on this tower."

Taliana shook off her momentary fear and as expected, sided with Argus. "I'm afraid I have to agree. We cannot leave Penwick undefended."

Andrella now had them exactly where she wanted. She fixed Taliana with a look of sympathy. "And I quite agree with you. I've been in this city for less than a day, but I've already fallen in love with it."

Taliana seemed taken aback, not expected that answer. Argus seemed surprised as well.

Andrella filled her voice with passion as she pressed on. "One day I'll be responsible for all the souls in Dunwynn. Yet, with my impending marriage, I also feel beholden to the people of Penwick."

Andrella covered her heart with both hands. "My greatest desire is to protect them all. I don't want to see another soul die at the hands of these foul creatures."

She spread her hands out in front of her, toward both sides of the table. "To that end, all I ask is to continue to borrow one of your airships. With it we can track down weapons of great power—weapons that can send these demons back to the Abyss from whence they came!"

She finished by slamming her fist down onto the table, something she had noted other members of the council doing to emphasize their points.

Her speech was met with a round of "Here, here," from the one side of the table and many of her companions. Even the Baron, Taliana, and Argus seem moved by her words.

Alburg apparently appreciated her performance, but not for the reasons she had hoped. The political-minded merchant stood and brought his hands together in a slow clap. "That was a very passionate speech, young lady. Quite moving, in fact. I can see that you'll make a fine duchess one day. However, we still have only the two airships, and they are to be the cornerstone of Penwick's defense."

Elladan had been quiet thus far, watching the political banter back and forth. He chose this moment to interject a crucial point. "But weren't you looking to buy more?"

Elladan finished with a pointed glance at Theramon. The violet-eyed immortal still sat next to Maya, his chin in his hand as he watched the proceedings with clear amusement.

"My offer is still on the table," Theramon responded with a nod to the bard.

Alburg, seemingly unperturbed, sat back down with a nonchalant wave of his hand. "Ah yes, but those negotiations are still in the works."

Aillinn leaned across the table and caught Alburg's eye. "Still, even you must admit there is merit to Andrella's words. If this threat were to get past Dunwynn, we would be hard-pressed to stop it at our own front door."

Alburg's expression remained impassive, but those words had struck a nerve with the Baron. "What are you getting at, Aillinn?"

A satisfied smile crossed Aillinn's lips, resulting in a scowl from Alburg. The Baron's brother then sat back and turned his attention to the Caverinus. "Wouldn't it be better to lend one of our airships to the Lady Andrella and company? They have already proven their worth." He swept his eyes around the table. "If they can find these weapons as they say, then we are buying ourselves insurance against the coming storm—a storm that could sweep away not just our city, but all of Thac if left unchecked."

Aillinn ended with his eyes once again settled on the Baron. Andrella marveled at how masterfully he handled his brother. She thought she could learn a thing or two from this man.

Unfortunately, Caverinus looked more nervous than usual. Lara was right. He was far too timid a man to make such an important decision on his own. His eyes appeared filled with guilt as he turned to Dunamal. "What say you, Alburg?"

Alburg's scowl faded into a smug smile, which he cast at Aillinn before answering the Baron. "Your brother and niece both make impassioned arguments, but I prefer to deal in facts. The fact is, neither ship has made it back here as of yet. Also, if I am not mistaken, they will need to be maintenanced before they can fly again." He turned an eye toward Kratos. "Isn't that correct?"

Kratos wore a dour expression, but responded truthfully. "Yes, it is."

Alburg practically crowed with delight. "See, even Kratos and I can agree on that."

Andrella felt the argument slipping away from them. They had come so close, only to be forestalled by the Baron's craven nature. Still, he hadn't completely denied their request, either.

Alburg then surprised them all with an unexpected overture. "Since it will take some time anyway, what if we have these fine folks help us by dealing with a threat much closer to home?"

The Baron's puzzled expression mirrored Andrella's. "What did you have in mind, Alburg?"

Dunamal waved a nonchalant hand toward the end of the table. "I would leave the details of that to Carenna and Taliana. However, if they were to successfully do so, I'm sure it would weigh in their favor with this council."

Andrella didn't quite buy Dunamal's indifference. She was certain he had something specific in mind—something that would not be all that easy for the companions to accomplish.

Caverinus, however, seemed thrilled by the idea. He slapped the arms of his chair excitedly, the guilt disappearing from his eyes. "That is an excellent idea, Alburg!" He peered across the table at Andrella. "The council meets again in five days' time, my dear. By then the airships should be ready and we'll revisit your request."

Andrella slowly rose from her seat, an uneasy feeling in the pit of her stomach. Still, she forced herself to execute a graceful curtsy. "Thank you kindly, Uncle Caverinus." She hesitated a moment, then decided to fire one last parting salvo. "I'll be certain to inform my other uncle, Kelvick, of your generosity in this matter."

A wave of uncertainty flashed through the Baron's eyes at the mention of the Duke of Dunwynn. "Um—yes, that would be— quite kind of you, my dear."

As Andrella turned to leave, a thin smile crossed her lips. Lara had been right. Dunwynn was definitely a weak spot for him and Andrella had scored a direct hit with that remark. Perhaps he would think twice before ultimately denying her request.

Andrella's gloating was cut prematurely short when Lloyd abruptly drew up beside her. "Where's Theramon?"

Andrella froze in her tracks. The bench where Maya and Theramon had been now stood empty.

8
DOUBLE TALK

Glo gulped—everyone's eyes now glowed violet

Seth didn't move a muscle as the others filed into the council chamber. He briefly thought about going invisible, but someone might spot the movement required to invoke the spell.

Aksel ended up being one of the last ones in line. For a brief moment Seth thought Aksel had seen him, but like the others, he seemed totally intent on entering the council chambers.

Once the door closed behind them, Seth did what he did best— waited quietly and inconspicuously, out of the direct line of sight. Minutes passed with no change other than the drone of muffled voices echoing through the closed door. Finally, after twenty minutes or so, the door to the council room opened again.

The continuing drone indicated that the meeting had not yet ended. Seth peeked out from under his hood to see who had the good sense to duck out early.

A young human with long blonde hair and the most distasteful robes Seth had ever seen exited the chamber. Other than his bad taste, Seth might have not given the man a second thought were it not for his companion. The little girl beside him looked just like Maya.

That meant the man had to be Theramon. Still, something seemed off about these two. Seth had seen far too many cons in his life to take things merely at face value. Thus, he chose to quietly observe them before doing anything.

Theramon stopped and rubbed his temples as if he had a splitting headache. The girl, on the contrary, seemed quite content, holding a doll out in front of her as if she were dancing. If Seth didn't know any better, he would think Theramon had little to no control over her.

As if to answer his question, Theramon muttered under his breath. "Can you please stop that incessant singing?"

The little girl stopped playing with her doll, her face forming into a pout. "But I'm not."

Theramon winced. "You are in your mind."

It was all Seth could do to stop himself from laughing. The great Theramon, the immortal psychic who could read and control minds, and who could possess bodies, had met his match in an innocent little dragon girl. On a more serious note, Seth no longer had any doubts the little girl was Maya.

"Hmph," Maya murmured, stamping her small foot on the floor.

Still grimacing, Theramon pointed a finger across the room toward the exit. A single word passed through his lips. "March."

Maya gave him a dirty look, then wrapped her arms around her doll and stomped off toward the exit. Theramon followed close behind.

Seth needed to move fast. Sliding from his seat, he glided through the maze of chairs and slipped into the main aisle just ahead of them. He propped himself against the throne room door, the corner of his mouth lifting ever so slightly. "If she's bothering you that much, I can take her off your hands."

Both Maya and Theramon stopped short. The former's pout

disappeared when she saw him, while the latter eyed him with cold amusement. "Nice try, but the girl stays with me until I get what I want."

Seth folded his arms across his chest. "And what's that?"

Theramon fixed him with a disdainful gaze. "Not something that you can give me."

Seth gave Maya a subtle wink, then shrugged at the golden-haired man. "Are you sure? Because you don't look so good."

Theramon began to wince once more. Maya must have gotten Seth's unspoken message and started to sing again in her mind.

Rubbing his temples, Theramon gazed from Maya to Seth, realization dawning in his eyes. "Oh, I see what you did there. Very clever." He narrowed an eye at Seth as if reassessing him. "You are not like the others."

"Hmph," Seth muttered. "Flattery will get you nowhere."

A cold smile spread across Theramon's lips. "Maybe we can do business after all. Give me the rune pattern to Tower of Night, and you can have the girl."

Tower of Night? Seth assumed Theramon meant the key to the force field at the top of the Marsh Tower.

Seth found it rather curious that Theramon would trade Maya for a chance to get at his sister. Yet that wasn't the only thing he found interesting. This entire time, Seth had been mind-linked to Glo, yet Theramon hadn't seemed to notice. Perhaps Maya's singing gave him more than just a headache—maybe it also interfered with his psychic powers.

Either way, Theramon was totally unprepared when Glo came flying across the throne room and clocked him across the chin with a fairly decent haymaker. To be honest, Seth hadn't expected it, either, but he found it absolutely hysterical.

Theramon staggered back from the blow. Catching himself on the last row of chairs, he glared at Glo as he wiped away the blood that had formed below his lip. "Feeling better now, I trust?"

Glo half-grinned and half-winced as he waved the hand he had hit Theramon with back and forth through the air. "Yes, as a matter of fact, I do."

Lloyd, Andrella, Elladan, and Aksel all caught up to them at that point. Lloyd looked at Glo with clear admiration. "That was some punch!"

Still nursing his hand, Glo's cheeks turned a bright shade of scarlet. "Thanks, but I think maybe I should stick to magic from now on."

Elladan placed himself between Theramon and Glo, holding his hands out as if to ward them both off. "Alright, now that we got that out of the way, how about we talk this out like civilized folks?"

Theramon adjusted his jaw, momentarily turning his head to the side as he spat blood. "As long as you can keep your barbarian wizard here at bay."

Barbarian wizard? Seth couldn't hold it back anymore. He burst out in laughter, nearly falling on the floor.

"Everything okay over there?" One of the council guards called over to them.

"Everything's fine!" Elladan yelled back. "Just a minor misunderstanding."

Theramon stood and readjusted his robes, a cold, superior smile returning to his face. "Very well—we can talk, but not here. I suggest we adjourn to my suite back at the inn."

Elladan gazed around at the others. No one seemed thrilled with the suggestion, but it was better than continuing their fight in the castle.

Elladan ushered Theramon ahead of them. "Lead the way."

Xellos Runell sat quietly in rafters of the Temple of the Ralnai, wondering how he had gotten into this mess in the first place. It had all started out as an innocent visit to Hagentree. Next thing he knew, he had retrieved a cold iron spike from the great tree, and in the process got himself cursed. Xellos had one year to find three Arcarion seeds and plant them in the fields outside Hagentree, or his life would be forfeit.

In truth, he only had himself to blame. Xellos' obsession with shiny objects, coins in particular, had done him in. Strangely enough, he didn't even need the money. His people, being forest dwellers and shapeshifters, really had no use for them. They lived as one with the land; it nurtured them and they nurtured it back in turn.

Thus, Xellos felt completely out of his element in the ruins of the human/elven city in the marshes, and now here in Penwick. The buildings of wood and stone these people built and lived in seemed so foreign, but none more than this enormous temple where he now waited.

Xellos spied Ves not long after entering the temple from the main chapel. From there, she went directly into one of the smaller side chapels, the one underneath the statue of a human god holding a sword and a lightning bolt.

When Ves exited the side chapel twenty minutes later, a blonde-furred human in golden robes confronted her. The moment she saw him, she backpedaled into the chapel, her face distorted with fear.

Xellos telepathically alerted the others as he invoked his cloak and dove from the ceiling. Moments later, he touched down behind the man and drew his bow in one swift motion.

"Back away," he told the man simply.

The man turned around and gave Xellos a start. He had violet eyes just like Elistra. The man's reaction to having an arrow pointed at him was also quite unexpected. He laughed at Xellos and waved a hand at him, as if shooing him away.

"Begone," the man said as if it were an afterthought.

A strange compulsion abruptly came over Xellos. Before he knew it, he found himself turned around and headed for the front door of the temple.

Glo rubbed his sore hand as they followed Theramon from the castle grounds. Punching him like that had perhaps been foolish, but gave Glo a keen sense of satisfaction, nonetheless. After everything the smug immortal had done to Ves, Maya, and his own sister, Elistra, he definitely deserved it.

Even worse, they had recently discovered that Theramon was the one behind the creation of the towers. He had convinced Naradon

to build them, but lied about their ultimate purpose. Instead of seal-
ing the demons away, they would have destroyed the entire world.

Despite feeling gratified, one thing still bothered Glo. Why hadn't
Theramon attempted to use his psychic powers? The last time they
clashed, he had possessed Maya, Andrella, and nearly Glo as well.
Something was definitely not right with this whole situation, but before Glo could dwell on it further, he heard Xellos' telepathic cry for
help.

Ves is in trouble!

Glo reacted out of pure instinct. Aksel, right in front of him,
froze in place at the tracker's warning. Glo grabbed him by the arm
and whispered, "Send for Cyclone."

Glo then traced a quick spell through the air, ending with the
words. *"Planum porta."*

As soon as the words left his lips, a blue, glowing, person-sized
oval opened in the air before him. Glo leapt into the portal, briefly
passed through the astral plane, and moments later appeared on the
steps leading up to the Temple of the Ralnai. He was just in time to
see a slim man with a bow and quiver exit the temple. Dressed in
the greens and browns of forest tracker, a shock of bright red hair
peeked out from under his thick hood.

That's Xellos. If Ves is in trouble, what's he doing out here?

Glo ran up to the tracker, but found him glassy-eyed, as if he
were in a trance. Focusing his mind, Glo peered beyond the veil and
received a shock. A thin mass of invisible tendrils extended through
the door of the temple and had wrapped themselves around Xellos'
head.

Glo had seen this type of mild psychic possession before. *That
looks like Theramon's handiwork, but how can that be? I just left him outside
the castle.*

Grabbing Xellos by the arms, he shook him while calling out his
name. As he did so, the tendrils loosened and finally fell away.

Xellos' eyes came back into focus. "Glolindir? What am I doing
out here?"

"You were under a spell," Glo explained simply. "What happened
to Ves?"

Xellos swiftly told him about the blonde-haired man with the violet eyes.

Theramon? How is that possible? Glo wondered. Either way, there was no time to waste.

"Come on!" Glo waved for Xellos to follow.

They rushed into the temple together, Xellos guiding them to a small chapel in the back dedicated to Alaric, the god of storms. Upon entering, they found the chapel empty except for two occupants. Ves stood with her back up against the wall, while a familiar figure loomed over her—a golden-haired man in sparkling gold robes.

"Theramon?" Glo paused, uttering the name in total confusion. "Or more like his doppelganger," he said aloud as the realization struck him.

Xellos did not wait for a response, immediately drawing his bow and shooting the interloper with an arrow.

Strangely, it didn't seem to faze him.

Theramon's doppelganger stood there with an arrow sticking out of his shoulder as if he could feel no pain. He then shifted his gaze to Xellos. "Well, that wasn't very friendly."

The doppelganger's eyes abruptly flashed violet. Beyond the veil, Glo could see mana flowing through his third eye. There was no motion or incantation, but instead a sudden release of power. Invisible tendrils lashed out toward Xellos and wrapped themselves around him like a noose.

Glo had to act fast. He swiftly traced a pattern through the air, pushing as much mana into it as he could muster.

"*Aqua Ruptis.*" As the words left Glo's lips, a powerful stream of water burst from his outstretched hands.

The deluge slammed into the doppelganger, knocking him over and pushing him across the room. With the doppelganger's concentration broken, the tendrils enveloping Xellos faded away into nothingness.

Knowing he had only bought them a little time, Glo ran over to Ves. He grabbed her by the hand and yelled, "Come on, let's go!"

Ves peered at him wild-eyed, but didn't move. She seemed

completely overtaken by fear. With no other recourse, Glo yanked her toward the door.

They exited the small chapel and only went a few steps down the aisle when the doppelganger appeared in the doorway. Anger filled his eyes as they settled on Glo.

"Now you've done it." The doppelganger's eyes flashed violet again, yet this time they projected an enormous amount of power outward.

Glo felt a huge wave of mana pass over them and flow out into the temple. The lights around the chamber flickered and then went out. Along with that, Glo felt the protective spells that encircled the place completely disappear.

All the temple-goers around them stopped in their tracks, then turned as one to face Glo, Ves, and Xellos. Glo gulped—everyone's eyes now glowed violet.

Forcing down his fears, the young elf placed himself between Ves and the doppelganger. "Leave these people out of it! They've done nothing to you."

The doppelganger glowered back at him, all pretense of civility gone. "I didn't want to bring the people of this city into it. This is on your head."

Glo, Ves, and Xellos were backed against the wall of the central altar dais as the temple-goers crowded around them. The young elf grappled with his conscience as he sought for a way to protect his friends without hurting these innocent people.

Xellos seemed to struggle as well. He held out his bow with a nocked arrow, pointing it this way and that, yet didn't have the heart to fire.

A hand wrapped around Glo's arm, then his other arm. He felt himself being pushed down. He struggled to maintain his balance, but there were too many of them. Xellos started to go down as well. Ves screamed.

With no other recourse, flames appeared at Glo's fingertips. He prayed to the gods for forgiveness as he pulled in the mana to release the spell.

Suddenly, a white circle of light flashed across the aisle around them. Glo felt the surge of magic and the folks holding them stopped in their tracks. They let go and pulled back, shaking their heads as if waking from a dream.

At the same moment, a fierce voice echoed across the vaulted ceilings of the temple. "Who dares to desecrate the Temple of the Ralnai?"

Over at the door to the main chapel stood a familiar figure in white robes. It was Thea, her eyes lit with white fury.

The doppelganger turned to face this new challenger. "Someone you don't want to cross, little girl."

With an almost negligent wave of his hand, he dispelled her magic. Up and down the aisle, the temple-goers again fell under his sway, their eyes turning violet once more.

Thea's voice grew hard as steel. "We'll just see about that."

Glo felt a great surge of magic as a white aura enveloped her body. The aura grew taller and wider, enveloping the temple-goers as it expanded across the aisle. Each person it touched was freed from the doppelganger's control, the violet fading from their eyes again.

The doppelganger's mouth twisted into a wicked smile as he drew in mana once more. His eyes flashed purple, and invisible tendrils shot out from his body straight for Thea.

"Watch out!" Glo cried in warning.

Thea must have seen them, too. She threw up her arms in a warding gesture, bracing herself for the imminent onslaught.

All of a sudden, a blue blur leapt from the altar dais above them. A long-handled axe swung out in front of it, cleaving the doppelganger's head clean from its shoulders.

Cyclone landed in front of the doppelganger as his body collapsed to the floor. Strangely, he no longer looked like Theramon.

Glo's stomach nearly turned inside out. This must have been someone Theramon had taken over, like what he had planned to do to Ves.

Up and down the aisle, the temple-goers began to wake up from the doppelganger's spell. However, Glo didn't quite believe it was over. The real Theramon was still out there.

Glo shot a quick warning to Aksel and Seth. After a brief telepathic exchange, Aksel bade him to get Ves somewhere safe.

Glo locked eyes with Thea. "Is there somewhere more secure we can go?"

Thea bit her lip as she eyed the fallen body and the still-dazed temple-goers. "I would have thought the temple secure." She hesitated a moment longer, then motioned to the door behind her. "Follow me. There's a back entrance behind the chapel."

The four of them fell in line behind the priestess as she led the way out of the temple.

9
MIND GAMES

What do you want with the sisters, anyway?

$\mathcal{A}$ ksel had heard Xellos' telepathic cry at the same time as
Glo. Yet with Theramon here, he couldn't imagine what
might pose a threat to Ves. Still, he agreed with Glo—
better to err on the side of caution.

As the wizard disappeared through his portal, Aksel
sent a mental message to Cyclone. *Ves is in trouble at the temple.*

Got it, came the immediate response. All went eerily silent after
that.

The rest of them continued to follow Theramon out across the
Lord's Square—the same plaza they had arrived in earlier this morning. Theramon appeared quite preoccupied, between holding onto
Maya and skillfully evading Elladan's questions. If he had heard their
telepathic exchange, he gave no indication. He didn't even seem to
notice that Glo had gone missing.

Weaving through the late afternoon crowds, the small group had just made it to the other end of the great plaza when Theramon came to an abrupt halt. He grabbed his chest and let out a low moan, his skin paling as he doubled over.

At the same moment, Glo broke the telepathic silence, warning them about what had happened at the temple. Aksel exchanged a worried glance with Seth as he told Glo to take Ves somewhere safe.

Meanwhile, Elladan hovered over the ailing immortal. "Are you alright? You don't look so good."

Theramon slowly straightened himself up, his violet eyes burning with hatred. "That's it. Say what you want here and now, or we are done."

Aksel couldn't believe his ears. With everything Theramon had done to his friends, he had a lot of nerve trying to turn this around on them. Still, this wasn't the time or place to pick a fight with the arrogant immortal. A number of folks had stopped to stare at them and innocent bystanders could get hurt.

Swallowing his pride, Aksel stepped forward, his hands raised in a calming gesture. "Hey, we just want to talk. You're the one who keeps attacking our friends."

A chilling smile spread across Theramon's face. "I didn't know talking was an attack."

"Tsk," Seth clicked his tongue. "Mind control is."

Elladan's brow knit into a faint frown as he looked from Aksel to Theramon to Seth. "Did we miss something?"

The others listened on in horror as Aksel gave them a brief synopsis of what had occurred at the temple. When he finished, their faces had darkened over.

Lloyd took a step toward Theramon, his hands on his sword hilts. "You son of a…"

"Lloyd, not here." Andrella grabbed him by the arm and swept her eyes around the plaza.

Lloyd followed her gaze to see that more people had stopped to stare at them. His expression grew pained as he wrestled with his emotions. A moment later, his hands dropped away from his swords.

"That's a good boy." Theramon mocked the honorable young man.

Andrella placed herself in front of Lloyd, leveling a stare at the smug immortal that could have melted a mountain of ice. "It's a shame that you constantly have to revert to these parlor tricks, but I guess that's all you can expect from one with such a limited mind."

Theramon grabbed his chest again, this time feigning his wound. "Ouch. Slings and arrows, my dear…"

All of a sudden, a small foot lashed out and kicked him in the shin. "Ouch!" Theramon cried for real this time.

Maya glared up at him, her normally cherub face scrunched into the meanest look she could possibly muster. "You hurt my sister, you meanie!"

Considering Maya's inert strength, Aksel surmised that kick hurt quite a bit. Still, Theramon seemed more unnerved than injured. Though Aksel couldn't be sure why, his control over Maya appeared to have waned.

"Losing your touch?" Seth wore a wicked grin as he needled the shaken immortal further.

A wild look flickered through Theramon's violet eyes, but it quickly disappeared. He took a step back, his voice taking on an ominous tone. "Perhaps you need a reminder of what I am capable of."

Things nearly escalated out of control from there. A deathly silence fell across the plaza and a cold wind kicked up out of nowhere. Aksel could feel the abrupt rise in Theramon's power. It was so potent, it practically made his skin crawl.

Lloyd placed himself in front of Andrella and drew his swords. Kara lined up next to him, her spear readied. A pair of daggers appeared in Seth's hands.

Aksel gulped. They were still surrounded by too many folks for things to go down without someone getting hurt. He opened his mouth to say just that, but Elladan beat him to the punch.

A lute appeared in the bard's hands, a soothing tune arising from its strings. "It's a shame you feel that way—especially when all we really want the same thing."

Theramon cast a disdainful gaze at the bard. "Really? And what's that?"

Elladan shrugged and fixed the immortal with one of his most charming half-smiles. "Why, to take down the demon tower, of course."

"That is true," Theramon admitted, his expression lightening ever so slightly.

Aksel knew better than to think the bard's magic had affected Theramon. Still, for some reason the immortal held himself back. Perhaps Seth was right. Maybe something was interfering with Theramon's powers. Still, it wasn't worth risking the lives of those in the plaza around them.

Aksel purposely marched forward and placed himself between Theramon and the others. He held out a hand in either direction, making a warding gesture with them.

"Stand down," he told his friends in as commanding a tone as he could muster. They all stared back at him, then one by one, sheathed their weapons. Seth was the last to comply.

"Whatever," the halfling muttered, the two daggers disappearing from his hands as if they had never been there in the first place.

Aksel took a deep breath, then turned around to face Theramon. "What do you want with the sisters, anyway?"

The anger in Theramon's eyes dissipated, replaced instead with a condescending smile. "Leverage."

That had not been the response Aksel expected. "Leverage with whom?"

Theramon's smile transformed further into a look of clear superiority. "Why, the girls' parents, of course."

Aksel felt a wave of confusion wash over him. *Why would Theramon need leverage with the sisters' parents?*

True, their father was Rodric Greymantle, one of the greatest wizards of all time. Yet Theramon's powers would probably be a match for Rodric's. Further, Theramon had that giant adamantine dragon...

Wait. Something clicked in Aksel's mind. He locked eyes with Elladan. "In Dreamweaver's chronicles, didn't it say that all dragons fell under the thrall master's sway except for one?"

"It does." Elladan responded with a knowing nod. "In fact, it goes further than that. It speaks of a mad storm dragon who fell beyond the Dragon Master's control—a dragon that was his eventual undoing."

Andrella had been listening intently to their conversation. After that last statement, her face abruptly lit up. "If I'm not mistaken, aren't storm dragons bronze?"

"Indeed," Elladan answered her with a sly smile.

"Also, wasn't Rodric Greymantle a key player in defeating the Thrall Masters?" Andrella pressed further.

Elladan smile spread into a grin. "Exactly what I was thinking."

Suddenly, all the pieces fell into place. Aksel now understood why Theramon was so afraid of the Greymantles' parents.

Theramon stared at Aksel with thinly veiled amusement. "So you finally get it?"

Aware that Theramon was trying to goad him, Aksel let the conceited statement wash over him without reacting. "Yes. The girls' mother is the same storm dragon that took down the Dragon Thrall Master. Together with her husband, Rodric, the two are a nearly unstoppable duo."

"Give the gnome a prize," Theramon said in an attempt at levity. Unfortunately, it came across as more condescending than not. When he saw no one laughed at his little joke, he grew serious once more. "I need assurances that they won't interfere with my plans."

"And what plans are those, exactly?" Andrella asked, matching his condescending tone with one of her own.

Theramon gave her a deadpan look. "I'm certain my sister has already told you about my 'evil' plans for this world. I won't bore you with the details," he finished with an inconsequential wave of his hand.

"So what now?" Seth stared darkly at the smug immortal.

Theramon met the halfling's gaze with a disdainful one of his own. "I am not a totally unreasonable man." He nodded toward Maya. "Give me what I originally asked for, and you can have the girl back."

Aksel had no idea what he had asked Seth for, but he didn't trust Theramon. He was a master manipulator and he didn't trust him in the slightest. "What about her soul?"

A sly smile crossed Theramon's lips. "Well played. Yes, her soul as well."

Though Aksel still had no idea what they were bartering for, he could see that Theramon would rather haggle than fight. Elladan must have realized it as well. The bard folded his arms across his chest and shook his head emphatically. "Sorry, friend, but you'll have to do better than that. You need to promise to leave the sisters alone from now on—no kidnapping, no mind control, no harm to them of any kind."

Aksel breathed a deep sigh as Elladan and Theramon hashed out the details of their negotiation. The immediate danger to the folks in the plaza was over. Still, one thing nagged at him.

Aksel stole over toward Seth and whispered quietly into his friend's ear. "So what exactly is it that Theramon wants?"

Seth let out a soft snort. "Just the key to the runic lock at the top of the Marsh Tower."

All sorts of alarms suddenly went off in Aksel's mind. If Theramon got the rune pattern to that lock, there would be nothing stopping him from capturing his sister.

With Elistra's life hanging in the balance, Aksel reached out telepathically to Glo.

Thea led them at a half-walk, half-run to the back of the main chapel. Moments later, Glo, Ves, Cyclone, and Xellos emerged into the temple grounds behind the massive Temple of the Ralnai.

Thea pointed to a gap in the walls that surrounded the grounds a short distance away. "That way leads to the river bridge. Once across, we can lose ourselves in the city."

Everyone fell in behind the priestess as they cut across the grass toward their destination. They had only gone perhaps a short distance though when a deep, rumbling voice called to them from above.

"What's going on?" Cal asked as he swooped down and landed directly in their path.

Glo quickly explained to the copper dragon everything that had transpired in the temple. He finished with, "I don't think Penwick is safe for the sisters anymore."

"I quite agree," Cal rumbled. "Perhaps it would be safer for them back in Lanfor."

Glo wasn't quite sure how he felt about that. After what Princess Anya had done to Ves, he wasn't sure Lanfor would be all that safe, either.

Ves seemed to mirror his thoughts. The young lady pointed back toward the temple entrance. "I'm not sure anywhere would be safe anymore."

Behind them, a group of people came pouring out of the back door to the chapel. Their movements appeared stilted, as if in a trance once more.

"Don't worry, I've got this," Cyclone told her as he took off in a run back the way they came.

Ves cupped her hands around her mouth and called after him, "Don't hurt them."

"No promises," Cyclone yelled back.

A moment later he plowed into the first group that had emerged from the chapel. In a fierce display of combat prowess, the hunter took them all down using his fists and the blunt end of his long-poled axe.

A few yards further back, the chapel door opened once more. With a huge leap, the hunter sailed through the air, landing directly in the path of the next group that emerged. Cyclone gave those in front a rough shove, pushing the entire line back into the chapel. He then slammed the door shut and barricaded it with the pole of his long axe.

Thea raised an eyebrow at Ves. "Charming friend you have there."

Ves responded with a wan smile and a shrug. "He sort of grows on you."

Glo snorted with laughter, but his amusement was cut short when Aksel contacted him. After hearing the terms of Theramon's deal, Glo felt his insides twist into a knot. While he absolutely wanted to save the sisters, giving up Elistra to her brother was out of the question. There had to be another way.

Feeling completely torn, Glo screamed out Elistra's name in his mind. A moment later, his grief was met with a psychic reply.

Yes, my love?

Uncertain what to do, Glo explained the situation to Elistra. Her response came without hesitation. *Save Maya.*

Glo felt his entire body go numb. *But… what about you?*

There was a brief hesitation before Elistra replied. *Don't worry. I'll be alright.*

Glo was no expert at psychic communications, but somehow she didn't sound all that convincing to him. *Well I won't. How can we possibly trust your brother?*

Make him give you his word, she responded immediately. *That is the one thing he won't break.*

Glo let out an audible sigh. *Okay, if you insist, but as soon as he's gone, you're teleporting me back to you.*

Their psychic link went abruptly silent. When Elistra finally responded, her thoughts were thick with emotion. *You know I can't do that. There are still things you must do out in the world.*

Glo began to insist, but then another idea struck him. *As you wish, my love,* he told her simply.

Stay safe, my darling, she responded softly, and then her voice was gone.

Glo contacted Aksel back and informed him what Elistra had decided. He also added an idea of his own that might just save them all in the end.

Seth watched with growing annoyance as Elladan and Theramon continued to haggle.

"I'm a patient man. Time means very little to me," Theramon boasted with clear arrogance.

A sly look crossed Elladan's face. "If that's the case, what could it hurt to let us take on the demons for you?"

As the irritating discussion wore on, Seth and Aksel finally heard back from Glo. Elistra's decision was an interesting one, far more noble than Seth would have guessed. Glo's idea on top of that was sheer brilliance, however. Seth found himself truly impressed.

Meanwhile, the negations had finally come to a head, with

Theramon appearing to capitulate. "Very well. I will leave the sisters alone for the space of three months. You have that time to take down the Demon Tower. Any more than that, and this world is done for anyway."

Before Elladan could agree, Aksel inserted himself between the two and looked Theramon directly in the eye. "Do we have your word?"

A faint smile crossed Theramon's lips. "I see you've been talking with my sister." He hesitated a moment longer, then added, "Very well, you have my word."

Seth folded his arms across his chest and fixed Theramon with a hard stare. "Same goes for Elistra."

That had been Glo's idea.

Theramon met Seth's gaze evenly, then responded with a small laugh. "Very well. You have my word on that, too. My sister will be left alone as well for the next three months."

The immortal gazed at him with an exaggeratedly innocent expression. "So, do we have a deal?"

"One more thing"—Aksel added quickly—"free the people of Penwick."

Theramon paused, his gaze turning briefly distant. After a few moments, he waved his hand in a negligent motion. "They are free."

In his mind, Seth heard Aksel ask Glo about the folks at the temple. Glo confirmed that they had all returned to normal.

"So do we have a deal?" Theramon asked once more, peering off through the crowd, trying his best to act nonchalant.

Seth traded a glance with Aksel, who nodded his agreement. The halfling pulled out a parchment Donnie had previously inked up for him with the combination to the tower. Seth strode over and held it out toward Theramon.

All of a sudden, the color drained from the immortal's face. He looked as if he'd seen a ghost. Seth swiftly followed his gaze, catching a glimpse through the crowd of a man wearing a robe with a strange symbol on his chest.

Theramon quickly recovered, but Seth thought he detected a look of dread in the immortal's eyes. As Theramon reached down to take the parchment, Seth quickly pulled it back.

"Maya's soul?" he reminded him.

Theramon huffed and gazed over his shoulder as he pulled out a crystal from his robes. Seth took it and handed it to Aksel.

"Is it?" Seth asked the little cleric.

Aksel cast a quick spell, then responded with a curt nod.

Seth once again held out the parchment for Theramon, but the latter seemed preoccupied with scanning the surrounding crowd.

"Do you want this, or not?" Seth prodded the violet-eyed man.

Theramon almost absently took the paper from Seth's hands. "A deal's a deal," he murmured quietly. With a wave of his hand, the crystal in Aksel's hand imploded.

A broad grin swept across Maya's face, her dimples showing once again. She grabbed the corners of her dress and twirled around in a pirouette.

"Ooh, I can dance again!" she exclaimed with joy.

In the meantime, Theramon backed away. In one swift motion, he spun about and bolted for a nearby hillock.

"Got to run!" he called out over his shoulder.

Overhead, a huge black shape dropped down out of the sky. People stopped and stared all over the plaza. Alarm bells rang out from the nearby castle.

As Theramon reached the top of the hillock, a huge black dragon swooped down and picked him up. Moments later, they were soaring back up into the sky together. Shortly thereafter, they all but disappeared.

"I wonder what was that all about?" Elladan drawled once they were gone.

Seth quickly explained to them about the strange man who had spooked Theramon. When he mentioned the symbol on the man's chest, Aksel nodded thoughtfully. "That's the symbol of the Mad God."

The Mad God? Seth thought wryly. *That's interesting.* He thought it would be highly amusing if the Mad God were actually 'mad' at Theramon.

10
THE LION'S SHARE

Behind me stands what remains of the Fountain of Lions

Ruka was angry—angry at Donnie for talking her into staying behind, and furious at Theramon for kidnapping Maya in the first place. She was mostly annoyed at herself, though, for falling for Donnie's stupid charms yet again.

The young dragon in human form sat slouched down on a bench in the common room of the Lucky Heroes, her arms folded across her chest. Donnie sat next to her, listening telepathically to what was going on with the others. She turned an irritated eye on him, but he merely responded with one of his toothy grins.

Ruka nearly slapped herself as she felt her cheeks redden. *He's turning me into a sap.*

Biting her lip, she folded her arms tighter and brooded on her unwanted reactions to the elf. That's when it hit her—the only way she was going to get over him was to face the truth—something at which she was terrible.

Donnie leaned in closer and whispered, "They're in the council now. Maya's there."

Ruka let out a thankful sigh. At least the scaleless tail-biter had brought her sister with him. She forced herself to smile at Donnie. "Thanks."

He nodded and went back to listening.

Ruka watched him out of the corner of her eye. His boyish good looks were quite appealing, but that wasn't what had attracted her in the first place. If she was being honest, he had been the first one to ever treat her like a woman. That had turned her head in a way she never thought possible.

Stupid, stupid, stupid, Ruka mentally berated herself.

She had developed a schoolgirl crush on him, but quickly found out how fickle he was when it came to women. She swore she would never let him sweet-talk her again, and yet here she was, waiting at the inn with him for the others to rescue her sister.

Donnie leaned over again. "They've left the council meeting and are confronting Theramon."

Confronting Theramon?

At those words, a deep-seeded hatred welled up from somewhere inside of Ruka. She had faced Theramon before, back on Anya's ship. He and that metal-headed puppet of his had crushed the powerful red dragon, Theriaxus, but neither of them had been able to touch her.

A stark realization abruptly washed over her. *It's because I'm different.*

Ruka was cursed—in fact, so was her entire family. The other dragons had taunted her about it all her life. Yet maybe that very curse was the thing made her immune to the likes of Theramon.

Spurred into action, Ruka leapt from her seat and grabbed Donnie by the hand.

"Whoa, whoa, whoa," he cried as she practically dragged him across the room. "Where are we going? They haven't rescued your sister yet."

"I... don't... care..." Ruka enunciated each word through gritted teeth. She dragged him outside the inn and glared at him. Somewhere off in the distance, the sound of thunder rolled across the sky.

Ruka put her hands on her hips and glared at Donnie, her words as hard as steel. "Theramon or not, I am going to see my sister. Are you coming with me?"

Donnie visibly paled. She had never used that tone with him before, but that was just too bad. It was high time he got used to the real her.

"Okay," Donnie agreed, realizing he wasn't going to win this time, "but we're going on foot. The last thing this town needs is another dragon flying overhead."

Ruka nearly bit his head off, but caught herself. He was right. The people here hadn't reacted all that well when they saw Calipherous.

"Fine!" she exclaimed, "but I'm not slowing down for you."

Before he could answer, she took off down the street and around the corner at a dead run.

Donnie had no idea what he'd gotten himself into as he tried to keep up with Ruka. He thought running would slow her down, but by the gods, she was fast on foot. Before he knew it, they had passed the temple and the tower that housed the magic school. Ruka flew up the bridge as she crossed the river that split the town, practically going airborne as she raced down the other side.

Donnie prided himself for being fast on his feet, but Ruka put him to shame. Try as hard as he could, she continued to pull farther and farther away. His breath came in ragged bursts as they finally entered the Lord's Square.

The plaza was normally packed with people this time of day, yet none bustled about. Instead, everyone had stopped and stared toward the southern end of the square.

Donnie followed their gaze just in time to see a huge black figure swoop down out of the sky. It snatched a second figure in gold from atop the lone hillock, then immediately swept upward at a steep angle. Donnie inwardly shuddered as he recognized that great black form. It was Theramon's pet—the giant adamantine dragon that had chased him and Ruka through the mountains, and nearly had him for a late-night snack.

Thankfully, Theramon and the giant dragon were now headed away from the town. Donnie breathed a sigh of relief—that was one creature he never wanted to see again. It was then that he noticed a group of familiar figures congregated at the base of the hillock.

Ruka must have seen them at the same time. She had stopped a few yards ahead of him, but now took off at a dead run for the group.

Donnie gulped down as much air as he could, then took off after her. By the time he caught up, Ruka had already swept Maya up into her arms. She hugged her so tight he thought the young girl's bones would break.

"Maya, Maya—I thought I had lost you!" Ruka cried, uncharacteristic tears streaming down her face.

Maya grabbed her sister's cheeks and stared at her with the seriousness of a child. "But Ruka, I'm not lost. I'm right here!"

Had Donnie not been gasping for breath, he would have made a smart remark. As it stood, he was more than happy to lean on his knees and refill his lungs. As he did so, he felt a hand on his shoulder.

Donnie peered up to see Elladan staring down at him. "Weren't you supposed to keep Ruka away from here?"

The winded elf gave his friend as cynical a look as he could muster at the moment. "You try"—he paused and gasped—"and stop her."

As the two companions chided each other, a blue oval of swirling energy appeared in the air about a dozen yards away. A moment later, Ves came spilling through the portal, followed by Thea, Xellos, and finally Glo.

"Maya!" Ves cried as she rushed up to join her sisters and flung her arms around the both of them. Maya wrapped an arm around Ves' neck and they all shared a three-way hug.

Donnie felt a warmth in his heart that he hadn't experienced in decades. All three of these girls had come to mean a lot to him, though not in the usual way he felt about women. Still, it was a bittersweet moment for him. Despite his strong feelings for all three of the sisters, he couldn't risk getting close to any of them. His curse might extend to women he cared about, and he'd be damned if he put any of them in danger.

A few moments later, a large copper dragon swooped down out of the sky and landed on the hillock not far from them. A familiar figure in blue sat squarely between the dragon's shoulders.

Ves, Ruka, and Maya all hurried over to greet Cal. The reunion was complete. The Greymantle sisters and their guardian were reunited once more.

Most of the others gathered around them, but true to his word, Donnie kept his distance. It was then he noticed the growing crowd at this end of the plaza. Most of the people had shuffled down this way to see the unusual gathering.

Still somewhat reluctant to interfere in the girls' moment, Donnie felt he had no choice. He made his way over to the others and tapped Elladan on the shoulder. "Don't look now, but I think we're drawing a crowd."

Elladan glanced over his shoulder, his eyes widening. "You're right, that's quite an audience."

The bard raised his voice and caught the rest of the group's attention. "Folks, this is definitely cause for a celebration, but I think it's getting a bit crowded here." He pointed a thumb over his shoulder.

As the others became aware of the crowd, Elladan leaned in close to Thea. "Is there someplace more private we can go? I have a spell handy for food and drink."

Thea grabbed her chin, her eyes growing distant as she mulled over his request. "Normally, I'd suggest the temple grounds for a picnic, but things might still be a bit hectic back there." A moment later she snapped her fingers. "I know just the place. Follow me."

Everyone fell in behind the priestess as Thea led them south, out of the square. Only Cyclone and Cal did not join them, the pair going airborne again to draw attention away from the others.

The green where the hillock rested ended a few blocks down. At that point, the street opened into another square nearly as large as the one they just left. Not nearly as crowded as the Lord's Square, this plaza had one major defining feature—a wide, multilevel circular fountain that sat in its center.

A lover of all types of art, Donnie was intrigued by what once must have been a magnificent piece. Unfortunately, where numerous statues must have once stood, now only crumbled stone remained. On closer inspection, the fountain appeared dry as a bone. Donnie felt a pang of grief at the sight of the ruined work of art.

Thea strode up beside him, then turned to address the entire group. "This is Lion's Square. Behind me stands what remains of the Fountain of Lions, once a landmark of Penwick." Her expression grew sad as she looked over the dried and crumbled monument.

Donnie completely understood how she felt. "How long has it been like this?"

"Since the pirate invasion," Lloyd explained, drawing up beside them. "My parents have tried to have it rebuilt, but we couldn't find anyone willing to take the job."

Donnie's inner artist screamed at him to offer his services, but he knew better. Sculpting was not his forte. Abruptly, an idea struck him. *Calipherous is a natural at shaping stone. Perhaps if I were to guide him...*

His ruminations were rudely interrupted by Elladan. "So where's this place that you want to hold our celebration?"

Thea ripped her eyes away from the fountain and waved for everyone to follow her once more. "This way."

She led them around the fountain, all the way to the south side of the plaza. A large, boarded three-story building stood at that end, an old sign hanging by one hook to a post jutting from the wall.

Donnie tilted his head sideways as he attempted to read the faded lettering. "Lions—Shar—in. Lions Sharon?"

Thea giggled at his attempt to make sense of the sign. "Lion's Share Inn," she corrected him.

Donnie shrugged. "That makes far more sense."

Lloyd tapped his sister on the shoulder. "This place? Are you kidding me?"

Thea wore an exasperated smile as she painstakingly explained her choice to him. "Well, it is empty after all—and it's not nearly in as bad a condition as the others."

"Others?" Andrella wrapped her arm around Lloyd's and peered quizzically at her sister-in-law-to-be.

Lloyd responded to her first. "Remember I told you the old

quarter of Penwick was nearly burnt to the ground during the pirate raids? Well, the council refuses to do anything about it."

"So Mom and Dad took it on themselves to renovate most of the old quarter," Thea finished for him.

Donnie let out a low whistle. "That must be costing them a small fortune."

Thea shrugged. "Almost all our family's money is tied up in renovating the old section of town."

"That's extremely noble of them," Andrella noted, "but why was Lloyd surprised that you picked this place?"

Thea grimaced, her eyes dropping to the ground. "Well, this inn was Eboneye's headquarters during the pirate raid."

Eboneye's headquarters? That definitely sparked Donnie's interest. Perhaps the old pirate had left some hidden treasure somewhere behind the walls of this place. Donnie rubbed his hands together with anticipation. "This I've got to see."

The front door had been sealed with a Wizard's Lock, but Thea knew the password. It opened into a spacious tavern room filled with the remains of numerous tables and chairs. Large cracks lined the walls and a thick layer of dust covered everything, but with a little clean-up, it would make an excellent place for an impromptu celebration.

While Lloyd went to get his parents, Donnie and the others cleared out the rotted furniture. Everyone then waited back outside so Glo and Andrella could clean out the dust with magical blasts of air.

As Donnie meandered over to the fountain, he spied Ruka leaning against the side. Catching her alone like this, he decided to broach a subject that had been gnawing at him ever since the incident in the Marsh Tower.

Donnie leaned next to her and said in a tentative voice, "Can I talk to you?"

"Sure," she replied after a moment's pause, trying to sound nonchalant, though her eyes betrayed her mixed feelings.

Donnie pulled the Ruchan from his belt and held it out to her with both hands. "I want—" he began, but his voice cracked with emotion. Mentally chiding himself, Donnie cleared his throat and tried again. "I want to—return this to you."

Ruka's face contorted with pain. "Why? What did I do?"

Donnie's heart wrenched inside his chest. He hated doing this to her, but he told himself it was for her own good. "It's not you. It's me. I'm not worthy of this."

Moisture welled in Ruka's eyes as she looked from Donnie to the dagger and back again. When she finally spoke, her voice was low and filled with anguish. "No, you're not. Not anymore."

She ripped the dagger from his hands and stormed away, back toward the inn.

Donnie's eyes trailed after her, the guilt eating away at his insides. *It's better this way,* he continued to tell himself, though it didn't really make him feel any better.

The guilt-ridden elf wallowed by the fountain until Cal and Cyclone finally caught up with them. It was nearly dinner time, the plaza mostly empty as the copper dragon landed in the square. The blue-clad hunter leapt from Cal's back and called out to Donnie, "Where is everybody?"

Donnie, still wrestling with his conscience, merely pointed toward the inn.

Cyclone gave him a curt nod, then went to join the others.

At the same time, Cal padded over to Donnie, his head weaving in all directions around the fountain. "What a shame. This must have been a beautiful sculpture."

Donnie's ears perked up at the dragon's comment, his sullen thoughts all but forgotten. A sly look crossed the elf's face as he fell into his best sales-pitch persona—the one he used when coaxing noble wives and daughters into having their portraits done. "It could be again, you know."

Cal snaked his large head down and came face-to-face with the scheming elf. "What do you have in mind?"

Donnie made a square with his fingers and scrutinized the broken fountain from end-to-end. "What if I were to paint a portrait of it in its original form—maybe even improve on it a bit?"

Cal tilted his head back and forth, a deep rumbling emanating from his throat. "You mean, as a guide of sorts?"

Donnie touched the side of his nose with his finger. "Exactly."

Cal's eyes turned distant as if lost in thought. "It's been a long, long, time since I've sculpted a piece of art. It might be a nice change of pace."

Still in sales-pitch mode, Donnie laid a hand on the dragon's scales. "So, do we have a deal?"

Cal paused a moment before rumbling his answer. "Yes, I believe we do."

"Excellent!" Donnie cried, no longer able to contain his enthusiasm.

"What's excellent?" Lloyd's voice sounded from across the square.

Donnie glanced over his shoulder just in time to see the young man returning with his parents. Caught off-guard, the embarrassed elf quickly came up with a plausible answer. "Why the food inside, of course!"

Covering his mouth with one hand, Donnie whispered to Cal, "Let's keep this between the two of us for now."

"Certainly," Cal softly rumbled.

Leaving the dragon by the fountain, Donnie led the Stealles into the tavern. The place looked completely different now. All the broken furniture had been removed and the tap room stood completely clean. Furthermore, Elladan had cast *Feast*, creating a banquet fit for a king.

A long, ornate table spread across the center of the room, decorated with a frilly lace tablecloth and seven lit candelabras. Fourteen matching chairs encircled the table, each in front of a fancy place setting. A huge selection of food lined the tabletop, including bisque, chowder, prime rib, lobster, chicken, fish, potatoes au gratin, sweet potatoes, corn on the cob, three different kinds of bread, butter, and herb salad. There were also apple pies, cherry pies, pudding, and a number of clear flasks filled with red and golden nectar.

Upon seeing them enter, Elladan bade everyone to be seated. Lloyd and his parents took the three empty chairs between Andrella and Thea. Elladan sat on the other side of Lloyd's sister, with the last empty chair between him and Glo.

As Donnie sat, he ruefully noted Ruka seated at the other end of the table between her sisters. Despite his convictions, the guilt-ridden elf caught his eyes drifting in that direction more than once. *It's better this way,* he reminded himself each time, though it didn't really make him feel any better.

11
INN OF THE
THREE SISTERS

It appears that you are losing control of your powers

The celebration of Maya's return had turned out better than Thea hoped. Lloyd's misgivings about this place had made her self-conscious at first, but after tidying up and celebrating thanks to Elladan's *Feast*, everyone seemed to be enjoying themselves now.

Even Ves' mood had markedly improved, although Thea could still detect a hint of that dark shadow still hanging over her soul. Other than that, Ruka seemed to be the only exception, the teen acting more sullen than usual.

Thea had eaten more than her fill when Elladan began piling food onto a second plate. She watched with keen interest as the pile slowly grew higher and higher.

"Do you have a hollow leg, or something?" she asked, the corner of her mouth upturning slightly.

Elladan chuckled as he continued with his culinary construct. "I wish, but this is not for me. There's a hungry dragon outside who still needs to be fed."

Once again, Thea was forced to reevaluate her opinion of this far-too-handsome elf. "If you're trying to score brownie points, you're definitely on the right track."

A half-smile split the bard's face. "My plan all along."

Once Elladan finished his 'tower,' he discovered its fatal flaw. It was far too tall and nearly spilled over as he tried to walk and balance it at the same time.

Thea, sensing the impending catastrophe, rushed to his rescue with a second plate. "Here. Let's put half of it on this."

With a bit of juggling, the two managed to split most of the food between the two plates. They only lost a tiny bit, some of which landed on Elladan's nose.

Thea reached over and scraped the vagrant mashed potatoes from the bard's face with her finger. She then shoved it into her mouth.

"Mmm," she murmured with exaggerated glee, "these taste a bit like elf."

Elladan burst out into laughter, but then caught himself. He cast a guilty glance at Thea's family, but no one seemed to notice his momentary outburst. Satisfied that no one else was listening, he fixed her with an impish smile. "Oh, so you know what elf tastes like?"

"Maybe," she responded with a mysterious grin, then strode through the door before he could ask anything further.

The large copper dragon had nestled himself right next to the broken fountain. His head popped up and he sniffed the air as soon as the two of them stepped outside.

Elladan held up his plate toward the dragon while simultaneously gesturing to Thea's. "Dinner is served!"

The two of them leaned up against the fountain as Cal genteelly ate his meal. Thea threw her head back and scanned the sky above. Night had fallen and the stars shone through the dark firmament like tiny sparkling jewels. It was a gorgeous sight.

"I was thinking about what you said earlier," Elladan broke the silence after a minute or so.

"Oh?" Thea said, still drinking in the night sky.

He paused a moment before continuing. "Is all your family's money really tied up in rebuilding the town?"

Thea shrugged. "Most of it."

"Can they really afford that?" Elladan asked.

This time Thea met his gaze. She could see the genuine concern in his eyes.

"They are stretching things a bit thin," she admitted.

That half-smile crept across his face once more. "What if I said I know a buyer?"

"Who?" The question had caught her by surprise.

Elladan pointed a thumb to his chest. "Me." He immediately corrected himself. "I mean us." He swept his hands outward. "I mean the group of us," he finished by pointing back over his shoulder toward the inn.

Thea felt her cheeks warm at the kind offer. She wondered whether he was really this generous, or if he was merely trying to impress her. "That's sweet of you, but the place still needs a lot of fixing."

Cal's head abruptly popped up from the second plate. The first sat lying next to it, completely cleaned of every last ounce of food. "I could help."

Elladan gave the dragon a grateful smile before returning his attention back to Thea. "See, Cal can help. Between him and the rest of us, we'll have the place fixed up in no time."

Thea couldn't help but smile at his enthusiasm. "Very well. I'll mention it to my parents, then."

"Good," Elladan said with conviction. "Now that that's settled, I have one more question for you."

"Oh?" Thea asked with just a touch of apprehension. She was really starting to like this elf, but hoped he wouldn't press things too fast.

Elladan patted the fountain behind them. "You said this was a landmark?"

Thea felt abruptly relieved, but at the same time experienced a touch of regret. She swiftly shook off the feeling and answered him. "Yes. It's very famous, but as I said, has been broken since the pirate raids."

Elladan peered over at the dragon who had just finished cleaning off his last plate. "Cal, do you think you help us fix this as well?"

Cal raised his head up to the same height as Elladan's, a laugh rumbling from deep within his throat. "Funny you should ask me that."

The dragon proceeded to tell them about his clandestine agreement with Donnie. When he was done, Elladan placed a single finger over his mouth. "We'll keep this just between us, then."

Thea put her hands on her hips and stared curiously at the elf. She knew he had something in mind, but wasn't sure quite what. "Okay. Spill it. What are you thinking?"

Elladan laughed. "I think you're getting to know me just a bit too well." He waved her and Cal closer and explained that the Baron wanted them to prove themselves here in Penwick. He ended by placing both hands on the fountain, and leaning over the edge. "While I don't see any threats in town, I'd say fixing up a bonafide landmark should weigh well with the Baron." His gaze grew wistful. "Plus, I have to admit, the artist in me hates to see something this beautiful broken."

For a brief moment, Thea had thought his motivations purely mercenary, but that last statement made her immediately retract that thought. This elf's feelings ran far deeper than she ever imagined.

Thea drew up next to him and gazed out over the fountain. Her heart swelled with pride, and maybe something more, as she imagined what it would look like fully restored.

Back inside the inn, Ruka still brooded over the unexpected return of her gift. *Her* dagger, made from *her* own scale, and he had the unmitigated gall to return it! Most of the smaller races would kill for a gift from a dragon, at least according to the legends. Yet Donnie had thrown the precious gift, a very part of her, back in her face.

While Ruka continued to grapple with her anger, Maya had finished her meal and climbed up onto the bar. The young girl began to sing and dance, swirling around in her pinafore along the length of the bar top.

"Maya, get down from there!" Ves called out, once again playing mother hen in absence of their own mother.

Maya paused in the midst of a twirl, a pout forming across her cherub face. "But Ves, I haven't been able to dance in what feels like ages! Can't I dance just a little bit? Please?"

Something inside of Ruka abruptly snapped. She turned on her younger sister and yelled, "You heard Ves. Get down from there!"

She emphasized what she said with a wave of her hand. Without warning, an electrical arc jumped from her fingertips and zapped one of the nearby pitchers. The glass container exploded, sending golden liquid flying everywhere.

"Ruka!" Ves exclaimed, her eyes going wide.

Up on the bar, Maya started to cry. "W—what did you ha—have to do that for? I was j—just trying to ha—have some fun," she managed between sobs.

Mortified, Ruka grasped her wayward hand and pulled it back. "I—I didn't mean to do that."

Something didn't feel right. Ruka's skin continued to tingle, much as it did just before she was going to let off an electrical discharge. She closed her eyes and tried to will the energy back below the surface, but it just wouldn't listen.

"May we examine you?"

Ruka's eyes snapped back open. Thea's mother stood a few feet away, staring at her with a mixture of concern and understanding. Glo stood right behind her, wearing the same expression.

"Please." Ruka managed between gritted teeth as she struggled to hold back the rebellious electricity dancing across her skin.

Lara stepped forward and carefully prodded the air around Ruka, her face going through all sorts of contortions as she did so. After about half a minute, she stepped back and briefly consulted with Glo.

"So—what's the prognosis?" Ruka blurted out, feeling almost as if she were going to explode.

Lara and Glo stopped talking, the former peering at her with clear sympathy. "Oh, I'm sorry my dear. It appears that you are losing control of your powers."

"I'm what?" Ruka almost shouted, the energy buildup seeming to grow with her agitation.

Two pairs of hands abruptly grasped her on either side. Ruka nearly jumped out of her skin, but then the wayward energy began to siphon from her. Her sisters now stood on either side, each holding one of her hands and pulling the excess energy away.

Maya gazed up at her shyly, a small smile emphasizing her dimples. "It's okay, sissy. I forgive you."

"Thanks," Ruka said sincerely before turning her attention to Ves.

Her older sister gave her an encouraging smile, before shifting her gaze toward Lara and Glo. "Do you have any idea what's making her lose control?"

The two wizards exchanged a brief glance before Glo finally answered. "It's just a theory, but we think it's related to her strong emotions."

"My what?" Ruka cried, her anger rising.

The energy around her responded in kind, surging again across her skin. Both Ves and Maya tightened their grip and helped siphon off the flow once more.

Feeling foolish, Ruka clamped down on her emotions. She ruefully shook her head and begrudgingly acknowledged the two wizards. "I guess you're right."

"I might be able to help with that," a gruff voice sounded behind her.

Ruka glanced over her shoulder to see Cyclone leaning against the bar, his arms folded across his chest. The dragon hunter ran his eyes over her body as if he could see the remnants of energy dancing all over her.

With most of the excess energy now drained off, Ruka let go of her sister's hands and spun about, fixing the hunter with a skeptical glare. "How?"

Cyclone nudged his head toward Ves. "I'm already training with your sister. Why don't you join us?"

Ruka felt the anger rise within her again and the electrical energy surge with it. Her arms went straight, her fists clenching as she strained to push down on both. After barely regaining control, she slowly turned to face her sister. "Oh really? And just when were you going to tell me about this?"

Ves averted her eyes, guilt written across her face. "We haven't exactly had the time—plus we haven't even started the training yet."

Ruka pursed her lips and narrowed an eye at her sister, but Ves would not meet her gaze. Yet even without her saying so, Ruka thought she knew what this was all about. It was that damn curse. Ves probably thought if she could shoulder the burden, then both she and Maya would be spared. It was a very Ves-like thing to do. Still, Ruka would be damned if she'd let her sister sacrifice herself for the two of them.

Forcing herself to be calm, Ruka pulled out the Ruchan and proffered it to Cyclone. "I accept your offer, but you must take this in exchange."

Cyclone scoffed at the dagger in her hand. "I don't use small weapons."

Ruka forced herself to be patient, her words coming out as if she were speaking to a small child. "I don't expect you to use it. It signifies a pact between us."

Cyclone lifted his chin higher. "What kind of pact?"

Ruka had not wanted to put it into words, but it appeared she had no choice. Briefly glancing around, she saw that everyone had gathered closer to witness their exchange. With a deep sigh, she answered his question, the words spilling out as fast as her lips could move. "If and when I become a storm dragon, you would be my rider."

Ignoring the murmurs that broke out around them, Ruka glanced at Ves. Her sister no longer avoided her gaze, her eyes hard as they met Ruka's stare. The two sisters stood there glaring at each other defiantly until Cyclone interrupted them.

"Agreed," the hunter said simply, reaching for the Ruchan.

Ruka handed the dagger to him, then looked back at Ves with a triumphant expression. She expected to see defeat in her sister's eyes, but instead saw only concern.

Ves gave her a wan smile, then spun on her heel and headed for the door.

As Ruka watched her go, her gaze fell on Donnie. The thin elf had a haunted look in his eyes, but he quickly turned away from her.

What Ruka had viewed as a triumph suddenly felt very hollow. *It's better this way,* she told herself, though it didn't really make her feel any better.

Thea was still feeling rather blissful when she spied Ves exiting the inn followed closely by the tall elf, Glolindir. Ves had appeared quite cheerful after Maya's return, but now seemed somewhat off once again. Perhaps it was the moonlight playing tricks on Thea's eyes, but Ves' skin appeared pale, and the darkness at the edge of her aura looked more pronounced.

Though Elladan probably couldn't see auras, he must have sensed something as well. He leaned in close to Thea and whispered, "They look like they could use a bit of cheering up."

The handsome elf stepped away from the fountain and waved to his companions. "Glo! Ves! Come over here. We have some good news to share."

Ves paused in her tracks, seemingly reluctant to join them. Glo must have whispered something to her to change her mind, because the both of them then came over to join them.

Elladan gestured toward the fountain. "Cal here has agreed to help us fix this thing up good as new."

Still somewhat stiff, Ves gazed from the fountain to Cal. "That's awfully kind of you, Calipherous."

Cal responded with an appreciative rumble. "Um, yes, well, I haven't done artistic sculpting in a long time, but I'll try my best."

"I'm sure you'll do great," Ves murmured, reaching out and fondly rubbing the copper dragon's snout.

Thea noted a tiny lifting of her spirits, but the darkness still clung to her aura.

"...but the real cherry is that we're buying the inn!" Elladan added with a magnanimous gesture toward the building behind them.

A single eyebrow rose on Glo's forehead. "We are?"

"Indeed," Elladan told his friend with a half-smile. He proceeded to tick off the reasons on his fingers. "First, we need a place to stay. Second, it would help the Stealles. Third, refurbishing the fountain and the inn might help our case with the Baron."

Glo thought about it for a moment or two, then shrugged. "All good points."

"Yet the best part is what we're going to call it," Elladan teased mysteriously.

"Oh, and what's that?" Ves asked absently, still rubbing Cal's snout.

"The Inn of the Three Sisters," Elladan stated with a dramatic flourish.

Ves stopped what she was doing and began to blush, the color returning to her skin. "That's—very sweet of you, Elladan." She reached out and grabbed his hands, a genuine smile gracing her lips. "I'm certain my sisters will love it."

Aside from her skin returning to normal, Thea noted the darkness around Ves receding. Elladan's surprise had indeed cheered her as intended. Now instead of looking ill, Ves merely appeared tired. The young lady let out a short sigh and gazed up into the night sky. "It is beautiful out here. I think a walk would do me good."

"Would you like some company?" Glo asked her.

Ves peered at him for a moment, then nodded. "Yes. That would be nice."

The tall elf extended his arm and the young lady took it.

"See you later," Ves called back over her shoulder as the duo strode off into the night together.

Thea watched them curiously until they left the plaza. The way their auras played off each other signified a closeness—a deep, abiding trust. Though not exact, she saw something similar between her mother and father. It made her wonder.

As soon as they were out of earshot, she whispered to Elladan, "Are those two a couple?"

A deep, lyrical laugh escaped Elladan's lips. "Those two? No." He shook his head emphatically. "Glo is head over heels over Elistra."

"Interesting," Thea murmured. She had heard mention of the seeress before, but not much else. Now her curiosity was truly piqued.

"Anyway, I think it's time we go inside and share the good news with everyone else," Elladan said, extending his arm the same way Glo had for Ves.

A warm smile spread across Thea's face as she laced her arm through his. "Very well, but on the way, you have to tell me more about this Elistra."

12
I DREAM OF GENIE

I doubt it's here to grant his wish

Elladan's announcement about buying the inn came as no surprise to Seth. He had, after all, convinced them to do the very same thing back in Ravenford. Still, calling this one the Inn of the Three Sisters was a nice touch. With all the crap Theramon had put them through, the sisters deserved a bit of recognition at the very least.

"Coming through!" Maya yelped as she leapt over the crack in the bar Seth was trying to mend.

"Sure, I'm only trying to work here," Seth huffed as she danced away down the surface of the bar.

Night had come and gone, with the new day's focus supposedly on fixing up the inn. They were getting the place ready for a grand opening, throwing a party to which the whole town would be invited. That was Elladan's idea, of course, as a way to schmooze the council.

Seth thought the whole thing overkill, but he had to admit he was starting to like the place.

Lara had given them the guided tour last night. The inn had three stories, a huge kitchen, a large pantry, and a full basement with storage for wine and ale. The top two floors contained all guest rooms, many of which housed doubles or even triples. A couple of rooms on the top floor opened onto a wide balcony that overlooked the plaza. All in all, the place had a lot of potential.

"Coming through again!" Maya cried as she made her back up the bar.

Seth threw down his hammer and folded his arms across his chest. "Remind me again how I got stuck babysitting you?"

Maya paused in her tracks, her hands on her hips as she gave him the evil eye. "I am not a baby!"

"Whatever," Seth grumbled.

Deep down inside, he knew he was the one being childish. Allowing Maya to play to a pretend audience seemed the best way to keep her busy while her sisters were out training with Cyclone. At the same time, Glo and Andrella had gone off to research purple worms and tunnels, or something like that, at the Hault School. Donnie had also shirked helping with the inn, off to the library for pictures of the original fountain or some such nonsense.

With nearly half the group gone, today's focus actually seemed to be anything but fixing up the inn. Thankfully, Aksel and Cal hadn't bailed on them, the duo working inside and out to fix the major cracks in the walls. Lloyd and his sister, Elladan, Kara, and Xellos also pitched in, fanning out to the other floors to clean and mend. Unfortunately, that left Seth as the only one to keep an eye on Maya.

While Seth didn't exactly see himself as the paternal type, this morning hadn't turned out nearly as bad as he thought. Maya mostly kept herself busy, and he got to imagine what it would be like to run the tavern. He had been thinking of settling down anyway and could think of worse places to do so than this inn.

Taking a deep breath, Seth gestured for Maya to continue up the bar. "You know what, go ahead. After all, we have to keep our guests entertained."

"Really?" Maya asked, her face scrunching into an adorable grin punctuated by dimples on either side.

"Sure, why not," Seth shrugged. "You do that, and I'll start serving up some drinks."

Maya glanced around the empty room, then back at Seth with a puzzled expression. "We are pretending, right?"

"Either that, or we're both crazy," Seth replied, circling his finger around his ear.

Maya giggled back at him. "You know what? You're funny."

She grinned at him again, then launched herself up the bar, singing along as she went.

A wry smile crossed Seth's lips. He'd been called many things in his life, sarcastic and far worse, but this was the first time anyone had called him 'funny.'

The sun had reached its zenith by the time Aksel and Cal finished mending the worst of the walls. Donnie returned at that point with a portrait he had made of the original Fountain of Lions. Cal, now completely intrigued, wanted to begin working on it immediately. Yet before he started, he insisted they help him put up a tent over the fountain so that no one else could see it until he was finished.

Afterwards, everyone took a break for lunch, then split up again to work on the inn. Aksel had been cleaning in the kitchen for maybe an hour when he heard Donnie call out from the tavern room.

"I found a hollow area behind a wall in the cellar!"

Everyone gathered back in the tavern, then followed Donnie down to the basement—everyone except for Seth. The halfling seemed uncharacteristically content working on the bar and watching after Maya. When Elladan mentioned secret doors and traps to him, Seth casually waved him off, claiming, "I'm sure Donnie can handle it."

Aksel thought Seth was being just a bit too cavalier. He distinctly remembered Donnie flubbing a poison trap in the assassin's lair underneath Vermoorden Keep. Still, if Seth didn't want to help them, Aksel wasn't going to force the point.

His halfling friend had been acting more moody than usual as of late. With his acerbic temperament, most folks might have not noticed, but Aksel did. He also knew better than to ask Seth about it. When Seth was ready, he would tell him.

In the interim, the rest of them followed Donnie down to the wine cellar. A long stone room, dozens of wooden racks lined the walls on either side. The racks themselves were mostly empty, with the exception of the occasional shattered or empty bottle. At the other end of the room, two huge kegs lay on pallets in front of the wall. Both of their tops had been smashed in and they lay empty.

"Someone really did a number on this place before they left," Elladan noted dryly.

Donnie led them to the wall between the two huge kegs. Aksel used his affinity for stone to examine the wall. The blocks here felt much newer than the ones on either side. Still, they were not that new.

Donnie hovered impatiently over him. "How long ago would you say it was sealed?"

Aksel glanced over his shoulder and narrowed an eye at the anxious elf. "You do know this is not an exact science?"

Donnie responded with one of those toothy smiles of his. "But you do have an idea, right?"

Aksel let out a brief sigh. "If I had to guess, I'd probably say a decade or two."

"Ah ha!" Donnie exclaimed, exultantly pointing his finger into the air. "Right around the time of the pirate invasion."

"Give or take." Aksel tried to temper the elf's enthusiasm. "We'll probably know more once I open this up."

The others backed away as Aksel weaved a spell to open up the wall.

"*Lapis Mutare.*" The magic released from Aksel's hands and infused itself into the stone blocks of the wall. He used it to create a small hole in the very center, then gradually widened it until he could fit himself through.

Elladan followed with a spell that sent four globes of twisting and spinning lights after Aksel. The lights revealed a smoothly hewn stairwell leading downward to a corridor below.

Aksel expanded the hole a bit more so the larger folk could fit through, then Donnie led the way down the stairs.

The corridor below wound around a bit before opening up into a small room with a door at the other end. Donnie cautiously entered the room, then immediately performed an about-face and rejoined them down the corridor.

"There are two iron golems in that room on either side of the door," Donnie told them in a hushed voice.

Iron golems? Aksel thought. *What would iron golems be doing down here below Penwick?*

Something abruptly jarred Aksel's memory. He waved a finger at Lloyd. "Didn't you tell us the Golem Thrall Master took over Penwick at one time?"

Lloyd responded with a solemn nod. "Just before the end of the Thrall Wars."

"Well then, maybe we should see what's behind door number one," Elladan drawled, nudging his head back down the corridor.

"Only one way to find out," Donnie exclaimed, his fear of the golems suddenly gone.

Donnie braved the small room once more. He quickly discovered that approaching the door brought the golems to life, yet backing away caused them to go inert again.

Lloyd, of course, wanted to fight. Kara seemed game as well, but Thea nixed the idea before Aksel could speak. Aksel had to admit it was refreshing to have someone else in the group who was willing to be the voice of reason.

Elladan put all thoughts of fighting to rest with a more practical solution. He opened a portal in front of them that led to the other side of the door.

After passing through, the small group found themselves in another smooth-hewn stone corridor. This one ran straight for a hundred yards or so before ending in an iron-bound door. The door turned out to be locked, but Donnie picked it rather handily.

Beyond the door lay a sizeable room with a large circular stone structure standing directly across from them. Intricate patterns were carved into the stone at regular intervals around its circumference.

Aksel thought they looked familiar, but would need to get closer to tell for certain.

"I've seen a circle like that before," Thea confided in a hushed voice, "but I think the markings were different."

"We've also got treasure," Donnie reported, pointing with a twinkle in his eye toward the wall to their left.

Against that wall stood five large barrels on either side of a stone table. A small chest sat all alone upon the tabletop.

Aksel briefly swept his gaze around the rest of the room. It appeared empty, but he had learned to proceed with caution in these types of situations.

"Lloyd, Kara, keep an eye on the door," he told the two warriors. "I'm going to have a closer look at that circle."

"I'm coming with you," Thea declared, seemingly as intrigued as Aksel.

Donnie rubbed his hands together in anticipation. "While you two do that, I'll go check out that chest."

The eager elf took off across the room before Aksel could utter a word of caution.

Elladan rolled his eyes up to the heavens. "I'll go keep an eye on him."

Aksel and Thea crossed the room together. As they drew closer, he thought he recognized the markings there—at least some of them, anyway. "I believe these patterns might be runes. Some of them bear a striking resemblance to the celestial alphabet."

Thea's eyes lit up with excitement. "I thought they looked somewhat familiar. Do you have any idea what they say?"

Aksel swept his eyes around the entire circle, looking for familiar letters, until he found a small section near the top. "I think that group spells out g-o-d."

"God," Thea repeated in a hushed voice.

Aksel continued around the circle until he spotted another familiar set of runes. "That's an 'l', not sure, a 'g'—I think that might spell light."

Thea's jaw fell agape. "God and light? Could this thing have something to do with Arenor?"

"Maybe?" Aksel stepped closer and touched the stone as his eyes reached the lower portion of the circle. "Though this feels very old and those runes might very well be ancient." He abruptly stopped as his hands swept over a hole embedded in one of the runes.

Thea bent down for a closer look. "Is that a keyhole?"

Aksel had been asking himself the very same thing, but before he could answer her, all hell broke loose.

"Damn." Donnie's voice echoed across the room.

Aksel spun about to see the chest on the table laying wide open with a stack of gold coins piled next to it. Donnie and Elladan back-pedaled from the chest as a large cloud of thick red smoke rose from it into the air.

The top half of the cloud coalesced into the upper portion of a well-muscled, humanoid creature with reddish skin, two short, pointed horns, and pulsing tattoos the color of hot lava. The bare-chested creature had nary a trace of hair on its hulking body which Aksel estimated to be twice the size of Lloyd's.

The creature fixed its coal-black eyes on Donnie, a contemptuous sneer across its devilish-looking face. Its deep voice boomed across the stone-walled room. "Who are you and what do you want?"

In typical fashion, Donnie immediately tried to bluff the intimidating creature. "I came to free you, of course."

Lloyd and Kara started forward, but Aksel called over for them to halt. While the creature certainly looked infernal, he recognized it as a djinn. They were indeed demon-like, but not quite the same as a demon.

Thea must have recognized it as well. She murmured under her breath, "I doubt it's here to grant his wish."

Aksel cast her a quick glance. Two long, curved daggers had mysteriously appeared in her hands. He tended to agree with her. They'd be extremely lucky to get out of this without a fight.

The djinn folded its massive arms across its chest and glared down at Donnie. "Very well. First, you must solve this riddle."

The creature's voice took on an unearthly tone as it recited a puzzle to its would-be 'rescuer.'

A harvest sown and reaped on the same day
In an unplowed field,
Which increases without growing,
Remains whole though it is eaten
Within and without,
Is useless and yet
The staple of nations.

Aksel was quite familiar with riddles. It was the primary way his goddess tested her followers. Still, he had never heard that one before.

Elladan sounded as baffled as he. "You want to repeat that, friend?"

"The riddle is only for him," the djinn declared, its tone deathly serious.

Elladan threw his hands up in a surrendering gesture. "Alright, alright. I didn't mean any harm."

"Don't worry, I've got this," Donnie assured his companions. The overconfident elf grabbed his chin, his other hand supported his elbow.

"Sown and reaped," Donnie murmured. "That implies ground."

"Plow and field, too," he added under his breath. "Eaten and staple might refer to crops, though, but then how does it remain whole? And how is it useless?"

Donnie's foot tapped furiously on the stone floor as he reviewed the riddle from the top again. The air grew thick with tension as the seconds slowly ticked by.

After his fourth time through, the djinn declared in an ominous voice, "Time's up. What's your answer?"

"Soil!" Donnie blurted out, pointing an accusing finger at the djinn. "The answer has to be soil!"

The djinn's dark eyes bore down on him, its voice more menacing than before. "Wrong."

With a wave of its hand, a huge, curved blade appeared out of thin air in front of the creature. The djinn grabbed the hilt of the weapon and pronounced in a deadly tone, "Prepare to die."

Yet before the creature could enact its sentence, two words familiar to Aksel rang out across the room. *"Sanctus Percutiat."*

Divine power rippled through the air as a column of white light shot down from the ceiling. The brilliant beam engulfed the djinn, causing it to cry out in pain. "Ahh, I can't see!"

Behind Aksel, Thea held both hands stretched out in front of her, her brow furrowed with concentration. She had reacted before anyone, striking the evil creature with divine holy power. That also meant...

"Quick, attack while it's blind!" Aksel finished his thought out loud.

Lloyd and Kara rushed forward, but before they could reach the djinn, Donnie had his blade out. He lunged forward and jabbed the creature four times in rapid succession.

The djinn flinched from each attack, blood now pouring from several gaping wounds. It swiped at Donnie with its huge sword, but the agile elf easily dodged back out of the way.

"Give up! There's more where that came from," Donnie declared with more bravado than was probably warranted.

Instead of capitulating, however, the djinn bellowed a woeful cry. "Brothers!"

In immediate answer to its plea, three more clouds of red smoke rose up from the open chest. All swiftly coalesced into djinns who looked remarkably similar to the first.

"Kill them all!" The first djinn commanded, pointing out Donnie and his friends.

Aksel knew they were in deep trouble the moment the other clouds first appeared. He frantically drew in his will with a fervent prayer to his goddess. *Soldenar, please give me the power to banish these unholy creatures.*

So be it! The words reverberated through his mind.

Divine power rippled throughout Aksel's entire being. He channeled the potent holy force into the pattern that appeared in his mind.

"*Resigno Magicae.*" Aksel cried as the holy power burst forth from his body.

A wave of mana flashed outward from where he stood in all directions. The rushing wave passed over Lloyd, causing the flames on his swords to wink out. The white tip of Kara's spear winked out as well.

The djinns' eyes went wide as the wave collided with them. There was a faint popping sound as all four creatures vanished in the wink of an eye.

Lloyd stared at Aksel in amazement. "What was that?"

"An antimagic field," Aksel huffed, suddenly feeling quite spent. It had not been the spell he prayed for, but it did banish all the creatures at once. Unfortunately, its effects were only temporary.

"Hurry, we don't have much time," Aksel warned.

Donnie immediately rushed over to the chest and dug his hand into it, down to his elbow. After rummaging around a bit, he pulled it back out. In his hand he held a smooth black pearl the size of an eye.

Thea let out a sharp gasp.

Elladan placed a hand on her back. "What is it?"

"It looks like—an eboneye," Thea stammered.

Elladan let out a low whistle. "Like the pirate?"

"Exactly," Thea recovered from her momentary astonishment. "That's how he got his name. Legend has it he plucked out his eye and replaced it with a pearl like this. It supposedly gave him the power to unite all the pirate clans."

Donnie held the pearl up over his head and squinted at it. "You don't suppose this is actually his eye?"

Thea shook her head. "I don't know."

"The way Mom and Dad tell it, Eboneye went down with his ship in the harbor," Lloyd told them.

"Maybe Glolindir or your mom could tell us more about it," Kara suggested.

"Good idea," Donnie agreed, pocketing the pearl for now.

Elladan then stepped outside Aksel's field and cast another portal spell. Everyone else went through before Aksel stopped concentrating on the antimagic field that surrounded him.

As he entered the portal, four red clouds reappeared behind him.

Seth finished fixing the bar and gave the tavern a critical once-over. Lloyd and Kara had brought over a few spare tables from the Stealle Academy. Elladan had even purchased a keg for behind the bar from one of the other inns. All in all, the place was starting to look like a real tavern.

The only thing that still looked out of place were the chandeliers. Eight of them hung across the length of the ceiling in pairs of two. All were covered with a layer of thick dust. They were a bit high for him, even on a tall ladder, so Seth improvised by casting a *spider crawl* spell upon himself. With hands and feet that would stick to any surface, the halfling climbed up the wall and across the ceiling to each in turn.

In the fifth chandelier, Seth found something interesting. An amulet sat inside one of the glass candle collars. He picked up the circular object and spun it around in his hand. Strange markings dotted its surface, almost like runes, though in no language he had ever seen.

Not knowing what to make of it, Seth pulled out a portal bag he had just purchased here in Penwick. These handy little things were small enough to carry, but connected to another plane and could store far more than it appeared from the outside. In fact, they were so handy, Seth had bought two of them. He bagged the strange amulet for now, thinking he would show it to Glo later.

Seth was on the next to last chandelier when Ves, Ruka, and Cyclone returned. Ves still seemed a bit withdrawn, but Ruka appeared to be in much better spirits.

She chuckled as they walked in the door. "That was a great idea—pretending the dummy was Donatello."

Seth snorted so hard, he nearly lost his grip on the ceiling.

Maya came running over to greet them. The four of them had just sat down when a blue spinning oval abruptly appeared in the middle of the room.

Donnie, Elladan, Thea, Lloyd, and Kara all came spilling out one by one. The last one through was Aksel, who cried out a warning, "Watch out, they're right behind me!"

All of a sudden, four red-skinned fire genies appeared in the middle of the tavern. As everyone drew their weapons, Ruka admonished Donnie. "What did you do?"

Donnie cast her a hurt look. "I swear this time it's not my fault!"

Seth groaned with annoyance. He had just finished cleaning this entire room. He yelled down at Donnie, "If anything gets busted in here, you're paying for it!"

Donnie paid him little heed, however, as the lead genie floated toward him and glared at the hapless elf. "Give us the eye and we'll spare your life."

"You'll have to catch me first!" Donnie cried, spinning on his heel and bolting for the door. All four genies flew after him, with Lloyd, Kara, Elladan, Thea, and Aksel on their tails.

Seth breathed a sigh of relief. At least his tavern would be safe.

Down below, Cyclone eyed the chase scene dubiously. "Think he needs help?"

Ruka sighed. "Probably."

Seth leapt down to the floor and reluctantly followed as everyone emptied out of the tavern.

Andrella had mixed feelings as she and Glo returned from the Hault School. Nearly ninety wizards were enrolled there, making it the largest magic academy Andrella had ever seen. The roster of books in the library proved even more outstanding, with entire sections dedicated solely to magic and history. Many of those books had been penned by Lady Lara Stealle herself.

Despite all that, Andrella felt disappointed, a feeling she decided to share with her mentor. "Do you think it's strange that we found so many texts on Naradon and the towers, but none of them even mentioned the tunnels or the purple worm?"

A soft chuckle escaped the tall elf's lips. "I can't tell you how many times I made similar complaints to my father. His response would always be something like, 'Research is not an exact science. Often when you are searching for one thing, you'll find out something else entirely. Yet knowledge is knowledge. What you discover one day might prove useful another.'"

Andrella giggled at the pompous sound of Glo's voice as he imitated his father. "Does he really talk like that?" she asked him in a confidential tone.

Glo's gaze dropped to the ground, his expression one of deep embarrassment. "Almost always."

Andrella felt bad for him. Her father had always been supportive, but apparently Glo's was just the opposite. Well, Glo had just cheered her up. Now it was her turn to do the same. She grasped him by the arm while wearing one of her brightest smiles. "We did find out some important things about rune weapons."

Glo pressed his lips together into an inverted smile and nodded. "That's true."

The two great demon-slaying swords of legend, Thesius' Soulbreaker and the Shin Tauri blade, had multiple great runes carved into their metal. According to the texts, these ancient runes carried vast power, enough to fell even the greatest of demons.

Glo's eyes took on a faraway look. "I just wish we had some clue as to the actual runes carved into those blades."

Andrella jostled his arm to get his attention. "But we do know who crafted them."

Both weapons had been crafted by master smiths. Renish, head smith of the great Barroth Forge, crafted Soulbreaker almost five hundred years ago, while the legendary swordsmith Tauriyama crafted the Shin Tauri blade just prior to the Thrall Wars.

This time Glo actually cracked a smile. "True again. Maybe…"

He never got to finish his thought. The two of them had just entered Lion's Square when shouts broke out from across the plaza.

"Watch out! Run for your lives!" Donnie came dashing out of the inn trailed by four fiery djinns.

Glo reacted immediately. The elven wizard weaved a spell through the air while yelling at Donnie to 'duck.' Two seconds later he unleashed a powerful spell with the words, "*Glacies Tempestas.*"

As Donnie hit the dirt, the wind swept up and clouds formed above him. The air turned frigid and great balls of ice began to pelt down on the hapless elf as well as the djinn. Donnie curled up into a ball, but within seconds, the four fire creatures winked out of existence.

"Yeah, you better run!" Donnie waved a fist at the air where the djinn had been, but then curled back up into a ball as the ice continued to pelt him.

Seeing the creatures gone, Glo waved his hands and the storm swiftly dissipated.

Andrella stared at him in amazement. "That was awesome!" She grabbed him by the arm again and tugged on it. "Teach me that one? Please?"

A genuine smile crossed the wizard's lips. "Absolutely—when you're ready for it."

Meanwhile, Donnie picked himself up and brushed the remaining snow off of his shoulders. His teeth still chattering, he called out to Glo, "Th—thanks, I think."

Everyone else had piled out of the inn and now gathered around the three of them.

The side of Seth's mouth lifted into an outrageous smirk. "First time I've seen Glo use anything but a fire spell."

Andrella winced. Her mentor had made some explosive mistakes with magic in the past. Seth never missed an opportunity to remind him of that.

Glo opened his mouth to retort, but stopped himself. Instead he just shook his head and muttered, "Never going to live that down, am I?"

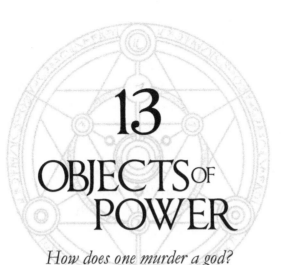

13
OBJECTS OF POWER

How does one murder a god?

W hat's going on out here?" Cal demanded, his head suddenly poking out through a tent flap.

With all the commotion, Glo hadn't noticed the huge tent in the center of the square. The dragon must have been in there this entire time, working on the fountain.

Ruka snorted, pointing a thumb at Donnie. "Bright boy here was being chased by a bunch of fire genies, but Glo snuffed them out with a blizzard."

"Hm," Cal rumbled, "I thought I felt a chill in the air."

Ruka folded her arms across her chest and leveled a withering stare at the hapless elf. "So what was this eye the genie was talking about?"

Donnie pulled a smooth black pearl out of his pocket the size of a humanoid eye.

Maya clapped her hands together. "Ooo, that sure is pretty…"

"…and powerful," Glo added. He could see a thick aura of black energy pulsing around it just beyond plain sight.

Elladan grasped him by the shoulder as Glo bent down for a closer look. "Thea was thinking it might be Eboneye's eye."

"Excuse me?" Glo wasn't quite sure he'd heard him right.

Lloyd swiftly related the story of the eboneye to him. Glo winced at the thought of someone plucking out their own eye.

"So where did you find this?" Glo asked when Lloyd finished.

Aksel described the room they discovered below the inn, and how it was protected by iron golems and the djinn.

Glo found the entire thing fascinating, especially the circular structure they discovered. "Sounds like it might be some kind of portal. The question is to where?"

"Ahem," Cal rumbled. "This is all well and fine, but some of us are trying to work here?"

"Oh, right. Sorry Cal," Ves apologized to the irritated dragon. She swept her eyes around the group and gestured back toward the inn. "Maybe we can continue this inside?"

"Excellent idea," Aksel concurred.

Everyone except Cal regrouped back at the inn. Seth poured a round of drinks as they all took a seat.

Thea then prompted Glo once again about the pearl. In truth, he had no idea the kind of power it would take to make one warlord of an entire pirate nation, thus he suggested getting Lara to look at it.

Glo and Andrella then related their failure to find out more about the tunnels or the purple worm. They did share, though, what they discovered about great rune weapons and the smiths who forged them.

When they were done, the entire room went silent. Elladan slowly drummed his fingers against the table, then sat back and stared at Thea. "You said before that the pirate invasion lasted close to three months."

Thea pressed her lips together and nodded. "Mm hmm."

"That's not normal," Donnie said with a certainty that spoke of firsthand knowledge.

"How so?" Glo asked, his curiosity piqued. The slim elf had always been closed-mouthed about his past, but if he knew more about the pirates, this was most certainly the time to share.

Donnie met Glo's gaze, but hesitated as if deciding just how much he wanted to share. "Well—by the mandates of Zesstara, the clans can't stay on land for more than three days."

"Mandates of Zesstara?" Glo repeated. He had read of the goddess of the sea, but never heard that term before.

Donnie let out a short sigh. "Yeah, well—the mandates are symbols—blessings—bestowed by the goddess on the leader of each clan."

"What happens after three days?" Lloyd asked.

Donnie shrugged. "The blessing runs out."

Glo found this all quite fascinating. Donnie claimed they were merely symbols, but apparently they had some sort of power of protection over the pirate clans. He wondered if there was something more to them than that.

Ruka leaned back in her chair and narrowed her eyes at the clandestine elf. "And just how do you know so much about pirates?"

Trying to be coy, Donnie gave her one of those toothy smiles. "Let's just say I spent a few years along the Dark Coast."

Maya, who had been twirling around the room this entire time, stopped next to Donnie and stared at him wide-eyed. "Ooo, does that make you a pirate?"

Donnie got up and knelt down in front of the girl, his voice taking on a distinctive pirate accent. "Aye, but in all my years, I've never seen a finer treasure than that pretty little face of yours." He finished by touching her nose.

Maya giggled, her laugh punctuated again by those cute dimples.

Meanwhile, Elladan continued to brood. "If they stayed beyond the three-day limit, then this key they were searching for must be mighty important."

"Key?" Glo repeated uncertainly. Had he been so lost in thought that he missed something?

Elladan's eyes seemed riddled with guilt as they fell on Thea. "Would you mind sharing with the others what you told me earlier about Eboneye's treasure? I think it might be important."

Thea seemed hesitant, but Lloyd reacted immediately. He shot up out of his seat, his face red as he knocked his chair backwards. "Whoa, whoa, whoa! That's a really sensitive subject there, buddy."

Glo was taken aback by Lloyd's reaction. In all the time they had been together, he had never seen him so upset with one of his friends.

Andrella appeared equally flustered. She stood up and grabbed him by the arm. "Lloyd!"

Thea placed her hand over her brother's and spoke in a calm, yet reserved tone. "It's okay, Lloyd."

Lloyd met his sister's gaze, still somewhat red in the face. "Are you sure?"

"Elladan's right." Thea responded with a hesitant nod, though the pained expression on her face spoke volumes.

A sudden flash of insight struck Glo. Lloyd had confided in him about how his sister and her friends had died when they were younger. It had happened during their search for Eboneye's treasure. Though they were all eventually resurrected, it had not been a pleasant experience for any of them.

"Sorry," Lloyd apologized to Elladan, then picked up his chair and sat back down.

Thea took a deep breath as if to steady her nerves. She then explained how the pirates had gathered every gem and jewel in the city in search of this crystal key.

Aksel adjusted his seat and then gingerly stroked his chin. "I wonder if this has anything to do with that keyhole in the portal below the inn?"

"I was wondering the same thing," Thea agreed.

All the pieces started falling into place in Glo's mind. He steepled his hands in front of his chin as he reviewed them out loud. "So this is what we know. The portal, if that's what it is, is decorated with runes in some variant of celestial. The stone itself is rather old, so it's a fairly good assumption the language is ancient celestial."

Aksel cocked his head to one side and pursed his lips together. "Go on."

"Your interpretation of some of the runes spells 'god' and 'light,'" Glo continued. "Once might think that reference is to Arenor, but considering the age of the stone, perhaps it is more likely related to Phobas."

Elladan's face lit up at the mention of the name. "Ah, the original God of Light. Didn't he disappear at the end of the Third Demon War?"

"You mean murdered," Kara declared in a harsh voice, before draining the rest of her ale and setting her mug down with a solid *thwump*.

Her definitive pronouncement had stunned everyone in the room. Elladan sat with his mouth hanging open. The blood drained from Thea's face. Aksel looked astonished.

"Murdered?" Glo repeated with an arched eyebrow. "How does one murder a god?"

Kara sat forward in her seat and placed her armored elbows on the table. Her eyes burned with a flame-like intensity as she swept them around the room. "What I'm about to say doesn't go beyond these doors—unless you want to undermine folks' faith in the Ralnai."

The angel's words were met with a round of silent nods.

"Good, then." She waited while those at the other tables got up and gathered around them in a tight circle. Once everyone had drawn in close, she pressed on with her story.

"When the Ralnai first ascended, they had not yet divested themselves of their petty mortal concerns. Thus, when the other gods began to look to Phobas for leadership, his brother, Amon, grew jealous."

Glo had studied the pantheons of other races and therefore was quite familiar with Amon, the Lord of Darkness. They had run into his evil disciples before, when searching for the baron's heart.

"During the third Demon War," Kara continued, "two of the seals on the chains that bind this world to the Abyss were broken. Amon tricked Phobas into believing that the Ralnai were mounting an all-out assault on the Third Abyssal Chain."

That didn't surprise Glo in the slightest. After all, Amon was also known as the Lord of Deceit.

"Phobas appeared in full aspect at that chain," Kara pressed on, "completely alone against a horde of demons and three demon princes. The raw power unleashed during that battle was so great that we could hear it halfway across the world."

"Whoa," Lloyd breathed, his eyes wide with awe.

Glo quite agreed with him. The battle must have literally shaken the world.

Kara's voice dropped to nearly a whisper, her eyes heavy with sadness. "Through his own sacrifice, Phobas destroyed the Third Abyssal Binding and most of the horde. Too late, his brethren gods arrived. After much grieving, they took up his remains and buried them somewhere in this world. The location of his tomb, however, remains a mystery to this very day."

A deep silence fell over the room after Kara's incredible revelation. Aksel and Thea both looked shaken to the core.

Glo sat back in his seat, stunned at what they had just learned. Yet in spite of that, it made him wonder. "Kara, who else knows about this?"

Kara refilled her mug with ale and took a huge swig before answering. "Aside from the gods, some of my host witnessed the aftermath."

Ves, who had been silent this entire time, finally spoke. "There are legends of it amongst my people as well. They had bonded with men to form the Storm Riders and fought alongside the Ralnai in that war."

That confirmed Glo's suspicions. Some folks did know of the death of Phobas. Further, since the god had fallen in battle, he would most likely have been buried in his full regalia.

Elladan nudged him in the arm. "What are you thinking?"

Glo locked eyes with his elvish friend. "I'm thinking about what Kara told us back in Lukescros—about *an object of great power that all demons fear* and how *it is hidden somewhere along the east coast of Thac.*"

Elladan's face lit up with understanding. "So you think that might be related to the tomb of Phobas, or maybe what's buried with him in the tomb?"

"Precisely," Glo affirmed.

The initial shock worn off, Thea's eyes now glowed with a strange intensity. "Any of Phobas' regalia would be considered holy relics. If my studies are correct, however, then two powerful artifacts disappeared with him: The Staff of Law and the Crucible of Souls."

Kara's eyes widened with amazement. "Those are mighty relics indeed. I could see the demons being afraid of one or both of them."

"I could also see the pirate clans wanting to raid the tomb of a greater god," Donnie added with a sly wink.

"The same could probably be said for the Golem Master," Glo noted.

The glow in Thea's eyes dissipated, her expression growing troubled. "It all seems to fit together, but I'd be more comfortable if we could decipher the rest of the runes around that supposed portal."

At that point, Seth pulled something from a portal bag and laid it out on the table in front of her. "What about this thing? Think it might help?"

Glo leaned in for a closer look. It appeared to be a circular amulet with a hole in its center and rune-like markings around the edges. Thea waved Aksel closer as she picked it up and spun it around in her hands.

Aksel circled around the table and drew up next to Thea. He examined the amulet for a few moments, then shook his head. "These markings are not the same as the portal downstairs."

Thea squinted at the object in her hand, tilting her head left and right. "I've seen markings like this somewhere before..." All of a sudden, her face lit up and she snapped her fingers. "I know where. The portal under the watchtower."

Glo's brow furrowed into a single line as he wondered if he had heard her right. "Another portal? Watchtower?"

A gay laugh escaped Thea's lips. She briefly described an abandoned watchtower at the south end of town, and a hair-raising experience she and her friends had there as youths.

When she was done, Glo felt even more confused. "No wonder everyone was searching this town. There seem to be portals hidden almost everywhere."

Thea laughed a second time. "Penwick has been around for a lot longer than most people realize."

Lloyd leaned across the table, his voice taking on a conspiratori-ally tone. "Mom says it's been around since before the fall of the Baleful Moon. According to her, it's been rebuilt more times than you can count."

Lloyd and Thea exchanged a knowing glance before she added one last thing. "One of her favorite quotes is *Not even the gods know what lies beneath the streets of Penwick.*"

Glo found the entire discussion astounding. *The tomb of a greater god? Ancient relics? Hidden portals?* Penwick had turned out to be a far more interesting place than any of them realized.

Aksel felt completely dumbfounded by all they had just discov-ered. Phobas, the original God of Light, was dead. Even more as-tounding, his body just might be buried somewhere in or around Penwick. As if that weren't enough, relics of great power had most likely been buried with him. The entire thing seemed surreal.

Aksel couldn't imagine finding that tomb, let alone wielding such mighty artifacts. He couldn't even begin to guess what his parents would have thought of all this. Both archeologists, they had lived for this kind of stuff. Unfortunately, he would never know. They disappeared on a trip along with his only uncle when he was still very young. The Church of the Soldenar took him in, and there he stayed until he met Seth and Glo years later.

Aksel's musings were cut short when someone else entered the tavern. A woman wearing a Penwick uniform called out to them, "Is Lord Lloyd Stealle here?"

Lloyd rose from his seat and waved to the woman. "Yes, over here."

The soldier rushed up to him, holding out a thick envelope in her hands. "I have a letter here for you from Lord Hightower."

Lloyd took the letter from the soldier and thanked her. He started to open it as she left.

Andrella hovered anxiously next to Lloyd, her eyes glued to the envelope. "Hurry up and open it already."

Lloyd had been trying to neatly open the envelope, but finally gave up and ripped it open. He pulled out a number of parchments folded together and read the first one out loud for all of them to hear.

Dear Lloyd,

I hope this letter finds you and your lovely fiancée in good health. I just received correspondence from Andrella's mother with grave tidings, I'm afraid. Please find that letter attached here. Let me know if I can be of any further assistance.

Sincerely,
Lord Lagerie Hightower

Grave tidings? Aksel did not like the sound of that.

Andrella must have felt the same. She grabbed the letter from Lloyd's hands and nervously flipped to the second page, also reading aloud.

Dear Andrella,

The Princess of Lanfor returned from her mission to the Demon Tower earlier today, and I'm afraid the news is not good. The Princess' ship crash landed just outside the keep and looks like a blackened and twisted mess. It appears they were scouting too close to the tower and were attacked.

The Dunwynn platoons were decimated. Not a one survived I'm afraid to say. Anya lost some of her people as well, while others were badly wounded in making their escape. Not even all of her dragons made it safely away.

We will keep the Princess and what's left of her crew here until they are all back in good health. In the meantime, please tell everyone to prepare carefully for the next assault on the tower. According to the Princess, there are some demon lieutenants there now. You will need to match their dark power with an equal power of light.

Please take care and be safe, my daughter.

Your loving mother,
Gracelynn

When she was done, Elladan let out a low whistle. "They took out Anya like she was nothing."

Lloyd wore a haunted expression, his voice sounding hollow. "All those Dunwynn men and women…"

For the second time in the space of an hour, Aksel felt numb. The loss of life was bad enough, but Elladan's assessment was chillingly correct. They had barely survived their own run-ins with Anya. How could they expect to take on a tower full of demons if she had failed so easily?

Kara's countenance had grown as grim as Aksel felt. "This does not bode well if demon lieutenants have now entered this world."

For the first time since they had entered the tavern, Cyclone showed a spark of interest in the conversation. "So, what kind of power are we talking? Like that demon we stopped them from summoning back in mountains?"

Kara peered over at the hunter, who stood leaning against the bar. "If you're talking about Salisma Tanj, I highly doubt it. She is one of the most powerful demon lieutenants in the Abyss. What they're referring to is most likely more akin to that undead red dragon we fought outside the Marsh Tower."

Cyclone's eyes lit up with clear interest.

Aksel, on the other hand, had heard more than enough. If demon lieutenants had entered their world, they were already far outclassed.

Everyone had begun talking at once. Aksel climbed up on his chair and called out over the din, "Alright!"

The room fell abruptly silent as all eyes turned his way.

"Now," he began, rubbing his hands together, "it's all that much more imperative that we prepare before going up against the Demon Tower." First," he ticked off on his fingers as he counted, "we should follow up on the forging of demon-slaying weapons. Second, we could really use more information on those tunnels and that purple worm. Third, we need to find out about these portals and the possible location of Phobas' tomb."

"Sure. Piece of cake," Seth commented, the corner of his mouth curved upward.

Aksel leveled a disdainful gaze at the halfling.

Kara stood and shouldered her spear. "In the meantime, I'm afraid I'll have to take my leave of you. I need to warn my order about these latest developments."

Aksel breathed a regretful sigh. Kara was a powerful ally, but deep down inside he knew she was making the right decision. "We more than understand. Thank you for all your help these last few weeks."

Everyone gathered around Kara to say their goodbyes. Just before leaving, she stopped at the door with one last warning. "A word of caution. Although we beat the Empress, those black robes that attacked Lukescros bore the symbol of the Undead Thrall Master. If he has truly risen, the undead incursions to come will make the Marsh Tower look like child's play."

14
BEST SMITH IN TOWN

Perhaps we should go back up front before you melt

Lloyd thought he knew all there was to know about Penwick, but he had been sorely wrong. From iron golems to hidden portals to even the tomb of a dead god, there was far more buried under his city than he ever imagined. All this time he'd thought his sister crazy, but now it appeared she had been right all along about 'hidden treasures.' It made him wonder if any of her other theories were true, such as the pirates working with a secret group in Penwick or a cabal of witches being behind the invasion in the first place.

Either way, it gave Lloyd a lot to think about. Much of it was still going through his mind at dinnertime back home. Donnie had surrendered the black pearl for Andrella to give to Lloyd's mom. Lara now held it up to the light, murmuring as she looked it over.

"Mm, this does exude quite a bit of power, but there have been many fakes over the years. I'd need to run some tests on it to be certain."

"Please, keep it," Andrella implored her. "It's probably safer in your hands anyway."

Lara pocketed the pearl, then patted Andrella on the hand. "You're such a sweet girl." She gave Lloyd an approving nod. "You did well finding this one."

Andrella blushed profusely. "Thank you, Lady Stealle"—she caught herself as Lara gave her a cautionary look—"I mean, Mom."

Andrella then brought up the sensitive subject of the tomb of Phobas. Strangely, neither his mom nor dad seemed surprised in the slightest.

Lloyd found the whole thing highly suspicious. He put his fork down and stared accusingly at his parents. "Kara said the tomb was supposed to be a huge secret. Just how do the two of you know about it?"

Lara exchanged a glance with Kratos, then laughed. "Oh my dear, Lloyd. It's only a secret from the general populace. The clergy has known about it since it happened, as do the bronze dragons, of which we happen to know a few."

Lloyd suddenly felt very foolish. Ves had known about the legend as well. Still, that meant his parents knew her far better than they were letting on. He breathed an exasperated sigh. "So what else aren't you telling me?"

"Oh, so many things," his mom answered, her eyes dancing with amusement.

Lloyd knew she was trying to be funny, but that didn't make it any less true. He eyed her for a few moments, then gave his dad a pleading look. "Dad, make her stop."

Kratos chuckled softly at his request. "Now Lloyd, you should know your mother better than that. She's a virtual vault of secrets."

Lloyd knew his dad was right. Between the council and her position as Head Wizard, his mom knew many things she couldn't share, some not even with his dad.

Lara watched him with a sympathetic smile. "There are a few things I can tell you, however. For instance, the tomb you seek has many false doors, as well as many real doors. Some just lead to more keys, both real and fake, that open other doors in other places. So finding it will not be all that easy."

Lloyd's head hurt from trying to follow all she just told them. "Thanks, Mom, I think."

He felt a gentle squeeze on his arm and turned to see Andrella smiling up at him. "What do you say we change the subject?"

Andrella proceeded to tell them all she and Glo had discovered about great runes and the forging of legendary blades. When she brought up the cold-iron spike, Kratos asked to see it. Lloyd went to retrieve it from his room and handed it over to his dad.

Kratos weighed the spike in his hands, then held it up to his eye and peered along its length. "This is mighty fine metal, very light and yet sturdy. If forged right, it will make a fine blade."

The word *forge* reminded Lloyd of something. "Dad, didn't you always say Mr. Bache was the best smith in town?"

Kratos flipped the spike over in his hands and eyed the other side. "Yes, but from what you've told me, I doubt even he has the talent to craft this into a blade."

Lloyd let out a deep sigh. He had hoped they might find a smith in Penwick. It would certainly have saved them time.

"His daughter, on the other hand…" Kratos murmured as he continued to eye the spike.

A wave of confusion swept over Lloyd. "You mean Amada? I thought she was studying abroad."

"Was," Kratos corrected him. "She returned shortly after you left and proceeded to forge some of the finest weapons anyone in town has ever seen."

Andrella pressed her lips together and gave him a single nod. "That sounds rather impressive." She fixed Lloyd with a pointed look. "Is this Amada an old friend of yours?"

Before he had a chance to answer, Lara responded. "Oh, she and Lloyd were friends growing up, but a few years back, her father sent her to Isandor to study metalworking."

"She sounds quite driven," Andrella said, sounding even more impressed than before. "Do you know who she studied with?"

This time, Kratos answered. "The best of the best—the Tauri-yama family."

Andrella's eyes lit up with recognition. "Tauriyama? The same Tauriyama who forged the Shin Tauri blade?"

Kratos laughed. "Unfortunately he's long dead by now, but his craft has been passed down through his descendants."

Andrella brushed the hair back from her shoulders and gave him a wry look. "Thanks, but I'm not that blonde."

"Touché," Kratos responded with a sly grin.

Andrella's expression grew serious once more. "So, do you think that this Amada would be able to forge a rune blade out of that spike?"

Kratos shrugged as he handed the iron spike back to Lloyd. "I'd say if anyone can, it would be her."

"Okay, then I'll take the spike to her tomorrow," Lloyd said, feeling hopeful once again.

Andrella stood and grabbed him firmly by the arm. "And I'm coming with you. This woman I have to meet."

Lloyd peered at her questioningly, but then she kissed him on the cheek and he forgot all else.

Andrella found herself more and more curious about this Amada Bache. Here was a girl who had grown up with Lloyd. She probably knew things about him Andrella might not ever find out. Deep down inside, she knew Lloyd would never keep anything from her, but it still wasn't quite the same as growing up with someone.

"It's this way." They had reached a corner and Lloyd pointed down the street, headed east.

"Where exactly is this place?" Glo asked, peering down the next block.

They had stopped off at the inn to tell the others what they learned the night before. When Glo heard they were headed to the smithy, he expressed interest in joining them. Andrella welcomed the idea. She didn't want it to appear as if she was hovering over Lloyd in front of his old 'friend.'

A short while later, they reached the eastern side of the city. This appeared to be a trade area with leatherworks, woodworking shops, and the like. Lloyd led them to a large building with a sign out front that read *Bache Metalworks*.

Andrella wasn't sure what had her more anxious as they entered the place—finding out more about Lloyd's past, or if this Amada could actually craft them a rune blade.

All sorts of weapons hung on display inside the front area of the building. There were swords, maces, axes, spears, knives, and other weapons Andrella had never even seen before. Like the proverbial kid in a candy shop, Lloyd seemed enamored by all of them.

A broad-shouldered, barrel-chested man, maybe in his late forties, stood behind a counter in the very back. He laughed softly when he saw the look on Lloyd's face. "Well as I live and breathe, it's Lloyd Stealle!"

Lloyd grabbed the back of his neck, a sheepish grin on his face. "Oh, hi there, Mr. Bache.

Mr. Bache came around the counter to greet them. Though his hair had started to thin and his temples showed a touch of gray, the man looked like he could still lift an ox. "Last we heard, you were out making a name for yourself. What brings you back to Penwick?"

Lloyd gave him a brief explanation about the Demon Tower, then introduced Andrella and Glo. The two of them then took turns explaining about rune swords. As they did, Lloyd pulled out the cold-iron spike and placed it on the counter.

Bache picked up the metal and examined it much the way Lloyd's father had done the previous evening. "There's something very strange about this metal," Bache murmured as he flipped it from end to end. "I think we need an expert on this."

"Follow me." Bache gestured as he exited from behind the counter. He stopped and waited for them in front of a door that led to the back.

The back area of the metalworks shop was exceedingly warm and rather dim. A few smith stations lined the walls with a couple of workers at them, but Andrella's eyes were drawn to the center of the room. A tall figure stood outlined there against the brilliant flames of a huge hearth. The clink of metal on metal pervaded the room, but the loudest sounds came from that figure as it slammed a large hammer down on a nearly molten piece of metal.

As they drew closer, the figure's features became distinguishable.

The smith was a tall blonde woman garbed in a sleeveless shirt and shorts. She was covered by a thick leather apron that exposed much of her muscular arms and legs.

As they approached, Bache called out to her, "Amada, you'll never guess who's come to call!"

Amada halted in mid-strike and glanced over her shoulder at them.

Wow, she is pretty, Andrella thought, not quite expecting that of a female smith. She immediately chastised herself for stereotyping the woman. As a diplomat and a future ruler, she should know far better than that.

Amada swept her eyes over the three of them until they settled on Lloyd. "Lloyd?" Her face lit up. "Lloyd!"

Amada dropped her hammer on the anvil, threw off her gloves, and then came over and caught Lloyd in a huge bear hug. The young woman was so strong that she practically lifted him off the ground.

Lloyd, his face a bright shade of scarlet, grunted his greeting in return. "It's—nice to see you, too—Amada. I see you've gotten—stronger."

Amada laughed as she set him down, then stepped back and looked him over. "You look like you're in pretty good shape as well."

Andrella was hard pressed to suppress a laugh. Lloyd appeared completely embarrassed by the situation. Unable to help herself, Andrella wore a wide grin as she cleared her throat. "Lloyd, aren't you going to introduce us to your 'old' friend?"

Lloyd glanced at Andrella, his face reddening even further. "Oh, um, yeah." He gestured toward Glo. "Amada, this is my friend, Glolindir."

Amada stretched out her hand to Glo. "Nice to meet you, Glo—linda was it?"

"Glow-linn-derr," Glo pronounced each syllable for her as he took her hand. From the way he winced, Andrella could tell he immediately regretted it. She had no doubt this Amada was as strong as Lloyd.

Lloyd then introduced Andrella. "And this is my fiancée, the Lady Andrella."

She had wondered how Lloyd was going to introduce her. He definitely got points for that one.

"Fiancée?" Amada repeated, her eyes widening. Her face broke out into a sudden smile as she extended her hand to Andrella. "Well then, congratulations!"

"Thank you," Andrella replied, ignoring Amada's hand, and executing a perfect curtsey instead. She wasn't going to make the same mistake that Glo had made.

Appearing somewhat amused, Amada retracted her hand and gave Andrella the once-over. "My, you are a pretty little thing, and that dress is gorgeous"—she took a quick glance around the room—"but maybe a dirty smithy isn't the best place for either of you."

Andrella peered down at her dress and ran her hands over it as she giggled. "Oh, this old thing? It may be pretty, but it's quite functional, too." She casually snapped her fingers and an aura of flame sprang up around her, courtesy of her Regalia of the Phoenix.

Caught by surprise, Amada stared unabashedly at the flames engulfing Andrella. After a brief pause, she broke out into a grin. "That is rather handy." She elbowed Lloyd in the arm, making him flinch. "I think I like this fiancée of yours."

"Amada, look here at what Lloyd has brought us." Bache held out the cold-iron spike to his daughter.

A sudden gasp escaped Amada's lips. "Is that what I think it is?"

"Cold iron," Glo affirmed, still rubbing the circulation back into his hand.

Amada took the spike from her father and examined it closely. "This is tempered with eldritch magic. You don't find iron like this growing on trees."

"Well, actually..." Andrella told her the story of how they acquired the spike.

When she finished, Amada appeared quite impressed. "So this came from the same tree as Soulbreaker? Very interesting."

Andrella could practically see the wheels turning in the smith's mind.

"We'll need a hot enough forge—and the right runes, of course," Amada murmured, her eyes focused off somewhere in the distance.

"We were thinking of the forge up at Supond," Glo said, trying to regain her attention.

Amada shook herself as if waking from a dream and grinned at the tall elf. "That would definitely do if you could get it up to five thousand degrees."

"So what you're talking about is red or gold dragon breath," Glo countered.

"Gold. Definitely gold," Amada corrected him. "Red might taint the metal. Still, it's a moot point without the proper runes."

That brought them back full circle to the problem of finding such runes. Still, something had been nagging at the back of Andrella's mind. "So Amada, we heard you studied with the Tauriyama clan in Isandor. Wouldn't they still have the same runes used for the Shin Tauri blade?"

Amada let out a pained sigh. "Had. The scrolls with those runes were stolen just before I came back. In fact, it's the reason they sent me away."

"They thought you stole them," Lloyd asked, his expression incredulous.

Amada shook her head. "It wasn't that. After the theft, they sent away anyone who was not part of the family."

"Were there any clues as to who stole them?" Glo asked.

Amada cast a quick glance around the room, but the other smiths seemed to be concentrating on their work. Even so, Amada motioned for all of them to follow her back out front.

Once they had all gathered around the back counter, Amada continued her story in a low voice. "Rumors say it was the pirates of the coast, but I'm not so sure."

"Why's that?" Andrella asked in hushed voice matching Amada's.

A wan smile spread across the smith's lips. "Let's just say that Isandor's recent alliance with Parthos has brought a few too many undesirables into the country."

Lloyd's expression grew puzzled. "Why would an upstanding nation like Isandor ally itself with known conquerors?"

The corner of Amada's mouth curled ever so slightly. "Isandor isn't exactly the great nation it once was. After the death of their

King and the loss of their greatest General, they've had a hard time with the pirate clans."

Lloyd made a sour face. "The Parthians do have a strong fleet, but I still think it was a bad move."

Andrella loved that about him—he was not the type to compromise his morals. Unfortunately, that left them back at square one when it came to finding these runes of great power.

Luckily, Mr. Bache had an idea. "You know, if it's rare items you're looking for, you might want to check with one of the merchant houses like Relvern or Dunamal. They do a lot of shipping up and down both coasts and might know something."

"Thanks, Mr. Bache," Lloyd said with an ironic smile, but getting information out of either of them might not be all that easy."

"Why don't you ask Alys?" Amada said suddenly.

"Alys," Lloyd repeated, his face lighting up. "That's brilliant! Why didn't I think of that?"

"Who's Alys?" Andrella asked. It was not a name she had heard any of the Stealles mention before.

Lloyd grabbed her hands, a broad smile on his face. "An old friend of the family—and Dunamal's daughter."

"Dunamal?" Andrella repeated. "The same Dunamal as the one on the City Council."

"That's him," Lloyd sighed.

"Don't worry," Amada assured her, "Alys is the exact opposite of her father. You can trust her."

Somehow, Andrella was having a hard time believing that. Still, she didn't want to contradict Amada, at least not to her face.

They left the cold-iron spike with the Baches and proceeded back toward the Inn of the Three Sisters. On the way, Andrella asked Lloyd to tell them more about this Alys Dunamal.

Lloyd seemed reluctant at first, but once he told them the story of what had happened on Thorn Isle, Andrella understood why. When he finished, Andrella had to wipe the moisture from her eyes. "Oh Lloyd, that sounds so tragic."

"It could have been worse," Glo noted in a soft voice. "At least your sister and her friends were all resurrected."

The three of them walked together in silence until they reached Lion's Square. Andrella then asked Lloyd the question that had been weighing on her mind. "So, do you think really this Alys will help us?"

Lloyd had been lost in thought, but now gave her an encouraging smile. "If anyone can, it's her. Still, I haven't talked to Alys since I left. Let me ask Thea and see what she thinks."

15

FAME AND FORTUNE

My family is cursed

The next few days flew by for everyone. Lloyd split his time between the Stealle Academy and the inn. Glo and Andrella fit in as much studying as they could in between repairs. Cal continued his clandestine work on the Fountain of Lions, allowing only Donnie in to see his progress. Ves and Ruka helped as well, when they weren't off training with Cyclone. They had to be careful, though, as the powerful lightning they threw around sparked rumors amongst the townsfolk of angry deities in the nearby woods.

Meanwhile, the work on the inn progressed. The walls were repaired and painted, the floors refinished, and the windows replaced. They bought all new furniture for the rooms, set up the kitchen, and fully stocked both it and the wine cellar. They also hired a cook, bartender, and a few barmaids.

Elladan had managed most of the purchasing and hiring, assisted by Seth of all people. The halfling had decided to take up the job of innkeeper, something which caught all of them by surprise. Still, with everything he was juggling, Elladan had little time to find entertainment for the grand opening. Of course he planned to perform himself, but he was hoping for at least one more act.

Surprisingly, it was Thea who came to his rescue. It turned out that her old friend Alys also happened to be a professional singer. Thus when Thea approached her about the stolen scrolls, she recruited her to audition as well.

Elladan waited with Lloyd and Andrella when Thea came waltzing into the tavern with a coppery-haired redhead on her arm. Garbed in an emerald green dress and a matching parasol that highlighted her eyes, Alys looked more like a lady of the gentry than an actual artist.

Thea wore a bemused smile as she introduced her companion. "Elladan, I'd like you to meet my old friend, Alys."

"Charmed, I'm sure," Alys said, holding out her hand like a refined noble.

"As am I, good lady," Elladan replied as he took her hand and executed a deep bow. He silently hoped that Thea hadn't just saddled him with a stuffy noblewoman who would only sing old boring standards. Still, he had the strangest sense he had seen this woman somewhere before.

A moment later, Alys caught sight of Lloyd and all pretenses flew out the window. Her face broke out into a dazzling smile that practically lit up the entire room.

"Lloyd!" she cried, launching herself at the young man. The two exchanged an exuberant hug, swinging each other from side to side. "It's so good to have you back!"

Andrella stood a bit behind the two, the slightest tinge of jealousy in her eyes. That all but disappeared, however, when Alys punched Lloyd in the arm. "You big lug. Thea said you went and got yourself engaged. Where is this gorgeous fiancée of yours?"

Andrella stepped around Lloyd's huge frame, a wan smile on her lips as she gave Alys a curt wave. "I'm right here."

Alys immediately let go of Lloyd and went straight in to hug Andrella. "You're as gorgeous as Thea said."

Andrella seemed caught off guard, but almost immediately warmed to the young lady. The two began comparing outfits and talking about fashion in general.

Thea leaned in close to Elladan and whispered, "Alys can be a bit of an acquired taste."

Elladan chuckled softly as he whispered back. "Well at least she isn't stuffy. I just hope she can really sing."

A smug smile spread across Thea's face. "Just you wait."

A short while later, Alys took the stage they had set up across from the bar. When she began to sing, the entire tavern went silent. All the workers stopped what they were doing and sat to watch the young lady on the stage. Alys started with a slow ballad, showcasing her rich, sultry contralto voice. Yet midway through the second stanza, she picked up the tempo and belted out a tune with the power to rival Elladan himself.

Thea nudged Elladan in the arm. "I told you she could sing."

"You weren't kidding," Elladan agreed. Her performance floored him for all those reasons, but also because it finally dawned on him where he'd seen Alys before.

When she was done, the entire tavern broke out in applause. Alys took a few bows, then came off the stage to rejoin them. She peered at Elladan with another one of those dazzling smiles. "Well, what did you think?"

"I think that you're *Angelfire*," Elladan pronounced definitively.

Andrella's mouth dropped open. "*The* Angelfire? The hot new performer who went on tour with Cassilla Nightbird?"

Cassilla was the most famous entertainer in all of Thac. Elladan had competed against her at the Lukescros Faire last year, just barely losing to her in the finals.

Alys giggled, her eyes dancing practically with a light of their own. "Yup, that's me."

Andrella grabbed Alys by the hands, pulled her down into the seat next to her, and proceeded to gush. "Oh, I adore everything about you—the songs, the costumes, the dancing. I so wanted to get you for my eighteenth birthday."

Alys' fair-skinned, slightly freckled face reddened at the incessant praise. "I'm very flattered. When was it?"

"A couple of months ago," Andrella told her.

Alys' face fell, her lower lip jutting forward just a bit. "I'm sorry. I would have loved to, but I needed some time off when I came back home."

Thea's mouth rose to one side as she nudged Alys in the shoulder. "You mean 'Pallas' time."

"Thea!" Alys yelped, her skin turning a bright shade of scarlet. She turned around and smacked her friend across the arm.

Andrella's eyes burned with interest at the tidbit Thea had just dropped. "You wouldn't be talking about your brother?"

Thea began to answer, but Alys covered her mouth. "That's enough, Thea!"

The two women mock-tussled with each other, then began to laugh and hug it out. It was heartwarming to see the closeness between these two. Up until now, Elladan hadn't realized what he was missing. It made him long for a closer relationship in his life.

Andrella went on to describe her party and how Elladan and Shalla Vesperanna had provided the entertainment. As it turned out, Alys had heard of both them and confessed to being a fan of Elladan's. "I really admire your style—the way you combine song, instruments, and dance."

It was Elladan's turn to blush. "Why thank you. Thank you very much." He was really starting to like this young lady. A sudden idea struck him. "Shalla and I had done a duet for Andrella's party. What would you say to the two of us doing one here?"

Alys' face lit up with excitement. She clapped her hands together with glee. "Really? I would absolutely honored." Alys peered over each shoulder then sat forward in her seat and held a hand to the side of her mouth. "The truth is I haven't performed since I got back home. I'm afraid I might be a little rusty."

Elladan arched an eyebrow at the young lady. "If that was your rusty, then I really need to work on my voice."

Alys gave him another one of those brilliant smiles. "Why Elladan, you say the nicest things to a girl." She peered at Thea with a mischievous smile. "I'd say this one's a keeper."

"Alys!" Thea yelped at her friend, her cheeks reddening more than a little.

The hint that Alys had just dropped filled Elladan with a warmth he had never felt before. *So she does think of me that way.*

A sudden pang of guilt washed over him. Elladan cast a rueful eye at Lloyd, but the young man didn't seem to be concerned in the slightest. He and Andrella joined in the fun, everyone taking turns teasing each other. Not being one to spoil the party, Elladan jumped in feet first.

With the upstairs mostly refurbished, everyone picked rooms at the inn but Lloyd, Andrella, and Cyclone. The latter preferred the quiet of the woods to the sounds of the crowded city. Those staying at the inn insisted that the sisters get the largest room on the third floor. The nicest room at the inn, it opened up to a wide balcony that ran the entire length of the building.

Elladan and Donnie took the next room over, while Aksel and Seth got the last room in front. Xellos was given the double room behind those two, with the idea that he and Martan would share it when he returned. They also reserved another room for Kalyn. Glo chose the only other single room on that floor, just behind where the sisters were staying.

The day of the grand opening, the door to the sisters' room lay open. As Glo passed by, Ves called out to him, "Glolindir, do you have a moment?"

Glo paused in the hallway and saw Ves sitting on her bed. They had been keeping company more and more these last few days, both of them enjoying quiet walks together along the riverside after dinner. Between her training with Cyclone and their evening constitutionals, Glo had noticed a marked improvement in Ves' aura. Yet even so, she still seemed more reserved than usual.

"Sure," Glo responded to her, parking himself in the doorway to her room.

"Come in," Ves motioned to him.

Feeling awkward, Glo hesitated, eliciting a small smile from her. "I don't bite—at least not in this form."

Glo arched an eyebrow. *Humor from Ves? That was something new.*

Entering the room, Glo noted two other beds, both made but empty. "Where are your sisters?" he asked, his unease growing.

Ves waved a nonchalant hand through the air. "Last I saw, Maya was prancing around on stage. Seth promised he would look after her."

Seth babysitting again? That's a surprise. Either he was mellowing with age, or someone had appropriately bribed him. Glo would bet money on the latter.

"And Ruka?" Glo pressed.

Ves shrugged. "She went down to the docks with Thea. Something about 'for old times' sake?'"

Still standing in the middle of the room, Glo shifted uncomfortably from one foot to the other. "So, what can I do for you?"

Ves huffed with exasperation as she motioned toward the empty bed across from her. "For the gods' sake, please sit down already?"

"Sorry," Glo winced, his cheeks growing warm with embarrassment as he set himself down on the bed.

Ves folded her hands on her lap and took a deep breath to calm her nerves. "See, this is exactly what I wanted to talk to you about. You just haven't been acting like yourself lately."

"Really?" Glo's eyebrows shot up his forehead. This had suddenly turned into a serious case of 'pot and kettle.'

"No, you haven't," Ves insisted with a firm shake of her head. "While I've enjoyed our walks, you are starting to make me feel uncomfortable."

Glo had no idea how to respond to that. Had he truly been acting different? "I—I don't know what to say," he stammered. "If it's become a problem, we don't have to walk together anymore."

A pained expression crossed Ves' face. She got up, strode to the door of the balcony, and peered out over the city. "No, that's not what I'm saying." She hesitated a moment as if searching for the words. "I think it is that you miss Elistra. While I do like keeping company with you, I don't want you to misplace any feelings you might be having."

If Glo had been embarrassed before, he now felt ten times worse. Not used to analyzing his own feelings, this forced him to take a good look at himself. He swiftly concluded that Ves was right. While ostensibly he thought he'd been trying to help her, instead he had been using her as a crutch to ease his own suffering.

Wringing his hands together, Glo dropped his gaze to the floor, no longer able to look directly at Ves. "I am truly sorry if it came across that way. You are right. I miss Elistra."

"That's a good first step," Ves said. She turned away from the door and strode over to where he sat. The next thing he knew, she had seated herself next to him on the bed and placed her hand over his. "Now how about telling me the rest of it?"

Glo slowly lifted his head to meet her gaze. The concern in her eyes appeared truly genuine. Feeling a bit better, he did his best to put it into words. "The first time Elistra disappeared, I was devastated. Yet since then, I've come to understand just how selfless she is. I do love her and I am trying to be strong, but it's not exactly that easy. It feels like we had just gotten back together, only to be ripped apart again." Glo breathed a heavy sigh, his eyes dropping to the floor once more.

Ves got off the bed and knelt down in front of him, still holding onto his hands as she caught his eye. "Thank you for sharing all that with me. It takes bravery to open up like that. I must admit that is an area in which I've also been sorely lacking."

Glo shrugged, a wan smile gracing his lips. "Trust me, that wasn't easy to put into words."

"Well, now it's my turn," Ves said emphatically. She rose to her feet and began to pace around the room. "I know I've been moody lately and it isn't just due to my troubles with Theramon."

Glo could see how difficult this was for her, thus he waited patiently for her to continue. He had to admit at being surprised when she went to close the door, but what she told him next more than explained her actions.

"My family is cursed," Ves began. She paced around the room, wringing her hands as she spoke. "There is a certain prophecy concerning the end of the world as we know it. It contains many references that you might recognize. One of them in particular mentions the eternal enemy that walks among us."

"Theramon," Glo spoke the name with thinly veiled anger.

"Yes," Ves agreed solemnly. "The prophecy goes on to detail many signs of the coming apocalypse, but also speaks of how it might be averted."

Glo had read entire books on prophecies in his father's library, but never came across this one. He sat on the edge of the bed, his curiosity firmly piqued. "Such as?"

"The first sign is the appearance of the Aes Aeris, the true heir of storms," she intoned as if quoting a line of prophecy verbatim.

"Aes Aeris," Glo repeated slowly. "That roughly translates to *bronze air* in the ancient spell tongue."

Ves stopped and turned to face him, her face drawn and her shoulders stooped as if some invisible weight sat upon them. "Subsequent passages are equally as cryptic, but roughly translate to this: the Aes Aeris is destined to go mad and become the most fearsome of storm dragons. That madness will be instrumental in the destruction of the enemy, but the cost is great. The Aes Aeris will never be sane again."

Glo listened carefully to her words, but still felt as if he was missing a piece of the puzzle. "So how exactly does this relate to your family?"

"Have you ever read the poem *Dragon Tears*?" she asked softly.

Glo in fact had read that poem. In it, Rodric Greymantle joins Thari, the berserker storm dragon, to face the Thrall Masters. Together they are forced to slay many of Thari's fellow dragons. In her grief, Thari goes to the Stones of Sorrow to die, but Rodric follows her and professes his love. The poem ends with Rodric performing forbidden magic to bind their spirits together in eternal death.

A chilling thought suddenly crossed Glo's mind. He stood and looked Ves in the eye. "When we first met, you introduced yourself as Vestiralana ta Yatharia—in other words, Ves, daughter of Yatharia. Would your mother's nickname happen to be Thari?"

"Yes," Ves answered, her voice barely above a whisper.

Everything fell into place at once for Glo. "So your mother was the berserker storm dragon referred to in the poem?"

"Yes," Ves responded again, her skin suddenly very pale.

"And because your mother went berserk, you're afraid that you, or your sisters, will become this Aes Aeris?"

Ves merely nodded this time. Moisture had welled in the corners of her eyes and it appeared as if she were going to cry. Glo immediately went to her and wrapped his arms around the young woman. She lay her head on his shoulder and silently wept into it.

Glo felt terrible. This prophecy had her all tied up in knots. Knowing Ves as well as he did, she was probably more concerned for her sisters than herself. Still, that just made things worse.

Glo gently patted her on the back, wishing there was something he could say to make her feel better. His mind wandered to what Elistra had shared with him about prophecy—how it was basically all a lie. She had told him there was no such thing as destiny or fate, only a myriad of possibilities based on the impact of individual events.

All of sudden, it dawned on him. The answer to soothing Ves was Elistra. He cried out for her in his mind.

Yes my love, came the response a moment later.

Glo silently explained to her what Ves had just shared with him. He told her how tortured she seemed and that he didn't know how to console her.

Hold on, came the simple reply.

Glo was hoping for a bit more than that, but swiftly stifled that thought as a sudden shimmering appeared in the air across the room. A few moments later, that shimmering turned into Elistra.

Glo's mouth dropped open. "Elistra, is that really you?"

"My astral projection," she corrected him. A slight frown crossed her brow. "I cannot do it for long, though."

She turned her gaze upon Ves, who had pulled back from Glo and was attempting to dry her eyes. "Glo explained to me what is going on with you and your family." A trace of guilt washed over her face. "I feel somewhat responsible."

Ves stopped drying her eyes and narrowed them at the visage of the seeress. "What do you mean?"

Elistra breathed a deep sigh. "It's a long story and we don't have much time."

The seeress briefly explained her eons-old battle with her brother and how prophecy was one of the weapons she used to keep him at bay. She ended with what she had previously told Glo—that prophecy was a lie.

Ves perked up with renewed hope. "Does that mean that one of us is not destined to go mad?"

A look of keen sympathy swept across Elistra's face. "Oh, my dear. As I said, there is no destiny. You and your sisters merely inherited your mother's mind."

Deep creases formed across Ves' brow. "So we will go mad?"

Elistra shook her head in exasperation. "That's not what I said at all. Let me try this again." She pointed at Ves with her index fingers steepled together. "You have a way of seeing beyond what most dragons can see. That is what made it so the Dragon Thrall could not control your mother, and the same goes for the three of you."

Ves cocked her head to once side, her expression riddled with uncertainty. "Then how did Theramon control me?"

Elistra briefly closed her eyes, her expression pained. "That is because unlike your sisters, you pride yourself on discipline. While that is good in many cases, it is not in this one. You need to learn to let go, to embrace your instincts. There you will find a power beyond the draconic, a power which will allow you to evade any attempts to control your mind."

Ves' expression grew even more confused. "But how do I do that?"

A knowing smile spread across the seeress' lips. "You've already started. Continue your work with the dragon hunter. He thrives on raw emotion and can teach you to let go."

Ves let out a huge sigh, her shoulders straightening as if a huge weight had been lifted from them. For the first time in a long time, a genuine smile graced her lips. "Thank you, Elistra."

Elistra smiled back, then suddenly swooned.

Glo and Ves instinctively reached for her. They were both surprised to find that she was solid.

Recovering quickly, Elistra waved them off. "I'm alright. I just can't stay much longer."

Ves leaned forward and kissed the seeress on the cheek. "Thank you again." She cast a furtive glance at Glo, a sly smile on her lips. "I'm going to give you two a moment alone."

Without another word, Ves walked over to the door and exited the room, pulling it closed behind her. As soon as she did, Elistra wrapped her arms around Glo and gazed at him with a wide grin.

Glo marveled at the sensation of feeling her in his arms. "I didn't think this was possible."

A gay laugh escaped Elistra's lips. "Normally it's not, but the power of the crystal makes it so."

Glo stared down into her violet eyes and found himself totally mesmerized. "Well, if that's the case, then let's make this count." He leaned in close and kissed her with unbridled passion.

16
GRAND OPENING

Did you know Alys could move like that?

That night, the grand opening of the Inn of the Three Sisters commenced. Lion's Square and the tavern room of the inn were packed with people from all over the city. A stage had been set up outside in front of the tent still covering the fountain. The Penwick Philharmonic spread out in front of the stage as the sound of musical instruments being tuned wafted across the square. Inside, Seth worked the bar while Donnie, Elladan, and Maya prepared for the evening's entertainment.

The rest of the companions gathered on the third-floor balcony awaiting their guests' arrival. Three tables had been set up across the wide terrace. Andrella sat at one of those tables with Lloyd, Glo, and Aksel. Ves, Ruka, Cyclone, and Xellos had been seated at the other until Ruka and Cyclone, neither fond of crowds, bolted for the nearby roof. The middle table currently sat empty, reserved for the City Council.

While they waited, Aksel reported that Martan's tribunal had gone well. He and Kalyn would set out for Penwick first thing in the morning.

"That's going to take them a week on horseback," Lloyd exclaimed.

"It can't be helped." Aksel shrugged. "The council would have had a fit if the Remington stayed in Deepwood to wait for them."

Shortly thereafter, Lloyd's parents arrived. Kratos informed them that both the Cloud Hammer and Remington had docked in Penwick. "Alburg is having every inch of them gone over to make sure they are undamaged," he finished with a wry smile.

"Wonderful," Lloyd grumbled. "At this rate, we're never going to pry them out of his grubby hands."

In truth, Andrella thought the same, but she had been raised in the art of diplomacy, and would thus never openly admit defeat. Still, politics was not his forte—at least not yet. So for now, she'd have to be strong for the both of them. Andrella placed her hand over his and gave him an encouraging smile. "Don't lose hope just yet."

Aksel expressed his faith as well. "I agree with Andrella. Let's see how tonight plays out first."

The conversation abruptly came to a halt at the arrival of the Baron of Penwick. His brother, Aillinn, accompanied him, as well as Carenna Hightower. To Andrella's surprise, behind them strode Alburg Dunamal, with Alys upon his arm.

Apparently she was not the only one shocked to see him. Aillinn made a comment similar to what Andrella had been thinking.

Unruffled, Alburg responded, "Why, I'm here to see my daughter perform, of course."

With the center table reserved strictly for council members, Andrella had saved a seat for Alys next to her. Though she tried her best to wheedle details of tonight's performance from the young lady, Alys remained staunchly quiet on the matter.

Alys had just stepped away when Thea arrived with a dashing young man on her arm. Garbed in naval uniform, he was the spitting image of Lloyd, with the exception of his longer hair and trimmer build. Andrella realized this had to be Pallas, Lloyd's older brother.

Thea introduced Pallas around. He turned out to be quite

charming, but when presented to Andrella, feigned confusion. "Lloyd, how did an oaf like you end up with this ravishing young lady?"

Lloyd, used to his brother's teasing, had an immediate comeback. "That's because I don't spend every waking moment out to sea like some folks."

It appeared as if Pallas had another jab on the tip of his tongue, but never quite got the chance to say it. Alys came flying across the terrace and practically threw herself into his arms. The kiss she planted on him appeared to have the double effect of embarrassing and enticing him at the same time.

Alys then dragged Pallas over to see her father. As it would happen, Alburg seemed pleased to see the young man. Andrella leaned in close to Thea. "I thought Alburg resented your entire family?"

Thea responded with a bemused expression. "Everyone except for Pallas." Apparently, Pallas had saved Alys from pirates not once, but twice.

Shortly thereafter, Alys excused herself and headed downstairs as the show was about to begin.

Darkness had fallen. The brilliant lights set around the square abruptly dimmed as a bank of thick fog appeared on the stage. Some pyrotechnics went off above the square, drawing the crowd's attention. As if out of nowhere, Donnie swung onto the stage and executed a deep bow, to the audience's applause.

With a bit of magical assistance, Donnie's voice boomed over the din of the crowd. "Thank you all for joining us at this evening at the grand opening of the Inn of the Three Sisters. We have some very special entertainment planned for you tonight. To kick things off, please welcome the incomparable Elladannnnn!"

Donnie backed off the stage as a dark figure walked through the mists. The lights suddenly came up and focused on the elven bard.

Elladan wore a pure white outfit with long fringes and spangled sequins interspersed throughout. He turned around, and woven into the fabric of his outfit was the heraldic of Penwick.

The audience went wild. Elladan posed in a few directions so that the entire crowd could see, then bellowed above the din, "Hello Penwick! Are you ready to make some noise?"

The audience roared in response. Elladan grinned, then summoned his lute as the orchestra began to play. The noise died down as he broke into the *Hounds of Hell*, a variation of one of his well-known songs. With his soulful voice, catchy lyrics, and flashy footwork, the consummate performer mesmerized the audience.

Near the end of the song, Lloyd leaned in closer to his siblings. "Everyone loved this at Andrella's party—except for the Duke of Dunwynn and his people."

"Seems pretty catchy to me," Thea replied, not taking her eyes off the handsome bard on the stage below.

Pallas seemed less enthusiastic, but the mention of the Duke got a rise out of him. "I'm no expert, but the crowd seems to like it. Plus, what would the Duke know about music anyway? He's too busy following the beat of his own drum."

When Elladan finished his number, he received a rousing round of applause and whistles. Ever the gracious performer, he gestured to the musicians in front of him. "How about another round of applause for the Penwick Philharmonic?"

A loud cheer went around the square for the hometown musicians. As Elladan receded back into the mists, Donnie reappeared on stage. "So what do you think of Elladan, folks?"

Another round of cheers rippled through the crowd.

"I have to tell you he's a good friend of mine, but those white outfits. Sheesh. I'd hate to have his cleaning bill." Donnie's attempt at humor elicited a few chuckles amongst the patronage. "We also have a special guest with us tonight." Donnie gestured to the side of the stage. "The newest phenomena to hit the entertainment scene, and a Penwick local, welcome the one and only, Angelllll-fiiiiiire!"

Donnie backed away as Alys took the stage in a lavish red gown decorated with yellow and orange flames. The audience grew hushed as the orchestra began to play a heartfelt ballad, *Fools Rush In*. One of Elladan's songs, Alys swiftly made it her own, her rich voice soaring above the plaza. So haunting was this rendition that it sent chills up Lloyd's spine.

A few times during the performance, Lloyd noticed Alys looking Pallas' way. In truth he had rarely seen Pallas blush before, but Alys seemed to have a way of getting to him.

When the song ended, there was not a dry eye left in the place. Lloyd covertly wiped the moisture from the corners of his eyes. He didn't feel quite so bad, though, when he noticed Pallas doing the same.

As the applause died down, Alys called out to the crowd, "What do you say we pick up the tempo just a bit, folks?" As the orchestra began a fast tune, Alys doffed her long skirt and flung it off the side of the stage. Beneath it she wore a skin-tight pair of red briefs that accentuated her smooth, well-toned legs.

Lloyd heard Pallas gulp. "Did it suddenly get hot out here?"

Alys moved across the stage with power and grace as she belted out a tune called *Dragon Heat*. Her movements were both fluid and electric, further enhanced with a bit of acrobatics. When she reached the chorus, Maya and Elladan appeared out of the mists behind her. The trio then began to dance in sync. Their moves were crisp, edgy, and exciting to watch. Not missing a beat, they stayed in perfect synchronization, harmonizing with Alys through each chorus thereafter.

When the song ended, the audience burst to its feet, giving the trio a standing ovation. The applause went on for quite some time, but when it finally died down, Thea couldn't resist teasing Pallas.

"Did you know Alys could move like that?"

Pallas' cheeks grew flush once more as he stammered over his words. "Yes—well—she is quite the acrobat. When those pirates had us cornered at Redune, I saw her knock out a witch with a flying kick to the face."

Meanwhile, Donnie had returned to the stage. "So what do you think, folks? That Angelfire is one hot performer." A few chuckles went through the crowd. "Anyway, speaking of hot, next we have some fireworks for you, accompanied by your own Penwick Philharmonic!"

The lights dimmed as Glo and Andrella took turns setting off sparkling pyrotechnics above the plaza. Each tried to outdo the other with fancier and fancier images in the sky. Glo finally topped it all with a fiery lion. Not to be completely outdone, Andrella added a pair of flaming swords below it.

"Touché," Glo capitulated to her with a broad smile. She had come a long way under his tutelage, something for which Lloyd was particularly grateful.

After that spectacular finale, the entire square lit up once more. The mist had dissipated, leaving a clear view of the tent behind Donnie and Elladan, who both stood on stage. "And now for the grand finale, we have a special treat for you," Donnie announced to the crowd. "A present from us to the City of Penwick," Elladan declared, gesturing toward the tent behind them. "Without further ado," Donnie went on, "we would like to present to you the artist Calipherous and his most magnificent work to date…"

"…the brand new Fountain of Lions!" Elladan finished with a flourish.

The duo separated as the tent flew up, revealing Cal next to the fully restored fountain. Three majestic lions sat around the fountain proper, looking so real that Lloyd half expected them to move. The crowd *oohed* and *ahhed* as water began to spray from the top of the center column. It flowed down to two intermediate basins and ended up in the wide reservoir at the fountain's base. All of a sudden, the water changed color from red to green, green to yellow, yellow to blue, and over again.

Boisterous applause rang out amongst the townsfolk, with rousing shouts of "Penwick! Penwick!" repeated over and over again.

Caverinus Avernos, the Baron of Penwick, appeared uncharacteristically emotional at the sight of the restored Fountain of Lions. Wiping a tear from his beady little eye, he turned his attention to the table where Lloyd sat. "You have done us a tremendous service this day in restoring this valuable piece of Penwick heritage."

"From where I'm sitting, I'd say they've done more than restore it—they've improved it," his brother, Aillinn, pointed out with a wink in the direction of Lloyd and Andrella.

Still somewhat emotional, Caverinus cleared his throat. "Yes, yes indeed. You are quite right, Aillinn."

"It was the least we could do, uncles," Andrella tactfully downplayed their accomplishment.

Ever the diplomat, Aillinn used her humility to their advantage. "You are too modest, niece. I'm sure this will weigh well in your favor toward borrowing of one of our airships."

The Baron appeared to be considering his words when Alburg stepped in. "I quite agree with Aillinn. This group has made an excellent overture. Still, the ships have only just returned and it will take a few days to maintenance them."

"It should only take two," Kratos immediately corrected him.

All in all, things appeared to be going quite well until Lloyd's brother went and stuck his big fat nose into it. "Pardon me if I am overstepping myself, but can someone please explain to me why we would lend an airship to anyone, let alone my kid brother?"

Old angers that had festered from years of teasing and tormenting welled up from somewhere deep inside of Lloyd. He glowered at his brother, ready to rip him another one, when he felt a restraining hand on his arm. He gazed at Andrella, the momentary distraction saving him from saying something he would most likely regret.

Thankfully, Thea confronted their brother before anyone else had a chance to speak. "How 'perfectly Pallas' of you," Thea railed at him, her tone scathing. "You have no idea what these folks have accomplished in the last few months, yet here you are ready to judge them against your impossible standards."

Pallas drew back with clear astonishment at the unexpected attack. It did not rattle him for long, though. After a moment's consideration, he sat back, folded his arms, and narrowed his gaze at Lloyd. "Very well, little brother, just what have you accomplished in these few months since you've been gone?"

A dozen responses immediately came to Lloyd's mind—none of them particularly nice. Yet before he could speak, he was cut off yet again.

"Ahem, if I may?" Ves had strode over from the other table, most likely having picked up on their conversation with her keen dragon hearing. The young lady appeared quite regal in her lavish bronze gown, arm-length white gloves, and moonstone-colored pearl necklace dangling across her neckline.

Pallas sat up in his seat, his face registering surprise at this clearly noble young woman who chose to speak for his brother. Remembering his manners, Pallas rose and bowed. "As you please, good lady."

Ves gave him a demure nod, then proceeded with a polite, yet at the same time withering lecture. "I am Vestiralana ta Yatharia Greymantle, daughter of Sir Rodric Greymantle, and these good people have shown nothing but bravery and kindness since we first met. I have witnessed firsthand their defense of Ravenford against a demonic cult. Further, they came to my aid when I had been callously abducted. And most recently, I had the honor of accompanying them as they wrested the tower in the marshes from an army of undead, led by the former Empress of Naradon herself."

Each accomplishment Ves listed rendered a visible blow to Pallas' superior attitude. Yet before he had the chance to comment, Andrella rose from the seat next to Lloyd and chimed in. "Not only did they save Ravenford from the Serpent Cult, but they also cleared it of a vampire infestation before we left. Furthermore, they moved heaven and earth to save my father from a merciless death. If not for your brother and our friends, my father would still be lying dead at this moment in our family crypt."

Those final points shattered what remained of Pallas' arrogant demeanor. Clearly stunned, he peered at Lloyd with a look of astonishment. "Did you seriously do all that?"

Lloyd's anger had dissipated at the overwhelming support he'd received from his friends. Yet he hadn't accomplished all that alone and wasn't about to take credit for it. "We did"—he said, gesturing to all those around him—"together."

That moment changed the dynamic between Lloyd and Pallas forever. His attitude gone, Pallas peered at Lloyd with something he had never seen before in his brother's eyes—respect. "I am truly sorry if I misjudged you, brother."

This was new territory for Lloyd. Having always been the brunt of Pallas' taunting and lectures, he had no idea how to respond. Strangely, it was Alburg who saved him from having to reply.

"Ahem," Alburg cleared his throat. "Indeed, they do appear to be quite capable. Perhaps while we are waiting for the ships to be refurbished, they can help with that issue you've uncovered, Carenna?"

Carenna Hightower had sat quietly at the council table throughout most of the evening. Now, with all eyes turned toward her, the Protector of Penwick beckoned for them all to gather around. "This needs to remain between us—we are trying to keep the people from panicking."

Lloyd exchanged a worried glance with the others. What could possibly be that bad that they needed to keep it from the townsfolk?

"Over the last few weeks, there have been a rash of disappearances in the hamlets just west of the city," Carenna continued. "We've sent out scouting parties, but found nothing. Then just this morning, a couple of townsfolk were reported as missing from the tenement rows along the western wall of the city."

Lloyd let out a low whistle as he remembered Kara's parting words. "Kara was right. It's started again."

Carenna narrowed an eye at Lloyd, the concern on her face obviously mounting. "What's started again?"

Aksel, in front of the others and closest to the table, explained what was going through all of their minds. "That's what was happening in Ravenford just before we discovered the vampire infestation. People started disappearing overnight."

Caverinus leaned over the table, his eyes glued to the little cleric. "Are you saying there are vampires in Penwick?"

This time Glo fielded the question, his expression grim as he detailed their previous experiences. "Based on the evidence at hand, I'd say it's highly likely. The folks who disappeared from Ravenford had been turned into vampires by the original one. By the time we tracked them to the catacombs beneath the town, their numbers had swelled to well over two dozen."

After hearing Glo's dire words, all the council members started talking at once. They all tried to get their point across, not listening to what anyone else had to say.

Lloyd put his fingers in his mouth and whistled loudly over the din. The cacophony of voices stopped as all eyes turned his way. Suddenly feeling awkward, Lloyd nonetheless plowed ahead with his impromptu speech. "Listen, there's nothing to worry about. Once we found their nest, we wiped them out in one quick battle. By the time we left Ravenford, there was no trace of any vampires in town."

Though Lloyd tried to sound cavalier about it, deep inside he knew it would not be all that easy this time. If these creatures were indeed minions of the Undead Thrall Master, then they were in for the fight of their lives.

"Well, Alburg, it appears you were right in enlisting these folks' aid," Aillinn noted with an ironic smile. "They obviously have experience with this sort of thing."

Alburg absently stroked his beard as he considered Aillinn's words. "Perhaps, but right now this is all just supposition. There may be another more reasonable explanation for these rash of disappearances."

Lara huffed at Alburg's denial of the most obvious solution to the evidence at hand. The side of her mouth was upturned slightly as she turned her gaze to Lloyd. "You might want to check the burial crypts beneath the old town graveyard. That's the largest grave site in the city."

Thea scoffed as well at Alburg's stubborn attitude. "If there's even a chance that this involves undead, then I'll be joining you."

Feeling suddenly relieved, Lloyd broke out into a grin as he wrapped an arm around his sister's shoulders. "It couldn't hurt to have a Priestess of Arenor on our side."

Aillinn, with a pragmatism to match Aksel's, finally put the conversation to rest. "Well, I'm not sure what else we can accomplish tonight, so how about we try to enjoy the rest of this evening?"

Caverinus let out a deep sigh. "You're quite right, Aillinn. Quite right."

17
MISSING PERSONS

Since when is 'fun' a word in your vocabulary?

Early the next morning, the companions prepared for another possible confrontation with the undead. As far as weapons went, they were in fairly good shape. The dragons certainly didn't need any, and neither did the spellcasters. Lloyd had a holy sword, Donnie a holy dagger, Cyclone just lopped off heads with his halberd, and Xellos had proved his bow effective against vampires more than once. Only Seth appeared to be lacking a proper weapon, so he gave Aksel one of his daggers for Thea to have blessed while the two of them consecrated vials of holy water at the temple.

Meanwhile, Seth accompanied Elladan on his rounds to pick up a few more useful items. First they headed to the trade district to get some wood to be whittled into stakes. On the way back, the two of them stopped in the east market to get some garlic. As they were leaving, they heard a commotion coming from a nearby wine shop.

"…over a dozen casks of wine! All smashed from the inside!" a frantic voice bellowed from inside the shop.

Seth halted in his tracks and cast a knowing look at Elladan. "That doesn't sound good." They'd run into the same thing in Ravenford, except that time it had been a single crate.

Elladan winced. "We'd better go check it out. If there are that many, the entire city could be turned in just a few days."

The owner of the wine shop, an older bald gentleman, had been talking to a pair of city guards. Elladan introduced himself and Seth as having been recruited by Carenna. At the mention of the Protector's name, the guards openly welcomed their help. The shopkeeper then started his story over for them, from the beginning.

The shipment in question had arrived just a few days ago, but the shopkeeper's assistant only discovered them just that morning. "It would've been sooner," the owner complained, "but the workers that handle the inventory haven't show up for work for the last two days."

Seth felt a sudden headache coming on. *Idiots! With a two-day head start, the vamps could have a small army of minions by now.*

With time being of the essence, Elladan paid a kid to go fetch Aksel and Thea from the temple. Meanwhile, Seth confronted the hapless store owner. "Show me these broken casks."

The shop owner led Seth and the guards downstairs into the wine cellar. Sure enough, they found thirteen broken casks in total, all with splinters jutting outward and lying all on the stone basement floor. "Yup, all burst from the inside," Seth pointed out the guards.

Seth reached inside one cask and pulled out a handful of dirt. Kalyn had reported finding the same thing in Ravenford—yet another thing confirming Seth's suspicions.

While the guards examined the rest of the casks, Seth looked around the rest of the cellar. A close examination of the floor revealed multiple sets of dusty footprints leading away from the casks. One set in particular appeared rather small and barefoot. "I hate halflings that don't wear shoes," Seth muttered to no one in particular.

Seth followed the tracks to a set of stone stairs that climbed up to a closed cellar door above. He called out to the shopkeeper, "Where does this lead?"

"That's a back alley where we do the loading and unloading," the man replied.

Just great, Seth thought to himself. *So the vamps slipped out of here with no one seeing which way they went.*

With no other leads, Seth had one last idea. He strode back over to the others as Elladan joined them. Seth told the bard what they had already found, then asked the owner, "Who delivered the casks?"

The owner frowned as he thought it over. "I'd have to check my records to be sure, but I think it was the Warnok brothers out of Lymerdia."

Realizing what Seth was looking for, Elladan pressed the old man further. "Do you know if they're still in town?"

The shopkeeper nodded. "Should be. It's a long trip back, and they'd want to reload their wagons with stuff to sell."

"Any idea where they'd be staying?" Seth pushed the old man, trying his best not to lose his temper further.

The owner grabbed his chin and peered up at the ceiling as he tried to recall. "Let's see. If I remember right, the Warnoks like to stay at the Merry Monkey."

"Which is where?" Seth asked, feeling as if he were pulling teeth from a baby dragon.

"Northwest side of town." One of the guards came to his rescue. "I can take you there if you want."

"Thank you," Seth said, forcing himself to take a deep breath.

Elladan nodded him on his way. "You go check out it. I'll wait here for Aksel and Thea."

"Just as well," Seth grumbled. "Someone with a brain needs to be here to meet them."

When Thea and Aksel got the word about the wine shop, they headed over there immediately. What they found was quite alarming. Multiple evil presences had been in that basement recently, all undead and some quite powerful. With things having gone from bad to worse, they sent word to the Stealle Academy and the Hault School for everyone to meet them back at the inn.

When they arrived at the tavern, Thea was in for a bit of a shock. Pallas sat at one of the tables waiting with Lloyd and his friends. Even stranger, Lloyd and Pallas seemed to be getting along with each other.

Her suspicions aroused, Thea approached her brothers. "Pallas, what are you doing here?"

Pallas turned to face her with a sardonic smile. "Did you really think I was going to let you and Lloyd have all the fun?"

Thea raised a single eyebrow as she folded her arms across her chest. "Really? Since when is 'fun' a word in your vocabulary?"

Pallas threw his hands up and laughed. "Fine, you caught me. I'm actually here to keep an eye on you. Is that what you wanted to hear?"

Thea gave him a sour look. "No, not really."

Ever since Thea had reached her teens, Pallas had played the role of overprotective brother. Any boy who even looked at her funny ending up running from the tip of his blade. At one point, she had to make him swear not to terrorize the boys in her group of friends. Still, she supposed she shouldn't complain too much. If it hadn't been for Pallas and Ruka, she and her friends would never have survived Thorn Isle.

While Thea confronted Pallas, Aksel went over to the stage to talk to a dancing Maya. "Where are your sisters?"

"They went to train with Cyclone," Maya answered without stopping. Since her performance with Alys and Elladan, the girl had become even more obsessed with dance.

Despite those still missing, they decided to bring everyone else up to date. Elladan began by explaining to everyone what they had found at the wine shop. Seth then added what he discovered about the caravanners. "All of them checked out two days ago, but their wagons are still parked behind the Merry Monkey."

"That's exactly the way they got into Ravenford," Andrella pointed out to Pallas and Thea, neither of whom had been there at the time. "Still, that was only one vampire and the empty wine crate had gone unnoticed for nearly two weeks."

Glolindir sat with his hands steepled in front of his face, his expression grim. "So this time we have more than a dozen vampires who have been loose in the city for two to three days…"

"…and a much bigger population to suck the life out of," Seth, sitting at the bar, finished for him.

"Which means we need to move fast," Donatello said, rising to his feet, looking ready to rush out the door.

Aksel gestured at the impetuous elf to sit back down. "Agreed, but first we need a plan." He gingerly tugged at his chin. "We should probably split our forces to cover more ground. The question is how?"

"We already know about the west tenements and the crypts beneath the old town graveyard," Glolindir deliberated out loud. He suddenly sat forward, his eyes lighting up as if he'd had a revelation. "Lloyd, you told us the old quarter nearly burnt to the ground. Is any of it still left standing?"

Lloyd shook his head. "It's mostly in ruins. What's left wouldn't be enough to hide a nest of vamps…"

"…and those that have been rebuilt are occupied," Thea continued where Lloyd left off. "If anything strange had been going on out there, we'd probably have heard something by now."

Glolindir pressed his lips together and nodded. "Fair enough. Are there any other structures in town that are abandoned but still fairly intact?"

Thea had just been thinking the same exact thing. "Well, there is the old watchtower I told you about."

"I'll go check that out," Seth said jumping down off his barstool and stretching his arms.

Aksel's brows knit into a single line. "Seth, did you just volunteer for something?"

"Better than searching through musty old crypts," Seth replied with a derisive snort.

"I'll go with him," Glolindir offered, though he didn't sound too thrilled about it. Thea had noticed a tension between these two, but hadn't quite figured out what it was all about just yet.

"I'll go with you both," Thea said. She knew the place better than any of them.

Elladan fixed Thea with one of his charming half-smiles. "I'll come, too."

The thought of Elladan joining them somehow gave her a measure of comfort. Before she realized it, she was smiling back at the elf.

"Count me in as well," Pallas declared.

Thea sighed, now feeling less comfortable. Of course Pallas would go where she went.

Lloyd stood and gestured toward Andrella. "We can go and check out the tenements."

"Good. I'll come with you," Aksel agreed with a firm nod. The little gnome then called out to Maya, who now sat glumly on the floor of the stage. "Maya, can you go get your sisters and Cyclone?"

The young girl immediately perked up at being given a task to do. "Sure, I can do that."

"I'll fill them in and let them know she's coming," Glolindir proposed. The tall elf held in his hands an amulet inset with a moonstone-colored pearl.

Thea had seen one of those before—in fact, she had one herself. They were called *Pearls of Friendship* and could be used to communicate over long distances with a likewise-bound pearl. After the incident at Thorn Isle, her mother had made a pair: one for Thea and one for herself.

"Also tell them to join us at the crypts," Aksel added after a moment's thought.

"Will do." Glolindir rose from his seat and went off by himself to contact the Greymantle sisters.

Aksel began tugging on his chin again, one eye on Donatello. "Someone should probably scout out the graveyard before they get there."

"I'll do it." Donatello said, rising from his seat with a sigh. From his reaction, it didn't sound like he thought the job all that thrilling. Yet Aksel had cleverly maneuvered the impulsive elf into volunteering for the less-than-glamorous job.

"Excellent," Aksel responded.

Thea had noted another dynamic revolving around Donatello and the rest of the group. Though not completely certain what prompted it, it appeared as if they were trying to protect the elf from his own reckless nature.

Aksel ended the planning session with a gesture toward Xellos, the only one left who hadn't been assigned a task. "That leaves you with me."

"Sure thing," Xellos said simply.

He's a strange one, Thea thought. Xellos hardly ever talked and mostly kept to himself. She felt as if he was hiding something, but had yet to figure out exactly what.

As a final thought, Aksel asked Glo to setup a telepathic mind link between the groups. Unfortunately, the reliability of the spell faded at distances greater than a mile. That meant that each group would in essence be on their own.

Lloyd had been anxious since they first heard about the missing persons last night. He'd be damned if he let what happened in Ravenford repeat itself here in Penwick. Thus he led the way to the western tenements and took the lead on questioning people in the area. Since this was his city, he felt it his obligation.

From what they heard, it sounded like more people had gone missing last night. To expedite things, Aksel cast a spell to track undead. The spell had a limited range, maybe a couple dozen yards, so the four of them roamed the streets in and around the tenement buildings.

Aksel's brow was furrowed in concentration, his wrists rolling in circles as he went. White light filled his palms and engulfed his weaving fingers. At one point, he stopped. "There's a trace of undead here. It's not that strong, but is fairly recent."

"How recent?" Lloyd asked, his eyes scanning the nearby buildings.

"A couple of days at most," Aksel answered.

The door to the tenement Lloyd had been staring at suddenly opened; someone in a dark hood stepped outside. The moment they saw Lloyd staring at them, the figure lunged back inside and slammed the door shut behind them.

Lloyd bolted across the street and up the stairs to the door through which the hooded figure had just disappeared. The door turned out to be locked, but Lloyd stepped back and kicked it down, then charged inside. He entered a dark hallway with a single door to his left and a set of stairs winding upward out of sight.

Lloyd debated which way to go when he heard Andrella's cry from outside. "Look, they're trying to escape on the roof!"

Lloyd swiftly invoked his flying cloak, then took off through the door and veered upward.

"That way!" Andrella pointed toward the south.

Lloyd rose up above the rooftops, and sure enough, spied a hooded figure with a sack on its back leaping from rooftop to rooftop two buildings down. The young warrior dove straight for the fleeing figure, quickly catching up and tackling it.

The sack went flying from the figure's back and tumbled off the roof and to the streets below. The others caught up to them and rifled through the fallen sack.

"There's nothing in here but candles, silverware, and a few other odds and ends," Andrella called up to him.

Lloyd ripped the hood off the fallen figure. It was a teen girl. Lloyd picked her up and looked her in the eye. "Miss, what are you doing with all that 'stuff?'"

The girl tried to look him in the eyes, but couldn't, instead staring down at the rooftop. "Times have been hard lately. Dad died last year and mom's been working to pay the rent, but it never seems like enough. So, I thought I would help out."

"By stealing all that junk?" Lloyd asked incredulously.

"Hey!" The girl found the courage to look him in the eye. "It helps pay the rent."

Lloyd found himself admiring the girl's spunk, if not her choice of profession. He folded his arms across his chest and tried to imitate his father's stern face. "What's your name?"

The girl hesitated before finally responding. "Luscinda."

Lloyd took a moment to think what his father would do. The answer came to him almost immediately. "Well, Luscinda, first you're going to return everything you stole."

"But…" she began.

"No buts about it," Lloyd cut her off. "After you do that, you head down to the Stealle Academy. You tell them Lloyd sent you and that they're to give you a job."

Luscinda's eyes widened into saucers. "For real?"

"It may not be all that glamourous at first," he warned. "They might just start you with cleaning floors."

Luscinda launched herself at Lloyd and threw her arms around his waist. "Thank you! Thank you, Lloyd—I mean, Mr. Stealle. As long as it pays steady, I don't care what I have to clean."

Lloyd grabbed the teen by the shoulders and grinned at her. "Be careful what you wish for. Anyway, how's about we go get that bag of yours?"

Lloyd put his arm around her waist and flew her down to the ground, where the others waited. He then explained Luscinda's story to them and what he proposed.

Aksel looked the girl over with a stern gaze, purposely deepening his voice. "I am a Cleric of the Soldenar, young lady. If any of what you told Lloyd here isn't true, I'll know it."

Lloyd knew Aksel well enough by now to know he was bluffing. He hadn't even taken the time to cast a spell. Still, Luscinda didn't know that.

"I swear it's true! All of it." Luscinda prostrated herself at Aksel's feet.

Aksel winked at Lloyd, then held his hands out to Luscinda. "It's alright, young lady. I detect that you do in fact speak the truth." He instructed Xellos to give her back the bag of stolen valuables.

Luscinda took the bag and threw it over her shoulder, her eyes still wide. "I'll return all of it. I promise."

Aksel made the sign of the Soldenar in front of her and spoke again in that deep voice. "I know you will. Now go, my child, and do the right thing."

Luscinda bolted away, calling over her shoulder as she went. "I will! I promise!"

When she was out of earshot, Andrella threw her arms around Lloyd. "That was a truly kind gesture. You'll make a great duke someday."

His cheeks feeling warm, Lloyd grabbed the back of his neck. "Duke? Me?"

"Someday," Andrella smiled, then she stood on her toes and kissed him.

"So do you really think she'll give all that stuff back?" Xellos asked.

Aksel shrugged. "Who knows?"

"I have faith that she will," Lloyd stated definitively. "But I will check at the academy when I get the chance to see if she took the job."

With the day quickly wearing on and still no sight of undead, the foursome decided to split up and head in opposite directions. Lloyd and Andrella went one way, while Aksel and Xellos went the other.

Not having Aksel's undead tracking abilities, Lloyd took to knocking on doors. At the third house down, a man answered dressed like a butler. There was a strangely detached quality to his tone and mannerisms. "The master should be returning soon. If you want to wait, I can serve you some tea."

Lloyd wasn't sure what to make of it. Folks who had been turned by a vampire tended to call that vamp 'master.' However, this strange butler could be just referring to his employer. Lloyd glanced at Andrella, but she just shrugged.

With no other leads, the two of them decided to enter the tenement. This place appeared to be a single dwelling with multiple floors. A center hall divided a sitting room on one side with a dining area on other. A set of stairs led up to the next floor.

The butler left Lloyd and Andrella in the sitting room, then disappeared down the hall to 'make some tea.' As soon as he was out of sight, the two of them began searching the house. The dining room proved empty. Down the hall led to the kitchen where the butler did appear to be boiling water.

The two of them then headed upstairs. They found a couple of bedrooms, one in particular with boarded up windows. Andrella lit her dress to provide some light, revealing a woman in the bed. She seemed quite pale, but it could have been the flickering shadows from the flames on Andrella's dress playing tricks on their eyes.

Andrella knelt over the woman and checked her pulse. Lloyd stood close by, ready for anything. "She's dead," Andrella whispered to Lloyd, her voice cracking as she slowly backed away.

Lloyd eyed the corpse suspiciously. "Or maybe she's undead."

He thought he saw a sudden movement. Acting out of sheer instinct, he flew straight up and crashed through the roof, shining sunlight down into the room.

"Lloyd, whatever are you doing?" Andrella cried after him.

"Get back! She moved!" Lloyd yelled through the hole in the roof. Realizing the sunlight was not hitting the woman, Lloyd dove back through the roof, crashing another hole in it right over her. Pieces of roof fell all over the bed and sunlight filtered in directly onto the body.

Lloyd landed next to Andrella, then pulled her further back as he eyed the corpse warily. However, nothing happened. As it turned out, she was just dead. In his panic, however, Lloyd had called out telepathically to Aksel. By the time the went back downstairs, Aksel and Xellos had joined them in the hallway.

The butler had let the two of them in. "Would your friends like to join us for tea? The master should be returning anytime now."

"Let me say a proper blessing first," Aksel responded.

"No—no need for that," the butler said, showing emotion for the first time since they met him. He started to back away as the little cleric weaved his hands through the air.

"*Averti Ab Malum*," Aksel repeated as the spell released. The mana rushed outward toward the cowering man. It encircled his body in brilliant white light about a foot from his skin in all directions. Though the light swiftly faded, Lloyd could still feel the magic radiating from the trembling butler.

As if waking from a dream, the butler abruptly fell to his knees. "Oh, thank goodness. That awful man put me under a spell and he did something horrible to the Mistress of the house."

Lloyd placed a comforting hand on the man's shoulder. "We know. We saw her. I'm sorry."

The butler proceeded to tell them the master only came at night. He did not know where he went during the day.

Leaving the poor man to his grief, the four of them retreated outside to confer on what to do next. Aksel wore a worried expression. "If the master comes at night, we should probably clear everyone out of these tenements."

Lloyd thought that over for a few moments. "That's a pretty big job, but if we can enlist the town guard, it should go quickly."

"That's a good idea," Aksel agreed. "Do you think you and Andrella can handle that? If there's a master vampire in town, it might be best for Xellos and me to join the others searching the crypts."

Lloyd didn't relish the idea of dealing with Taliana, but it couldn't be helped. "That shouldn't be a problem. You two go ahead." He and Andrella then went off together to find the nearest town guard.

18

THE OLD WATCHTOWER

*Spiked crystals extended from all its joints, across its shoulders,
and out of the top of its head*

Lloyd and Thea hadn't been kidding about the old quarter being burnt to the ground. Torn and crumbled buildings stretched as far as the eye could see, and jagged pieces of charred stone still riddled the edges of the cobblestone streets. Blackened streaks marred the sides of what once had been shops and residences. The broken and scorched remains reminded Seth of the ruins they'd seen in the City of Tears.

"Those pirates don't do things halfway," Seth commented from the window of the coach Thea had flagged down for them. With the watchtower along the coast south of the city, and time of the essence, it seemed the prudent choice.

"No, they don't," Pallas replied, his voice tinged with anger. Lloyd's older brother sat wedged between Seth and Glo on their side of the coach.

"From what Lloyd has told us about your navy, they'd be fools to come anywhere near Penwick these days," Elladan pointed out from the opposite seat, where he sat next to Thea.

"Yes, they would," Pallas responded in a flat tone, not reacting to Elladan's attempt to lighten the mood.

Seth had to stifle a laugh. From the moment Thea chose to sit next to Elladan, the elf was on Pallas' shit list. After that, nothing Elladan did made a difference, but Seth found it funny watching him try.

Despite the cramped conditions, the carriage ride was definitely worth it. They reached the south city gate in far less time than it would have taken on foot and were already headed down the south coastal road.

The road paralleled a steep cliff that reached down to the azure seas far below. Crashing waves hit the jagged rocks along the craggy shoreline, sending up white spray in all directions. A few miles down the coast, the top of a crumbled tower appeared over the next ridge. The road turned slightly inland, running along a broken stone wall that encircled the ruined tower.

The carriage pulled up in front of a pathway that led uphill toward the wall. Seth, Pallas, Glo, Thea, and Elladan all disembarked, the latter pausing to pay the driver a few extra coins to wait for them there.

Thea led the way up the path, to a wide break in the wall where a gate might once have hung. Beyond lay a courtyard overgrown with long weeds, wild brush, and some rather spooky looking trees.

An old well sat in the center of the yard. Seth peered over the edge, but could see no sign of water or the bottom. He picked up a nearby pebble and dropped it, in waiting for the splash. It never came.

"Well, that's not disconcerting at all," he muttered to himself.

"What happened to this place?" Glo asked, peering up at what remained of the watchtower.

"Cannon fire," Pallas answered as if it should have been obvious.

Thea placed her hands on her hips and gave her brother a cautionary look before elaborating further. "The top was blown off during the pirate invasion, and the third floor collapsed in on the second. Only the first floor and the basement still remain."

Seth spied an iron-bound door at the base of the tower. He pointed it out to the others. "Is that the only entrance?"

"Yes," Thea said, striding up to the doorway. "There are no other doors or windows on the first floor."

Seth followed her, scanning the base of the tower as he went. He observed a few cracks in the wall, but they were too small for a person even of his size to climb through. A vampire, however, could turn gaseous and fit through the tightest of spaces.

The door itself had a mark above the handle that looked like some sort of rune. Glo bent in for a closer look. "Is that a wizard's lock?"

"My mother's handiwork," Thea acknowledged. "This is one of the first places my friends and I checked when hunting for Eboneye's treasure."

"I remember Mom being pretty mad about that," Pallas commented with a smug smile. He seemed to love pointing out his siblings' shortcomings. Seth wondered how well he would take it if the roles were reversed.

"What happened in there?" Glo asked, with a hint of trepidation in his voice.

Thea took a moment to cast her brother a dirty look, then answered the elf's question. "We found a portal like the one below the inn. This one, however, had a powerful crystal guardian."

"Do you have any idea where the portal leads?" Elladan interjected.

Thea shrugged. "We never got close enough to find out. Once that guardian showed up, we beat a hasty retreat."

"Then Mom sealed it up so no one else could get into trouble in there," Pallas continued to taunt his sister.

Thea ignored him this time.

"If any vamps went in there, wouldn't they wake the guardian?" Elladan pointed out the obvious.

Thea shrugged a second time. "Maybe, but I don't know for certain. Let's find out if anything 'wicked' has come this way first." She gave him a sly wink, then started to cast a spell.

"*Deprehendere Malum.*" As the words left her lips, white light extended from her palms and encircled her hands. Thea raised them, her wrists rolling in circles as her brow furrowed with concentration.

"Something definitely passed through here recently," she said after a few moments. "Make that two somethings."

"How strong?" Glo asked with mounting concern.

"Fairly strong," Thea replied as she ended her spell and rubbed her temples.

"Vamps?" Elladan guessed.

"One way to find out." Seth inspected the lock on the door. It was a standard pin and tumbler. Normally it might take him a couple of seconds to fiddle with the pins, but with magic reinforcing the lock, it wouldn't be quite that easy.

He'd wrestled with it for about a minute when Glo made a comment. "Need some help there?"

Seth cast an acerbic glance at the wizard. "It's fine." He grappled with it for maybe thirty seconds longer until finally the last pin fell into place.

Click.

A wide smirk spread across Seth's face as he pushed on the handle and the door swung open. He ushered everyone forward with a dramatic flourish. "After you."

Thea pressed her lips together into an inverted smile and gave him a sharp nod. "Very impressive. Not just anyone can bypass one of mother's spells."

"Don't compliment him too much," Glo warned her. "It'll go to his head."

"Too late," Seth countered with a wicked grin.

Darkness pervaded the inside of the watchtower until Glo lit the end of his staff with a spell. A wide, circular room stretched out before them, maybe twenty yards or so in diameter. A pile of rubble lay at its very center, directly beneath a wide hole in the otherwise solid ceiling. Large chunks of stone filled that hole, making it impossible to see the floors beyond.

A stone stairwell rose upward across from where they stood. A half-wall extended from the stairway base, suggesting another flight headed down. Seth went to inspect both. As expected, the way up was completely blocked by more rubble. The way down, however, was clear.

Seth led the way as they descended the stairs, with Thea and Glo right behind him. The flight down wound nearly halfway around the building. Seth counted forty steps from top to bottom. The stairwell opened to a small corridor with a door at its other end.

Seth went to examine the door and found a mark similar to the one on the entrance above the handle. He narrowed an eye at Thea. "I guess your mother really doesn't trust you."

"She was a bit of a wild child," Pallas commented, with a droll expression on his face.

"Not everyone grew up as perfect as you, Pallas," Thea retorted with a withering stare.

"True," Pallas agreed with a mirthful snort.

"Alright, you two. Are we doing this or not?" While the two of them had been bantering, Seth had just about picked the lock. He punctuated his success with a satisfying *click* of the last tumbler.

"That was fast," Glo noted with an arched eyebrow.

"What can I say? I'm a quick study," Seth replied with a smug smile.

"Alright then, how about we prepare with a few spells of our own?" Elladan waved his hand in the air and a golden-brown lute suddenly appeared in it.

The bard proceeded to cast a few spells on himself and his comrades. Seth and Glo did so as well. When they were done, multiple Seths and Elladans stood in the hall with them, Pallas looked sort of hazy, and everyone appeared to be moving in fast motion.

Seth pushed the door open. A large room lay beyond, spread farther out than the light from Glo's staff could reach. Seth caught a hint of a checkered marble floor and thick columns, when multiple torches suddenly flared to life.

A circular chamber stretched before them, the same size as the one on the first floor above. Columns rose across the room at regular intervals, each with a burning torch of its own. The ceiling must have been rather tall, for it lay hidden in the shadows above. Two large urns sat in the center of the room, about ten feet apart. A large circular stone structure stood on the opposite wall of the chamber. The intricate patterns carved around its edges reminded Seth of the amulet safely tucked away in one of his portal bags.

The only other thing that immediately caught Seth's eye were the pieces of crystal strewn all about the marble checkered floor. "Is that our crystal buddy?" he whispered to Thea.

"I'm not sure," Thea whispered back. "Last time, we never even made it into the room. As soon as we opened the door, the guardian came charging at us."

"That's strange," Glo murmured. "I wonder what changed this time?"

"Maybe it had a run in with vamps?" Elladan made a tentative guess.

"Probably best then that I go first," Pallas announced. He slid past the others and paused to draw his sword—a long, sleek, curved blade whose pommel he gripped with both hands.

As soon as he started forward again, Seth threw his arms out and hissed, "Wait."

Pallas stopped in his tracks. "What is it?"

Seth knelt down and peered at the floor. Something didn't look quite right about the marble squares right in front of them. He put his face to the floor and eyed it carefully. Sure enough, those first few squares appeared raised compared to the others.

"Pressure plate," Seth whispered as he scanned the walls around the door. Sure enough, there was a wire painted the same color as the stone wall running up from the floor alongside the door jamb.

Seth motioned to Glo. "Can I borrow your staff?"

Glo hesitated a moment, raising an eyebrow. "Sure," he said finally, though he didn't sound all that thrilled about it. Nonetheless, he passed the staff to Seth.

Carefully leaning through the doorway, Seth shone the light upward toward the ceiling. About two dozen feet up, he spied the base of a large stone slab about the same width as the door.

A wry smile crossed Seth's lips as he handed the staff back to Glo. "It's a nice little trap," he whispered. "You step on the plate and *bam*, a stone block falls in front of the doorway, trapping you inside with Mr. Crystal over there."

"Can you disable it?" Pallas asked with a trace of skepticism in his voice.

Seth put his hands on his hips and glared at the tall human. "Can your mother fly?" It was a rhetorical question. All wizards learned the fly spell as soon as they were experienced enough.

Without another word, Seth pulled a sharp knife from his belt. He leaned out, grabbed the wire, and cut it with a quick flick of his wrist. Just to be safe, Seth immediately backpedaled into the hallway. *Nothing happened.*

The halfling stepped into the room and placed his weight on the pressure plate. It depressed; still nothing happened. He jumped back into the hall, but the stone block did not fall.

Seth made a show of dusting his hands off while casting a self-satisfied glance at Pallas. "Child's play."

"Not bad," Pallas acknowledged with a begrudging smile.

"Hold on a minute," Glo said from behind them. "I've got a hunch."

Seth felt the magic build, and then the wizard's spell released out into the room. The crystal pieces across the floor began to glow white, signifying they were magical. Interestingly enough, so did the two urns.

"Guess that answers that," Elladan stated dryly. "The real question is, what do those urns do?"

Seth shrugged. "One way to find out."

Seth cautiously stepped into the room and approached the urn on the left. As he drew closer, a black flame sprang from it. One of Seth's shadow images drew too close to the flame and abruptly winked out. "Well that's not disconcerting at all," Seth murmured as he backed away.

Meanwhile, Pallas approached the second urn. A white flame sprang from this one, sending waves of heat across the room that Seth could feel even from ten feet away. Pallas swiftly retreated from the urn.

Curious, Seth tried to circle around the outside of his urn. Still, no matter how much distance he tried to give it, the black flame reappeared and snuffed out another one of his shadow images. After the fourth attempt, all of his images were gone.

Out of images, Seth folded his arms and stared at the others. "So now what?"

Glo cocked his head to one side and stared from one urn to the other. "I wonder," he muttered to himself. Before anyone could stop him, the wizard strode forward toward the center of the room.

Seth watched with fascination as the black flame rose in one, but immediately receded as the white flame rose in the other. This kept happening on both sides, both flames canceling each other out.

Glo finally reached the midway point between the two urns, then stopped and turned to stare at the others with an amazed expression. "Well what do you know? It worked."

Seth had a smart-ass remark on the tip of his tongue, but it died on his lips as the crystals all around the room began to shake. As one, they lifted up into the air and flew toward Glo.

"Watch out!" Thea cried.

The flying crystals formed into a swirling vortex around the startled wizard. Glo's quick thinking was probably the only thing that saved his life. The wizard cast a frantic spell, shooting up into the air as the mass of swirling crystals closed in around him. He barely cleared the top of the vortex when the whirling rocks slammed together, forming into a crystalline creature.

Towering over them, the vaguely humanoid guardian reached nearly twice the height of Lloyd's brother. Broad shoulders capped its bulky frame, sweeping out to almost half the creature's height. Spiked crystals extended from all its joints, across its shoulders, and out of the top of its head. Two cold blue glowing eyes stared out from its otherwise featureless face. Flexing its hands into huge blocky fists, the crystal guardian swiped at the elven wizard floating just above its head.

Barely dodging out of the way in time, Glo pointed a finger at the massive creature and sent a searing bolt of lightning cascading down toward it.

Crack!

Thunder reverberated through the chamber as lightning split the air in two. Yet just before it connected with the guardian, the bolt suddenly fizzled out.

"Immune to lightning—check," Seth noted with a wry grimace.

Pallas rushed in and swiped at the creature twice in rapid succession across its one leg, chipping off crystalline fragments with each swipe. He dodged one bulky fist, but got hit with a backswing as he tried to retreat. The blow sent him flying across the room, landing halfway to the door in a heap.

"Pallas!" Thea cried, immediately retaliating with a spell. A ray of white light shot from her outstretched palm, slamming into the guardian's torso. The impact cracked the creature's 'skin,' sending crystal fragments flying in all directions.

All of a sudden, a pool of black liquid appeared beneath the guardian's feet. The creature struggled to maintain its balance, but lost the battle and fell to the floor with a resounding *thud* that shook the entire room.

Near the door, Elladan chuckled. "The bigger they are…" *Pool of Grease* was one of the bard's favorite spells, something he tended to use at the most advantageous of times.

This instance was no exception. His clever tactic gave Thea a chance to revive a stunned Pallas. At the same time, Glo pelted the guardian from the air with a barrage of purple projectiles. Each missile hit the creature with an audible *thud*, widening the cracks in its already fractured leg and torso.

While all that was going on, Seth turned invisible. Further, he cast *spider crawl* on himself and stole past the urns to end up behind the downed creature. As the golem began to rise to its feet, Seth rushed in and jabbed a sharp knife into the same leg that Pallas and Glo had previously attacked.

Seth dove out of the way as the creature swiped at where he had just been. That turned out to be a mistake for the guardian. Between the swift movement, the greasy pool, and the damage it had already taken, the leg gave out from underneath it and the crystal creature fell to the ground once more.

Finally up again, Pallas did something Seth had only seen Lloyd do to date. Sword readied, he disappeared from where he stood, and a moment later reappeared astride the fallen body. Pallas hoisted his long blade and brought it down with incredible force, straight into the guardian's chest. The blade sunk to its hilt into the unprepared creature.

Cracks fanned out in multiple directions from the site of that mighty blow, swiftly spreading across the guardian's torso. The creature shuddered violently, then shattered into dozens of fragments that fell to the ground in a cascade of crystals.

Pallas had leapt off just in time, skidding backwards across the floor, just outside the black liquid pool. Impressively, he managed to remain on his feet. Glo landed next to Pallas as the others all gathered around.

"Well that was fun, but let's not do it again," Elladan commented dryly.

Pallas stared at him with a deadpan expression. "You have a strange definition of fun."

Seth agreed with Elladan, but they weren't out of the woods just yet. He gazed at Thea. "So, any sign of them vamps?"

Thea shook her head. "I've been tracking it since we first entered the watchtower, but so far there have just been traces."

Glo, in the meantime, seemed intrigued by the portal across the room. He held a hand out to Seth. "In that case, can I see that amulet?"

Seth hesitated for the briefest of moments, then pulled out a portal bag and rummaged around inside of it. "Damn, wrong one," the halfling exclaimed. He pulled out a second portal bag and reached his arm inside of that one, finally pulling out the amulet.

Glo arched an eyebrow at the halfling. "You have two portal bags?"

Seth shrugged. "I figured they're so handy, why not? Still, it's a pain to dig through two." All of a sudden his face lit up. "What if I were to put one bag inside the other?" His eyes took on a faraway look. "Or why stop there? You could put a bag inside a bag inside a bag…"

Wincing at the thought, Glo cut him off before he went any

further. "…I don't think it would work that way. I think it would be more likely to blow up in your face."

Seth glared at Glo before handing him the amulet. "Killjoy."

The wizard took the amulet and proceeded across the room. Everyone else followed, though Seth did so warily. Something about this entire thing didn't quite feel right to him.

Glo and Elladan examined the runes around the portal. At the very bottom, Elladan discovered a slot embedded in one of the runes. He asked Glo for the amulet and lined it up; it appeared to be about the same size.

"I don't think that's a good…" Seth began as Elladan pushed the amulet into the slot. He never got the chance to finish his warning.

A humming sound filled the room as the portal came to life. A bright purple glow emanated from the center of the ring and Seth felt himself being tugged toward the portal. It took every ounce of strength he had just to stand his ground.

Glo and Elladan weren't so lucky. Near the portal, the tug must have been stronger and the two elves were being dragged in.

"Help!" They both cried in unison.

Pallas rushed forward and grabbed an arm with each hand, but only delayed the inevitable. Though he strained with all his might, all three of them were now being pulled in together.

"I… can't… hold… them!" Pallas groaned through gritted teeth.

"Hang on!" Thea cried. She clamped her eyes shut, deep creases forming across her brow. Despite the pull from the portal, Seth could feel the energy build around the priestess. A few moments later, her eyes snapped open and she thrust her hands outward.

"*Nullam depelle.*"

As soon as the words left her lips, the mana rushed forth. A circle of violet light engulfed the elves, Pallas, and the portal, accompanied by a soft sound like the shattering of glass. All at once, the tug stopped and the portal went dark. Glo, Elladan, and Pallas went flying backward. ending in a heap in front of Seth and Thea.

Seth stood over the trio and clucked his tongue at Elladan. "Didn't your mother ever tell you, 'Don't go sticking things where they don't belong'?"

Elladan met the halfling's gaze, his face turning beet red as his eyes drifted toward Thea. He just as quickly looked away.

Thea, somewhat red-faced as well, swiftly changed the subject. "Yes, well, besides that, we've learned two things. One, any vampires who had been here are long gone, and two, this tower still isn't safe." She gazed imploringly at Glo. "We should reseal it. Can you do the honors?"

Glo gave her a begrudging look as he rose from the floor and straightened out his robes. "I could, but it would better if someone with more experience, like your mother, did so."

Thea shrugged. "Fair enough. I'll send for her, but in the meantime I think we should close this up."

"Good idea," Glo said, still dusting himself off.

While Seth agreed, he didn't really want to wait around for Mama Stealle—especially if there was a chance the others would run into vamps. He peered at Glo with as innocent an expression as he could muster. "Yeah, about that…"

Glo had known Seth long enough to realize what was coming. The elf sighed. "Alright Seth, what is it?"

Seth tried hard not to grin. "Maybe you should just lock it up anyway for now. Thea's mom can always put her own spell on it later."

Glo thought about it for a moment, then nodded. "I hate to admit it, but you're probably right."

This time Seth did grin. "Aren't I always?"

19
GRAVE MATTERS

*Undead did pass through here—a major presence, in fact,
and quite recently*

Donnie didn't like graveyards. Even in the bright of day, they were ominous places, stark reminders of death. Still, he had promised to scout out the place before the sisters arrived. Though he had to keep them at arm's length, he could still protect them, and that's just what he intended to do.

The Olde Town Graveyard was possibly the largest Donnie had ever seen. He had already traversed the equivalent of five city blocks just searching for the entrance. When he finally found it, rows upon rows of gravestones stretched out before him. Some appeared in reasonable shape, but others had cracks and chips, the names on those stones faded with time.

"Apparently they weren't kidding when they named this place," Donnie murmured to himself.

Walking paths led in several directions, but tall trees and thick

bushes blocked most of his view. Donnie realized it would take forever to scout out this place, but he had an idea. The building next to
the entrance stood three stories high. Donnie climbed to the rooftop
and surveyed the entire yard from there.

Nestled between the gravestones and foliage, Donnie spied three
large buildings. He quickly drew himself a map and went in search of
those places. The first one turned out to be the gravekeeper's quarters, but no one appeared to be home at the moment. The second
was the Avernos Family Tomb, all locked up and sealed tight. The
last building appeared to be a large mausoleum.

A set of stone steps led up to a doubled-doored entrance, surrounded on either side by thick white columns. A domed roof capped
the structure, with the symbol of Arenor affixed atop. A plaque stood
at the base of the stairs. Donnie read the inscription aloud. "Here
Lies Those Who Fell During the Battles of Penwick."

The building was a chilling reminder of the death that accompanied those invasions. Donnie was glad he left the pirate clans before
the raid on this city. So many lives lost on both sides—and for what?
Gold? Jewels? Even if there were some fabled treasures of the gods
hidden somewhere in Penwick, had it truly been worth all the loss
of life?

Donnie's ruminations were cut short when he spied the broken padlock on the double doors leading into the mausoleum. He
climbed up the steps to investigate. The thick padlock had been nearly snapped in half.

Donnie's anxiety rose a level. *Whatever did this must be really strong.*

The anxious elf carefully opened the mausoleum door and
peeked inside. Light filtered down from the dome above, revealing a
wide chamber. A memorial monument sat on a raised dais in its very
center. Dozens of stone tombs lined the walls on all sides, with the
exception of an archway in the very back. Donnie knew he should
investigate further, but didn't exactly relish the idea.

"What'cha doin?" A high-pitched voice sounded behind him.

Donnie nearly jumped out of his skin. He spun about, ready to
either fight or run, but immediately felt foolish as his eyes focused
on the diminutive form of Maya. Below her, at the base of the stairs,

Ruka, Ves, and Cyclone watched his dismay with varying levels of amusement.

"You're looking a little pale there, ace!" Ruka called up to him while wearing a wicked grin.

Donnie fixed her with a look of exasperation before holding up a finger to his lips. He galloped down the stairs, stopping to grab Maya by the hand, and met the rest of them at the bottom. He pointed a thumb over his shoulder.

"There's definitely something going on in that mausoleum." Donnie swiftly explained about the broken lock.

"Well then, let's see," Ves said, stepping past him. She climbed to the top of the steps, Donnie and the others following close behind. When she reached the top, Ves raised her hands and cast a spell.

"*Deprehendere Inmortuos.*" As she spoke the words, white light appeared in her palms and encircled her hands. Rolling her wrists in circles, Ves frowned with concentration. After a few moments she stopped, her expression grim. "You were correct. Undead did pass through here—a major presence, in fact, and quite recently."

Donnie gulped. "A major presence?"

"Yes," Ves affirmed, her expression neutral.

"So what's the plan?" Ruka asked, her arms folded as she stared at Donnie expectantly.

The anxious elf took a deep breath to calm his nerves, then made a staying motion with his hands. "You guys wait here. I'll go check it out."

Donnie slipped through the door and carefully crept across the chamber. The eerie silence that pervaded the room did little to allay his already frayed nerves. He cautiously skittered around the memorial, passing the walls of stone tombs. When Donnie finally reached the open archway, he discovered a staircase going down; the stairs disappeared into darkness below.

A sudden noise made Donnie's heart practically leap into his throat. He glanced over his shoulder and saw Cyclone, Ruka, Ves, and Maya all standing a few paces behind him. Donnie took a moment to catch his breath, then spoke in a harsh whisper, "I thought I told you to wait?"

Cyclone merely glared back at him. "Never agreed to that."

Donnie almost threw a fit, but caught himself. There was no reasoning with the headstrong hunter once he made up his mind. Further, Ruka seemed to be taking great pleasure in Donnie's torment. The elf sighed. "Fine, but be quiet."

In the meantime, Ves continued to search for traces of undead. "The presence is stronger here," she announced after a few moments of concentration. "They definitely passed this way."

Donnie glanced back down the stairs. Despite his keen elven vision, there was no seeing into the total darkness below. He didn't like this one bit. Still, he had promised to protect the girls and wasn't about to back out now.

The uneasy elf started down the steps when more voices echoed across the chamber. Donnie halted in his tracks. Over by the entrance, three figures entered the mausoleum.

Donnie's hand went to his sword hilt, but he withdrew it seconds later. Garbed in overalls and carrying shovels, all three figures appeared to be gravekeepers. The lead man called out to them. "Who are you? How did you get in here?"

Donnie moved to the front of the group and spoke for them. "We're here on the Baron's behest and found the lock to this mausoleum broken." As the gravekeepers drew up to them, Donnie noted that the first two looked like twins. "Have you seen any strange folks wandering about?"

"I haven't," the lead gravekeeper said. He turned to the man who looked just like him. "Have you, Zsamaal?"

Zsamaal shook his head. "No, Waan, I haven't."

Ruka drew up next to Donnie and glared at the gravekeepers. "Pale folks with intense eyes?"

Waan and Zsamaal just shook their heads, but the third gravekeeper paled under her stare. Without warning, the man spun on his heel and bolted for the entrance. Cyclone took off after him and caught him in seconds, dragging the man back to face the others.

Waan and Zsamaal seemed perplexed at their coworker's actions. "Troika, why did you run?"

Troika didn't respond, however. Instead, he rolled himself up into a ball and began rocking back and forth.

Cyclone pulled on Troika's collar and raised his fist. "Answer the question." Before he could do anything further, Ves stepped forward and placed a hand on his fist.

"Let me," she said in a calm voice. Cyclone peered at her, then lowered his hand, stepped back, and folded his arms across his chest.

Ves stood over Troika and traced an unseen pattern through the air. When she finished, she cast a spell with the words, "*Averti Ab Malum*." A brilliant white light encircled the gravekeeper's body about a foot from his skin in all directions. A moment later, the light faded.

Troika stopped rocking back and forth and sat up straight, his eyes wide. Ves then repeated the question. "Can you tell us now why you ran?"

Fear shone in Troika' eyes. "I was compelled by the 'Mistress.'"

Ves placed a comforting hand on Troika's shoulder. "It's alright. You are safe now."

Sudden hope replaced the fear in the man's eyes. "Really?"

Ves gave him a warm smile and nodded.

Ruka stepped around Ves, drawing Troika's attention. "What did this 'mistress' look like?"

"She was beautiful, actually, with raven hair, dark eyes, and porcelain skin," he told them, his voice tinged with awe.

"Thank you," Ves said warmly. She then turned to Waan and Zsamaal. "Take your friend to the temple and stay there for now. This graveyard is not safe at the moment."

"Y-Yes ma'am," they replied in unison. The two men helped their friend up and escorted him out of the mausoleum.

Ves watched them go, then straightened her dress and faced the others. "Well at least now we know what we're up against."

"Somehow I don't find that very comforting," Donnie replied with an ironic smile. Taking a deep breath, he then resumed his descent down the dark stairs. All of sudden he froze in place. Something moved in the shadows below. "Something's down there," he warned the others.

"I've got this!" Maya cried with delight. She cast a quick spell that sent four globes of spinning and twisting lights careening down the dark staircase.

The lights revealed a pale halfling crouching at the base of the stairwell. When he saw the lights, he hissed at them, revealing two pairs of fangs in his upper and lower jaws.

A blue blur suddenly swept past Donnie. Cyclone raced down the stairwell, halberd poised above his head. The little vamp hissed again, then abruptly disappeared in a puff of smoke. Donnie had heard that vampires could shapeshift into many forms, including smoke, but he had never seen it until now.

Cyclone chased after the puff, swearing as he went. "Get back here, you little…"

"What's going on?" A familiar voice drowned out Cyclone's cries. Aksel, with Xellos right behind him, came running toward them across the chamber.

"We found a little vamp," Ruka explained in a matter-of-fact tone. She pointed a thumb over her shoulder at the staircase. "Mr. Happy down there is trying to swat him with his giant meat cleaver."

At the bottom of the stairs, Cyclone still tried in vain to chop the smoke with his axe. All of a sudden, the smoke funneled into a crack in a pipe along the wall. Moments later, it was gone.

"Damn!" Cyclone swore, adding a few more expletives that Donnie hadn't heard since his days on the pirate coast.

"Any idea where that pipe goes?" Aksel asked.

Donnie shook his head. "Not really. The gravekeepers might, but we had to send them away."

Aksel responded with a grim nod. "Yes, we know. We ran into them on the way here. In fact, that's how we found you."

"So are we just going to let that little vamp get away?" Cyclone called from down the steps.

"No," Aksel said definitively. The little cleric climbed down the stairs followed by the rest of them. A short corridor led from the bottom of the stairwell to a door. Aksel pointed it out to Donnie. "You check that way with the others. Xellos and I are going to track down that halfling."

Xellos eyed Aksel as if he were crazy. "And how are we going to do that?"

"The same way he did." Aksel pointed to the pipe, his expression deadly serious.

Donnie shared Xellos' confusion. "Isn't that a little small for the two of you to fit in?"

"Not if we turn to smoke like that vampire," Aksel answered simply.

"You can do that?" Cyclone suddenly seemed interested.

"I have a spell for it," Aksel explained.

"Can you turn me, too?" The hunter asked eagerly.

Aksel pressed his lips together and shrugged. "Well, I was thinking more me and Xellos. I need to turn us to smoke and back, and Xellos is the best tracker we know."

Xellos didn't quite seemed thrilled with the idea. He cast a plaintive gaze at Donnie.

Donnie had to admit he agreed with Xellos. The idea of being changed into smoke seemed rather disconcerting. Donnie put his hands up in a warding motion. "Don't look at me. You're the one who led us through the mists around the Marsh Tower."

"Alright." Xellos gulped. "Is this going to hurt?" He winced at Aksel.

"Of course not," Aksel assured him. "I'll turn us both, then you lead the way through the pipe."

Xellos stiffened and spoke through gritted teeth. "Okay. Go ahead."

Donnie felt kind of sorry for the tracker, but at the same time thought, *Better him than me.*

Moments later, Aksel's spell had turned them both to smoke. The two distinct puffs rose into the air, then filtered into the crack in the pipe and disappeared from view.

It felt strange having no eyes, but still being able to see. Aksel had read about this. Smoke forms used tactile senses to gather information about their surroundings. Thus his 'sight' was a translation in his mind of what he actually felt.

Aksel followed Xellos' smoke form through the pipe before they came up to a section where a second pipe split off to their right. Xellos paused for a few moments, as if deliberating which way their quarry went. Finally, he chose the pipe that branched. The two of them followed the next pipe until it ended at a 'T' intersection. After a moment's pause, Xellos chose to go right again.

Aksel marveled at the tracker's uncanny ability to find his way. It was as if he had some 'sixth sense' beyond the rest of them. It made Aksel wonder as to Xellos' true origin, but he wasn't about to pry into his personal life.

They followed this new pipe a short distance before the sound of voices reached their 'ears.' It came through another crack just up ahead. "Intruders! We must warn the Master and Mistress."

Master and Mistress? Things were getting worse by the moment.

Aksel followed close behind Xellos as they filtered through the crack into another room. Despite the darkness, he found he could sense quite a few things. This was a large area, with a high ceiling above and a circular protrusion in the floor just below them—a well, most likely. He could also sense three beings in the room, possibly via the heat of their bodies.

One of the beings was half the size of the other two. That had to be the halfling. Aksel found he could even get a sense of their shape. Of the two larger figures, one was a man and the other a woman.

"How many?" The woman asked.

"Five," the halfling replied, holding up a handful of fingers. "One of them is a brute with a huge axe. He nearly chopped off my head!"

The man laughed. "That would be a shame. You're short enough as it is."

"I'd still have more brains than you," the halfling retorted.

"Stop fighting, you idiots," the woman chastised them. "We need to report this as soon as possible."

"He started it!" The halfling grumbled.

Ideally, Aksel would have liked to inform the others before taking on these creatures. Still, he knew it would be best to stop them from reporting to their Master and Mistress. Making a quick decision, he floated down behind the well while they were still arguing. Xellos followed him.

Aksel broke the spell which turned them to smoke, and the two of them resumed their normal forms. Hunched down behind the well, the little cleric knew what he had to do. He traced a pattern through the air, invoking the spell as soon as it filled with mana. "*Vocare Creatura Leo.*"

"Who's that?" The woman cried out.

At the same moment, the air between them began to glow. A white light filled the room, forcing the vampires to cover their eyes. The light swiftly took shape, forming into two white semi-transparent lions. Though the light dimmed, it illuminated the area around them enough that Aksel could see the vampires.

All three had eerie, red glowing eyes. Aside from the halfling, the two other vamps appeared human. Dressed in dark clothes, they both had long, dark hair and skin that appeared pale in the dim light.

"Watch out!" The halfling screamed as both lions surged forward.

The first lion pounced on the small vamp and swiped at it with a large glowing paw. The halfling immediately turned to dust. The second lion launched itself at the man, but he caught it by the front paws and began to wrestle with it.

All of a sudden, an arrow whizzed past both Aksel and the lion, embedding itself directly in the man's chest where his heart should have been. An inhuman scream erupted from the man's throat just before he turned to ash.

As the two lions focused on the woman, she shifted into smoke. They swiped at her with their huge paws as she flew overhead, but it did little good. Before anyone could stop her, the lady vamp disappeared down the well.

Aksel peered after her, but all he could see was a metal grate a few feet below. Beyond that he could hear the sound of lapping water.

With the battle over and their purpose fulfilled, the lions vanished and the room grew dark once more. Aksel pulled out a diamond-shaped pendant, the symbol of his goddess, and touched it while speaking a single word. "*Lux.*"

The pendant began to glow with a soft yellow light that spread out across the room and down the well. Aksel could now see brackish water a few feet below the grate.

"That was easy," Xellos commented as he went to pick up his arrow.

"Those were only spawn," Aksel replied as he searched the well with his eyes to see where the woman might have gone. "A true vampire would be much harder to kill."

"Duly noted," Xellos said as he leaned over the well beside Aksel. "So, do we follow it?"

Aksel spied the edge of a broken pipe extruding from the side of the well just above the water line. He was sorely tempted to go after her, but in the end decided against it. "No, I think it best if we regroup with the others. The gods only know how many vampires and spawn there are down here."

Xellos shrugged, then went to the door. He stopped for a moment to listen, then opened it. A hall ran perpendicular to the doorway. Both ends stopped at a door a few yards down. Xellos paused for a moment, then went left down the corridor, with Aksel right behind him.

The door at this end of the hall turned out to be locked. At that moment, Aksel wished he had brought Seth with them.

Xellos, his ear to the door, waved Aksel closer. "I hear voices."

Aksel put his ear to the door and now heard it too. It sounded like their friends. Aksel banged on the door and called out to them.

20
INTO THE CRYPTS

Why don't you just announce to the vamps that we're here?

onnie still felt a bit guilty about pushing Xellos to go with Aksel, but in the end it worked out for the best. Xellos was truly the better tracker, and it also allowed Donnie to continue watching out for the sisters. The overprotective elf cast a covert eye at each of them. Ves still appeared more reserved than usual. Her run-ins with Anya and Theramon had surely taken a toll on her, but Donnie had a sense it was more than that playing on her mind.

Ruka fluctuated between overly sarcastic and quietly brooding. Though neither were exactly out of character for her, it was a wide swing in her personality. Donnie inwardly winced, knowing that he had been largely responsible for what she was going through. Only Maya seemed like herself, gaily twirling about in her white pinafore dress.

Realizing there was little he could do to assuage either Ves or

Ruka, Donnie did what he did best. He rubbed his hands together and flashed them all a pearly smile. "How about we check out that door, like Aksel asked?"

Donnie's sprightly overture was met with a series of grunts and half-smiles, but he didn't allow that to dissuade him. He went to examine the door and found it locked. A simple pin-and-tumbler mechanism, he picked it in less than thirty seconds.

Maya's twirling lights flitted through the open doorway, revealing a long room filled with more stone tombs and two more doors on either side. The room ended in a corridor that continued on out of sight. The pipe from the stairwell ran along the right wall, but Donnie spotted a branch just before it reached the door.

Ruka must have spotted it as well. She walked over toward the door and nudged her head at it. "Bet they went this way."

Ves stopped just behind her sister and fixed her with a skeptical stare. "You're a fortune teller now?"

"Maybe she's spent too much time with Elistra," Donnie said with a wink at Ves. He was rewarded with a bit of a smile, the first chink he had seen in her emotional armor since Maya's return.

Behind them, Cyclone grumbled with impatience. "Straight or right, I don't care. Just pick one already."

Donnie was saved the trouble of choosing by a sudden banging on the door, accompanied by a muffled cry. He thought it sounded like Aksel's voice, but Ves confirmed it with a nod to her sister. "I guess you were right."

"Told you so," Ruka responded with a satisfied smirk.

Donnie gave her a begrudging smile. "Maybe Elistra did rub off on you."

The door was locked, but Donnie picked in no time. He pushed it open and sure enough, there stood Aksel and Xellos. Aksel described their encounter with the three vampires, ending with the one that got away down the well.

When he finished, Donnie had an idea. "Which direction would you say that pipe was pointing?"

"Back down this corridor," Xellos answered with certainty.

Donnie knew better than to question Xellos' uncanny sense of direction. "Well then, what say we follow this corridor and parallel that pipe?"

"Sounds like a plan," Aksel agreed.

Donnie led the way down the side corridor to the door at the other end. This door turned out to be locked as well, but again Donnie picked it in no time. Beyond the door, they found a set of stairs that descended further into the crypts. Donnie led the way down to a short hall that ended in an iron gate.

Cyclone pushed his way forward and sheathed his halberd behind his back. "I've got this," he said, flexing his fingers together in front of him.

"Can I watch?" Maya asked, trying to slip through to the front as well.

Ves put her hand out in front of the young girl, warding her off. "Maya, stand back. Ruka's new 'rider' is going to break the gate."

Ruka fixed Ves with a look that could have melted stone.

"Oooh, can I have a rider?" Maya asked, her eyes as wide as saucers.

"No, you can't," Ves responded in a tone that precluded any further argument.

Maya folded her arms and stamped her small foot, her face forming into a cherubic pout. "Hmph, I never get to have any fun."

The crux of the conversation sent Donnie's mind spiraling. He had seen Cyclone accept Ruka's dagger, but had something more happened between them since? Even if it did, why should it matter to him? He had no hold over Ruka. She was better off without him. Still, for reasons he could not fathom, the thought of Ruka and Cyclone together gnawed at his gut.

While all this went through Donnie's mind, Cyclone heaved against the gate. The hunter was rewarded with the sound of bending metal until the iron gate finally buckled from his herculean effort. The gate went clattering to the ground, the deafening sound echoing up and down the entire corridor.

"Tsk," Ruka glared at Cyclone as she clicked her tongue. "Why don't you just announce to the vamps that we're here?"

"Better than all this sneaking around," Cyclone grunted back.

Donnie exchanged a glance with Ves, who responded by rolling her eyes to the heavens. He realized at that point he had nothing to worry about. These two would kill each other before they would ever get together.

Despite the racket the gate made, no one showed up to confront them. With no other recourse, they continued on down the corridor, with Donnie again leading the way. Maybe a few dozen yards farther, they came across an intersecting hallway.

Donnie peered down all three paths, but something didn't seem quite right. He waved the others forward. "You might want to take a look at this."

Everyone joined him at the intersection, including Maya's twirling lights. The orbs shone down all three halls, ending in each at a wall of darkness about a dozen yards from where they stood. The light seemed unable to penetrate any farther past those walls. In fact, none of their eyes—elf, gnome, dragon, or even the uncanny Xellos, could pierce that unnatural darkness.

"Must be a spell," Aksel mused aloud.

"Maya, try sending your lights through one of them," Ves coached her sister.

Maya complied by sending the twirling and spinning lights at the wall directly ahead. Unfortunately, they disappeared into the darkness with no trace of light seeping through.

Aksel pursed his lips together. "Maybe I can dispel it?"

He began to trace a spell through the air when Xellos interrupted him. "You might want to try the one to the right." The tracker pointed out a set of wet boot prints leading off down that corridor. About halfway to the wall of darkness, the footprints stopped and faced the side wall. From there, they then continued on and disappeared into the dark.

Donnie went to investigate and discovered a hollow section behind the wall. He pressed against a few of the stones until one gave way and swung outward. Embedded into the wall behind the stone, he found a lever.

"Well that doesn't look ominous at all," Donnie noted with irony. The lever sat in the downward position. He flipped it back up and was rewarded with a metal grating sound from somewhere beyond the darkness.

As a dragon, Ruka felt in very little personal danger from these invading vampires. The concern she had was more for the people of this city. They didn't deserve to be dominated or enslaved like mindless puppets. Ruka had seen firsthand, in the City of Tears, what that could lead to. She wasn't about to let that happen here in Penwick.

Though her main focus lay in saving this city, Ruka found herself distracted. Despite having killed any feelings she had for him, Donnie's very presence seemed to annoy her. Even Cyclone was starting to grate on her nerves. While she appreciated his help in regaining control of her powers, the human hunter showed little restraint of his own. Not that she thought dragon males were any better—she found them to be a boorish lot.

What Ruka really wished was that things could go back to the way they were before. She vowed that once these undead were gone and the demons banished, she would gather her sisters and resume the search for their lost father.

While Ruka had been brooding, Aksel tried to dispel the darkness. Unfortunately, his spell had no effect. Whoever had created the darkness did so with a great deal of power. In fact, even now Ruka could feel the magic radiating from it.

Aksel gingerly tugged at his chin. "Perhaps a sunlight spell might work?" The little cleric weaved his hands through the air in a complicated pattern. Ruka could feel the magic building to a rather impressive crescendo.

"*Solis.*"

As Aksel's spell released, the mana rushed forth through the veil of darkness. It coalesced somewhere beyond the wall, forming into a sizable ball of magic. The light from that ball pierced the veil the same way the moon illuminates the dark of night.

A wide room appeared beyond the veil, sloping downward out of sight. Donnie led the way forward, with Ruka and the others trailing not far behind. At the bottom of the slope they came to another iron gate. Thankfully, this one had a padlock on it.

"I've got this," Donnie announced before Cyclone got any more bright ideas. Ruka would have killed the hunter if he pulled another stunt like before.

The darkness ended beyond the gate. Once Donnie opened it, they all filtered out into the next corridor. The trail of wet boot tracks reappeared here, leading them to the next intersection, where the tracks turned left.

At the end of that hall stood an open archway with light filtering out toward them. Aksel whispered to Maya, "Extinguish your light."

Maya made the orbs disappear with a flick of her wrist. Ruka was impressed. Her little sister was getting pretty good at magic.

"Stay here while I check this out," Donnie advised them. The slim elf then crept down the hall so silently that even Ruka couldn't hear him. He returned shortly and whispered his findings. "There are three people in there that I could see. One is a dwarf with an axe. The other two are humans, one carrying a great sword and the other a bow."

"What are they doing?" Aksel whispered back.

Donnie shrugged. "They appear to be just sitting there in the center of the room, with their backs up against a stone coffin."

"Well that doesn't sound creepy at all," Ruka commented with a soft chuckle. Her comment lightened the mood a bit which ,was exactly what she had intended. *Life was so absurd at times that you had to laugh at it—either that, or go crazy.*

"Let's get closer," Aksel decided.

They all followed Donnie down the hall as silently as possible, stopping a few yards from the archway. Ruka could now see the three people Donnie had mentioned, situated exactly as he described.

Ves quietly cast a spell. Her hands lit up with white light, which she then turned toward the archway. A few moments later, she whispered to Aksel, "They are not evil."

Aksel nodded his understanding. "Still, what are they doing down here and how did they get past that darkness?"

Ruka thought he raised a good point. "Not to mention that third vampire must have come through here," she added after a moment's thought.

"Ruka's right," Aksel agreed. "If they're not vampires, then they might be dominated. Either way, let's be prepared."

With everyone in agreement, Donnie led the way. Xellos and Cyclone went next, with Ruka, her sisters, and Aksel bringing up the rear. When they reached the doorway, Donnie halted while Xellos and Cyclone fanned out to either side.

Ruka now got a better look at the room. It was larger than they first thought, with more stone tombs embedded in the walls. Two more figures wearing robes stood on either side of the room and appeared to be examining the tombs.

With everyone in place, Donnie pulled one of his cheesy greetings. "Howdy, gents." He waved to the folks in the room and gave them one of those toothy grins. "You wouldn't happen to have seen any vampires down here?"

The folks in the center of the room scrambled to their feet, while those on the sides spun about. "N-No. No. No. Nope." Came the multiple replies.

Aksel cast a spell to discern the truth and immediately announced, "Watch out! They're lying."

Before anyone else could react, Donnie and Cyclone rushed forward. Cyclone handily clocked the guy with the great sword, dropping him like a sack of potatoes. Donnie launched himself at the dwarf's feet, taking his legs out from under him. The dwarf went sprawling onto the ground, his axe clattering away across the crypt floor.

Still a bit leery about her powers, Ruka drew the short sword hanging at her side. The sentient sword, Inazuma, was like family to her—an annoying old grandfather, to be exact. However, he did have a nice ability to store her lightning charges and cast them as bolts of his own.

Using the sword, Ruka sent a bolt of lightning cascading across the room at the robed figure on their left. The bolt stunned the unprepared man, knocking him out cold. Ruka grinned at Inazuma. "Looks like we haven't lost our touch."

"Oh, so you're finally speaking to me again?" the sword asked in a disparaging tone.

Ruka immediately regretted using the sword. "Not now, grandpa," Ruka replied, sheathing it before he could chastise her further.

In the meantime, Xellos had shot the person on the right. That person, however, turned out to be a mage. An angry red ball appeared in the mage's hands and shot across the room, directly at the doorway.

Ruka reacted instantly, as did Ves. The two of them grabbed Aksel and yanked him out of the way, simultaneously placing themselves in front of the little cleric. A moment later, the ball of fire struck. It expanded out into a hemisphere of flame, engulfing both Ruka and her sister. Had Aksel been hit, it might have hurt him, but Ruka and Ves barely felt it.

Moments later, when the flames died out, Ruka dusted a few ashes off of her leather outfit. Ves did the same with her dress. The mage stood there gaping at the two young women, until Cyclone clocked him across the jaw. Meanwhile, Donnie had taken out the bowman. That ended the brief fight.

Ruka quietly surveyed the scene. All the people lay either wounded or unconscious, but no one had been killed. Considering none of them were actually evil, they hadn't deserved to die anyway. Still, it had taken finesse and restraint to pull something like this off. She had forgotten how good-hearted her friends could be when the need arose. Maybe she had judged them too harshly.

Aksel had them gather all the wounded and unconscious into the center of the room. He then weaved a pattern through the air, ending his spell with four words. *"Magicae Circuli Contra Malum."*

The magic released and a white circle engulfed the folks they had just fought. The circle swiftly faded, but Ruka could still feel the magic radiating outward from where they lay. Those who were still awake shook themselves as if waking from a dream.

Ves and Aksel went to heal their wounds while the dwarf explained their story. "I am Davik, a Priest of Arenor from the town of Blackwood just south of Lymerdia." He gestured to the men who had been seated next to him, both who were still out cold. "That's Edd and Tedd Warnok. They own the caravan that arrived in Penwick a couple of days ago. In fact, we were all on that caravan."

"Let me guess, you were dominated by the 'master' and 'mistress,'" Donnie interrupted before the dwarf could say more.

A look of surprise crossed Davik's face. "Yes. How did you know?"

"He gets around," Ruka commented, directing a slight smirk at Donnie.

Donnie glanced her way and winked. Ruka sighed. She should have known better. He was an incorrigible flirt and would never change.

Davik's expression grew grim. "Those two are a vampire Lord and Lady. They are very powerful. To make matters worse, they have in their possession an ancient artifact called the *Eye of Amon.*"

"That doesn't sound good," Donnie said wryly.

"It's not," Davik agreed. "It is a powerful scepter that can create darkness at will, suck the life force from people, and shoot death beams. To work, however, it needs to be charged with the lives of living beings."

"That's just plain sick." Ruka huffed, her stomach nearly turning.

Ves and Aksel had both gone pale; Cyclone wore a more ominous expression than usual. Even Donnie was suddenly serious.

"Do you know where this Lord and Lady are now?" the elf asked the dwarven priest.

Davik shook his head. "Somewhere here in these catacombs, though I don't know exactly where."

Ruka's concern for the people of Penwick had escalated to a whole new level. It was one thing to be made puppets, but another entirely to be 'fuel' for some magic weapon. Of course, what would you expect from an artifact named for the Ralnai Lord of Darkness?

Once Aksel and Ves finished healing the wounded, the five of them gathered to discuss next steps. Neither Aksel nor Ves felt comfortable leaving these folks alone here in the crypts.

"Maya and I can escort them out of the catacombs," Ves offered.

"That's a good idea," Aksel agreed. "While you're doing that, we should probably get everyone else down here. It's imperative we take out this vampire Lord and Lady as soon as possible."

"I agree," Ves said, her countenance nearly as grim as Cyclone's.

She glanced at Ruka. "Contact Glolindir and have him gather the others in the graveyard. Once we get these folks to safety, we'll lead them all back down here."

"Sure thing," Ruka said, impressed at her sister's sudden take-charge attitude. She had not seen Ves this fired up since they first set out to find their father. It was a shame it took something like this to get her going, but it was good to see the old confident Ves again, even if just for a little while.

While her sisters escorted the others out, Ruka went to contact Glo with her pearl of friendship.

21
PROTECTOR OF PENWICK

He had to do better. Nothing less was an option

allas Stealle had always demanded perfection, especially from himself. Anything less was an invitation to those who would harm others. He had already seen far too much of that in his short life. Even now, the dreams still haunted him.

Thick smoke hung like a grey veil in the air. Scarlet flames leapt from windows and danced across rooftops. Black husks of crumbled, burnt-out buildings sent smoke in all directions.

Corpses were strewn all about, some piled in great, decaying mounds. Cries and shouts echoed around every corner, mixed in with the ring of steel on steel. Dark shadows fled down side streets, some accompanied by cries of death.

Dozens of black-hulled ships sat in the harbor, as if watching the carnage with delight. The flags that flew atop their sails filled all that saw them with a sense of dread—the Clans of the Pirate Coast.

Pallas had only been six at the time, but visions of the pirate invasion were forever etched within his brain. He had sworn afterwards that no one else would die by the hand of those dread pirates. He worked and trained every day since, climbing the ranks of the royal navy and mastering the path of the spiritblade.

"It's done," Glolindir announced as he climbed up into the carriage. The elven wizard had resealed the watchtower after their failure at finding any vampires inside. "So where to now?"

Thea touched a finger to her chin. "I think I'd like to see how Lloyd's doing."

Pallas wanted to retch. She had coddled their baby brother since he was in diapers. He thought it a major contributing factor to Lloyd's slow progression at just about everything. Thus, it came as a shock to hear all Lloyd accomplished since he'd been away. "He's a big boy now. I'm sure he's just fine."

Thea bit her lower lip, a habit Pallas had come to recognize as a tell for when she was nervous. "You're probably right."

"If these vampires are anywhere in town, my money is on the crypts," Pallas pressed further. It was his mother's suggestion, and she seldom proved to be wrong.

"That's where we found them in Ravenford," Elladan just had to add, with that infuriating half-smile.

"It does make the most sense," Glolindir agreed, sitting with his hands steepled in front of him.

Pallas appreciated the wizard's input. He seemed rather intelligent, much like his mother. He could have done without the bard's opinion, though. Something about the overly handsome elf just rubbed him the wrong way.

"I'm with Thea," Seth chimed in. "Let's rule out these other places first."

Pallas sighed. That's all his sister needed to hear. He could see by the look in her eyes, her mind was already made up. "Fine. Let's go."

As the carriage took off back toward Penwick, Pallas' mind drifted back to his own accomplishments and failures. As a spiritblade, he was on par with Carenna, both second only to his father. Further, at the age of only twenty-six, he had attained the coveted role of

Captain of the Avenger, the finest warship in the fleet. Yet despite all that, his sister and her friends had died under his watch five years ago. Had it not been for the young dragon lass, Ruka, they would all still be dead.

Further, despite his best efforts, the town of Redune had suffered at the hands of the pirates less than a year ago. While in the end, Pallas saved Alys and the town, he nearly lost everything in a duel with a mere pirate captain. Pallas still berated himself to this day. He had to do better. Nothing less was an option.

The journey to the tenements seemed like it took forever. When they finally arrived, they found the town guard escorting residents to a waiting line of wagons. Pallas spied Taliana coordinating the apparent evacuation and approached her. "What's going on here?"

Taliana directed another group to a wagon before answering his question. "Your kid brother and his fiancée found a dead woman and a person who claims to have been possessed. I'm having it verified, but for now, Carenna and I thought it best to clear out the tenements."

Despite Taliana's attempt to downplay the situation, Carenna's involvement said otherwise. The Protector didn't get involved unless things were serious.

Picking up on that as well, Thea questioned Taliana's glib reply. "Where is this dead woman now, and how are you having the possession verified?"

Patience not being her strong suit, Taliana huffed at being questioned. "I had both taken to the temple. I'm sure your fellow clergy can handle it." She paused for a moment, the corner of her mouth upturning slightly. "Of course, feel free to go and assist them if you wish."

"I'm sure they can handle it," Thea responded, a dangerous edge to her voice.

The two women locked eyes, each staring the other down. Though she didn't know it, Taliana was playing with fire. The two had been bitter rivals back at the Stealle Academy, but time and again, Thea had bested Taliana on the training floor.

Taliana probably thought she had the edge these days, but

unbeknownst to all but a very few, Thea had not neglected her studies. She was just as sharp today as she had been back then.

Pallas decided to step in before this turned into a bonafide grudge match. "Carenna, did you say? Where is she?"

Taliana held Thea's stare for a moment longer before tearing her eyes away to face Pallas. "She's helping with the evacuation, along with your brother." Her gaze momentarily strayed past Pallas. "Oh look, here they are now." Pallas followed her gaze to see Carenna, Lloyd, and Lady Andrella escorting another group of people toward one of the wagons.

"Now if you'll excuse me," Taliana said in a dismissive tone. She strode away down the line of wagons, officiously directing guards and residents as she went.

"That woman..." Thea began, catching herself before saying anything further.

"We ran into her at the council," Elladan confided. "She's a real 'peach.'"

Thea grinned at the bard, her anger swiftly fading. Though Pallas still didn't like him, he had to admit the elf seemed to have a positive effect on his sister.

As soon as they finished their escort duties, Lloyd, Andrella, and Carenna came over to join them. Never good at hiding his emotions, Lloyd appeared surprised to see them. "What are you guys doing here?"

"We struck out at the watchtower," Seth answered rather succinctly. Pallas found himself rather liking the halfling's candor.

Peering past Lloyd, Pallas noticed Carenna staring right at him. There was a strange look in her eyes, but it disappeared almost immediately.

"If you're here to help, we're almost done," Carenna said brusquely. Her irritable reaction left him feeling confused.

Pallas and Carenna had been good friends and often sparring partners at the academy. Yet in the last few years, she had proven to be difficult at times. Still, at other times she reverted back to the old friendly Carenna. Pallas could never quite make sense of it, so he stopped trying.

Before he had a chance to reply, Taliana called over to Carenna. "Have you seen either Smythe or Whison?"

Carenna pursed her lips together, her eyes unfocusing as she thought it over. "No. As a matter of fact, I haven't seen them for a while now."

"I saw them headed toward the southmost tenements," Lloyd interjected.

Taliana approached them and narrowed her gaze at Lloyd, as if she were grilling a suspect. "How long ago was that?"

"Hmm," Lloyd hummed as he tried to recall. "Probably almost an hour ago. Do you want us to go look for them?"

Before Taliana could answer, they were interrupted yet again. A carriage came barreling down the street and barely stopped right in front of them. The door swung open and Alys Dunamal stepped down out of the carriage.

She looked absolutely stunning in a teal blue gown that perfectly accented her bright copper-colored hair. Her emerald eyes lit up as they focused on Pallas. "There you are! I've been looking all over town for you."

"Wonderful. Is the entire gentry suddenly slumming it here at the tenements?" Taliana sniped under her breath.

Carenna seemed equally unenthused. "Alys Dunamal? To what do we owe the pleasure?" From the way she pronounced that last word, it was obvious she meant the exact opposite.

Alys unfolded the parasol she carried, threw it over her shoulder, then sauntered over, stopping right in front of Pallas. She waved a single finger at him. "I told you I wanted to help you find those poor missing people," she explained with a sudden pout, "but you left without me."

Pallas found his cheeks growing hot and his tongue tied. Luckily, his sister saved him from answering. "We couldn't all just wait around until noontime for you to get up out of bed, Alys," Thea responded, only half-teasing.

Alys fixed her best friend with a winsome smile. "Oh Thea, don't be like that." She waved a nonchalant hand through the air. "Anyway, I'm here now. What can I do to help?"

Both Taliana and Carenna looked like they had scathing answers to Alys' question, but neither got the chance to say it. "Hold that thought," Glolindir abruptly interrupted them all. "I just heard from Ruka. Apparently they found some folks down in the crypts."

"What folks?" Taliana asked curtly.

The elven wizard shook his head. "She didn't exactly say. Ves is bringing them out now and they need to get to the temple. They also think they may have found the vampires' nest. They want us to rendezvous with them at the graveyard."

"Well then, let's go!" Alys cried before anyone else could speak. "My carriage is at your disposal."

"Yes, please go," Taliana added with obvious relief. "The town guard can handle the rest of this."

"If you're sure," Lloyd responded, not looking quite convinced. Pallas actually agreed with him for once. He thought Taliana was being rather shortsighted about not needing their help.

"I'm sure," Taliana replied, motioning them all toward Alys' carriage.

Lloyd shrugged, then offered his arm to Andrella, escorting the lady toward the waiting carriage. Pallas was impressed. Lloyd had picked up manners somewhere along the way.

Alys laced her arm through his. "Shall we?" Pallas felt a warmth flow through his body where their arms touched. It had been this way ever since he rescued her from the pirates at Redune.

A sudden tug on his other arm made him pause his tracks. Carenna stood on the other side of him. "You want me to come with?" Once again, she had reverted to the old friendly Carenna.

Pallas considered her offer for a moment. She would definitely be an asset in battle, but what if something truly happened to those missing guards? "No. It's probably best if you stay here. I'm sure the town guard could handle regular problems, but they'll need you if there are any vampires involved."

Carenna's cheeks reddened slightly. "You're probably right."

Alys whispered to him on the way to the carriage. "I'm glad you told Carenna to stay behind. You don't need her anyway—especially when you've got me!"

Her face lit up in a bright smile that made him laugh. "Alys, you are incorrigible."

They arrived at the graveyard entrance just as Ves and her little sister exited with a group of haggard-looking folks. They piled those people into the carriage, then Alys instructed the driver to take them to the Temple of the Ralnai.

As they drove off, Alys let out a gay laugh. "Father is going to just 'love' it when he finds that I loaned his carriage to that motley crew. He'll probably have it fumigated."

Pallas exchanged a wry smile with Thea. Alys had a good heart, but could be an acquired taste at times.

"Either way, thank you for your help, Alys," Ves said with a grateful smile. Immediately afterward, the expression on her face reverted to a grim one. "Now then, there's no time to lose. Please follow me."

The young lady spun on her heel and marched back into the graveyard, everyone else falling in behind.

22
DEVILS IN THE DARK

*Something snapped inside of Pallas when he saw the body
at the vampires' feet*

Lloyd's mind was elsewhere as Ves led them down into the crypts. The people of Penwick were in terrible danger, based on what she had told them. Being drained or turned by a vampire was bad enough, but to have your very soul sucked out of you sounded absolutely horrifying. Still, this wasn't their first time facing vampires. He and his companions had routed a nest of them in Ravenford, and back then they didn't have half the force they had now. This time, they'd be going into battle with the dragon sisters, a dragon hunter, an expert archer, an auric priestess, and the second-best spiritblade in all of Penwick.

Normally Lloyd might have been intimidated by his brother, but with all that lay at stake, he welcomed it. In fact, he decided to say just that. He maneuvered himself within whispering distance of both his siblings. "I'm really glad you're joining us. This could prove to be tough."

Pallas emitted a bemused snort. "If even half of what they say you've done is true, then I could say the same." He placed a hand on Lloyd's shoulder and shook him roughly. "I guess all those years of my pushing you finally paid off," he said with a smug smile.

Lloyd's eyes went wide as the meaning behind his brother's words sunk in. All those years of teasing, calling him 'lead bottom,' and those torturous extra drills for him alone, all that had actually been to drive him to excel? Lloyd suddenly saw his brother in a whole new light. He was still a prick, but he meant well in his own way.

"Thanks?" Lloyd responded, uncertain about this new territory he had entered into with his brother.

Thea, on the other hand, didn't appear to have any doubts. She placed a hand on both their shoulders and whispered. "It's nice to see you two finally getting along, but Pallas, you're still an arse."

"Love you, too, Sis," Pallas grinned back at her.

When they hit the area of magical darkness, Thea cast a spell that allowed them to see through it. Not long afterward, they caught up with the others. Aksel and Elladan had a brief discussion about strategies, then laid out a marching order.

Seth and Donnie took the lead, immediately followed by Lloyd and Pallas. The casters stuck to the middle, with the Greymantles and Cyclone bringing up the rear. Two doors led from this room. Aksel told them the one led to a dead end, so they ended up going through the other.

The path they followed wound further down into the crypts. They passed through dark corridors, steep stairwells, and more locked doors until finally coming out into a wide passage. The party spread out as they continued down the broad corridor, ignoring smaller tunnels and more stairs on either side.

"Ahhhh!"

A woman's scream echoed down the passageway from somewhere up ahead. Lloyd exchanged a brief glance with Pallas, and then they both took off at a dead run. A few dozen yards down, the passage opened into a wide chamber. Both he and Pallas had lit their blades, revealing another one of those areas of deeper darkness just ahead.

More screams came from within that darkness, accompanied by

strange chanting. Lloyd then heard a hiss, followed by the words, "Warm blood." A second later, a woman leaped out of the darkness directly at him.

Luckily, Lloyd had been expecting it. Time slowed as he stilled his mind and reached inside for that spark of spirit. As soon as he touched it, the world blurred around him. A moment later, he reappeared behind the leaping woman and lashed out at her with both of his blades. Fire seared her pale skin, causing her to shriek in pain.

Pallas gave him a begrudging nod. "Not bad, little brother."

Before Lloyd could respond, a second vampire vaulted out of the darkness at Pallas. Instead of teleporting out of the way, Pallas used a different spiritblade technique to fade back into the shadows. As soon as the vampire flew past him, he popped back out and sliced the creature across its torso with his fiery katana.

Meanwhile, the first vampire lunged again at Lloyd. Lloyd ducked under the attack and caught her with another swipe of his blade. The vamp screeched as she spun about, but abruptly went still as an arrow caught her in the chest. Her eyes went wide for a brief moment, and then her entire body crumbled to dust.

Seeing its brethren's fate, the second vampire leapt back up into the shadows with a loud cry, "Master, we have guests!"

Behind them, the rest of the companions poured out of the tunnel. Thea traced a pattern through the air and unleashed a powerful spell at the darkness. A brilliant light shone forth from the deeper dark, swiftly spreading out across the area. The silvery light revealed a huge chamber, its ceiling easily fifty feet above their heads. The other end of the vast chamber remained invisible, despite the wide area illuminated by the moonlike orb.

Lloyd's eyes focused on a large raised platform in the center of the room. A group of sinister figures had gathered up there, intermixed with what appeared to be Penwick town guards. In their center stood an extremely handsome man garbed in black formal wear, accompanied by a stunning pale-skinned woman wearing a long, black skin-tight gown. Lloyd could not be certain from this angle, but it appeared as if a body laid before their feet. The head and shoulders of a dark-armored figure rose just behind the comely duo.

Stairs rose on either side of the chamber, leading to walkways that ran along the walls; those walkways led to bridges that crossed over to the center platform. A line of nearly a dozen people stood on either walkway, unmoving as if in a trance.

"All those people..." Andrella gasped in horror.

"...like lambs to the slaughter," Donnie murmured, sounding equally stunned.

Lloyd felt both outraged and confused at the same time. There were far more people down here than had been reported missing, not to mention the mysterious presence of those town guards. Yet none of that truly mattered, for they were all in terrible danger.

"Not if I can help it," Pallas said through gritted teeth. The sudden rise in his brother's energy spurred Lloyd into action. Pallas went vaulting across the room and up the staircase to the left. Following suit, Lloyd invoked his flying cloak and soared up across the chamber to the walkway on the right.

Glo watched the scene unfolding before him with a mixture of astonishment and revulsion. Bathed in the silvery equivalent of moonlight, it appeared almost surreal. Yet that body at the vampires' feet attested to the reality of the situation. Furthermore, Glo could sense a terrible energy radiating from the scepter in the vampire lord's hand.

For a moment, Glo thought he was going to be sick. He detested vampires for draining the life from people or turning them into more undead, yet this was far worse than that. Destroying someone's very soul and using it to fuel an evil artifact? Though on a much smaller scale, that was as bad as Theramon and his seven towers. It's what the demons in the one tower were currently doing to their prisoners.

As if a switch had been flipped, Glo's revulsion suddenly turned into white hot anger. *No! I will not let this happen.*

Lloyd and Pallas had reacted first, with everyone else right behind.

"Free the prisoners!" Aksel barked as he sprinted after Lloyd.

"I've got the other side!" Thea cried as she took off after Pallas. An aura of white light sprang up around the priestess, enveloping her entire body as she ran. That light spread out in all directions, completely negating the darkness around her.

Maya and Ruka both shifted into dragon form. With the expertise of an acrobat, Alys somersaulted onto Maya's back. Simultaneously, Cyclone leapt high into the air, landing on Ruka while cutting off a dumbfounded Donnie. Both dragons then took off for the platform. At the same time, Xellos shot upward, racing for the ceiling.

Glo reacted out of pure instinct. "Wall off the people!" he shouted to Andrella while tracing a frantic spell through the air.

They had trained together so much as of late that Andrella immediately understood him. "I've got the right!" she shouted back as she, too, traced her pattern. Both wizards punctuated their spells with their palms forward and two harsh words. "*Murum Ignis.*"

Dual curtains of shimmering scarlet flames sprang into existence on either end of the platform. The fiery walls rose twenty feet high, effectively cutting off the platform from either walkway. Dark figures at the edges of the platform screamed and backed away from those flames. That left just a few vampires on either bridge or on the walls above the walkways.

At that point, the chanting stopped. The dozen or so town guards moved to the front of the platform with a number of sinister figures right behind them. The dark armor stepped forward, placing itself directly in front of the vampire lord and lady. With all now in position, the battle had begun for the lives of the innocent.

When Alys Lynde Dunamal originally tracked down Pallas, she had no idea what she was getting herself into. Her plan had been to spend more time with him and strengthen their growing bond. If she were truly lucky, she might even finally get him to admit his feelings for her.

Alys had been enamored with Pallas since she first laid eyes on him at the Stealle Academy. Sheltered by her father, she began to sneak out in her pre-teens. Drawn to the school, she soon met Thea and then Pallas.

Pallas struck such a dashing and heroic figure that she was

immediately smitten with him. As fate would have it, he had saved her life twice since then—at Thorn Isle, and more recently at Redune. He had become her own personal knight in shining armor.

Yet this little jaunt had not turned out at all how she planned. From the graveyard to the crypts to these disgusting tunnels beneath the city, Alys began to second-guess herself. Maybe this hadn't been the best idea after all.

When Alys saw those people lined up like 'lambs for the slaughter,' she forgot all about her plans. Something welled up inside of her, a long-buried anger she had not known still existed.

Alys had felt like a prisoner her entire life. She also knew a bit about death. Yet if she had heard correctly, the fate these people faced was worse than dying. When their souls were gone, they wouldn't get to sing with the angels like she had done during her short demise.

Alys was no hero like Pallas, Thea, or even Lloyd. Still, she wasn't about to let that happen to these poor folks if she could help it—and she wasn't exactly powerless.

Alys acted on pure instinct when she saw the girls change into dragons. The gown she had chosen to wear today had been tailor-made for the stage. Just as she had done during last night's performance, she tore off the rip-away skirt and set off at a dead run for the dragon that was Maya. Vaulting at the last moment, Alys somersaulted through the air and landed on the dragon's back.

Alys winced. The dragon's scales were harder than she anticipated and her legs chafed. Still, it was a small price to pay if it got her into the battle faster.

"Where to?" Maya cried, sounding excited at having a rider.

Alys pointed toward the left stairwell. "Follow Pallas!" She tightened her grip as Maya rose into the air, but any nerves she experienced immediately dissipated as they sped forth.

This is exhilarating! For a moment, Alys fancied herself a dragon rider, like the old storm riders of song and legend. Yet then reality settled in. Up on the walkway, Pallas rushed through the line of people, straight for the bridge. Though she had no doubt of his prowess, multiple vampires might be more than even he could handle.

Alys leaned forward in her seat and cried to Maya, "Take us down toward that bridge!"

"Do you want me to lightning-bolt the vamps?" Maya asked eagerly.

Alys thought it over for a moment. All the songs she knew about dragons agreed on one thing—their breath-weapons took a while to charge. "No, save it for when we really need it."

Maya sounded disappointed and confused. "What are you going to do, then?"

"Just get me close enough and duck your head," Alys replied mysteriously.

As Maya swooped down toward the bridge, a vampire leapt from the wall to block Pallas' path. The master spiritblade ducked under its attack and paid it back by slicing its arm off. The creature turned to flee, but Pallas skewered it with his blade and it burst into flames.

Reaching the bridge, Maya pulled up just a few yards away and hovered there. A huge wall of violet flames had sprung up between the bridge and the platform. The three vamps on the bridge had been attempting to breach the wall of fire, but now turned to face this new adversary.

Alys took a deep breath, pulling in the magic through her diaphragm. She then directed it up through her lungs and out through her throat. The resulting sonic cry blared forth and slammed into the unsuspecting vamps like a battering ram. Between the power of her wail and their acute hearing, the creatures reeled from the onslaught.

Trained to sustain long notes, Alys pressed her sonic assault. Shaken by the relentless cry, one of the vamps staggered backward and flipped over the railing and off the bridge entirely.

Finally having run out of breath, Alys took a moment to breathe. With the wailing stopped, Maya swung her head about and gazed at Alys in awe. "Ooo, can you teach me to do that?"

Meanwhile behind them, Thea reached the entranced people. Shining like a holy beacon in the dismal darkness, she cast a spell encircling those folks with a white light and broke their trance. Urging them on, Thea began to usher those folks away from the fight.

At that moment, Pallas reached the bridge. Of the two remaining vamps, one recovered and rushed to engage him. Desperate to keep the second one at bay, Alys launched into another assault. Focusing on the single vamp, she drove it back toward the railing and also sent it careening off the bridge.

She abruptly stopped when Maya's head swung up to face her. "Duck!" the young dragon cried.

Alys flattened herself against the dragon's back as a bolt of lightning leapt from Maya's maw and went cascading just overhead. Alys cast a quick glance behind her, just in time to see the bolt connect with a vamp behind her, also on Maya's back.

The vamp shrugged off the bolt, but Alys was ready. Using Maya's spine for support, she lashed out with both legs in a double kick that caught the vampire in the gut. The creature went flying off Maya's back to the floor far below.

"Nice move!" Maya giggled. "You have to teach me that one, too."

Alys grinned at the girl, but her smile swiftly faded. Over on the bridge, Pallas was in trouble. The last vampire had him by the throat and hoisted him up into the air. Instead of fighting back, however, her love appeared to wilt under the vampire's grip.

Alys froze in horror. *It's draining his life!*

With Pallas growing weaker by the second, Alys had to do something. Given little choice, she slammed the duo with another sonic cry.

Something snapped inside of Pallas when he saw the body at the vampires' feet. That had been one of his people, a life snuffed out under his watch. He had failed that person, but he could still save the other innocents lined up on either side of the platform.

Summoning his spirit, Pallas pumped energy into his legs and took off at a dead run for the stairwell on the left. Out of the corner of his eye, he saw his brother streak through the air for the walkway on the right. Lloyd had proven to be surprisingly capable so far. Pallas just prayed he could save the folks up there.

Taking two steps at a time, Pallas vaulted up the stairs and sprinted down the walkway until he reached his fellow townsfolk. Weaving through them, he pushed for the head of the line and the vampires beyond.

Someone with brains, Glolindir most likely, had put up a wall of fire between the bridge and the platform. That effectively separated their foes, allowing Pallas to take on just a few vampires at a time.

As he broke through the line, a vampire dropped down from the wall, landing in front of him. Pallas deflected the creature's attack, taking off its arm in the process. He then destroyed it with a quick thrust of his flaming sword.

Hearing footsteps behind him, Pallas chanced a glance over his shoulder. Glowing like some holy goddess, Thea had followed him up here. *Good,* he thought, *she can save our people while I take care of these vile creatures.*

As Pallas made for the bridge, a large figure suddenly swooped down from above. Though he hadn't seen one in four years, he immediately recognized it as a bronze dragon. This one was smaller than Ruka, though, so he guessed it had to be her little sister. The real surprise was who sat straddling the dragon's back.

Alys!

Pallas inwardly groaned. Once again, the impetuous girl had put herself directly in harm's way. She had done the same exact thing back at Redune, though Pallas had cautioned her otherwise.

Pallas winced when he realized what was coming next. Alys let loose a shrill wail at the three vampires standing on the bridge. Pallas had his doubts as to whether her voice would affect vampires, but it worked surprisingly well. She even pushed one right off the bridge.

Pallas reached the bridge himself just as Alys ended her wail. The nearest vampire recovered quickly and launched itself at Pallas. This creature seemed different from the last one. Pallas could sense its energy, and it was far greater than its brethren.

Pallas dodged its two-clawed attack and struck back with swift, controlled strikes of his own. This creature was fast, but Pallas could match its speed.

The two of them went back and forth, twisting and dodging and striking out at each other. Pallas was careful to avoid those claws. He knew full well that a hit from a vampire would drain his energy.

The creature then made its first and last mistake. It threw itself at Pallas with both arms at once, trying to catch him in a bear hug. Pallas ducked under the attack and brought his flaming katana straight up into the vampire's chest and out through the other side.

Confident he had won, Pallas chanced a quick glance over at Alys. Her last wail had been cut short and that worried him.

Another vampire had somehow managed to land on the dragon's back; the dragon immediately retaliated with a lightning bolt. The vampire shrugged it off, but then in an amazing feat of acrobatics, Alys double-kicked the creature right off of the dragon.

Pallas felt a wave of relief flood over him, but it was cut short when something gripped him by the throat. He had made a rookie mistake. This vampire had not burst into flames like the first one.

Pallas strained to retract his sword, but his arms suddenly felt like lead. The vampire fixed him with a wicked grin as it pulled the katana out of its chest and threw it to the floor. It then tightened its grip and hoisted Pallas up into the air.

With his energy waning fast, Pallas knew he had little time. He tried to call upon his spirit to teleport out of the vampire's grasp, but the energy he brought to the surface just as swiftly drained away.

Fading fast, Pallas had nearly run out of options. If he couldn't teleport, maybe he could fade into the shadows? Pallas prepared to muster his spirit when he was hit full force with a high-pitched shriek. It felt as if his body had been struck with a physical blow. The pressure on his ears was tremendous.

It must have been worse on the vampire, though. The creature's entire body began to shudder as it tried to hold onto Pallas, but after a few seconds lost its grip.

Pallas fell to the floor. He felt as if he could barely move, but forced himself to concentrate. Though the pressure on his ears was excruciating, he somehow managed to reach his spirit. Slipping into the shadows, Pallas breathed a thankful sigh. The pressure wasn't nearly as bad in there.

The vampire had clamped down on its ears and turned to face Alys. It prepared to leap at her and the dragon, but the dragon responded with a sizzling lightning bolt. This bolt seemed far greater than the last, momentarily stunning the vampire.

Realizing it wouldn't last long, Pallas mustered the last remaining vestiges of his spirit. Forcing himself to his feet, he came out of the shadows, grabbed his sword, and stabbed it straight through the vampire's back.

The vampire thrashed at him, but Pallas wouldn't stop. Focusing his will, he lit the sword on fire and poured all of his remaining energy into the flames. The flames grew hotter and hotter, turning from red to yellow to blue. His body screamed for him to stop, but he couldn't. Everyone was counting on him. Alys was counting on him.

Somehow, the vampire did not die. It continued to thrash on his sword, trying frantically to wriggle loose. Already at his limit, something broke inside of Pallas.

Visions of Penwick on fire passed before his eyes. Smoke everywhere, dead bodies, burnt-out buildings, black pirate ships—the nightmares that haunted him almost every night.

Pallas screamed. He pushed past everything and went deeper inside than he ever had before. There, deep within his very core, he found a white hot-spark of spirit. Desperate, Pallas reached out and touched it.

The intense power rushed through his body and out into his sword. The flames turned white hot, and all of a sudden the vampire exploded. The force of the blast sent Pallas reeling backward and everything went black.

23
EYE OF AMON

Now they wanted to destroy the souls of all these innocent folks

Seth hated vampires even more than politicians. They sucked the life out of you, lived in the darkest of places, and were a pain in the ass to get rid of if you didn't know how. Actually, the more he thought about it, vampires were a lot like politicians.

Seth snorted to himself as he chased Aksel up the stairs, though in all honesty, none of this was funny. At least one person had already died, and more would surely follow. *Not gonna happen,* Seth promised himself. *Not if I have anything to say about it.*

Seth spotted two vampires clinging to the wall up ahead. Lloyd must have seen them, too. The young warrior flew directly for them, scraping the wall with the tip of his blade. A stream of fire sprang from the sparks where his blade met the wall. It raced ahead of him, catching both vamps and lighting them on fire.

That's new, Seth thought to himself. He had never seen Lloyd do that before, but he definitely approved.

As the vamps above them burned, Aksel reached the folks idly standing on the walkway. The little cleric cast a magic circle and woke them up from their trance.

"Follow me!" Aksel waved them all back toward the stairway.

The people heard him and started to comply, but unfortunately, so did two more vamps on the bridge ahead. Seth weaved his way through the crowd, turning invisible as he came out on the other side. He knew he was no match for the two vamps, but he'd do his best to slow them down.

Right above them on the wall, the two vamps continued to burn. Lloyd came back around for a second pass, strafing through the pair with his gleaming holy blade. Both vamps turned to dust.

Meanwhile, the vamps chasing after the people had reached Seth. Seth flattened himself against the wall as the first one passed, but threw his entire body at the ground in front of the second one. Rolling at full speed, he took the vamp's legs out from under it, causing it to stumble and take the other one down with it.

That ought to slow you down, Seth thought with grim satisfaction.

As the two vamps struggled to untangle themselves, Lloyd touched down in front of Seth. He dusted the first vamp with a single thrust of his holy blade, but the second one was another matter. It had already regained its feet and moved in quickly, striking at the tall warrior.

Seth suddenly realized what they were fighting. *Those other vamps were just spawn. This one's a true vampire.*

Thankfully Lloyd had learned his lesson from fighting vamps back in Ravenford. He expertly parried the swift attacks, not letting this one touch him. He then employed a defense strategy, letting the vamp attack, dodging or parrying, and slicing back.

Wow. Lloyd's using his brain for once, Seth thought wryly.

While Lloyd kept the vamp busy, Seth had an idea. He pulled out a stake from his pack, and hugging the wall, stole behind the vamp. Seth then waited for his opportunity. He was finally rewarded when Lloyd caught the vamp with a quick slice from his holy blade. The creature flinched and Seth pounced.

Leaping up, Seth stabbed the creature in the back, right behind where its heart would have been. The stake sank deep into the vamp, eliciting a strangled cry from the creature.

Seth let go and rolled away as the vamp struggled to reach the stake sticking out of its back. It was too late, though. A second later, the vampire crumbled to dust.

Donnie had seen death before, but losing one's soul was an entirely different matter. There was no coming back from that. When Lloyd's sister lit up that huge chamber, it became obvious one person had already met that terrible fate. Seeing more people lined up to face the same doom rendered Donnie almost speechless.

Andrella mirrored his thoughts. "All those people..."

"...like lambs to the slaughter," Donnie finished for her.

Initially stunned, Donnie's numbness abruptly turned into rage. These creatures had gone too far. First they turned Alana into one of them. She then tried to kill her own brother, and Donnie had been forced to dust her. Now they wanted to destroy the souls of all these innocent folks.

No! Donnie swore to himself. *Not while I live and breathe!*

Donnie instinctively ran for Ruka when she shifted into dragon form. Yet Cyclone beat him to it, leaping ahead of him onto her back. Donnie watched dumbfounded as the two of them took off together. Their constant pair-up was really starting to annoy him.

Tearing his eyes away, Donnie observed that Maya had also shifted and now flew off with Alys on her back. Strangely, Ves had not. Instead, the young lady took off at a dead run down the center of the chamber. Curious as to what she was up to, Donnie followed.

At the base of the platform directly ahead of them, Donnie spied an opening. It appeared to be a tunnel that led all the way through to the other side. Ves was headed straight for it.

Donnie abruptly realized what she was up to. *She's going to flank the enemy!*

Marveling at the intelligence of the young lady, Donnie continued to follow. As they approached the platform, however, a deafening shriek rang out above them.

Donnie glanced up to see Maya hovering there with Alys on her back. The young lady appeared to be attacking those on the bridge with some sort of extremely loud sonic magic. A few moments later, a dark figure fell from the bridge.

While Ves continued on toward the tunnel, Donnie halted and watched as the fallen figure slowly rose to its feet. *That's definitely a vampire,* he realized.

Knowing Ves could handle herself, Donnie started toward the creature. The vampire hadn't quite noticed him yet. Instead, it went to the wall and began climbing back up toward the bridge.

"Oh, no you don't!" Donnie yelled up at it.

The vampire paused and turned to look at him, a loud hiss escaping its throat. As Donnie drew close, it tried to leap down on him, but the agile elf rolled out of the way. Coming up into a crouch, Donnie spun about, poised to meet the next attack.

The vampire swung at him, but Donnie ducked beneath its grasp and brought his holy dagger straight up into its chest. The vampire let loose an unearthly shriek, then turned to dust.

Without warning, something grabbed Donnie from behind. He tried to wriggle out of the vice-like grip, but found he could not. Worse, he was growing weaker by the second.

Must be another vampire, Donnie reasoned. If he didn't break free soon, he'd be a goner. Try as he might, though, he could not break the vampire's death-like grip.

Just when he thought all hope was lost, Donnie felt something beneath his feet. A pool of dark liquid had suddenly appeared there and grew wider by the second. Realizing what it was, Donnie spoke the words to invoke the magic of his boots. "*Aranea Repere.*"

Donnie had gotten *Boots of the Spider* from a chest in the Golem Master's monolith. Like the spell, they made his hands and feet stick to almost anything.

Bracing himself, Donnie prayed the vampire would lose its balance. Sure enough, its footing slipped and it momentarily loosened its grip on Donnie.

In one swift motion, Donnie spun about and stabbed the vampire straight through the heart. The creatures shuddered for a brief moment, then crumbled to dust.

Holding his knees while breathing in gulps of air, Donnie cast a glance toward the entrance to the chamber. Elladan stood there gazing back at him with a thumb up in the air. Donnie reciprocated the gesture.

Leave it to Elladan, Donnie thought wryly. This was probably the fifth time he could think of that the bard had saved the day with *Grease.*

Suddenly, another vampire fell from above. Donnie raised his hands to the heavens in disbelief. "What is it, raining vampires?"

Donnie still felt drained, but he had no choice. He had to fight. The vampire would catch him for sure if he tried to run.

Rapier in one hand and dagger in the other, Donnie began to circle the creature. The vampire lashed out at him, but he was just able to avoid its strikes. Still circling, the exhausted elf waited for the creature to overextend itself.

When it finally did, Donnie parried and executed a feint with his rapier. The vampire dodged the weapon, but couldn't stop in time to avoid Donnie's dagger. The holy dagger found its mark and the last vampire crumbled to dust.

"Whew, that was…" Donnie gasped between breaths. He never quite finished the sentence, though, as his body gave out beneath him.

Cyclone was a dragon hunter from a long line of hunters, dating way back to before the Thrall Wars. From the time he could hold a spear until his father disappeared hunting a red, Cyclone had been trained to fight dragons. Thus it was weird for him to now be 'friends' with a couple of bronzes. It was even stranger to now be hunting vampires by their side.

Cyclone was not one to share his feelings. Hell, he wasn't even sure he had any. If he did, he hadn't been raised to acknowledge them. Still, even he couldn't ignore the spectacle now laid out before them.

A dozen or more dark figures stood on the central platform, along with about the same number of town guards. They all surrounded a fancy-dressed couple with what appeared to be a body at their feet. Cyclone's gaze was drawn to a large, dark-armored figure just behind the strange couple. Sure, he noticed the people in danger on either side of the platform, but there was something he definitely wanted to fight.

Not far in front of Cyclone, Maya and Ruka shifted into their true dragon forms. Certain the others would save the people, Cyclone leaped into action. He vaulted past the others and jumped onto Ruka's back.

Ruka seemed momentarily startled, but quickly recovered with a snarky comment. "I'm headed down the middle. You good with that, hot shot?"

"Exactly where I wanted to go," Cyclone responded with grim excitement.

Without another word, Ruka lifted off. The large bronze flew up to a height halfway between the platform and the ceiling. Though she couldn't reach her full speed in this enclosed area, they closed with the platform in a matter of seconds.

The guards had lined up in front of the platform. They had a chance for maybe one volley of arrows before Ruka was upon them. Those who managed to get off a shot fared poorly, as those arrows just bounced off her hard scales.

As Ruka strafed over the guards, she let loose with a sizzling bolt at the fiends hiding behind them. Cyclone followed immediately afterward by launching himself off of her back. The hunter landed in a crouch on the exact spot where she had just blasted.

Cyclone found himself right in the midst of a number of vampires and shadowy creatures. A few of the closer things lashed out at him, but he merely shrugged off their attacks.

Cyclone stood and swung his halberd in a wide arc all around him. The axe blade sliced through a few of the things, forcing them all back and away. A few tried to sneak in past his arcing blade, and one or two did manage to strike him, but a couple of shadows went poof for their trouble.

All of sudden, a bolt of lightning sizzled a shadow that had been reaching for him. A moment later, the large bronze pounced on all the creatures to his one side. Lashing out with her claws and tail, she knocked a few more of the creatures away.

Somewhat annoyed, Cyclone barked at her as he destroyed another shadow with his halberd. "Hey, watch where you're going! You almost landed on me."

"I knew exactly where I was landing—and you're welcome!" Ruka snapped back.

Without warning, Cyclone, Ruka, and all the creatures around them found themselves engulfed by a frigid blast of ice and snow. The wind that accompanied it was so fierce that Cyclone had to cover his eyes. It only lasted for a few seconds, but when the wind stopped, all the shadows had disappeared. The only things still left standing were Cyclone, Ruka, and a few vampires.

"Wow. No honor among these things," Ruka commented dryly.

Wiping the snow from his eyes, the hunter lashed out at the nearest vampire. He neatly beheaded it and caused it to crumble to dust. Yet as he brought his axe back around, something hit him really hard.

Cyclone skidded backward through the snow before managing to stop himself. The dark-armored figure now stood before him, its arm raised for another blow.

"Is that all you've got?" Cyclone barked back at the dark armor.

Angry at himself for letting his guard down, Cyclone let the anger wash over him. He felt it seep through his body, his limbs growing stronger, and his skin growing harder.

Lightning flashed around them, but Cyclone had become fixated on the dark armor. It came forward and swung at him again, but this time Cyclone blocked the punch and swung back at it with his halberd. The creature's armor rang from the resounding blow, sending it skidding backward and popping off its dark helmet.

Atop the armor now sat a huge orange head that looked strangely like a pumpkin. Cyclone stared at it in disbelief. "What in the seven hells are you?"

"Ves!"

Ruka's sudden cry broke Cyclone's fascination with the pumpkin-headed monstrosity. Glancing past it, he saw the fancy-dressed man pointing a scepter at the head of a huge bronze dragon that towered over him. The scepter emitted a black ray that enveloped the dragon with the same colored aura.

Cyclone watched with astonishment as the dragon's eyes rolled upward. The dragon then fell out of sight, landing with a huge thud that caused the entire platform to shake.

Cyclone couldn't believe his eyes. Had that guy just taken down a huge dragon with that wimpy little scepter? Not to mention, that dragon was Ves. They were sort-of friends. Should he be feeling something about that?

Ruka certainly did. The large bronze roared with sudden rage and sent a bolt of sizzling lightning careening at the fancy-dressed man. A moment later, a barrage of red rays streaked down from above and hit the man in rapid succession. Those rays were immediately followed by a volley of arrows.

The man reeled from the multiple attacks. Yet before anyone could move, the man, the woman, and the pumpkin headed monstrosity were enveloped by a dark sphere. As rapidly as it appeared, the sphere contracted and disappeared. All three figures had vanished.

Cyclone was livid. "Son of a…"

The rest of his curse was cut short as Glolindir landed in front of him, holding Lloyd's sister in his arms. The priestess radiated a brilliant white aura that fanned out in all directions. As soon as that light touched any of the remaining vamps, they screamed and exploded into dust.

With the last vamps gone, Ruka took off in the direction of her fallen sister.

Elladan had experienced many things in his long life, both good and bad, but nothing appalled him as much as what these vampires were now doing. Callously using someone's soul to power an artifact was pure evil. Then again, so were vampires, so he guessed that was to be expected.

The bard watched with pride and admiration as his friends charged forth to do battle. Thea, in particular, absolutely amazed him, surrounded by that brilliant glow like some sort of goddess from the heavens.

Though Elladan sometimes wished he could do more, he wasn't a fighter. So instead, he did what he did best. He summoned his lute and played a quick tune to bolster his companion's courage as they leapt into battle. During the fray, he even cast a strategic spell or two where he thought it would help the most.

The first spell had been on the near-dozen guards who moved to the front line ahead of the dark creatures. Elladan surmised that the vampire lord had dominated them into acting as a shield for his other minions. The cowardly move irked Elladan to no end.

Some of the guards fired at Ruka as she went by, but that quickly proved fruitless. The rest traded shots with Xellos, who hovered up near the ceiling. The tracker masterfully wounded the guards and managed to dodge their return fire.

Still, Elladan thought it only fair to even the odds a bit. So, he cast a *Confusion* spell on the line. Before they knew it, at least half the guards were attacking themselves or each other.

The second spell had been a pool of grease beneath Donnie, and a vamp that had him in a compromising position. His timely intervention turned the tables and put Donnie back on even footing with the creature.

Elladan got a bit distracted after that, as Aksel and Thea herded the prisoners toward the entrance to the chamber. Unfortunately, those folks had begun to panic and trounced over each other in an effort to escape.

Elladan came to the rescue by playing a soothing tune to calm the frantic folks' nerves. As soon as the music wafted over them, the prisoners quieted down. Aksel and Thea then safely ushered those folks out of the chamber.

Thea came back shortly thereafter and touched Elladan's arm as she passed. "Thank you," she said with a brief smile.

Elladan blushed ever so slightly. "My pleasure."

The lovely priestess was soon gone again, flying into the thick of battle with the aid of Glo and Andrella. Elladan was livid when everyone on the platform, including the town guards, were hit with the vampire's icy blast. He was stunned when Ves fell, then cheered with glee when they finally routed the enemy. "Yeah! You better run." Yet in the midst of all the pandemonium, it dawned him that he had forgotten all about Donnie.

Searching the ground at the base of the platform, Elladan's gaze fell upon an inert form. *That's Donnie!* Realizing that everyone else was busy, Elladan took off at a run down the corridor toward his fallen friend.

When he reached him, Elladan checked Donnie's breath. Thankfully he was still breathing. Reaching into a pouch at his belt, Elladan pulled out a pungent herb and placed it under Donnie's nose.

A few moments later, Donnie's eyes fluttered open. He coughed, then grabbed his head and gingerly rubbed it. Donnie then sat up and gazed at Elladan, a thin smile crossing his lips. "Did anyone get the number of that wagon?"

24
FORK IN THE ROAD

I think I know where you can find those scrolls

lys watched in horror as the vampire exploded and sent
Pallas flying. Her poor love went careening backward
into the chamber wall, where he crumbled to the floor
in a heap. Forgetting all else, Alys launched herself off
Maya's back, spanning the distance to the bridge in a
single leap.

Distraught, she rushed to Pallas' side and checked for a pulse.
Her heart nearly skipped a beat when she didn't feel one, but then
she realized she had grabbed his wrist backwards. Flipping it over,
she held her breath as she checked again.

There it is! Alys sighed, fighting back the tears that streaked her
face. Thanking the gods, she slipped her hand behind his head and
gently cradled him in her arms. Without realizing it, she hummed a
soft tune that her mother had sung to her every night when she was a
child. Alys remembered little of her mother, but the tune had stayed
with her until this very day.

Suddenly, Pallas stirred. Alys gently caressed his face. "Pallas, are you alright?" her voice squeaked with fear.

Pallas' eyes fluttered open and after a few moments focused on her. A wan smile crossed his lips. "Why is it lately that every time I get hurt, the first thing I wake up to is your lovely face?"

Alys felt her cheeks turn hot. "You—you think I'm lovely?" she stammered, not daring to breathe.

He slowly reached up and brushed her cheek. "Yes, I do, in fact."

Alys really had to fight back the tears this time—tears of joy. She beamed down at him, grabbing his hand and holding it tight against her face. She suddenly remembered all that just happened, and her smile tilted sideways. "Sorry about the wailing."

"No"— Pallas grunted as he sat up—"You did the right thing." He grabbed her hands and met her eyes with a sheepish grin. "I don't think I would have survived without your help."

Alys' heart sang as she stared into his intense brown eyes. As if with a will of their own, their lips slowly gravitated together. Alys lost herself in that passionate kiss, a kiss that she had only experienced in dreams until this very moment.

Once the prisoners had been ushered to safety, Glo and Andrella flew into battle, the former carrying Thea with him. Glo's heart leapt into his throat when the vampire lord felled Ves. He instantly retaliated along with Ruka, Andrella, and Xellos, their combined attacks driving the master and mistress away. Seconds later, Thea destroyed the remaining vampires in an epic display of raw holy power.

As soon as the platform was cleared, Ruka flew off to check on Ves. Glo itched to follow her, but hesitated as Thea scrutinized an obviously battered Cyclone. "Are you okay?"

Cyclone responded with a typical snort. "I'm fine. Go help the dragon."

Thea's eyes strayed past the hunter to the fallen guards. "What about them?"

Cyclone shook his head. "They're beyond your help."

Thea still seemed uncertain, but Cyclone was insistent. "Fine. I'll get the gnome to look at them if it'll make you happy."

"You better." Thea narrowed her eyes at the hunter, then grabbed onto Glo's shoulders.

Glo wrapped an arm around Thea's waist, then took off for the other end of the platform. Clearing the edge, they found both Maya and Ruka standing over the prone form of the huge bronze dragon.

"Ves, wake up," Ruka shook her sister. Though she acted calm, Glo detected a nervous edge to her tone.

"Sissy, please wake up!" Maya pleaded, not hiding her anxiousness in the slightest.

"Let me see her!" Thea cried as she and Glo landed. Both girls stepped back, reverting to human form to make room for them.

Thea went to Ves' side, her hands feverishly running over the fallen dragon's body. After a few moments, she let out a deep sigh and gave the sisters a wan smile. "She's alright—just knocked out."

Maya leapt into Ruka's arms and let out a loud yelp. "Wahoo! Sissy's fine! It'll take more than some stupid vampire to hurt our big sister!"

Ruka hefted Maya in her arms, her lips twisting sideways. "You got that right."

Perhaps Ves heard the ruckus, for a moment later she began to stir. Her head popped up, swiveling around on her long, serpentine neck. "What happened? Where is that vampire?"

"He got away," Glo informed her.

"Are you alright? You fell down." Maya squeaked at Ves.

Ves peered at the little girl, then shifted to human form, her eyes wavering with emotion. "I'm—okay," she replied, gingerly rubbing the back of her head. "Just knocked me out for a minute."

Ruka stared at her sister skeptically. "You sure? That death ray was no joke."

Ves grunted as she rose to her feet. "You're telling me."

Any further conversation was interrupted as shouting rang out across the chamber. Fearful that the vampires had returned, Glo prepared for another battle. He breathed a sigh, however, when Carenna and Taliana appeared from the other end of the chamber, trailed by a troop of town guards.

Glo arched an eyebrow at the approaching crew. "Where did you come from?"

Carenna stopped short as she reached their side, pausing to take a breath. "We went searching for those missing guards. What we found was a tunnel leading from the basement of one of the southern tenement houses."

Andrella placed her hands on her hips. "So that explains how the guards and the prisoners got down here before us." Glo had actually been wondering the same thing.

Taliana narrowed an eye at her. "Guards? Prisoners? Explain yourself."

"Follow us. I'll explain on the way." Andrella motioned for them all to follow.

Glo marveled at how well Andrella handled the rude captain. She patiently described their encounter as they ascended to the platform, answering every one of Taliana's curt questions. Were it left to him, Glo was quite sure he wouldn't have been so forthcoming.

When they reached the top, they found that Cyclone had kept his word. Aksel was now there examining the fallen guards, along with the rest of the companions and the townsfolk they saved.

Aksel called out to Thea. "Lend me a hand! Some of them are still alive."

Thea cast a dark glare at Cyclone as she rushed ahead to help Aksel. Meanwhile, Andrella finished her story. When she was done, the townsfolk confirmed her tale. Apparently the missing guards had dragged them all down into the catacombs.

Taliana stared at them incredulously. "My guards?"

"They had little choice," Glo defended them. "A vampire's will is very powerful. Only the strongest of minds can resist it."

Despite his explanation, Taliana did not quite seem convinced. Still, any further discussion on the matter was cut short by Thea. "We've managed to stabilize them for now, but we really should get them to the temple."

Carenna gave her a firm nod. "Right. And these people as well," she motioned toward the townsfolk. "They look like they've been through hell."

Thea wrestled with mixed emotions on the way to the temple. She felt sad for the guards who died, and was still concerned for the few who nearly had. At the same time, she felt extremely thankful that Ves and the others were alright.

Cyclone could have easily been killed, throwing himself into the midst of things. Donnie had run off on his own and now had the bruises to show for it. Yet what surprised Thea the most was to see Pallas leaning heavily upon Lloyd on their way out of the catacombs. It was unlike 'practically perfect' Pallas to depend on anyone, especially their kid brother.

Perhaps even more strange, Alys had her arms wrapped around Pallas' waist as if they were a couple. Furthermore, her prudish brother didn't seem to mind at all. Her curiosity getting the better of her, Thea drew up beside Alys and narrowed her gaze at her older brother. "What happened to you?"

Pallas made a sour face. "I was stupid—that's what."

Thea did a double take. *Pallas admitting to a mistake? That's a first.*

"You were brave," Alys chided him, "protecting me and Maya from that vampire."

Pallas shook his head. "I should never have underestimated it in the first place."

"Same thing happened to me first time I fought a vampire," Lloyd said with obvious chagrin. "It drained so much of my lifeforce that I started to turn grey."

"You looked distinguished," Andrella stated firmly from the other side of Lloyd.

Thea had reservations at first about Andrella, thinking she might be just another spoiled noble. Yet Andrella had proven her wrong, showing far more substance than Thea had originally imagined.

An embarrassed grin crossed Lloyd's face. "Yeah, well, either way it taught me a lesson."

Pallas gave Lloyd a begrudging nod. "I agree. That's a lesson I won't soon forget."

Though he didn't show it, Thea could tell just how impressed Pallas was with Lloyd. So was she, in fact. Lloyd had come a long way in these last few months. Thea had to admit to herself, he wasn't the same reckless kid who needed looking after.

When they reached the temple, Thea was surprised to find High Priestess Sirus waiting for them. A tall woman with long blond hair, Sirus had an air of quiet serenity mixed with steel resolve. The High Priestess swiftly dispatched healers to help those who had been injured. She also assigned a second group to check out everyone else.

Once that had been taken care of, Sirus thanked and dismissed Carenna and Taliana. Afterwards, she turned her attention to Thea and Aksel. "I interviewed that first group you found in the catacombs. After what they told us, I suspected you might be returning with more injured."

The sense of sadness that Thea felt before returned. "Unfortunately, we couldn't save everyone."

Sirus placed a hand on Thea's shoulder and met her gaze with an understanding smile. "We are not gods, my child. We can only do our part, no matter how small."

Thea found her words reassuring. Still, she would mourn later for those who lost their lives.

Aksel cleared his throat and detailed what he had seen of the battle. Thea then supplemented it with her own observations. When they finished, Sirus appeared quite pensive. "So this master and mistress disappeared? I think perhaps it best we look further into that."

Sirus invited them both back to her office. There they waited, while the High Priestess lit a few white candles and then sat back and closed her eyes. Her hands on her desk, palms up, Sirus sat in quiet meditation for the better part of half an hour.

Aksel and Thea waited patiently, knowing that any divination the High Priestess received would require the utmost quiet. Finally, Sirus' eyes fluttered open. "Well I have good news and bad news. The good news is that neither this master nor mistress are anywhere in Penwick. The bad news is that I have no inkling of where they are."

Thea sighed. As long as those two powerful vampires were at large, Penwick would be in danger. Still, there was not much they could do about it at the moment. Thanking Sirus, the two of them left to seek out the others. They found them all seated in and around one of the many gazebos that decorated the temple grounds.

Lloyd and Andrella sat hand-in-hand in one of the seats in the gazebo. Surprisingly, Pallas and Alys sat similarly in the seat opposite from them.

Will wonders never cease? Thea thought wryly. Alys had been chasing Pallas ever since they were pre-teens. It appeared that after all this time, she had finally caught him. Thea felt her heart melt just a little bit at the welcome sight. Though sometimes erratic, Alys was warm-hearted and genuine. She was exactly what her exceedingly serious brother needed.

Ves and Ruka sat on the steps of the gazebo while Maya pranced around in front of them. Glo, Donnie, and Elladan rested on the grass nearby, the latter playing a jaunty tune for Maya. Cyclone and Seth both sat a little ways apart from the others, each against the trunk of a nearby tree. Even Cal had joined them, the copper dragon taking up most of the lawn on the opposite side of the gazebo.

Everyone had received a clean bill of health, though the healers recommended rest for the lot of them. Thea then reported what the High Priestess told them. When she was done, Lloyd got up and began to pace around. "So now what? Those vampires could be back at any time, the demons are still out there, and we're still no closer to finding the great runes for slaying weapons."

At Lloyd's words, Alys abruptly sat up and snapped her fingers. "That's what I forgot." She jumped out of her seat and took Thea by the hand. "It's what I originally came to tell you. I think I know where you can find those scrolls."

Everyone gathered around as Alys told her story. She had over-heard a conversation between her father and one of his confidants. Apparently, the rune scrolls that were stolen from the Tauriyama clan had shown up in the hands of one of the Clans of the Coast. Duna-mal was looking to buy them, but someone with a lot of money had already beat him to it. The exchange was to take place within a week's time somewhere out on the dark coast.

Thea felt an old tinge of excitement stir at the mention of the pirate clans. This was the third or fourth time this week the subject had come up. Each time, it had sparked memories of her past life. Thea had thought that all behind her, but maybe the gods were trying to tell her something.

Aksel stood pensively stroking his chin. "It's imperative that we get those scrolls, but I don't think it wise to leave Penwick just now, either."

Donnie raised his hand and let out a long sigh. "I'll go to the pirate coast. I'm the most familiar with it."

Ves gave the reluctant elf an encouraging smile. "Might I suggest stopping in Lanfor first? The Queen always seems to know what's going on along the coast."

Ruka snorted. "Translation—she's got a big spy network."

A soft chuckle escaped Elladan's lips. "Sounds like my kind of Queen." He nudged Donnie in the side. "Maybe I'll come along for the ride. After all, someone needs to keep an eye on you."

Calipherous lifted his head off the lawn and peered at Ves. "We should go as well. The last time I was there, the Queen requested to see the three of you."

Ruka got up and stretched her arms wide, a yawn escaping her lips. "We probably should." She narrowed an eye at the elves. "If Donnie and Elladan are going, someone needs to keep an eye on the both of them."

Donnie gave her a weak smile, but Elladan grinned. "Touché."

Cyclone rose from his tree trunk and came to stand in front of Donnie. "So, these pirates—are they strong?"

Donnie eyed him as if he were crazy. "Thirteen clans with over a hundred ships, dark witches, and lord captains that could give the best swordsman a run for their money? You tell me."

Cyclone mulled over his words for a moment or two, then nodded. "Count me in."

Thea fought the urge to say that she would go as well. She knew more about the pirate clans than anyone else in Penwick. She might even know as much as Donatello, though she suspected he knew more than he was saying. Still, Thea had just been ordained an Auric Priestess, and her duty was here to the people of Penwick. What would Sirus say if she suddenly wanted to pick up and leave for the other side of the sea?

Aksel let out a sigh of relief. "That should work. The rest of us will stay and track down the vampires. In the meantime, we should go and report to the Baron—especially since it looks like we'll need that airship."

25

RAIDERS OF THE DARK COAST

You can't tell me you're not having qualms about leaving Penwick

ndrella was determined to get that airship. She wouldn't let anything stand in her way this time—not Alburg nor the Baron himself. Good people had already died at the hands of those vampires. She couldn't imagine how many more would suffer the same fate once the demons set forth from the tower.

The council needed to see reason. Andrella would make them, or at the very least, play on their heartstrings. That's why she invited Alys to join them for this meeting. From what Thea told her, Alburg had a hard time saying no to his daughter.

The entire council was already in session when they arrived. Carenna and Taliana had gone ahead and reported to the Baron. Caverinus, in turn, called the rest of the council together.

Aksel, Elladan, and Glo filled in the details of the battle in the catacombs with Pallas backing up their story. Andrella then relayed the ill fate of the Lanfor and Dunwynn assault on the Demon Tower. Alburg did not seem happy at all to hear that news, most likely because it ruined his original ploy of letting Dunwynn handle the tower.

Aillinn immediately picked up on the point, staring directly at Alburg as he drove it home. "Well, I guess we won't be depending on Dunwynn after all."

Alburg said nothing, his expression sour as he stared back at Aillinn.

Lara then picked up the ball. "These demons grow more powerful every day. If we don't act soon, we might never be able to stop them."

Andrella gave her a grateful nod. "Exactly our thoughts. That is why we want to send part of our company to Lanfor by airship. Our sources informed us of a set of rune scrolls that have recently surfaced along the coast. Those scrolls could be used to forge weapons of great power."

By the look on his face, Andrella's statement had caught Alburg by surprise. It only lasted a moment, however. He gazed at Alys, a thin smile unexpectedly crossing his lips. "Well played, daughter."

Alys responded with an impish grin. "I learned from the best."

Their decision to bring Alys along paid off. Obviously mollified, Alburg gave up the battle. Still, the devious merchant managed to tip the scales in his favor. He addressed the Baron in a tentative tone. "Your excellency, since they are going to borrow one of our ships anyway, we should probably take advantage of the situation."

Caverinus stared at Alburg with a puzzled expression. "How so?"

A sly look crossed Alburg's face. "Why, by making it a diplomatic mission, of course."

Caverinus visibly brightened at the idea. "Excellent suggestion, Alburg. And whom do you suggest we send to entreat the Queen on our behalf?"

Alburg gestured toward Pallas. "I think young Captain Stealle here might make an excellent envoy. The council could craft up a proposal to the Queen for him to deliver."

Caverinus practically crowed with delight. "Excellent suggestion again, Alburg." The Baron shifted his gaze toward Pallas. "What say you, Captain Stealle?"

Mixed emotions played across Pallas' face. He did not seem thrilled about leaving Penwick at the present time. Like a true soldier, however, he squelched his emotions and bowed. "It would be my honor to represent Penwick in this manner, your highness."

Caverinus slapped the arms of his chair emphatically. "Then it's settled. When are you planning on leaving?"

Pallas glanced at Kratos. "What's the status of the airships, Father?"

Kratos pressed his lips together as he mulled over the question. "The Remington is still being refurbished, but I believe the Cloud Hammer could be made ready for the voyage by first thing in the morning."

Caverinus rubbed his hands together in anticipation. "There you have it. You'll leave tomorrow at first light."

Thea still didn't know what to do. Despite multiple hours of meditation and prayer, she still felt conflicted. Her duty to the people of Penwick was clear, but she couldn't shake the nagging feeling that she belonged with the others on their mission to the coast. After getting nowhere on her own, Thea finally decided to consult with the High Priestess.

Though later in the day, Sirus was still in her office. When she saw Thea at her door, she appeared pleasantly surprised. Sirus pushed aside the pile of parchments in front of her and motioned toward one of the chairs across her desk. "Thea. Come in, my child. Please sit down."

The smile on her face swiftly faded as she noticed the pensive state of her late-day visitor. She sat forward in her chair and eyed Thea with obvious concern. "Tell me, what is troubling you?"

Thea took a deep breath and painstakingly explained her dilemma, including her knowledge of the pirates, her concern for the people of Penwick, and even her thoughts about her younger brother. She stressed that she knew where her duties lay, but couldn't resolve the inner conflict she felt.

Sirus listened patiently and quietly until Thea was done. Once she had finished, Sirus sat back in her chair and clasped her hands together in front of her. "Overall, I'd say you're mostly correct."

"Mostly?" Thea raised an eyebrow.

A knowing smile spread across Sirus' lips. "To the best of my knowledge, you and your mother are indeed the foremost experts on the pirate clans in all of Penwick. Further, I think it good that you recognize your younger brother can now take care of himself. However," Sirus paused to take a breath, "I think you are being rather shortsighted in defining your 'duty' to the people of Penwick."

"Shortsighted?" Thea's brow knit into a frown. "Please explain, your worship."

Sirus came around the desk and sat in the chair next to Thea. She grabbed each of her hands and held them in her own. "You believe the duty of an Auric Priestess is to protect and heal the people of this city."

"Isn't it?" Thea cocked her head to one side, not sure she was following the High Priestess' words.

Sirus met her gaze with that same knowing look. "Tell me this—do you believe the only way to protect your people is to stand guard over them?"

This time both Thea's eyebrows shot up her forehead. She had been so focused on her 'duty,' that she was missing the bigger picture. "Well, when you put it that way, it does sound rather foolish."

"Not at all," Sirus admonished her. "You are still new to this. So," she paused for emphasis, "now that we've established that, how do you think you could best serve your people?"

Thea took a deep breath and stated what she had been feeling all along, but was too caught up in her own preconceived notions to recognize. "By using my knowledge of the pirate clans to help the group going to the coast. Also, to keep that group safe and help them return with those much-needed scrolls."

Sirus patted her on the hand and rose from her seat. "See, my child? Now, that wasn't so hard, was it?"

Actually, considering her duty-filled background, it had been a huge hurtle for Thea. Still, she wasn't about to contradict the High Priestess. So instead, she merely stood and sighed. "Thank you, your worship."

Sirus smiled and made the sign of the god of light in front of her. "Go now, my child, and may the blessings of Arenor follow you all on your journey."

Fortress Hightower stood at the northwestern end of the city, the great gray stone fortress and its single thick tower a cornerstone of the city's defenses. From the time it was built, after the Parthian invasion, this bastion of Penwick had never fallen. Most recently, its wide tower had become an excellent place to dock large airships.

Pallas stood atop the fortress watching the reflection of the newly risen sun cut a gleaming swath of orange from the horizon to the shore. Still stunned at being nominated envoy to Lanfor, Pallas nonetheless struggled with the thought of leaving Penwick just now. With their strong army and navy, a Lanfor alliance would definitely help in the perilous times ahead. Yet Pallas had always sworn to protect Penwick. How could he leave now when the city faced such insidious danger?

Lloyd stood a short way off, surrounded by his new companions. His little brother had come a long way in these last few months. In fact, he had fought even better than Pallas against those vampires. His friends had proven quite capable as well. Between those staying, his parents, and Carenna, it might not be the worst thing if Pallas left the city for a short while—especially if it were to secure a safer future for them all.

Pallas' somber musings were cut short as Thea arrived with their parents. Strangely, she seemed to be carrying a good-sized travel bag. His curiosity piqued, Pallas went to meet them. Before he could say anything, however, his mother pulled him into a tight embrace.

An abbreviated hug, she let go a few moments later. "Promise me to be careful out there, Pallas."

Pallas had to admit the sign of affection took him by surprise. His mother was not normally given to emotional displays. Trying to keep things light, he grabbed her by the shoulders and gave her a wry smile. "Aren't I always?"

"I seem to remember having to patch you up after that fracas at Redune," Thea said with thinly veiled amusement.

"A scuffle which won him his captaincy," Kratos reminded her.

"He'll be fine," Lloyd declared as he strode up to join them. "After all, he's got nerves of Stealle!"

Mom and Dad exchanged a pained expression while he and Thea both groaned. Apparently Lloyd still hadn't quite outgrown family name puns.

Lloyd proffered his hand to Pallas. "Good luck, bro."

"Thanks." Pallas took his brother's hand and had to double-check himself. Lloyd had grown awfully strong since he'd gone away.

"Yes, good luck out there, son," Kratos repeated, holding out his hand as well. Pallas took it, noting with surprise that his brother was nearly as strong as his father. "I know you'll do us proud," Kratos murmured as he let go.

"I'll do my best," Pallas replied, not knowing what else to say. First his mom and now his dad? He was not used to receiving praise or affection and it really made him uncomfortable. Thankfully, Lloyd changed the subject, saving Pallas from any more awkward moments.

"That's an awfully big bag you've got there, sis," Lloyd noted, mirroring Pallas' thoughts from earlier.

Thea stared down at the bag in her hands. "You think so?" Without warning, she hoisted it at him. "Then how about loading it on board for me?"

"Whoa!" Lloyd yelped as he nearly dropped it. "Are you going, too?"

The corner of Thea's mouth rose slightly. "No. I just packed this thing for my health."

Pallas grabbed his chin and pretended to look her over. "Your forearms do look a bit bigger."

Thea put her hands on her hips. "You're in a chipper mood this morning."

Pallas shrugged. "It's a beautiful morning and we're about to board an airship. What's not to like?"

Thea eyed him suspiciously. "Come on, Pallas. I know you too well. You can't tell me you're not having qualms about leaving Penwick with this ongoing vampire problem."

Pallas folded his arms across his chest. "What about you? Didn't you just become an Auric Priestess? How does Sirus feel about you leaving?"

"Strangely, she gave me her blessing," Thea replied. She sounded almost as surprised as Pallas.

Any further conversation halted as Alburg Dunamal arrived atop the tower. Alys accompanied him, looking absolutely stunning in a teal-blue full-length gown. Her coppery hair appeared almost ablaze in the light of the morning sun.

Thea leaned in close and whispered to him with clear amusement. "We'll let you say your farewells to the Dunamals." His family departed as Alburg and Alys came over to greet him.

Pallas barely noticed their departure. Something had changed between him and Alys since yesterday. He wasn't quite sure what to call it just yet, but whatever it was, he definitely wanted it to continue.

Alburg handed him a diplomatic pouch containing letters of correspondence for the Queen of Lanfor. He wished him luck, then discreetly excused himself, leaving Pallas and Alys alone.

Alys peered up at him, her face somewhat flushed. "I really wish you didn't have to go."

Pallas gave her a wan smile. "It was your father's idea."

A pout formed across Alys' lips. "I know. Trust me, he got an earful about it."

Pallas' smile spread into a grin. "I'm sure he did." He grabbed her hands and held them in his. "Listen, I won't be gone that long. Once I get back, we can take up where we left off."

Alys raised an eyebrow, her face reddening just a bit more. "Oh, and where's that?"

Pallas pulled her in close, then bent down and kissed her on the lips. A few moments later, he pulled back and said, "There."

Alys grinned from ear to ear, her smile lighting up the top of the tower. "I think I like 'there,'" she said in a soft voice. "Can we go 'there' again before you go?"

The way she said it practically melted his heart. "Of course," Pallas said tenderly as he leaned in and kissed her once more.

Glo felt strangely unsettled this morning. When he left his home of Cairthrellon, he never expected to see much of his fellow elves again. Thus, running into Elladan and Donnie out here on the coast had been quite the shock. True, neither was exactly your typical elf, but in the short time they had spent together, the three of them had become like brothers.

During the course of their stay in Penwick, Glo had made brooches for his friends. Similar to the sisters' pearls, they would allow for telepathic contact over short distances. He now handed out three of those brooches: one to Cyclone and the other two to Elladan and Donnie.

Usually priding himself on his intellect, Glo wasn't very good at dealing with anything involving emotions. That had never been quite so apparent as how he handled Elistra's disappearance. Though he'd gotten better since then, Glo still had a long way to go. Thus he was rather stiff in his goodbyes to his elven friends.

When he was done, he stepped back and bade the two a well-known elven farewell. "*Aa' menle nauva calen ar' ta hwesta e' ale'quenle*". Roughly translated it meant: *May thy paths be green and the breeze on thy back.*

Donnie exchanged a wry look with Elladan. "He does know we'll be traveling by water?"

Elladan elbowed Donnie in the side. "You know these *Galinthral* elves. They spend their days stuck in their towers, never setting foot in the real world."

Glo arched an eyebrow at the pair. "You do know that's exactly why I left home in the first place?"

Elladan and Donnie both broke into laughter. They then stepped forward and embraced their serious elven friend. "You think after all this time with us, he'd have developed a sense of humor," Donnie murmured to Elladan.

Elladan chuckled. "It's that damn flaxen hair. It's unnatural for an elf and sucks all of the fun out of you."

Glo hung his head and finally laughed as well. "You two—what am I ever going to do without the both of you?"

"Have some peace of mind for a change?" Ruka's voice sounded from behind him.

Glo glanced over his shoulder to see Ves, Ruka, and Maya all standing there. Maya came running up and leapt up into Glo's arms. "I'm going to miss you, Mr. Glo," she declared emphatically.

Glo felt his cheeks grow warm. "I'm going to miss you too, little Miss Maya."

Ruka, her arms folded across her chest, gave him a curt nod. "Yeah, you didn't turn out half bad"—she paused a moment and glared at Donnie—"for an elf."

Glo could practically feel Donnie wince behind him. Whatever Donnie had done to offend her, she was never going to let him live it down.

As Glo put Maya down, Ves drew up to him. Ruka grabbed Maya by the hand and said to her sister, "We'll see you on board."

"We better get going as well," Elladan nudged Donnie.

"Oh, right," Donnie caught Elladan's not-so-subtle drift. The two elves also departed, leaving Glo and Ves alone.

Ves peered up at him with a tentative smile. "We've come a long way from Cape Marlin." It was the place where Glo and his friends first met the three sisters.

"Yes, we have," Glo replied, feeling suddenly uncomfortable. He tried to cover it with a bit of humor. "Thankfully I haven't blown up anything since then."

Ves laughed for what might have been the first time since her ordeal with Theramon. "That was some show you put on. In fairness, who knew the goblins had stored all that oil at the top of the lighthouse?"

Glo joined in with her, laughing at the absurdity of the situation. After the merriment died down, Ves' expression grew serious. "I want you to know you will be missed. You have been a true dragon friend."

She stepped forward, placed a hand on his arm, then stood on her toes, and kissed him on the cheek. Glo's face felt hotter than before. He was certain his skin had turned as bright as a lobster.

As Ves pulled away, he touched his cheek where she had just kissed him. He stood there, awkwardly searching for something to say. "You—and your sisters—have become like family to me." The word family jarred something in his memory. "I have not forgotten our original promise. Once this is over, we will help you find your father."

Ves' expression turned grim. "I have this strange feeling that we'll find him when we finally face these demons."

Glo's heart abruptly went out to this brave young woman. She tried so hard to be strong for her sisters, but he had seen the chinks in her armor. She was just barely an adult, yet the responsibilities she had shouldered would be a lot for anyone.

Glo grabbed her by the hand. "Then we'll liberate him together," he said in all earnest.

Ves stared at him for a moment, then abruptly threw her arms around him. She hugged him so tight he thought he was going to burst. When she finally let go, he inhaled sharply, his ribs feeling sore, but thankfully intact.

Ves gave him a wan smile as she wiped a bit of moisture from her eyes. "The gods bless you, Glolindir," she said softly. She then straightening her shoulders and strode off toward the waiting Cloud Hammer.

Glo watched her go, wondering at what he had done to earn the friendship of such an amazing young woman.

26
THE LOST VILLAGE

What kind of magic would it take to teleport an entire town?

Glo closed the door to his room at the Inn of the Three Sisters. He sat on the bed, feeling strange to be back here without the sisters around anymore. Half the rooms on this floor were now empty, with a good portion of their company winging their way across the sea.

Still, he did not have the time to dwell on it. They had stayed to protect this city from the vampire master and mistress. In order to do so, they needed answers, and he believed he knew exactly who to ask.

Elistra! Glo cried with his mind.

No need to shout, my love, came the immediate reply. Moments later, a familiar shimmering appeared in the air in front of him. The violet sparkles soon coalesced into the form of his beloved.

Elistra came forward, wrapped her arms around his neck, and kissed him ardently. Swept up into the passion of the moment, Glo completely forgot why he had called her here in the first place.

A few breathless kisses later, Glo pulled her down on the bed next to him and grinned. "It still amazes me that you can appear here in solid form."

A mischievous smile crossed the seeress' lips. "I've gained a bit more control over the crystal," she said as she walked her fingers up his arm, "which means I can stay longer."

"Oh, really?" Glo arched an eyebrow at her. "Just how long is that?"

"Why don't we find out?" she said, cupping his cheek with her hand.

Glo took her hand and kissed it, then sighed. "Much as I'd love to, I really need to ask you something first."

Sensing his distress, she closed her eyes and brushed her hand over his forehead. "You need to know the whereabouts of this Master and Mistress."

"Yes," Glo said, marveling at how easily she had picked that out of his brain. "Can you help?"

"We shall see." Elistra sat up on the bed, crossed her legs, and closed her eyes. Her hands gently draped over her knees, palms up, as her face went still.

Glo watched her in silent fascination, wondering at what she was seeing. He didn't have long to wait. A minute or so later, she began to murmur.

"I see mountains—tall black peaks."

Glo immediately recognized the range she to which she referred. "The Korlokesels."

"Yes," she said, still in her trance. "There's a dark area—covered by clouds—unmoving clouds."

Glo found that rather interesting. It sounded like magical cloud cover, something a vampire might use to blot out the sun.

"There's a structure beneath the clouds—a great spiraling tower." Elistra paused a moment, then shook her head. "No, make that a castle. A grand crenellated castle—with spiraling towers."

Glo edged closer to her. "Can you see anything more?"

The seeress' brow furrowed. "I see dark creatures flitting about— shades—wraiths—ghosts—and vampires."

"That has to be it," Glo declared emphatically. Still, the Korloke-sels were a long range, running from Hagentree in the south all the way up to Dunwynn in the northeast. "Do you know exactly where in the mountains?"

Elistra's brow knit even further. "Follow the Penderbun—up to the three forks. Take the northernmost branch. Follow that—to its source."

With a deep breath, Elistra's eyes snapped open. "Did you get all that?"

"Yes—" Glo began, but halted as she swooned into his arms.

"Are you all right?" Worried, he laid her down on the bed.

All of sudden, she broke out into a grin. "Got you!' she cried, pushing him over and rolling on top of him.

Glo shook his head and gave her an exasperated smile. "You are incorrigible. I thought you had worn yourself out."

"Not quite just yet," she said playfully, her face now inches away from his, "but I'm willing to try."

Glo let out a momentary laugh, then pulled her in close, and lost himself in the warmth of her sweet lips.

Alys felt absolutely euphoric at the sudden turn in her relationship with Pallas. For years she had hoped and dreamed of this very moment. Now that it had finally happened though, she almost couldn't believe it. Still, the experience had been bittersweet. No sooner had Pallas kissed her than they were saying their goodbyes.

Furthermore, Thea had left with him, leaving Alys without her best friend. Thank the gods for Lloyd and Andrella. As soon as the Cloud Hammer disappeared over the horizon, the two of them grabbed her and dragged her back to the inn with them. The three of the sat at a table in the tavern room next to the bar, talking about what to do next.

Lloyd leaned across the table. "I heard you handled yourself pret-ty well against those vampires. Like it or not, you're now part of the group," he said with a boyish grin.

Alys felt herself blush. She grabbed his arm and gave it a gentle squeeze. "Thanks, Lloyd. I appreciate that."

She and Lloyd had grown close when Alys first returned to Penwick. With Thea rapt in her holy studies, and Pallas busy as the new
captain of the Avenger, Alys found herself spending more and more
time with their kid brother. It was she, in fact, who convinced Lloyd
to go out into the world and make a name for himself.

Andrella grabbed Alys' other hand. "That's right," she declared.
"You and I are going to be best friends."

Alys beamed back at her. She could really use a confident right
now, and Andrella was more ladylike than Thea had ever been.

"If you ask me, she's an improvement over Elladan and Donnie,"
Seth called over from behind the bar. The halfling's approval caught
Alys by surprise, and everyone else for that matter.

"Seth, are you okay?" Aksel asked with feigned shock. "I can't
remember the last time you cared for anyone joining us."

"Hmph," Seth murmured as he picked up another glass to dry.
"At least she won't be hitting on every girl that goes by." The halfling's comment elicited laughter from the entire group.

Alys found herself warming up to all the members of this little
company. In truth, she wanted to help protect her city. In doing so,
she would be honoring Pallas, and as Lloyd said, she had already
proven herself in battle. She proved herself useful yet again when
Glo came downstairs with news from his seeress girlfriend.

The castle the elven wizard described sparked something in Alys'
memory—something that she had learned during her time at the
Bardic College in Lukescros. "That sounds a lot like the lost village
of Ravenar."

A single eyebrow rose on the tall elf's forehead. "Ravenar? I'm
not familiar with that one."

"It's an old legend about a town with a great crenellated castle like
the one you just described." Glo, Aksel, and Seth came and sat at the
table as Alys continued. "According to the legend, the castle is run by
a dark master—a fiend who feeds on people."

"Sounds about right." The corner of Seth's mouth turned upward.

Alys grinned at the halfling. She really liked his wicked sense of
humor.

Lloyd narrowed an eye at her. "How do you lose an entire village?"

Alys laughed. "That's the strangest part of the legend. Apparently, the entire town moves from place to place. It never stays in one spot for more than a few days."

Lloyd let out a soft whistle. "The entire town? What kind of magic would it take to teleport an entire town?"

"I'd hazard a guess it's not teleportation," Aksel mused as he stroked his chin.

Glo steepled his hands together in front of him. "Probably not. I'd say something more akin to plane shifting."

Andrella tapped her chin with a single finger. "Maybe through a dark plane?"

"That would make the most sense," Aksel said, with an approving nod.

Alys marveled at how quick they all were and how well their minds worked together. More and more she felt she was going to like working with these folks.

Aksel placed both hands on the table and swept his gaze across everyone seated there. "I'd suggest we go see the Baron immediately. I think we should take the fight to these vampires before this Ravenar moves again."

While Aksel went to request an impromptu audience with the Baron, the others split up on separate missions. Lloyd sought out his father, Andrella went to find Lara, and Alys ran to get Alburg. Thus, with Aillinn and Carenna already at the keep, they had already gathered a majority of the council.

In keeping with their previous dealings, Andrella did most of the talking. This time, it didn't take much to convince the council, though. Even Alburg saw the sense in a preemptive strike against this dangerous enemy. His only stipulation was that they did not leave Penwick undefended.

Carenna objected, but Kratos surprised them all when he declared, "I agree with Alburg."

Alburg cast a suspicious glance at his fellow councilman. "You do?"

"Yes, in fact," Kratos said, standing from his seat and leaning on the table. "That is why I'm going to lead this expedition myself."

Lloyd's jaw nearly dropped. With his responsibilities to the council, navy, and the academy, it had been years since his father led any kind of mission.

"We'll take the Remington," Kratos continued, "and since the Avenger is in port, I'll take her complement of spiritblades as well."

Lara stood and met her husband's gaze. "Well if you're going, so am I," she declared flatly, "and I'll bring some wizards from the school."

Caverinus sounded quite impressed. "That's very commendable of the both of you. I daresay we can trouble Sirus to provide us with a few of her priests and priestesses."

Though Lloyd was equally impressed, he saw a gaping hole in their strategy. Unable to contain himself, he also stood and spoke up. "Forgive me for interrupting, but we've fought this enemy before. I don't think a direct assault is quite going to work."

All eyes in the room turned toward Lloyd. He suddenly felt very uncomfortable, and gingerly rubbed the back of his head. "I mean, I'm just saying."

Kratos broke out into a wide grin. "No, no, you are correct in your assessment. What we're putting together is a strike group to act as a diversion…"

"…while we sneak into the castle and deal with the vampire lord and lady," Aksel finished for him.

"Exactly." Kratos gestured toward Aksel.

A sheepish smile spread across Lloyd's face. He should have known that his family and friends would already have a plan.

"How soon can you leave?" Caverinus asked anxiously. These vampires appeared to truly have the Baron spooked.

Kratos peered at Lara, that wordless communication passing between them that Lloyd had observed so often in the past. After a few seconds, his father returned his attention to the Baron. "I'd say we should be ready to depart by early this evening at the latest."

Aksel held some major concerns about what they might face in the town of Ravenar. If it indeed moved around as Alys described, who knew what manner of minions the vampire lord might have acquired during his travels. That pumpkin-headed creature, for example, was like nothing any of them had ever seen before. If they weren't prepared for what lay ahead, someone could end up dead, or worse.

Aksel had shut off his emotions after losing his family. Thus, he never had any close friends until he met Seth and Glo. Yet with that friendship came the possibility of once again losing people he cared about. Being the leader of this group further magnified his fears. The responsibility for keeping them all safe squarely laid upon his shoulders.

So after the council meeting, Aksel decided to personally go and confer with Sirus. She happened to be teaching at that moment, but due to the gravity of the situation, her assistant led him to the class. The instruction took place outdoors, beside the gazebo where the companions had gathered the day before. Aksel watched with keen interest as Sirus taught her students to manifest an aura of light. He had seen firsthand how effective that could be against undead.

As soon as the High Priestess saw him, she had her assistant take over for her. Sirus then strode over to meet him, her countenance grave. "Cleric Aksel. I understand you may have found the location of this vampire master and mistress."

Aksel responded with a grim nod. "We believe so. The Baron has sanctioned an assault on this 'roving town' while we know its current location. We are doing our best to plan for all contingencies, but with so little information, we don't know exactly what we'll be facing there."

"I see." Sirus motioned for him to follow her on a path leading away from the class. "Walk with me."

Aksel followed the High Priestess toward a garden area decorated with beautifully trimmed hedges and colorful flowers. Sirus continued their discussion as they went. "If it will help, I can send my assistant, Tran, with you. She is an auric priestess." She paused a moment and tapped her chin. "There is also Balor. He is an auric priest. Still, neither of them is battle-hardened like Thea."

Aksel grimaced. "That could be a problem. While they would certainly be helpful on the ship, I was hoping to have someone accompany us into the castle who could project that aura."

"That is a problem." Sirus' brow furrowed, deep creases forming across her forehead. After a few seconds, a glint appeared in her eyes. She clasped her hands together and pointed her fingers at Aksel. "I could teach you how we manifest an aura. Since you do not worship Arenor, it wouldn't be quite the same, but it might be worth a try."

Aksel peered around at the flowers and hedges, giving it some thought before answering. "If you have the time, I'm willing to try, but we are planning to leave by early this evening."

Sirus rolled up the sleeves of her robe. "Well then, we have our work cut out for us." The High Priestess went to inform her assistant of their plans, then led Aksel to her office for some intense private instruction.

A few hours later, an exhausted but satisfied Aksel left the temple. While he'd never be a Priest of Arenor, he could now manifest a holy aura in short bursts. Hopefully, that would be enough.

As anticipated, the Remington set out just before sundown. The airship appeared similar to a seafaring vessel, but there were no masts or sails visible above the deck. Instead, a bright blue ring of pulsing energy encircled the ship at the ends of three long fins near the aft. The hull, crafted from the sacred grove in Hagentree, kept the ship aloft, while the ring propelled it through the skies.

Aside from Tran and Balor, they had a full complement of spiritblades on board, as well as three wizards from the school of magic. Aksel stood at the prow of the ship as they swiftly left Penwick behind. Over the mountains to the west, the setting sun painted the sky a burnt orange. Though it seemed impossibly far from here, Kratos assured them that the journey would only take five to six hours.

Sirus had helped him to alleviate two of his major concerns: manifesting a holy aura and bringing along a total stranger. The 'stealth' team needed to be a well-knit group if they were going to survive this mission unscathed. As it stood, he was taking a chance allowing

Alys to join them. Still, Aksel had seen firsthand how effective her voice could be against vampires. The way he saw it, the debilitating effects made it well worth the risk.

"You look wound tighter than one of them Dunwynn turds in a crowd of elves."

Aksel nearly jumped out of his skin as Seth leaned up against the rail next to him. "Whoa. Next time a little warning, please?"

Seth let out an amused snort. "So, what's got your drawers all in a bunch?"

Aksel sighed, then explained to Seth all that had been weighing on his mind. When he finished, the corner of Seth's mouth lifted ever so slightly.

Aksel narrowed an eye at his friend. "Okay, what about that did you find amusing?"

"I was just thinking too bad Donnie wasn't with us. I wouldn't exactly mind losing him," Seth ended with a wicked grin.

Aksel's head began to ache. He grabbed his temples and rubbed them with his fingertips. "You're not helping, Seth."

"I wasn't trying," Seth said with little to no compunction, "but if you're that worried, why not just scout out the place first?"

Aksel fixed Seth with a questioning stare. "Are you offering?"

"Mmm," Seth murmured hesitantly, "I was thinking more you and Xellos. He's got those eagle eyes, and you were studying that spell to see through magical darkness."

Aksel pressed his lips together and nodded. "You have a point."

Seth grinned. "Yeah, I know. I'm a fricking genius."

"Now that doesn't look suspicious at all," Xellos whispered to Aksel.

The pair had left the Remington docked a few miles back and flown ahead in that smokey form they'd used in the crypts. With the aid of the light from a crescent moon, they discovered a small vale hidden beneath a layer of clouds at the base of the mountains. Despite the night winds that blew through the area, these clouds did not move at all.

"Let's take a closer look," Aksel told his non-corporeal companion.

This higher order version of the smoke spell allowed them to generate their own wind. They used that ability now to propel themselves closer to the mysterious vale. When they reached the edge, it became apparent that the dark clouds touched all the way to the ground.

Aksel descended to the edge of the vale and turned solid once more. The little cleric then traced a complex spell pattern through the air.

"*Verum Aspectu.*" As the words left his lips, the mana flowed from the pattern upward and into his eyes. There was a momentary flash of light, but when it cleared, Aksel found he could see right through the bank of dark clouds. A small village lay before them with a tall spiraling castle on one end, and a large structure like a fort on the other. Aksel relayed what he saw to Xellos, who now stood on the ground next to him.

"That fort sounds like it could be a problem," Xellos murmured.

Aksel had been thinking the same thing. "We should probably check it out."

The duo shifted back into their smoke forms, then Aksel led them into the dark clouds. Once they passed through the mists, the entire village became visible to normal eyes. Xellos took the lead now as they flew over the fort.

The large stone structure seemed different from the rest of the town, almost as if it had come from somewhere else entirely. A thick outside wall made up the bulk of the exterior. Tall domed towers stood at three of the corners, while a massive square bastion rose at the fourth. The domes and bastion were well lit, but the walls only sparsely so. Still, Aksel spied dark figures roaming the length of the parapets, far too many for his liking.

Xellos brushed up against him. "There's a crack in the roof of the nearest dome."

Aksel squinted and spotted the thin line to which Xellos referred. "Let's check it out."

The duo floated over to the dome. The crack ran up and down the curved roof for a length of about six feet, expanding to almost three inches in some spots. Aksel peeked through it and found he could see inside the dome.

Below him lay a huge round chamber. A large pedestal stood in its very center, with a statue upon it that looked like a dwarf. Wound around the pedestal itself was another statue, this one of a dragon. Aksel took a closer look at the dwarf's face. *That's Larketh!*

Aksel had seen a portrait of the Golem Thrall Master back at his monolith in the Darkwoods. This statue appeared to be the spitting image of him. As Aksel pondered the existence of the strange effigy, a set of double doors opened at the floor of the chamber. Three people entered the room: a man and woman garbed in robes, and a man decked out in full armor.

The woman carried in her hand a fist-sized glowing golden orb. The orb made a strange thrumming sound that the acoustics in the dome magnified. As they drew directly beneath them, Aksel got a better view of all three figures. Each wore the symbols of Amon and Cel, the Ralnai Lord of Darkness and Lady of Death. *These are most definitely not your virtuous type of clergy folk.*

Aksel watched with fascination as the priestess held out the glowing orb in front of the dragon statue. She pulled on the top and bottom of the orb, popping it open and turning it. As soon as she did so, the dragon's eyes opened and began to glow.

Mesmerized, Aksel looked on as the dragon unwound itself from the base of the pedestal. It put out its paw and lifted the priestess up to face the statue of Larketh.

"That's not disconcerting in the slightest," Xellos remarked.

His words roused Aksel from his trance. "I think we've seen enough. Let's go back and tell the others."

27
WORSHIPERS OF THE GOLEM MASTER

The chamber had a statue of the Golem Master
with a dragon at its base

Seth just wanted this whole thing to be over. This little journey of theirs combined two of the things he hated the most: vampires and being dragged all over the place. It was bad enough hunting vamps beneath Penwick, but now they had to chase them halfway across Thac? Seth started to wonder if he would ever get to retire at this rate.

Aksel and Xellos had been gone for almost an hour now. Seth kept watch at the prow of the ship and was the first to spot the twin clouds of smoke whisking their way back in their direction. He alerted the others just in time for them to gather as the duo reappeared on deck.

When Aksel reported what they found, it threw things into an uproar. The new girl, Alys, seemed to take the news personally, almost as if it were her fault. "But—but the legends never said anything about a fort."

"Tsk," Seth clicked his tongue. "Neither did Elistra, and she's supposed to be psychic."

As anticipated, his comment got a rise out of Glo. The wizard glared at him for touching on his precious seeress. "Maybe you want to go to the Marsh Tower and wrestle with that crystal?"

Seth met the elf's gaze with a deadpan stare. "I don't even want to be here."

Usually it was Aksel who broke up their bickering, but this time Lloyd's mom beat him to it. "Honestly, no one's perfect. We'll need to improvise based on this new information."

Even more surprising, Lloyd appeared deep in thought, and even asked a salient question. "You don't think that dragon can fly like a real one, do you?"

Seth just couldn't resist commenting. "With our luck, definitely."

Aksel gave him a sour look, but the usually quiet Xellos cut him off. "You know, there were two more towers just like the first."

Glo did that weird thing where one of his eyebrows rose up his forehead. "Are you saying those other towers might have similar statues in them?"

Xellos shrugged. "Wouldn't surprise me."

Lloyd's dad had been listening quietly to the entire discussion. He finally spoke up, making more sense than the lot of them. "I don't think we can take the chance. If that dragon can fly, it could easily damage this ship. If there are more than one, they'd tear us apart."

Seth wanted to applaud the man. Now here was someone with common sense.

Too bad Lloyd didn't inherit any of it. Instead, he stared at Kratos with clear disappointment. "You're not planning on giving up, are you, Dad?"

Kratos met Lloyd's gaze evenly. "I don't want to, son, but I have to think of the safety of everyone on board this ship."

Seth wanted to shout with glee. He thought for certain they'd turn around and head back at that point, but then Andrella stuck in her two bits. The fledgling wizard absently tapped her chin as she spoke. "I think it would be okay if we could just get our hands on that golden orb…"

"...and hope that's the only one," Seth added pointedly. Back in the ruins on Stone Hill, they found two of Larketh's golems, each controlled by a plain gold ring.

Seth experienced a brief pang of sorrow. After obtaining the rings, they had managed to take control of one of the golems. Seth had even affectionately named it 'The Boulder.' It had been destroyed, however, when Dunwynn invaded Ravenford. To this day, Seth still missed the big stone guy.

"Still, Andrella has a point," Aksel said, furiously tugging his chin. Seth silently shook his head. He knew where this was going, and it certainly wasn't back to Penwick.

Having made up his mind, Aksel rubbed his hands together. "So new plan. The stealth team goes to the fort first. We get that orb and also check out the other towers."

Kratos gave him a curt nod. "Very well. Once you've grounded those dragons, signal us and we'll come in with the Remington."

Seth wanted to scream. Even Lloyd's dad had lost his mind. Well, if no one else was going to say it, Seth most certainly would. "Sure. Easy peasy. What could possibly go wrong?"

Less than half an hour later, the 'stealth' team, now all in smoke form, hung over the dome with the crack in its roof. Unfortunately, there was no one in the chamber below.

Almost as unfortunate, Seth could still hear Glo's voice, thanks to those damn brooches he had passed out to everyone in the group. *"Maybe they moved on to one of the other towers?"* It wasn't the worst idea the wizard ever had, but Seth certainly wasn't going to tell him that. Glo had a big enough ego as it stood.

They all followed Aksel over to the next tower, taking care to stay out of the lights coming from the yard below. When they got there, Aksel used a spell to shape a small hole in the roof. As they feared, the chamber had a statue of the Golem Master with a dragon at its base. Still, there was no sign of the dark clergy.

"Third time's a charm?" Andrella thought, rather unconvincingly.

"There's nothing charming about this situation," Seth thought wryly.

Once again, they all fell in behind Aksel as he floated over to the last dome. Aksel created a hole in this roof as well, and they all peered inside. Sure enough, there stood yet another statue of the Golem Master with a dragon.

If Seth still had a head, he would have shaken it. *"Wonderful. There's three of them."*

The priestess Aksel previously described stood at the statue's base, flanked by the priest and cleric in fullplate.

"Along with the unholy trinity," Glo pointed out.

Under other circumstances, Seth might have laughed.

"If we're lucky, they'll have all three control orbs on them," Aksel commented. Even in this form, Seth could hear how skeptical he sounded.

"Only one way to find out," Lloyd remarked, filtering through the hole and into the chamber below. Everyone else followed suit until only Seth remained behind.

"I still think this is a bad idea," Seth declared before finally trailing after the others.

They all followed Aksel down to the opposite side of the statue from the dark trio. On Aksel's mark, everyone turned solid.

Seth immediately went invisible and fanned out in a wide arc around the statue. Xellos and Aksel went in the same direction, while the others circled around the other side, with Lloyd in the lead.

All of a sudden, one of the men cried out, "We've got company!"

The priestess' shrill voice echoed across the chamber, "Hold them off!"

Lloyd had just come into view when the priest cast a spell on the tall warrior. Two glowing blue bands surrounded Lloyd's body, immobilizing him in place. At the same time, the man in armor cast a spell upon himself. His body seemed to separate in two, the twin images slightly overlapping each other.

Suddenly, a pair of arrows whizzed by Seth. They headed directly for the priestess, but bounced off some invisible barrier about a foot away from her body. The priestess completely ignored them, raising the golden orb in her hand in front of the face of the dragon statue.

A chill ran up Seth's spine as the dragon's eyes snapped open. A dull glow emanated from them, growing brighter by the second. If someone didn't do something fast, they'd all be in deep trouble.

Seth started for the priestess when he felt the tingle of magic pass over him. The air before him suddenly stirred and whipped up into a huge cone of wind. The cone swiftly bore down on the priestess and swept her up into its vortex. It dragged her across the room, far away from the dragon statue.

Seth breathed a sigh of relief as the dragon's eyes abruptly went dark.

Andrella's heart lurched in her chest when the evil priest froze Lloyd in place. Thankfully Glo reacted immediately, unfreezing him with a counterspell.

The moment Lloyd could move again, he launched himself at the heavily armored cleric. Unfortunately, his blades just passed through the man's strange double image.

Andrella had heard of this before. It was a sort of glamour, an illusion making the person extremely hard to hit. She flinched as the huge man swung back at Lloyd with a large two-handed blade, but thankfully her nimble fiancé tumbled out of the way.

Determined to help, Andrella pulled in her will and traced out a simple but effective spell that never missed its target. "*Nullam Telum.*" Three glowing purple projectiles leapt from her fingertips and arced across the room, directly for the armored man.

Thud. Thud. Thud. All three projectiles slammed into her target, each with a concussive force that momentarily stunned the man.

Just when she thought she had evened the odds, the priest stepped forward, pulled a green orb from his robes, and slammed it into the ground. Magic erupted from the glowing orb, in the form of translucent skeletal heads with long, wild white hair. Those heads swept across the room in a wide circle, each uttering a piercing scream of dread horror.

Andrella suddenly felt very sick. It quickly worsened, driving her to her knees. She felt like her entire insides were going to leap out of her throat. Just when she thought she was going to burst, Alys stepped in front of her.

A loud cry erupted from the singer's throat to match the screams of the wailing heads. It rose in power, driving back the sickness that had overwhelmed Andrella. A few seconds later, the skeletal heads faded away. Alys halted her retaliatory scream and cast a glance over her shoulder. "Are you alright?"

Still feeling a bit queasy, Andrella managed a weak smile. "I think so."

"Good," Alys said, staring off to one side, "because I don't think your wizard friend fared quite that well."

Andrella followed Alys' gaze to a purple and flaxen heap just a few yards away. A shiver ran up Andrella's spine. "Glo!" The tall elf had been caught by that wailing attack without the benefits of Alys' sonic shield. He now lay on the ground unmoving.

Andrella grabbed the brooch on her chest and screamed with her mind. *"Aksel! Glo's down!"*

"Where?" came the little cleric's immediate reply.

"Over by me and Alys," Andrella responded.

"Be right there," Aksel assured her.

His words allayed her fears for the moment, but they immediately returned as Alys pointed out a new danger. "Watch out! That cleric is casting a spell."

Andrella watched with growing trepidation as the heavily armored figure invoked an incantation. Three shadowy wraith-like figures emerged from the floor directly in front of him. The shadows floated across the chamber, heading directly for Alys and Andrella.

As soon as Aksel got the message about Glo, he took off around the back of the statue. As he went, the spritely gnome issued one last command to the elemental he had summoned. A moment later, the wind-born creature flung the priestess from its vortex. The disoriented woman sailed across the chamber, slamming into the wall on the opposite side of the room.

Meanwhile, the priest and cleric were preoccupied trying to hold off a frenzied Lloyd. The young man moved like a second whirling dervish, avoiding both of their attacks and striking back at the heavily armored man from different angles. Unfortunately, none of his blows landed.

As Aksel came out from behind the statue, he witnessed a frightening sight. Three wraith-like figures bore down on Andrella and Alys. Alys retaliated with a howling scream that visibly slowed the creatures' advance. Andrella then shot one of the wraiths with a sizzling ray of fire. Less than a second later, a pair of arrows streaked down from above and miraculously embedded themselves into the creature's shadow-like form.

The wraith threw its head back, its mouth hanging open in a silent scream. A moment later, its body evaporated in a dark puff of smoke.

Aksel stopped following the battle at that point. He had reached Glo and frantically ran his hands over the elf's body.

Aksel breathed a thankful sigh. Glo was still alive. With a brief prayer, white light surged from the little cleric's palms, bathing his friend in potent healing energies.

Glo woke up to a sudden scream. Across the room, the priest who felled him clutched desperately at his back. The diminutive form of Seth stood behind the dark-robed figure, dagger still in hand and a wicked smile on his lips.

Glo exhaled a thin laugh. "How many casters does that make that Seth has slain?"

Aksel shrugged. "Honestly, I've lost count." He peered intently into Glo's eyes. "How do you feel?"

That was a very good question. Glo had been hit with a horrific spell designed to kill anyone in its path. By all rights he should have been dead, yet other than a slight case of nausea, he actually felt fine.

Glo deftly rose to his feet. "Surprisingly well for someone who just heard the *Wail of the Banshees*. Speaking of wails…"

Alys and Andrella stood completely unharmed just a few yards away, the former holding off a pair of wraiths with her sonic cry. Glo marveled at the power of the young lady's voice. It had somehow negated the dark priest's deadly spell, even saving Glo from the worst of its effects.

Abruptly everything in the room went dark. Glo could feel the presence of magic in the sudden cloak of darkness. He began a pattern to counter the spell, but stopped when Aksel beat him to it.

"*Solis.*"

The mana from the cleric's spell rushed forth through the cloak of darkness. It coalesced somewhere above, forming into a sizable ball of magic. The darkness fled from the light of that ball, the entire chamber now flooded with its brilliant rays.

Glo's eyes immediately focused on the double doors to the chamber. One of them now hung open, the tail end of the priestess' robes disappearing from sight on the other side.

Glo immediately bolted after her, preparing a dangerous spell as he ran. It was risky, but he had to try. They needed that golden orb—*orbs*, he corrected himself—or their entire mission was for naught.

Reaching the door, Glo ran out and saw the priestess already far into the yard ahead of him. Her cries rang out as she tried to alert the fort to the intruders. No one seemed to have noticed her as of yet, but they were quickly running out of time. Leveling a finger at the priestess, he held his breath as he invoked the spell, praying that he had gotten the complicated pattern right.

"*Adiuuatur.*" A thin, green ray lanced from his finger across the yard and struck the retreating priestess square in the back. A strangled cry escaped her lips as her body vaporized before his eyes. Only a few wisps of smoke remained where the priestess had once stood.

The golden orb she had been holding fell to the ground and rolled back in Glo's direction. He might have caught it, except for the sharp pain that abruptly lanced up his arm.

Glo grabbed his wrist and peered at his hand. The entire thing looked badly burnt. The spell had partially backfired on him after all. In fact, he was lucky to be alive.

While Glo was preoccupied with his hand, the orb rolled right past him, back toward the open doorway.

Seth felt a keen sense of satisfaction after stabbing the dark priest. The lousy bastard had nearly killed his friends with that damned green orb.

Now what? Seth wondered as he surveyed the battlefield. Lloyd seemed to be getting nowhere against that cleric. Unfortunately, Seth's daggers would have little effect on that heavy armor.

Those wraiths, however, were another matter. Alys' cry had slowed their advance, but she had already used it to counter that death spell. Though she valiantly tried to hold them off, her voice had begun to crack.

His mind made up, Seth quietly advanced on the wraiths. The darkness did little to deter him, but it was immediately countered anyway with a ball of *Sunlight*. Intent on his prey, Seth ignored Glo as the tall wizard sprinted past him.

A moment later, Andrella let loose an impressive bolt of lightning. Thunder rolled across the chamber as the deadly spell ended one of the two remaining wraiths. At the same time, two arrows whizzed down from above, embedding themselves into the last wraith's shadowy form. Seeing that it was semi-solid, Seth whipped his own dagger at the creature's back.

The dagger landed with a satisfying *thwack*, causing the creature to arch its head toward the sky in pain. Its silent death knell was punctuated by the creature exploding in a puff of black smoke.

The only adversary now left standing was that armored cleric. Seth practically snorted with glee as Aksel rammed his wind elemental into him. Caught off guard, the cleric was stunned.

Lloyd took advantage of the situation to use one of those crazy spiritblade techniques. He paused a few moments, his pupils growing abnormally large before launching a particularly devastating blow. Lloyd's black blade hit its mark this time, cleaving the dark cleric practically in two. The armored figure fell to the ground with a resounding clatter and laid there unmoving.

Seth put his hands on his hips and glared at Lloyd. "Why didn't you just do that in the first place?"

Lloyd's reply came out in gasps as he caught his breath. "That one—takes a bit—longer."

Andrella swept her gaze around the chamber, her brow furrowing. "Where's Glo?"

Aksel's eyes widened with sudden recollection. "He went after the priestess!"

They all vaulted for the door, but Seth paused to cast a quick spell. *"Tempore Duplo."* Moving twice as fast as normal, Seth blew by the others and reached the open doorway first. He came to a halt just outside as a familiar-looking golden orb rolled up right to his feet.

Seth bent and picked up the orb while gazing around the courtyard. The dark priestess nowhere to be seen. Glo stood there all alone, nursing his charbroiled hand.

Seth practically chortled with glee as the others emptied out of the chamber. "That's what you get for playing with fire."

Glo glared daggers back at him. "It wasn't a fire spell."

Seth juggled the golden orb in his hand as Aksel went to heal Glo. "Well, hopefully this was worth it."

All of a sudden, the roof behind them burst open and a huge stone dragon went flying up into the night sky, turning east in the direction of the waiting Remington. A few moments later, the other two domes burst, those dragons following the first.

Seth turned his gaze upon Aksel with a deadpan stare. "Guess I spoke too soon."

28
STONE DRAGONS

The fracture erupted into a jagged rift that stretched in front of the three dragons

Andrella watched in horror as the three stone dragons burst forth from the domed roofs of the surrounding fort. This was her fault. It was she who suggested capturing the golden orb in the first place. Yet she had been dreadfully wrong about it stopping the dragons. Now the people on the Remington would pay the ultimate price—including Lloyd's parents!

Frantic, Andrella turned to Glo, but he seemed to be paying no attention to what just happened. "Glo!" she cried, tugging anxiously at his robes. "Don't just stand there. We need to do something!"

Glo fixed her with an intent stare. "I just did. I warned Lara about what was coming, and told them to get out of here."

Embarrassed, Andrella let go of him and tried to flatten his robes where she creased them. "Sorry. I forgot you set up a telepathic bond with her before we left."

"So now what, geniuses?" Seth stood with his arms folded, staring accusingly around the group. "Are we just stuck here in vampireville?"

Seth brought up a good point. What were they going to do? A sudden idea came to Andrella. She tapped Glo on the arm. "What if we portal to the ship?"

Glo shook his head. "It's too far for a portal spell."

Andrella gave him a sour look. "I know that. I meant a chain of portals."

"A chain of portals?" Glo repeated, arching an eyebrow. "That just might work."

"Well, whatever we do, we better do it soon," Xellos said, his eyes fixed on the yard behind them.

Andrella followed his gaze and nearly jumped out of her skin. A sea of red eyes had appeared throughout the yard, the nearest headed their way. Gulping, Andrella steeled her resolve. "Guess it's now or never."

The young lady focused her will and opened a portal in the air before them. Everyone leapt through, with Lloyd and Andrella going last. When they got to the other side, they were in the woods and Glo had already opened the next portal.

"You first," Glo told her.

Andrella leapt through, with Lloyd right behind her. She immediately began to open the next one. They kept this up a few more times, crossing the forest in a matter of minutes.

Andrella had just started to feel exhausted when they caught sight of the Remington in the night sky. The ship had turned around and was just getting underway.

"Hurry!" she encouraged Glo, but the elf had already opened the next portal. Andrella immediately leapt through and forced herself to cast one more spell. It was rough going, but she put everything she had left into it.

As soon as the blue oval opened in the air before them, Lloyd lifted her into his arms and charged through. The two of them spilled out onto the deck of the Remington in the middle of a mixture of surprised spiritblades and crew.

Lloyd threw his hands up in the air and cried, "It's just us!"

"Everyone hold your positions!" Kratos' deep voice rang out across the deck.

Moments later, after the last of them came through, Andrella flicked her wrist and closed the portal. Glo, looking as exhausted as she, leaned on his knees and grinned at her. "That was—exhilarating."

"Yeah, not too shabby," Seth admitted begrudgingly.

Andrella feigned shock. "A compliment from Seth? Whatever is the world coming to?"

"Hmph," Seth muttered. "Don't let it go to your head."

"We've got fliers to the stern!" a voice cried from the lookout, halfway up the vertical fin.

Everyone flocked to the rear of the ship. Off in the distance, the light of the moon glinted off three V-shaped figures. In the short time Andrella watched, they appeared to grow larger. "They're closing fast!" she cried in dismay.

Glo shook his head. "They're traveling at top speed. There's no way we can outrun them."

"Prepare for battle!" Kratos bellowed out the order.

While the crew got ready for the upcoming fight, the rest of them anxiously watched the approaching dragons. Lloyd moved closer to Andrella and wrapped his arms around her.

"We'll get through this," he said encouragingly. She knew he meant it, but was still not sure how.

Andrella wracked her brain for something they could use against these dragons. She reached over and tugged Glo's sleeve as a thought occurred to her. "Do you think they have breath weapons like real dragons?"

As Glo mulled over her question, Lara put in her two bits. "The Golem Master had never been known for doing things halfway. So my best guess would be yes."

"But we still have weapons and spells that travel over farther distances," Andrella insisted.

"True," Glo answered this time, "but remember—these aren't just dragons. These are golems. Most spells won't work against them, and arrows wouldn't hurt them, either."

Andrella let out a forlorn sigh. "You're right, of course." She knew as well as he that golems were immune to most forms of magic.

"Still, we've fought golems before and won," Lloyd reminded them.

Glo let out a nervous laugh. "Also true."

"I think there are riders on those dragons," Xellos suddenly burst out.

Everyone peered intently at the closing figures. "He's right," Seth confirmed a moment later.

"They're probably vampires…" Aksel surmised.

"…which means the sun is our best chance at the moment," Lara murmured, peering behind them.

Andrella followed Lara's gaze. Ahead of them to the east, the horizon was beginning to show signs of the day to come. Andrella felt a momentary spark of elation—but would it be in time, and would the dragons stop for their riders?

Lara seemed to think so. Her mother-in-law-to-be leaned over and whispered to Alys. A moment later, the singer's voice boomed out across the deck. "Admiral Stealle! Take us up as high as we can get!"

Lloyd's father, now by the wheel, glanced back over his shoulder. He looked from Alys to Lara, then gave them both a firm nod. "You heard the lady, take us up!" he barked at the navigator.

The deck of the ship slanted backwards as the Remington veered on an upward trajectory. Andrella cast a glance behind them and saw the dragons following suit. They were getting closer now, nearly in bow range by her best estimation.

The Remington continued its desperate climb, with the dragons continuing to close. At the same time, off to the east, the horizon grew brighter and brighter.

The wizards from the magic school began casting spells at the oncoming dragons. A barrage of purple projectiles and bolts of lightning leapt from their hands, but they seemed to have little effect on their targets.

"Hold off," Lara ordered them. "I'll tell you when and what to try." The three stared at the head wizard, quite obviously embarrassed.

The dragons had drawn so close now that Andrella could clearly see the red of their riders' eyes. "They're nearly in breath range," Glo announced. As if in response to his statement, two of the dragons opened their maws. Andrella could see sparks of electricity at the back of the one creature's throat while a liquid bubbled in the other's.

"Lightning and acid," Andrella murmured nervously.

Lloyd drew her protectively to his chest as the dragons seemed ready to strike. All of a sudden, a shaft of light shot across the sky. Andrella pushed away from Lloyd and stared out at the horizon. The top edge of the glowing sun had just peeked over its edge, flooding the sky with its brilliant light and pushing back upon the darkness.

Cheers rang out across the deck. Andrella turned back toward the stern and saw the dragons had fallen back. Orbs of darkness suddenly appeared, engulfing both rider and dragon alike. The three dark orbs backed off to a distance of about thirty yards, and from there paced the Remington.

Andrella let out a deep sigh. They were safe—for now, at least.

Aksel's stomach was tied in knots. Their entire plan had been blown to shreds. Not only had they missed the opportunity to end the vampire lord, but they had nearly lost everyone he cared about in the process.

The fault lay squarely on his shoulders. He should have realized just how slim a chance they had of succeeding. Yet now wasn't the time for blame. They were in an untenable situation and needed a way out that didn't risk everyone on board.

At least everyone's spirits had risen. Andrella beamed at Lara. "I think you saved us."

"For now," Lara agreed, mirroring Aksel's thoughts. "Still, we're not safe just yet. They'll resume their attack once night has fallen."

"What if we just head back to Penwick?" Alys asked, as if it were the obvious thing to do.

Lloyd fielded her question. "I'd hate to think what those things could do to the city if we lead them back there."

An embarrassed smile crossed Alys' lips. "I guess I didn't think of that."

While they'd been talking, an idea began to brew in the back of

Aksel's mind. He waved Xellos over from the rail. "Do you think you could hit those orbs from here?"

Xellos gazed at the trailing globes of darkness as if measuring a shot, then shrugged. "Sure."

Glo met Aksel's gaze, his eyes filled with curiosity. "What exactly do you have in mind?"

Aksel walked back to the rail and leaned over it as he answered. "Have you ever heard of a light arrow?"

"Only in fairy tales," Lara answered before Glo had the chance.

Aksel wore a sly smile as he glanced between her and Glo. "Well, I think I might have a way to bring that 'fairy tale' to life."

"Oh, this I've got to see," Seth said, folding his arms.

Aksel had Xellos take out three of his arrows and cast the *Sunlight* spell upon each of them. The arrowheads glowed with a brilliance to match that of the rising sun.

"Amazing," Andrella cooed.

"Quite clever," Lara agreed.

"Indeed," Glo added.

"If it works," Seth pointed out.

"Let's find out," Xellos replied as he nocked one of the arrows and drew his bowstring. The expert archer adjusted his aim three times before letting the first arrow fly. He then fired the other two in rapid succession.

Aksel held his breath as the shafts sailed across the skies toward the dark orbs. As the first arrow pierced the leading orb, the darkness abruptly popped out of existence. A moment later, the other arrows hit their marks with similar results.

The vampires, now exposed to the sun, swiftly went up in flames. All three dragons were now left riderless. Still, they continued to follow the Remington.

"So that worked," Seth admitted with a begrudging shrug, "but there's one thing I don't get."

Aksel narrowed an eye at his friend. "What's that?"

Seth pointed his thumb over the rail at the trailing dragons. "Since those vamps are gone, why are they still hanging back?"

"They're still following the last order they were given," Glo answered before Aksel had a chance to think.

"So," Seth drawled, "what if that last command was 'hang back and follow the airship'?"

Aksel mulled that over for a moment. He wasn't exactly an expert when it came to golems, but he did have some previous experience commanding 'The Boulder.' "I'd say we can't take that chance. The last command could have been a bit more complicated: something like, 'hang back and follow until dark, then attack the airship.'"

"That's quite plausible," Lara agreed.

"So what do we do now?" Alys asked pensively. Up until now, she had listened silently to the conversation, but Aksel had the distinct feeling she wasn't used to being quiet.

"If you retrieved that golden orb, I could take a look at it," Lara offered.

Seth had hung onto the orb since they left Ravenar behind. He now pulled it out of his portal bag and proffered it to Lara. After a cursory examination, she determined it required an invocation to the dark Ralnai god, Amon. Therefore, it was of little use to them.

With no idea of what to do next, Aksel leaned against the rail and stared at the three dragons trailing behind them. The others lined up on either side of him, all watching the dragons as well. Aksel lost track of time until Lara finally broke the silence.

"There is something I could try," she said, gently tapping her chin, "but there's no guarantee it would work.

"What is it?" Andrella asked, a glimmer of hope in her eyes.

"I could open a rift to another plane in front of the dragons," Lara answered hesitantly. "The only problem is I'm not sure how big I can make it. It might not catch all of them."

Andrella's brow kneaded into a frown. "Couldn't you just cast it again?"

"It's a seventh-order spell," Glo explained. "Between the complicated pattern and amount of mana it would require, I'd daresay Lara could only cast it once—maybe twice, at most."

Lara patted the tall elf affectionately on the hand. "Once, Glolindir, but I do appreciate your confidence in me."

Aksel tried to think of another option, but nothing really came to mind. "If you're willing, I think it's worth a try," he told her.

Lara took a deep breath, then motioned for everyone to stand back. "Very well, let's see what this old girl can still do." The pattern Lara traced through the air seemed far more complicated than anything Aksel had witnessed before. Furthermore, the amount of mana she poured into it made his hair stand on end.

"*Planum Rima.*"

When Lara finally released the spell, he could practically feel the vast amount of mana whooshing through the air toward the dragons. It coalesced directly in front of the lead one, fracturing the very sky. Lara snapped her hands out in front of her and made a separating motion with them. The fracture erupted into a jagged rift that stretched in front of the three dragons.

A deep, unsettling blackness peered out from that rupture. Aksel found it difficult to stare at, as if the very essence of that plane were the antithesis of life in this one. Sweat poured from Lara's brow and her arms shook as she struggled to hold open the rift.

"Look!" Xellos cried all of a sudden.

A winged figure appeared on either end of the rupture. It was two of the stone dragons! They had swerved in time to avoid the rift.

Her outstretched arms shaking uncontrollably, Lara finally let go. The rupture slammed shut, disappearing without a trace. The lead dragon now gone, the other two fell back in formation.

Lara let out a heavy sigh. "Sorry I couldn't make it bigger."

Lloyd put an arm around his mother. "It's okay, Mom. You did great…"

"…and now there's one less dragon," Andrella added with an encouraging smile.

With two dragons still on their tail, Aksel returned to his brooding. Glo, Andrella, Lloyd, Alys, and Lara had all gone below to rest. Aksel should have joined them as well, but didn't think he could sleep at the moment.

The sun had been up for almost an hour when they passed the eastern edge of the Darkwoods. The plains beyond stretched as far as the eye could see, following the Penderbun all the way to the eastern horizon. The flat land sparked an idea in Aksel's mind. It would be risky, and they'd need to test something first, but it just might work.

Aksel went to propose his idea to Kratos. A short while later, the Remington slowed and came to a full stop. As Aksel suspected, the dragons maintained their distance.

Aksel absently stroked his chin. "Well, at least we know that part will work."

"Tsk, I still think you're nuts," Seth said, clicking his tongue derisively.

Aksel met his friend's gaze evenly. "If you have a better idea, I'm open to suggestions."

Seth threw his hands up in front of him. "Not my problem if you want to get yourself killed."

Glo felt exhausted. That frantic portal-hopping stunt had done both him and Andrella. Lara, also feeling drained, guided them, along with Lloyd and Alys, to staterooms below decks. Glo now sat on his bed, ready to fall into a deep trance, when he heard his name.

Glo?

That sounded like... *Elistra?*

His response was met with a mirthful laugh. *How many other people talk to you in your head?*

More than I'd care to admit, Glo sighed.

We'll have to have a chat about your sanity when we get a chance, Elistra chided him playfully, *but for now, we have bigger problems.*

Oh, like what? Glo asked, suddenly wide awake.

Like the energies flowing around that castle. If I'm reading them right, they seem to indicate it will be moving again shortly, Elistra responded.

Glo felt a sinking feeling in the pit of his stomach. *When?*

There was a slight pause before she answered. *My best guess would be around sundown.*

That sinking feeling turned into a chill up his spine. *What are the odds it'll show up in Penwick?*

I'd say pretty good, Elistra responded grimly.

Glo got up from his bed. *I should go and tell the others. Talk later?*

You can count on it, Elistra promised.

As Glo traversed the ship's corridors, he felt the Remington come to a stop. Lara came out of her stateroom, as did Lloyd, Andrella, and Alys.

"Why'd we stop?" Alys asked Lloyd.

Lloyd shrugged. "I don't know." He turned to Lara. "Mom?"

Lara shook her head, her expression puzzled. "I don't know, either. Let's go and ask your father." She led the way up to the main deck, the rest of them trailing close behind. When they got there, they found Kratos with Aksel and Seth gathered around the ship's wheel.

As they drew up to them, Glo distinctly heard Seth say, "Not my problem if you want to get yourself killed."

Lara repeated the question on all their minds, to which Andrella added, "...and who's getting themselves killed?"

Aksel let out a brief sigh, then explained his idea on how to get rid of the stone dragons. Glo thought it over for a few moments, then gave Aksel a grave nod. "I'd say, let's give it a try."

Andrella folded her arms, her eyes shifting from Glo to Aksel. "Well, I agree with Seth. You're both crazy..."

Alys wrapped her arm around the young lady. "...and I agree with Andrella."

Glo peered at both ladies with a wan smile. "Unfortunately, I don't think we have much choice." He swiftly repeated what Elistra told him. When he finished, a dark cloud hung over them all.

Alys in particular was quite distraught. Her eyes filled with tears as she peered at Lara. "We have to do something! I promised Pallas we'd look after the city while he was gone."

It was now Andrella's turn to wrap her arms around Alys. Lara then grabbed the distressed young lady by the hands. "We will, dear, I promise," she cooed softly.

Kratos wore a grim expression. "We don't have much time. If we head back now, we should reach Penwick just before dark."

Glo had assumed as much; his mind had already jumped ahead to Aksel's plan. "It would have to be high enough to work..." he mused aloud.

"...but not so high as to get you both killed," Lara added, her eyes filled with grave concern.

The two of them put their heads together and calculated the optimal height to execute Aksel's plan. Once they agreed, they told Kratos. Kratos had the navigator bring the ship to that height. The dragons followed as anticipated.

Meanwhile, Glo, Aksel, and Andrella prepared themselves. The three of them lined up at the stern with everyone else gathered around. Once the Remington came to a stop, Kratos joined them.

"We're ready," he announced in a grim voice.

Andrella's face had gone ghastly white. "I just hope you two know what you're doing." Without another word, she hugged Glo and then Aksel.

Lloyd placed a hand on Glo's shoulder. "I wish I could go in your place."

Glo gave him a weak smile. "So do I."

"I still think you're nuts," Seth said to Aksel. The corner of his mouth upturned slightly, but his eyes softened. "Just try not to die."

"I'll try," Aksel replied.

Alys, having composed herself, gave them both a reassuring smile. "Let me see if I can bolster the both of you." She hummed a soft tune, her song laced with magic.

Glo felt his tiredness fade somewhat. He attempted a warm smile in return, though his voice cracked as his nerves got the best of him. "Thank you, Alys."

Andrella met his gaze with a solemn nod, then the both of them began to trace familiar patterns through the air. Once the patterns had filled with mana, they released their spells in unison. "*Planum porta.*"

Two shimmering blue ovals appeared in the air before them. At the same time, accompanying blue ovals appeared in the air above each of the hovering dragons.

Glo and Aksel nodded to one another, then each jumped through a portal. A moment later, Glo appeared on the back of a stone dragon. The dragon didn't seem to notice him, but Glo took no chances. He immediately began to cast his next spell.

Still feeling somewhat tired, Glo struggled to complete the complicated pattern, but in the end he managed to finish it. Mana flowed into it, then rushed outward in all directions as he released the spell with the words, "*Resigno Magicae.*"

The mana created a bubble around him ten yards in all directions, sucking all the magical energy out of it. Below him, the stone dragon abruptly went still. Its wings stopped beating and it began to drop toward the ground far below.

Glo hung on for dear life, his only chance depending on the stone dragon taking the brunt of the fall. Time seemed to slow. Glo peered up at the Remington. Half the friends he had made were up there. The rest were probably somewhere over the sea, on their way to Lanfor.

Below him, the ground drew closer.

He thought of his mother back in Cairthrellon. She'd have a heart attack if she saw what he was doing now. He thought of his father. He'd have berated Glo for not finding a better solution.

The ground below was coming up fast.

A pair of violet eyes appeared in his mind. The face behind them was perhaps the most beautiful he had ever seen. He hoped to the gods he got a chance to see it once more—touch it once more.

Glo braced himself as they were about to hit. He thought he saw a flash of violet, but then there was a huge *thud* as the stone dragon gave out beneath him. The air was knocked from his lungs and everything went black.

29
SPHERE OF DARKNESS

*A huge spinning sphere of darkness appeared over
the Old Graveyard*

The world around Glo appeared fuzzy when he first opened his eyes. A blurry blonde head hovered over him at the edge of his eyesight.

"Elistra?" he croaked, his throat incredibly dry.

His query was met with a shy giggle. "Not exactly—but I'm just as relieved as she would be to see you awake." The woman bent down and hugged him. Dull aches and pains wracked his body as she did so.

"Th-thanks," Glo managed, trying not to flinch.

The woman immediately let go. "I'm sorry. I should have realized you'd still be sore."

"It's alright," Glo assured her. He sat up and blinked until his vision finally cleared. They were in a stateroom. Andrella stood staring at him with obvious relief. He shook the cobwebs out of his head. "What did I miss? Did we destroy the dragons?"

Andrella sat down on the bed next to him and placed her hand over his. "We did, in fact. They each broke into over a dozen pieces after slamming into the ground." She said it without any emotion, as if reporting an everyday occurrence.

Glo narrowed an eye at the young woman. "Isn't that a good thing? Why don't you sound very enthused?"

"Because you and Aksel scared the hell out of us!" she cried, smacking him across the arm. Glo winced from the mild strike, his body still sore from his ordeal. Andrella stood and paced around the small room, her hands waving around frantically as she went on. "You two were a mess. Thank the gods Tran and Balor were able to heal you, but you've been out cold for hours."

Behind the anger, Glo could see the real concern in her eyes. "I'm truly sorry for putting you through all that."

"Not just me," Andrella corrected him. "Everyone was worried. Lloyd and I have been taking turns watching over you, while Seth wouldn't leave Aksel's side."

Glo's eyebrows shot up his forehead. *Seth watching over Aksel? Would wonders never cease?*

"How is Aksel?" he asked aloud.

Andrella walked over and gazed out the porthole. The sky still shone a bright blue, though Glo had no idea the time of day. "He woke up a short while ago. He came in here to check on you first, then went to see how things were progressing."

Everything Elistra had told him about Ravenar came rushing back to Glo at once. "That's right!" he cried, throwing off the covers and swinging his feet over the edge of the bed. "So, where do things stand?"

Andrella strode back toward him and made a staying motion with her hands. "Things are moving along just fine without you at the moment. Lara, Kratos, and the clerics have been in contact with the folks in Penwick. They know what's coming and are mobilizing the city forces as we speak."

Glo responded with a closemouthed laugh. "I should have known you'd all have things well in hand."

"Exactly," Andrella said in a tone a mother would use with a wayward child. "So you just worry about recovering your strength. We're going to need it once we arrive in Penwick."

"Yes, ma'am!" Glo grinned and gave her a mock salute.

Andrella stuck her tongue out at him in response. With the tension broken, they both broke out into full-bellied laughter. Once it died down, he remembered what she had said about him being out cold for hours.

Glo narrowed an eye at her. "So what time is it, exactly?"

Andrella cocked her head to one side and pursed her lips. "A couple of hours before sundown. According to Kratos, we should be arriving in Penwick in an hour or so."

The news startled Glo. It had been before noon when they took care of the dragons. If that were true, then he had been out cold for at least six hours, if not more. The thought of the dragons brought something else to the forefront of Glo's mind. "By the way, just before we hit the ground, did you notice a flash of light?"

Andrella peered up at the ceiling and tapped a finger to her chin. "No—can't say that I did. We were still far away, though." She eyed him quizzically. "What did you see?"

"I'm not sure." Glo shook his head. The violet color he had seen, however, made him think of Elistra. He felt the sudden urge to check on her. He gazed at Andrella tentatively. "Could you give me a few minutes?"

Andrella met his gaze with a warm smile. "Of course. Take all the time you need. I'll let the others know that you're okay." She leaned over and kissed him on the cheek, then left the stateroom, closing the door behind her.

Glo took a few moments to clear his mind, then called out to Elistra. Strangely, there was no answer. He tried again. *Elistra!*

Glo? Her reply sounded strangely weak.

Are you alright? He asked, suddenly worried.

Drained, she responded. *I tried protecting you and Aksel—but it took everything I had.*

Glo now felt more worried than before. *Will you be okay? Do you need me to come there?*

There was a short pause before she answered. *I'll be fine. Just… need… to rest.* She sounded as if she were drifting off.

Okay. Glo agreed reluctantly. *Call me if you need me.*

There was another short pause. *Will do.*

Glo thought that was the end of their conversation, but then she groggily called out his name. *G—Glo?*

Yes? He responded.

Be... careful.

Lloyd had been really worried about Glo and Aksel. Ever since his sister's death and resurrection, he'd been fearful about losing someone he cared about. He'd done his best to suppress those feelings, but things had gone almost too far this time. Thankfully that priest and priestess were able to heal them. Still, Lloyd swore to do all in his power to prevent something like that from happening again.

The sun hung low above the tops of the western mountains as the Remington pulled into the sky dock at Fortress Hightower. Things were already on the move in the city below. Lloyd's parents had contacted the Baron hours ago to warn him of what might be coming. They agreed to move everyone to relative safety—the consecrated grounds of both the temple and this fortress.

Though Fortress Hightower was nigh impregnable, the temple grounds had not been built to withstand an invasion. Thus, Lloyd's mom spoke with the top wizards from the magic school and tasked them with setting up defenses around the grounds. At the same time, his father worked out a plan with Carenna. She went to mobilize both her forces and the students from the academy. Meanwhile, Kratos had the fleet route back to port any ships close enough to aid in the city's defense.

As soon as they disembarked, Lara headed over to the temple with the wizards, priest, and priestess. Meanwhile, Kratos took the spiritblades from the Remington to help set up street checkpoints and move people to safety. That left Lloyd and his friends alone at the top of the fortress. With only a short time left until nightfall, they split up to keep watch. Xellos, Seth, and Aksel observed the countryside to the north and west, while Lloyd, Andrella, Glo, and Alys watched over the city proper.

Alys nervously tapped her fingers on the crenelated parapets as they peered out over the city. "Oh, I hate waiting like this."

Lloyd responded with a closemouthed laugh. "Me too."

"I was never much good at it either," Andrella confessed.

"The worst part is the not knowing," Alys went on. "This thing could pop up anywhere after sundown."

"What about you, Glo?" Andrella called over to the wizard. He had been unusually quiet and kept to himself since his near-death experience.

Glo turned his gaze in their direction, though his expression still appeared far away. "Sorry, I was a bit preoccupied. What were you all talking about?"

Andrella briefly related the conversation to him. Afterwards, Glo pressed his lips together into a wan smile. "My father used to always ride me about my lack of patience. So, I believe you can lump me in with the rest of you."

Lloyd was glad to see his friend smile again, even if it was a poor one. "So, where do you think this thing is going to show up?"

The elf's brow knit into a frown, deep creases forming across it. "That is a good question. Neither teleportation nor plane shifting are an exact science. Still, those vampires were already here once, so that would help them home in on the location."

"Are we really sure they're coming?" Alys asked anxiously. "I mean, we're going to look awfully foolish if they don't show up."

Lloyd had actually been wondering the same thing. Unfortunately with so many lives at stake, they just couldn't take that chance. "I think I'd rather look foolish and the city be safe," he stated with firm conviction.

Andrella laced her arm through his and gave him a peck on the cheek. "And that's why I fell in love with him," she said with a sly glance at Alys.

Andrella's playfulness distracted Alys from her fears. "They were raised right," Alys agreed with an impish smile.

Lloyd felt his cheeks growing warm. He gingerly rubbed the back of his neck. "If I keep on listening to the two of you, I won't be able to get my head through a doorway."

Alys' eyes glinted with glee. "Isn't he cute when he gets all flustered?"

"Definitely," Andrella agreed, her eyes also dancing with amusement.

Though embarrassed, Lloyd couldn't complain too much. Andrella had artfully broken the tension that had descended upon them. Thus, Lloyd did his best to keep the conversation light. "Maybe I can use my 'cuteness' to charm this vampire lord into giving up."

Alys and Andrella both giggled. The former touched her chin with a single finger as she appraised him. "Charming someone is my domain. Plus, I think you might have more luck with that lady vampire."

They managed to keep the banter going for a while longer after that. They even pulled Glo into it, eliciting a real smile from the otherwise distracted elf.

Everyone grew quiet, however, as the last rays of the setting sun disappeared behind the mountains to the west. As the blanket of night swept across the eastern sky, a huge spinning sphere of darkness appeared over the Old Graveyard at the western end of the city.

Even from halfway across the city, Lloyd could feel the vast amount of energy radiating from the immense globe. Squinting at it, Lloyd perceived what appeared to be the top of a tower inside. "Are my eyes playing tricks on me, or does anyone else see something in that sphere?"

"It's that castle from Ravenar," Xellos declared definitively. He, Aksel, and Seth had come over to join them.

Alys' voice was filled with awe. "So the legends are true. The castle does move from place to place."

Everyone else seemed astonished except for Seth. "Yeah, yeah, it's a roving castle," the halfling scoffed. "So now what, geniuses?"

Lloyd set his jaw, not taking his eyes off the castle in the darkness. "Now we get ready to fight."

Seth supposed he shouldn't have been surprised that the entire castle appeared inside the city. After all, Elistra had teleported them

directly into the town square. Still, if he was going to stay in Penwick—assuming there was still a city left standing once all this was
over—then Seth would need to have a serious talk with Lloyd's mom
about boosting their magical defenses.

For now, he trailed silently behind the others as they headed toward the temple. Aksel wanted to know a bit more about the dark
sphere before they decided on their next steps. Seth thought it a
smart move, especially after their last disastrous attempt to infiltrate
the castle.

Moving through town proved faster on foot, especially with all
the checkpoints setup along the way. The town guard had makeshift
blockades of barrels, boxes, and even furniture on almost every corner within the city. Seth noted spiritblades and clerics mixed in with
the forces at each.

When they reached the temple grounds, they had to wait for a
crowd of townsfolk being ushered inside by a group of spiritblades.
Lloyd recognized some of the blades from the school. They informed
him that his father had spearheaded the evacuation of the town.

Once inside the temple grounds, the companions found fortifications well underway. A second barrier had been hastily constructed
just behind the main gate. Small makeshift bunkers now stood along
the walls at regular intervals. Casters could be seen intermixed with
the guards at each of these stations.

As soon as they arrived, a priest escorted them directly to the
High Priestess' office. Sirus sat behind her desk with her eyes closed,
but nonetheless ushered them inside. "Please come in. I will be with
you in a moment."

Seth exchanged a surprised look with Aksel, then shrugged and
found a spot to lean against along the wall. Andrella and Alys both
took seats while the rest of them mimicked Seth. They waited in silence for the High Priestess to finish her trance. Luckily, they didn't
have to wait long.

About a minute later, Sirus' eyes fluttered open. "It is as we suspected. The sphere itself is a rift to the Plane of Shadows. That is
how they bypassed the city defenses."

Glo let out a long whistle. "That explains why we could feel it halfway across the city. The amount of mana required for a rift that big has to be enormous."

"We all felt it," Sirus agreed somberly, "but it hasn't come through quite just yet. It will likely take most of the night for the castle to re-form here in the material plane."

"At least that buys us some time," Andrella noted grimly.

Lloyd appeared lost in thought. "Is it just the castle? Big as that sphere is, I don't think it's large enough for the entire town."

"I only saw the castle," Xellos confirmed.

Glo steepled his hands together—another annoying habit he had when that big brain of his was whirring. "It probably would take too much energy to move the entire town and bypass the city's defenses."

"So that means the fort didn't come with them," Lloyd stated the obvious.

Seth saw where Lloyd was going with this. He decided to try and squelch any ideas before they went and did something stupid. "I wouldn't get my hopes up too much. They probably moved all the vamps inside the castle before they left." Lloyd's face fell at his words, but unfortunately the damage had already been done.

"Either way, Lloyd brings up a valid point," Glo picked up where Lloyd left off. "If we can just travel to the Plane of Shadows, we might be able to infiltrate the castle."

"Like the last time?" Seth scoffed. "That didn't go so well, if you remember." Unfortunately, his words fell on deaf ears.

"I could take us there," Aksel announced, completely ignoring Seth.

Before he knew it, they had all agreed on Aksel's plan. Seth made one last attempt at reason, but doubted any of them would listen. "Let's just get one thing straight—this isn't any 'infiltration.' I guarantee you the place will be teeming with vamps and worse. We're going to have to fight our way through."

Aksel met his gaze with a grave stare. "You're probably right."

"Oh, I know I'm right," Seth responded with a slight smirk.

"Either way, may you all go with the blessings of Arenor him-self," Sirus pronounced. She tried to smile, but her eyes betrayed just how dire she thought their plan to be.

Seth continued to brood to himself as they left Sirus' office behind. He couldn't think of any way to stop his idealistic friends from going through with this crazy assault. Still, this was not quite the same as their march on the Marsh Tower. Back then they had the two dragons with them, and that nutjob hunter. This assault would be far more difficult, if not downright deadly. If they were going to survive at all, they would need to be far more creative.

Some outlandish ideas crossed Seth's mind as they trekked across the temple grounds. He rejected a few outright, but one definitely had potential. Unfortunately, there might not be any coming back from it.

Seth mentally shrugged. *Ah well, you were planning on retiring after this anyway.*

30
PLANE OF SHADOWS

They 'fell' from that vast emptiness into a place of total darkness

Aksel experienced mixed emotions as they marched across the temple grounds. Their last attempt to breach this castle had not gone so well. In fact, it nearly cost him and Glo their lives. Yet in only two days, a few vampires had captured or turned over five dozen folks. If an entire castle of these creatures were set loose upon the city, Penwick could end up being the next City of Tears.

Just before leaving the grounds, they ran into Lara. She listened gravely as they informed her of their plans, but in the end agreed that desperate measures were in order. Before they left, she cast a telepathic link spell with Lloyd, Andrella, and Glo, cautioning them that it wouldn't work between planes. She then surprised Lloyd with a fierce hug and the words, "Be careful, my son."

Lloyd rubbed the back of his neck, his face turning nearly as red as his armor. "I promise, Mom."

With all the checkpoints along the way, crossing the city went slower than Aksel would have liked. At one blockage in the Lord's Square, they came across Carenna overseeing the fortifications. Apparently they had just missed Kratos, who had headed out with a group of spiritblades for another sweep of the city.

When they informed Carenna of their plans, her expression grew wistful. "I wish I could go with you."

Lloyd surprised them all with his insightful and diplomatic reply. "Your blade would be a great help, but I think that what you're doing here is just as important."

Carenna responded with a grim smile, then drew her blade and saluted them. "Gods' speed to you, my friends. May Arenor watch over you all."

It was the second time someone had invoked the God of Light's name in their favor. Aksel certainly appreciated it. With the mission they were about to embark on, they would need all the blessings they could get.

The group grew silent as they set out once more. There was none of the usual banter, everyone as somber as Aksel. Even the talkative Alys had gone quiet. The companions reached the other side of the city without further interruption. As they rounded the corner before the graveyard, the astonishing sight brought them all to a halt.

Andrella gasped. "I thought that thing was huge from across town, but from here it's absolutely enormous!"

The sphere of darkness sat in the midst of the graveyard, obscuring everything including the large mausoleum, a number of tombs, and hundreds of graves. "It isn't solid just quite yet," Glo informed them, "but once it becomes so, it will crush everything beneath it."

"Then we better make certain that never happens," Lloyd said, grinding his fist into his other hand.

With time of the essence, they hurried into the graveyard, not stopping until they reached the very edge of the sphere. Aksel could feel the dark energies whirling around inside. It looked unsettling, reminding him of the rift that Lara had created earlier that day.

This is no time to be squeamish, Aksel told himself. He shook off the disturbing feeling and barked out instructions to the others. "Alright, form into a circle and join hands."

Alys gazed up at the huge sphere towering over them, her jaw agape. "Are—are you sure we can do this?"

Already holding onto Andrella, Lloyd grabbed her hand with his free one and held it firm. "We can if we all work together."

"He's right," Andrella added in a reassuring tone. "That's how we defeated the Empress at the Marsh Tower."

Their determination heartened Alys' resolve. She gulped, then forced herself to smile. "Okay then, let's do this."

Aksel silently hoped they were right. There were fewer of them now than when they raided the Marsh Tower. Seth, Glo, Lloyd, Andrella, Xellos, and now Alys—the original four who had started this journey, plus the Lady of Ravenford, the uncanny tracker, and the fiery songstress. Aksel wished the three sisters and Cyclone were here as well, but their mission was even more important. In fact, the fate of the world hung in the balance.

With a quick prayer to the Soldenar, Aksel traced a complex pattern through the air. Mana poured into the symbol, filling it with energy. Once it was done, Aksel grabbed the free hands of both Alys and Seth, then spoke the words to invoke the spell. "*Planum Iter.*"

As the mana emptied from the pattern, it raced around the circle of friends. A spinning vortex of purple energy formed in their center and slowly expanded until it engulfed them all. The world around them abruptly disappeared, replaced with a vast black emptiness dotted here and there with distant sparkling lights. They seemed to be traveling a great distance, yet nothing appeared to be moving around them. A short while later, without warning, they 'fell' from that vast emptiness into a place of total darkness.

Aksel felt strangely disoriented as they landed in the midst of the complete blackness. It was an out-of-place feeling, as if this realm were trying to reject his very existence.

"Nice homey place you brought us to," Seth noted with a slight curve to the side of his mouth.

Aksel didn't exactly disagree with him. Strangely, they could all see each other in the darkness, as if each of their bodies radiated its own light. Aksel forced down that repulsive feeling and tried to focus on the mission at hand.

"There's the castle," Xellos said, pointing directly behind Aksel. He followed the tracker's gaze, his eyes focusing on the very same structure they'd seen in Ravenar.

Surrounded on all sides by high walls, multiple towers of various heights comprised the tall spiraling structure. A lighted building over the main gate connected two spires that stood on its either side. More spires appeared behind those, the two tallest connected via an enclosed bridge more than halfway to the highest peak. A particularly wide tower, similar to the one at the fortress in Penwick, sat in the corner opposite the main gate.

Dozens of windows lit up the castle, augmented by the plentiful lights that lined the walls. Myriads of dark figures could be seen roaming across those parapets. Farther up, large shadows occasionally passed the lights of the upper windows of the keep.

Despite its overall ominous appearance, the sight of the castle made Aksel feel more grounded in this otherwise empty place. Yet just as he started to feel more comfortable, the gates of the castle opened. A horde of zombies poured out through those gates and headed straight in their direction.

"Looks like we've got a welcoming committee," Seth noted dryly.

Glo arched an eyebrow at the halfling. "You and I have very different definitions of the word welcoming."

The horde continued to pour from the gates. Aksel quickly lost count of them, but estimated their numbers to be in the triple digits.

Glo rubbed his hands together nervously. "I think perhaps we might be safer in the air."

Andrella stepped out in front of him and rolled up her sleeves. "While you do that, I'll give our guests a warm welcome." Both wizards traced their spells through the air and cast them simultaneously.

"*Murum Ignis.*"

"*Omnes Fugere.*"

The mana released in two different directions at the same time. A circle of energy swept out over the group, leaving Aksel with a tingling sensation. He suddenly felt lighter than air, as he did when in smoke form. However, this time he was still solid.

The second wave of energy spread out in front of the rushing zombie horde. A shimmering curtain of scarlet flames sprang up in front of them, stretching nearly fifty feet in either direction and reaching upward about twenty feet into the sky. The unthinking and unfeeling zombies raced into the fiery wall, only to burst into flames and wither into burnt husks.

Glo cocked his head to one side and gave his pupil an appreciative nod. "Nicely done."

Andrella executed a half-curtsey and smiled back at him. "I learned from the best."

"H-how do you steer this thing?" Alys blurted out all of a sudden.

Aksel turned to see the young lady suspended about three feet above the ground, but awkwardly tilted off to one side. She flailed wildly with her arms and legs, desperately trying to right herself.

"Don't fight it," Lloyd cried as he floated up next to her. He grabbed Alys by the waist and ever so gently straightened her out. Once she was steadied, Lloyd let her go and floated back a few feet away.

"Now do what I do," Lloyd instructed her in a calming tone. His arms fanned out to either side at a forty-five-degree angle. Alys' expression grew serious, her brow furrowing with concentration as she mimicked his movements.

"It's like a bird," Lloyd explained, "except you don't flap your arms. Watch." He shot up into the dark sky and proceeded to execute a loop-the-loop over the top of them.

The sight brought Aksel back to the time when Lloyd first got his flying cloak. The young man had been a natural even then, immediately taken to the air and buzzing the camp of the Black Adders.

"Wow!" Alys cried, clapping her hands with glee. She seemed as impressed now as they all had been back then.

"Yeah, yeah, he's a regular mini-dragon," Seth said with a scathing snort, "but I think you're forgetting about something." The halfling pointed a thumb over his shoulder back in the direction of the castle.

Behind them, Glo had joined in with Andrella, catching the zombies in a pincer movement between two firewalls. Aksel had witnessed them do the same thing on the bridge that led to the Marsh Tower. Like then, the two wizards roasted dozens of zombies in between the two walls.

Yet that was no longer their only problem. A group of shadowy forms, slightly less dark than the blackness around them, had broken away from the castle and were now flying their way.

"Get behind me!" Lloyd cried out as he swooped down from above. His blades burst into flame as he took up a point position in front of the others.

With only a few of the zombie horde left, Glo and Andrella lifted into the air. The two wizards fell into formation on either side and slightly behind Lloyd.

Aksel counted just over a dozen of the shadowy forms headed their way. From this distance, he couldn't tell exactly what they were, but being caught on the ground was probably not the best idea. "Line up behind them!" he shouted to the others.

The rest of them rose into the air, with Xellos and Aksel behind the wizards. Seth and Alys brought up the rear, the latter following Lloyd's advice and reasonably falling into formation.

As the shadows drew closer, Xellos was the first to identify them. "They're wraiths!" he cried out in warning.

A slight shiver went up Aksel's spine. These were the same creatures that dark cleric had conjured back in Ravenar. Alys had managed to keep those three at bay, but this time there were far more of them.

The greatest danger from these soulless creatures was their touch. It could drain the very life from a living being. Aksel called out a warning to the others. "Whatever you do, don't let them touch you!"

The two leading wraiths went straight for Lloyd. Andrella wasn't having any of it, though. She leveled a finger at one of the wraiths and fired off three red-hot rays in rapid succession. All of the rays connected with a sharp sizzling sound, the last one causing the creature to halt in its tracks. It raised its head upward in a silent cry, then disappeared in an explosion of black smoke.

Glo hit the second wraith with a similar barrage, resulting in the same outcome. Before the smoke had cleared, however, two more wraiths crashed through the misty remains of their comrades, both zeroed in on Lloyd.

Unfortunately for them, Lloyd was more than ready. Aksel had seen it enough times to know when the warrior was about to use a spiritblade technique. Lloyd went still for a moment, then abruptly shot forward between the two wraiths. His body spun with such speed that the flames from his two blades appeared to form a solid ring of fire around him.

Lloyd caught both wraiths with that spin attack, hitting them multiple times as he drove through their midst. Like the first two, both these wraiths disappeared in an explosion of black smoke.

Having learned their lesson, the rest of the wraiths veered off. They did not stop, however. Instead, they kept their distance and formed a ring around the companions.

"Form up into a tight circle!" Aksel shouted. The companions did as he said without question, facing outward and tightening their ranks.

Aksel was fearful of this sudden turn of events. If all the wraiths came at them at once, someone was sure to get hurt. Yet just when he thought things would get ugly, help came from an unexpected quarter.

"That one's not a wraith!" Xellos cried.

Aksel peered where the tracker pointed, toward the figure closest to the castle. Narrowing his eyes, he saw that Xellos was right. Though floating in mid-air, the figure appeared human—a balding human, in fact, dressed like a butler. Aksel realized it was a vampire, but he almost preferred it to the wraiths.

The vampire butler made a summoning motion with his hand. "This way. The master awaits."

Aksel was taken aback. *Did this creature just offer to take us directly to the master?*

"Tsk." Seth clicked his tongue with a contemptuous nod toward the surrounding wraiths. "What about your friends?"

The butler's expression turned to one of obvious disgust. "They are no friends of mine. If you hurry, however, we should be able to outfly them."

Aksel swiftly swept his gaze around the encircling wraiths. They appeared to be edging closer. Deep in his bones, he knew they only had a matter of seconds before they all swooped in. Following his gut, the little cleric made a split-second decision.

"Go!" he cried to the others.

The butler took off. Glo and Andrella started after him, but Lloyd hung back as the two nearest wraiths tried to cut them off. A shrill sound suddenly cut through the quiet of the dark plane. It slammed into the wraith on the one side, stunning it and making it falter. Xellos immediately hit it with a barrage of arrows, causing it to explode.

Aksel caught the wraith on the other side with a blinding ray of searing light. The beam rattled the creature, giving Lloyd the opening he needed to finish it with his holy sword.

"Now go!" Aksel screamed as loud as he could.

Lloyd went first. Glo and Andrella each grabbed one of Alys' hands, and sped after him with the young lady in between. Xellos fell in behind them, with Aksel and Seth bringing up the rear. The rest of the wraiths immediately gave chase.

The companions were able to maintain their lead as they flew over the castle walls. Below, Aksel spied a wide courtyard stretching from the gate to the main keep. A set of double doors unexpectedly swung open in front of the stone building. A troop of about a dozen butlers and maids trotted out, lining the landing and wide stairs on either side.

"Well that's not suspicious at all," Seth noted ominously.

Aksel peered behind them to see the wraiths were not far behind. He met Seth's gaze with a plaintive stare. "I don't think we have much choice."

"See you on the other side, then!" Seth cried with a thin smirk.

The butler landed in front of the doors and motioned for them to follow him inside. Lloyd landed next, taking up a defensive pose. The array of butlers and maids did not move.

Andrella, Glo, and Alys landed next to Lloyd. Still the butler and maids held their ground. Xellos, Aksel, and Seth landed a few seconds later with the wraiths right behind them.

Before anyone could stop her, Alys stepped forth and let loose a sonic barrage into the air. She caught the incoming wraiths with her howling scream, stunning those in the lead. As the wraiths faltered, the maids and butlers rose up and tore into them.

Seth let out a low whistle. "Whew. Looks like there's trouble in vamp paradise."

Aksel was as surprised as Seth. "There does seem to be two factions here." For the moment it appeared to be playing in their favor,
but Aksel knew better than to count on it lasting.

The entryway behind them opened into an elegant wide foyer. A
black-and-white marbled floor and ornate pillars accented the chamber. Three sets of doors led from the room, one on either side, and
a set of double doors in back that sat between a pair of curved stairs
that climbed to a railed landing above.

The butler walked over to the back doors and opened them, revealing a large, glowing circular disc. The disc sat inside a cylindrical
shaft that appeared to lead to the keep above.

The butler stepped onto the disc, then stood to one side, and
ushered them to follow him. "This way, please."

The companions tentatively approached the disc, wary of their
surroundings. No more creatures showed up to harry them, however.

As they gathered around the double doors, Alys seemed particularly reluctant. "Is that thing safe?" she whispered nervously.

Glo placed a hand on her shoulder, his tone filled with compas-
sion. "I'm sure it is. We rode a similar disc through the Golem Master's monolith. It was perfectly safe." Alys gave the wizard a warm
smile, and gratefully squeezed the hand that rested upon her shoulder.

Aksel remembered that disc as well. It floated up and down a
comparable shaft, activated by a set of magic words. In that case, the
words had been in Dwarven. Aksel wasn't about to assume this disc
would driven by the same language.

Lloyd placed himself firmly between the vampire butler and the
others as they embarked onto the disc. Aksel noted that Alys still
held tight onto Glo's hand. It was as if she expected the disc to drop
out from beneath them at any moment. Under other circumstances,
he would have found the sight amusing.

Once everyone had situated themselves, the butler closed the
doors to the shaft and spoke a single word. "*Ndu.*"

It was then that Aksel realized Seth was missing. Still, that was not
his greatest concern. The disc began to slide effortlessly down the
shaft. Something about that didn't quite sit right with him, though—
he'd assumed the vampire lord would be waiting for them in his

throne room. If so, that should be situated either on the ground floor or on one of the upper floors. *Why are we going down?*

The butler stood at the front of the disc with his gloved hands folded behind his back. Aksel narrowed his gaze at the back of the vampire's balding head. "Are we still going to see the master?"

Not turning, the butler gazed over his shoulder at Aksel, his nose raised in the air as he fixed him with a snooty stare. "He will see you soon enough."

Aksel didn't like the sound of that at all. Neither did anyone else on the floating disc. Everyone tensed, Lloyd's hands going to his sword hilts.

A knot growing in his stomach, Aksel pressed the snobbish vampire. "What exactly do you mean by that?"

The butler opened his mouth to answer, but never got the chance. His body abruptly crumbled to dust. Seth stood on the other side of the dusty pile that was left, a stake pointed at where the vampire's heart had previously been.

Aksel frowned at his halfling friend. Seth responded with a wicked grin. "It was a boring conversation anyway."

With a shake of his head, Aksel turned to Glo. "Do you know how to run this thing?"

Glo replied with a single word. *"Pusta."* The disc came to a smooth halt. A thin smile spread across Glo's lips. "It responds to an ancient dialect of elvish."

Seth folded his arms across his chest. "Well then, genius, how about taking us up?"

"Amba," Glo said, not batting an eye at the halfling.

The disc began to rise through the shaft, soon passing the closed doors that led to the foyer. The disc continued to rise upward until it reached the very top of the shaft, coming to a halt before another set of closed double doors. Lloyd tried them, but they were locked.

Seth pushed his way in front of the tall human, shooing him away in a soft voice. "Move over and let an expert handle this." The halfling pulled a pick from his pouch and inserted it into the lock. After fiddling with it for a few seconds, he was rewarded with a sharp *click*.

"Child's play," Seth murmured, glancing back over his shoulder with a smug smile.

Aksel half-smiled and half-sighed in return. "Great, Seth," he said in a hushed voice. "Now how about checking out what's on the other side?"

Seth shook his head, his smile fading. "There's no pleasing some people," he muttered under his breath.

Everyone went completely still as the halfling put an ear to the door. After half a minute or so, he stood back and shook his head. "Nothing," he whispered.

Though it appeared the coast was clear, they had all been through too much to take that for granted. Everyone lined up as if ready for battle. Lloyd drew his blades, Xellos nocked an arrow to his bow, Glo and Andrella prepared to cast spells. Aksel and Alys stood in the back, ready to lend a hand if necessary.

Seth nodded to Lloyd, then pushed the door open and ducked out of the way. Before them lay a long, red-carpeted hallway with another set of double doors at its other end. Decorative pillars lined the sides of the hall, with pictures of what appeared to be nobles in fancy outfits hung between each. Other than that, the hall was empty.

Lloyd peered quizzically over his shoulder at Aksel. Though the hallway looked clear, looks could be deceiving. Aksel decided to continue with caution. "Stay in formation and move slowly."

The entire group moved as one into the hall. As they passed the first set of pictures, goosebumps formed on Aksel's skin. The pictures' eyes seemed to be following them.

"Watch out!" Xellos cried. A moment later, the people in the pictures, or more correctly, translucent versions of them, jumped out into the hallway and closed on the companions.

Everything happened at once. Lloyd sliced the nearest ghost with his holy sword; it disappeared with startled cry and a sudden popping sound. Aksel did a burst of light like Sirus taught him, causing the rest of the nearby ghosts to also evaporate.

Alys stepped up next to Lloyd and stunned the ghosts down the hall with her sonic cry. Glo, Andrella, and Xellos then picked them off with rays and arrows. With the last ghost gone, everyone breathed a sigh of relief.

Seth's mouth twisted to one side. "Well, that was fun."

Glo fixed the halfling with an acerbic stare. "You and I also have very different definitions of the word fun."

The rest of the trip down the corridor proved uneventful. Seth went ahead to check the next set of doors. He lifted the end of the carpet, exposing a pressure plate. After careful examination, Seth disabled the springs on the plate and then safely unlocked the doors. When he pressed his ear to them, however, his face took on a strange expression.

"What is it?" Aksel whispered.

"It sounds—like music," Seth responded with obvious confusion.

"Let me have a listen," Alys said. She stooped down next to Seth and put her ear to the door. Her eyes went wide and then she nodded. "Seth's right. It is music—orchestra music."

Aksel didn't know what to make of that. They had faced some strange things in these last few months, but an orchestra was certainly not one of them. Unfortunately, they were running out of time. With no other good options, Aksel made a command decision. "We open this door like the others. Everybody form up."

They took the same positions as before, then Seth pushed the door open. What they found behind those doors caused them all to gape and stare.

A small balcony spread out before them. An ornate curved staircase led down to a large ballroom a flight below. About two dozen couples stood on the dance floor, twirling and whirling around each other. Across from the companions, on a twin balcony, stood three people in fancy clothes watching the people dance below.

As soon as the door opened, the music stopped. After a few moments of confusion, a voice boomed out over the din from the balcony opposite them. "It appears we have company."

All eyes turned upon the companions as the room went deathly silent.

31
DANCING WITH THE VAMPIRES

"I think we just crashed a vampire ball."

Andrella had been to balls before, but none quite like this. The ballroom itself was rather exquisite, with beautiful white marbled columns, a glossy checkered wooden dance floor, and a number of sparkling chandeliers with easily two dozen candles each. Though all the people were dressed quite immaculately, they were also all quite obviously vampires.

"I think we just crashed a vampire ball," Alys said with hushed astonishment.

Things happened fast after that. Xellos immediately targeted the man on the balcony opposite them with a barrage of arrows. Though not the vampire lord they had faced in the catacombs beneath Penwick, Andrella figured him to be some sort of lord.

At the same time, Glo invoked a spell which spread mana over all the companions. Everything suddenly slowed around her except for her friends. Taking advantage of her new speed, Andrella joined with Xellos in pelting this vampire lord with a trio of fire rays. As the last ray leapt from her fingertips, Lloyd soared into the air and Seth disappeared from sight.

Though slowed in comparison, the vampire lord responded with a lightning bolt directed at both Andrella and Xellos. The bolt careened across the room at a pace that outmatched even their accelerated movements.

Andrella braced herself. This was going to hurt—a lot. The bolt was nearly in her face when something collided with her. Andrella slammed into the floor, the wind expelling from her lungs.

Lloyd's heart skipped a beat as the bolt of lightning streaked straight for Andrella. He spun about in mid-air to dive for her, but there was no way he could reach her in time. At the very last second, Aksel knocked her out of the way, taking the brunt of the sizzling bolt, along with Xellos. Both of them were jarred and seared, but managed to survive the blistering barrage.

Angered by the attack, Lloyd pulled up short and turned toward the man in the balcony. *How dare he target Andrella!* Yet before he could move, the two women beside the man both cast spells. One brought up a wall of wind in front of the balcony. The other, however, pointed her finger directly at him.

Her eyes locked with his, and Lloyd's body went rigid. A cold voice whispered in his mind. *Kill your friends.*

Chills ran up his spine as he railed against the hold she had upon him. *I won't,* he thought back angrily, though he still could not move a muscle.

A wicked laugh echoed through chambers of his mind, followed by that same cold voice. *Yes, you will.*

Lloyd felt his body begin to move on its own. Though he fought against it, his body turned to face his friends. Sweat poured from his brow as he struggled, but to no avail. His body just wouldn't listen.

A desperate thought came to him. If he could just reach his spirit, maybe he could throw off the witch's hold. Stilling his mind, he prepared to dive down inside of himself. Yet his sudden calm had an unexpected side effect.

There was a sudden flash from the ring on his finger and a strange energy coursed through his skin. It was the ring Lyrwen had given him—the ring of *mind shielding*. That energy pushed back on the presence in his mind, forcing loose the grip it had on him.

No! the voice wailed.

As quickly as it had taken him over, it was gone. Lloyd was free and in control of his own body once again. Seething with anger, he wanted to punish both the man and the woman in the balcony. Yet just below him, the vampires were rushing the staircase that led up to his friends.

The man and woman would have to wait. Right now his friends needed him. Without another thought, Lloyd dove down toward the crowd of vampires, reaching inside for his spirit as he went.

The sight of the elegant ballroom filled with so many vampires made Alys freeze. Who was she kidding? She was just a stage performer, not a battle-hardened veteran like Lloyd, or even Andrella. What could she possibly do here other than get in the way?

She nearly turned and ran at that point, but then she heard Pallas' voice in her mind. *I don't think I would have survived without your help.*

That made Alys pause. She had saved him, hadn't she? As if in answer to her question, Lloyd's words played through her mind. *I heard you handled yourself pretty well against those vampires. Like it or not, you're now part of the group.*

She was now part of the group. Lloyd had said that. He had faith her and so did Pallas. Andrella and Aksel seemed to as well. *She couldn't just let them down. She wouldn't!*

Freed from her inner turmoil, Alys saw the vampires gathering at the base of the staircase. A few of them charged upward, with more falling in behind. Her nerves once again intact, Alys stepped to the top of the stairs and drew in a deep breath.

At the same time, she pulled the energy in through her diaphragm. It traveled upwards through her lungs and throat, coalescing around her vocal chords. The energy causing them to vibrate faster and faster until they reached a fevered pitch.

Alys then opened her mouth and pushed out the energy with a high-pitched cry. The resulting force slammed into the climbing vampires, bringing them to a screeching halt halfway up the staircase. Paralyzed by their sensitive hearing, the lead vampires covered their ears and staggered backwards into those behind them.

As the vampires fell over each other, Lloyd dove down at them with the same fiery spin attack he had used on the wraiths. Alys abruptly cut off her cry just as Lloyd plowed into the vampires. He bowled through them, knocking some down and dusting a pair before arcing back upwards.

A moment later, Seth appeared in front of the vampires and staked one in the heart. On Alys' left, Xellos let fly a trio of arrows and caught the vamp next to Seth directly in the heart. It, too, crumbled to dust, just like the one Seth had just staked.

Aksel then appeared on her right and let loose a powerful spell with two words. "*Circulus Inmortuus.*" Alys could feel the magic rush past her down the staircase. White circles formed around many of the vampires, lifting them all up into the air. Shrieks of pain erupted from their throats before the lot of them burst into clouds of dust.

When the dust settled, only two vampires remained on the stairs. Seth expertly staked one of them and Xellos pierced the other's heart with another trio of arrows. The stairs were now clear, but a crowd of vampires still remained on the ballroom floor.

Since they walked through the door, Glo's attention had been pulled in all different directions. After accelerating his companions, his focus fell on the vampires in the opposite balcony. Casters all three, their efforts created more havoc than the dozens of vampires on the ballroom floor.

Glo had begun a globe of protection until Aksel pushed Andrella out of the way. While it would have stopped any further bolts, it would have tied Glo down to shielding the others. He next began a spell to free Lloyd until that ring of mind-shielding went off, saving him the trouble.

While Glo had wasted his time with half-cast spells, the others handily cleared the stairs of vampires. Still, they were far from out of the woods. Across the way, the man and women were casting again. Looking beyond the veil, Glo analyzed the patterns they traced. The one spell was not an immediate threat, but the other two would cause them serious problems.

As the spells released, Glo shouted a warning to his friends. "Get ready for a whole mess of flying vampires!" Two circles of magic appeared around a dozen of the vampires on the floor. Moments later, all those vampires lifted off into the air.

The last spell covered the opposite balcony in a shroud of darkness, but Glo couldn't worry about that now. Instead, he cast the fly spell upon himself. Andrella, back off the floor, wisely did the same for Aksel.

In the meantime, Lloyd plowed into the flying vamps with that spinning flame technique of his. He broke their ranks and hurt quite a few, even dusting one of them in the process. His luck had run out, though, as one of the vamps took off after him.

"Watch out, Lloyd!" Andrella cried. That vampire was too close behind him. If it got his hands on him, it could drain him of his life force. If that happened to Lloyd now, they wouldn't stand a chance against the vampire lord.

Glo lifted off and flew after them, targeting the trailing vamp with the most powerful spell he could think of. "*Adiuuatur.*" A thin, green ray lanced from Glo's fingertip and struck the vampire square in the back. Its sudden shriek was cut short as its body vaporized before his eyes. Only a few wisps of smoke remained in the air where the vamp had just been.

Lloyd immediately banked around and saluted Glo with a sheepish smile. "Thanks! I wasn't sure I could shake him."

Glo turned about just in time to see Aksel plummet into the midst of the remaining airborne vamps. A brilliant white light erupted from the cleric's body, catching most of the creatures in its wake. Glo had to shield his eyes, but when he looked again, almost all of the airborne vampires were gone.

Only two now remained. A trio of fiery rays caught the one and incinerated it. A trio of arrows zeroed in on the other's chest, turning it to dust in mid-air.

Though they had killed nearly two dozen vampires, another two dozen still remained. The battle was still far from over.

Once the stairs had been cleared, Seth did a quick head count. There were still three dozen vamps left, not including those three on the balcony. Something needed to be done quick to even the odds.

Sweeping his eyes around the ballroom, Seth noted the stage now empty. That gave him an idea. Cloaking himself in invisibility, he leapt over the side rail and hit the floor rolling. Seth then ran to the stage. Climbing onto it, he cast a quick spell to enhance his voice, then uncloaked himself.

Seth had to momentarily shield his eyes when Aksel lit up the whole ballroom, but once the aerial battle was over, he proceeded with his plan. Clearing his voice, Seth said the first thing that came to his mind that might annoy a vampire. "What do you get when you cross a midget with a vampire? A vampire that bites you in the kneecaps."

The two dozen vamps still left on the floor peered his way with obvious confusion. Apparently his little 'joke' had fallen flat.

A moment later, a frigid blast of ice and snow erupted from the darkened balcony. It caught the airborne Glo, Aksel, and Lloyd in its wake, but Alys managed to block the blast with that incredulous voice of hers. When the snow and ice disappeared, Alys, Andrella, and Xellos stood untouched. Unfortunately, the others had not fared so well.

Still, Seth went ahead with his plan, hoping that Aksel would catch onto it. He cleared his throat and tried one more jab. "How do you say goodbye to a vampire? So long, sucker!"

That apparently got their attention. About a dozen vamps turned his way and rushed the stage. The other dozen tried for another assault on the stairs.

Seth began to worry as the maddened throng closed in on him. He thought for certain Aksel would get his plan, but now he wasn't so sure. Seth backpedaled as the vamps climbed onto the stage. This wasn't going at all how he planned. He grabbed his cloak as the vampires closed in on him, but Seth was now surrounded. Even if he turned invisible, he'd be hard pressed to get away.

Caught in the midst of a sea of red eyes, Seth thought to himself, *this is it*. His father always said his smart mouth would be the end of him. It turned out the old man was right.

Seth ducked down, waiting for the inevitable. Dozens of hands were reaching for him when all of a sudden a pillar of blinding white light erupted from the stage below. It shot up to the ceiling above, making it impossible to see.

Shielding his eyes, Seth crawled his way out of the blinding pillar. When he finally made it, he found himself alone on the stage except for a dozen piles of dust.

After being hit with that blast of frigid cold, Glo had enough. Chilled to the bone, he forced himself to trace a pattern through the air and fill it with mana. *"Murum Ignis."*

A curtain of scarlet flames sprang into existence within the darkness that shrouded the opposite balcony. Screams erupted from within the shroud, filling Glo with a keen sense of satisfaction.

At the same time, on the floor below, the remaining vampires had split into two groups. Seth had used his talent for being annoying to draw off half the vamps. The other half rushed the stairs, right into another one of Alys' devastating cries.

While Aksel took care of the vampires around Seth, the stunned vamps on the stairs were hit with a merciless barrage of fiery rays and arrows. Lloyd then landed behind the remaining vamps, and with two quick, savage blows, cleanly lopped off each of their heads.

Over on the opposite balcony, the screams had stopped. The shroud of darkness fell, revealing the balcony to be empty. Glo doubted the vampires had perished in those flames, but nonetheless it left him feeling vindicated for all the trouble they had caused.

Almost everyone had been wounded in the ballroom battle. As it turned out, Aksel's pillar of light had the nice side effect of healing injuries. Thus, he had everyone gather on the stage.

Seth still stood next to the pillar, looking more than a bit frazzled. The halfling breathed a heavy sigh. "Next time someone invites me to a vampire party, remind me to pass."

"Now there's something we can both agree on," Glo said with a half-hearted chuckle.

After taking a ten-minute bath in the pillar of light, everyone had completely recovered. Two doors now lay before them below the balcony where they entered the ballroom. The door on the left led to a spiral staircase going down, while the door on the right led to a similar staircase going up. After a short discussion, they decided to take the stairs leading upward.

Falling into the same formation they had used before, the companions cautiously ascended the stairs. On the next flight up, they found a landing with another locked, iron-bound door. Everyone prepared for battle as Seth picked it and pushed it open.

Beyond the door lay another plush red-carpeted hallway. Instead of pillars and paintings, this one was lined with statues of people with swords and spears. Glo cast a quick spell to detect magic. The statues along the entire hall lit up.

"That's a hard pass," Seth said, slamming the door shut and re-locking it. No one argued with him.

Continuing their climb, the companions soon came across a tall, arched paned-glass window. As Glo peered through it, the hairs on his neck stood on end. Outside, the darkness had begun to fade, replaced instead with a shadowy vision of the city of Penwick. That could only mean one thing—the castle had already partially crossed from the Plane of Shadows to the Material Plane.

"Well, that doesn't look good," Seth said, mirroring Glo's thoughts.

Glo winced as he swept his eyes around the group. They all appeared anxious. Lloyd and Alys in particular had haunted looks in their eyes. Still, there was no getting around the truth. "I'm afraid Seth's right. We're running out of time."

32
TRUE MISTRESS

*A gargantuan figure rose from the chamber floor and
purposely made its way toward them*

Seth was getting really tired of this stupid keep. The place was one big, obnoxious maze. *They couldn't just have a single set of stairs leading to the top of the keep?* No, that would be way too easy. Not to mention they were quickly running out of time.

As annoying as Glo could be, he definitely knew his stuff when it came to magic. If they didn't find this vampire lord soon, Seth had little doubt that Penwick would fall for a fourth and probably last time.

After leaving the window to the outside behind, the company pressed on to the next landing. There they found yet another door, which of course was locked. Seth shook his head as he went to pick it. "Doesn't anyone trust anybody else in this keep?"

"Vampires aren't exactly known to be a friendly lot," Glo pointed out.

"Tsk." Seth clicked his tongue. "Ya think?"

With a mild *click* he picked the lock. Once again everyone lined up, ready to fight. Seth pushed the door open and stood back, but the hallway behind this door appeared to be empty. There were no paintings or statues in sight, only another door at the other end of the corridor.

Seth carefully led the way down the hall, searching for traps as he went. Surprisingly, he found none. Of course this door was locked as well, but as Seth went to pick it, he heard sounds coming from the other side.

Seth put an ear to the door and listened intently. Sure enough, he heard voices, and they were growing louder by the second.

Seth stepped back and whispered to the others, "We've got company."

Lloyd lined up on the other side of the door, while Seth moved to the other side and turned invisible. The others moved back down the corridor and got ready to shoot and blast.

Seth could now hear the voices right through the closed door. A moment later there was a soft *click* and the door slowly swung open. A pompous voice wafted through the opening that strangely reminded him of Sir Fafnir of Dunwynn.

"Who does he think he is, summoning me?" The 'man' behind the voice wore a fancy tunic decorated with some sort of heraldry. He was quite obviously some sort of noble. "Just because Vanalor let him watch the place in his absence, doesn't make him Lord of the Keep."

Vanalor? Why did name sound familiar? Seth filed the thought away for now. Glo would definitely know. The elf was like a walking encyclopedia.

A man and woman dressed in regular clothes trailed behind the noble. They were most likely his servants. The vamp noble peered back at the two, still prattling on as they stepped through the doorway and into the hall. "If the bootlicker hadn't betrayed Jinkolothos in the first place..."

"Master, look!" One of the servants interrupted him as she pointed down the hall.

The vamp noble spun about, his mouth agape as his gaze fell upon the rest of their group. Seth took that as a cue to launch himself at the nearest servant's back. He staked her in the heart from behind, dusting her instantaneously. At the same moment, Lloyd appeared from behind the door and beheaded the other servant.

The vampire noble now stood alone. Yet before anyone could lay a hand on him, he puffed into a cloud a smoke.

"He must know the way to the throne room! Don't let him get away!" Aksel cried. Yet, that was easier said than done. The cloud of smoke retreated back through the door and down another spiral staircase.

Seth cast a quick spell to double his speed and took off in hot pursuit. He followed the vamp cloud in a wild chase that zigged and zagged throughout the castle. He lost count of how many dimly lit corridors and flights of stairs the creature led him down. Along the way, they passed uncounted side corridors with shadowy forms and lesser vamps. He didn't even want to think about what might be trailing him at this point.

Seth continued to follow the cloud into what appeared to be a dungeon-like area. An iron-barred grate blocked the corridor ahead. The vamp passed through it unimpeded, of course, with Seth left just standing there. He searched around wildly for a lock or a lever, but there was none in sight on this side of the bars. Thankfully, he didn't have to wait more than a couple of seconds for the others to catch up.

"Where'd he go?" Lloyd asked, huffing a bit as he caught up to him.

Seth pointed toward the iron grate behind him. "Through there, genius."

Lloyd gave him a sour look. "I mean after that."

"Oh," Seth smirked. "To the left at the end of the corridor." Seth waved his hands at the iron grate. "Think you can move this thing?"

"That'll take too long," Glo said as he, too, finally caught up to them. "Probably best to just portal through." Before he could even start a spell, though, a blue oval appeared in the air in front of the grating, and a second one at the other end of the corridor.

"Way ahead of you," Andrella said with a bit of a smirk herself.

A pained expression crossed Glo's face. "I'm surrounded by smart asses."

"Not for long," Seth cried as he leapt into the portal. As soon as he came out the other end, he scanned the left corridor. He was just in time to catch a glimpse of a smoky cloud funneling through the keyhole of a door some distance down the hall. Once the others came through, he pointed it out to them.

As Seth expected, that door was also locked. Everyone lined up again as he picked it. With a nod to the others, Seth pushed it open and stood back.

A dimly lit room lay beyond the doorway, filled with what appeared to be seven stone sarcophagi. As soon as Lloyd stuck his head inside, six vamps leapt out at him. The young warrior dodged out of the way as Alys let loose with a powerful wail.

She knocked the vamps back into the room, then stopped to allow Aksel to enter. The little cleric placed himself into the midst of the vamps, then lit himself up like a Festivus tree. The blinding light dusted almost all of the vamps.

The others ran in after him, all except for Seth and Xellos; the two of them exchanged a glance. Xellos shrugged. "That room's kind of small, and bows aren't exactly great in close quarters."

Seth grinned back at him. "That's alright. At least you have an excuse."

The truth was that Seth figured the rest of them had this battle without him. Plus, he still wasn't completely convinced something else hadn't followed them. As it turned out, he was right. A figure dressed like another butler appeared down the corridor from the direction they had come.

Seth pointed it out to Xellos. "Don't look now, but we have more company."

Xellos quickly nocked an arrow and trained his sights on the approaching vamp. He held his shot, however, as the butler stopped and threw up his hands. "Wait, please don't shoot me!"

Seth and Xellos exchanged a puzzled glance. That was the first time either of them had heard a vamp beg for mercy. Xellos frowned at the vamp. "Why shouldn't I?"

The butler tried to sound officious, but couldn't hide the slight quake in his voice. "I'm here representing the true mistress of this castle. She would like to speak with you."

Seth carefully fingered the stake he held hidden beneath his cloak. "Right—and why would she want to do that?"

The butler raised his nose ever so slightly. "Let's just say she has no love for the current 'Lord' of the keep."

Seth flashed back to the vamp noble's words just before the ambush. *Just because Vanalor let him watch the place in his absence, doesn't make him Lord of the Keep.* It didn't take a brainy wizard to figure he was talking about the vampire lord. Yet from what they'd seen and heard, the vamp lord had made some enemies in this castle. If that were the case, they might be able to take advantage of that fact.

Seth narrowed his gaze at the pretentious butler. "This mistress of yours—she wouldn't happen to know how to get to the throne room?"

The butler stiffened and fixed him with a withering stare. "Of course she would. This was her castle before that upstart took over."

Once again, Seth recalled the vamp noble's words. *If the bootlicker hadn't betrayed Jinkolothos in the first place...* It did seem to confirm what this butler was saying.

Inside the room, things had gone quiet. Seth took a quick peek and found the others standing around a single sarcophagus in the center of the chamber. There were no vamps in sight.

Seth called out to his friends. "You done in there?"

Aksel turned to look at him. "Sort of. We took care of the rest of the vampires, but that noble is still hiding in his sarcophagus. We were just about to pull him out and interrogate him." As he spoke, Lloyd sheathed his swords and placed his hands on the lid of the stone coffin.

Seth cocked his head to one side, the corner of his mouth rising slightly. "Well, we might not exactly need him after all."

Aksel's brows knit into a single line. "Why not?"

Seth motioned for Aksel to join him in the hallway. The others followed, except for Lloyd, who remained to stand vigil over the sarcophagus. When Aksel saw the butler he momentarily froze, but Seth waved him farther down the hall.

After Seth finished explaining his story, Aksel pensively stroked his chin. "So you think this butler can take us to this true mistress, who in turn can point us to the throne room?"

Seth folded his arms and shrugged. "Something like that."

Glo placed a hand on Seth's forehead. "I thought you didn't trust anyone. Are you sure you're feeling alright?"

Seth slapped the elf's hand away and grunted. "I don't trust anyone, but do you have any better ideas, genius?"

Alys, standing next to Andrella, shifted nervously from one foot to the other. "Not sure if my opinion matters, but I'm afraid we're running out of time."

Seth could see the haunted look in her eyes. He actually felt sorry for her. After all, her friends and family were out there, even if her father was that creepy Alburg guy. Seth might have felt the same if this were his city and his own family weren't rotten to the core.

Aksel gazed at Alys with keen sympathy. "Everyone's opinion matters—and you're right, we're running out of time. I just wish there was some way we could be sure this butler was telling the truth."

A sly smile crossed Andrella's lips. "I think I might have an idea."

They all followed as she approached the butler. She stopped just beside Xellos and took on the air of a courtly lady. When Andrella spoke, her tone reminded Seth of that pompous turd, the Duke of Dunwynn. "So, my good man, you claim this mistress of yours can direct us to the throne room?"

The butler's snooty attitude immediately faded, replaced with one of fawning servitude. "Why yes, good lady, indubitably."

Seth wanted to yak right then and there, but kept his mouth shut.

Andrella touched her chin with her finger, then peered at the door they had just exited. "Well then, I guess we won't need that simpering fool anymore. I don't suppose you'd mind if we simply stake him?"

Seth snorted out loud. Glo was right. Andrella was turning into another smart ass. He most definitely approved.

The butler peered at the entrance behind them, then covered his mouth with the back of his hand and proceeded to laugh. "Forgive me, good lady, but Lord Icharion? The mistress never liked him anyway. He was a bore in life and the afterlife."

"Very well, then you will wait for us here," Andrella told the butler in a dismissive tone. Once inside the room, she placed her hands on her hips and gazed at the others. "Well, what do you think?"

"I think you're way too good at imitating that pain-in-the-ass uncle of yours," Seth noted with a wry smile.

Andrella mimicked his expression. "I know, right?"

Lloyd stared at her with a puzzled expression. "What's going on? And who were you talking to out there?"

Andrella gently patted his face as she briefly explained the situation to him. When she was done, Lloyd gritted his teeth and anxiously ground his fist into his palm. "I can't say I like it, but Alys is right. If we don't do something soon, there might be no Penwick left to save."

Aksel had begun to pace back and forth, but Glo seemed to have made up his mind as well. "Much as it pains me, I have to agree. The transition to the material plane is already underway."

Aksel stopped and stared at Glo with narrowed eyes. "How much time do we have?"

Glo pursed his lips together and shook his head. "There's no way to know exactly. It could take anywhere from a single hour to a few hours."

A pained expression crossed Aksel's face. He let out a deep sigh. "I guess we have no choice, then—we follow the butler."

After taking care of the vamp noble, they all returned to the hallway. Andrella, flanked by Lloyd and Xellos, motioned the butler onward. "Very well, good man. Lead the way to this mistress of yours."

The butler executed a deep bow. "Very good, your ladyship."

Seth followed in silence as the vamp butler led them deeper into the keep. They may have run out of options, but he was no fool. He didn't intend to meet this 'mistress' totally unprepared. Thus as they trekked through the gloomy halls, Seth discreetly prepared one of his more outlandish ideas.

Aksel felt a growing uneasiness as they descended further into the keep. The failure of their previous mission still weighed heavily on his mind, and this one only seemed to be getting worse by the minute. Still, they had little choice. Lloyd had been correct in his assumption. If they did not do something soon, there would likely be no Penwick left for them to save.

That possibility kept Aksel from saying anything. Instead, he followed along quietly as the butler led them down the dimly lit halls and steep winding staircases of the vampire keep. He lost track of the twists and turns along the way, until their journey finally ended at the bottom of a particularly long flight of stairs.

Around the next corner, the companions found themselves in a vast underground chamber. Layer upon layer of hewn stone blocks comprised the walls of the immense chamber. Massive carved stone pillars reached aloft to the ceiling far above. Dim light filtered down from overhead, yet most of the floor of the great chamber lay hidden behind a thick bank of fog.

Seth eyed the butler suspiciously. "So where's this mistress of yours?"

The vampire raised his nose at Seth. "She's here."

"Kindly announce us then," Andrella ordered in a regal voice.

"Good lady, she already knows you're here," the butler responded as if it should've been obvious. Without another word, he strode forth to the very edge of the mists.

Aksel didn't like the sound of that. In a chamber this size, that fog could be hiding almost anything. This mistress could have an entire army waiting in the mists to ambush them. "Be on your guard," he whispered to the others as they tentatively followed the pretentious vampire.

Aksel lagged behind, however, stopping to trace out a complex spell pattern. "*Verum Aspectu.*" As the words left his lips, the mana flowed out of the pattern and upward into his eyes. After a momentary flash of light, the fog bank faded before him, revealing a sight that made him blanch.

A gargantuan figure rose from the chamber floor and purposely made its way toward them. The ground beneath them shook with its every step, forcing them all to watch their balance.

"Wh-what is that?" Alys asked, her voice on the edge of hysterics.

"It's an undead dragon," Aksel responded, the dread in his voice paling in comparison to how he felt inside.

They had fought such a creature back in the City of Tears, yet this dragon was far larger still. Easily eighty feet long, its massive bones extended from the top of its serpentine neck to the tip of its long, sinuous tail. The tattered remains of huge bat-like wings fanned out from its back, though the color had long been drained from them. Two massive bony horns swept back from the top of its skull, framing the hollow sockets where the creature's eyes once had been.

Seth vaulted at the butler. A stake appeared in his hand as he held it up to the vampire's chest. "Just what are you trying to pull?"

Though he sounded indignant, the butler's skin turned even more pale, if that were possible. "Wh-why nothing. This is the true mistress of the keep—the Lady Jinkolothos."

As if on cue, the fog parted above the butler. The dragon's enormous skull slowly emerged from the mists, towering over them astride its thick skeletal neck. The hollowed sockets where its eyes should have been fixed upon them from above. Its massive jaw stood slightly open, revealing rows upon rows of huge, razor-sharp teeth, each one easily the size of a gnome.

The ominous sight sent chills up Aksel's spine. Alys took a few steps backward, gibbering in fear. Lloyd's hands went to his sword hilts; Xellos unslung his bow. Glo and Andrella, much like Aksel, stood frozen in place. Even Seth seemed taken aback, though he'd probably never admit it out loud.

Something happened then that precipitated a string of ultimately disastrous events. Seeing Seth momentarily distracted, the butler tried to pull away. Reacting out of pure instinct, Seth jammed the stake in his hand directly into the vampire's heart. With a sharp cry, the butler turned to dust, his remains falling to the floor.

Everyone went still. A moment later, the silence was broken by an earth-shattering roar. It was so powerful that Aksel could feel his very bones shake. The dragon's mouth opened, its voice cold yet strangely feminine. "Is that how you treat my hospitality—by destroying one of my servants? Very well, then one of you will take his place."

The mists parted further, revealing a cold blue light in the dragon's chest. It raced up the skeletal neck and formed into a large, brilliant ball at the back of the dragon's throat. A second later, a glacial
blast burst forth from that massive maw, straight down at the unwit-
ting companions.

Aksel found himself at a complete loss. *How had things spiraled out
of control so fast?* Time seemed to slow around him. Glo had begun to
cast a spell, but it wouldn't be in time. Lloyd hunkered over Andrella,
trying to shield her with his body. Seth and Xellos were in mid-tum-
ble, trying to get away from the blast.

An earsplitting scream erupted in the midst of them all. It was
Alys, her sonic cry rushing upward to collide head-on with the glacial
blast. For a few seconds it looked as if Alys' sonic shield would hold,
but then the arctic breath overwhelmed it, sweeping it aside as if it
were a child's toy.

Yet, Alys had bought them a bit of time, at least enough for Glo
to cast. A translucent globe of shimmering mana formed around the
tall elf, stretching nearly a dozen feet in all directions. Glo held his
hands aloft as if propping up the impromptu barrier. At the same
time he cried over his shoulder, "Lloyd, get them out of here!"

The barrage of ice and sleet slammed into the edge of the globe,
pressing relentlessly down upon it. The translucent sphere began to
bend beneath the weight of the dragon's breath.

At the same moment, Lloyd grabbed Andrella and rushed to
Alys' side; the songstress had been knocked out cold after her sonic
shield shattered. The spiritblade placed a hand on them both, then
went still as he reached into his soul.

Suddenly the globe broke. It shattered into a million pieces and
sent Glo staggering backward. A moment later, the glacial blast
slammed into the ground, engulfing everything in its wake.

Aksel nearly choked. He doubted anyone could have survived
that arctic blast. Just then, something caught the corner of his eye.
Lloyd, Andrella, and Alys lay on the ground just a few yards away
from him.

Aksel breathed a sigh of relief. *Lloyd must have teleported them out of
the way at the very last moment.* His relief lasted only a moment though.
Glo.

The glacial blast finally subsided and the subsequent snow cloud swiftly settled. A layer of snow and ice now covered the ground in a twenty-foot radius. Near the center stood a solitary figure that looked remarkably like an ice sculpture. It took a moment for it to register in his mind, but Aksel quickly realized that it was Glo! The elf had been frozen solid by the dragon's arctic breath.

Aksel's heart thumped wildly in his chest as his greatest fear was realized. He had lost someone once again—this time a dear friend.

Seth was mortified—not that he had dusted that vamp, mind you. He had always intended to do so, just not in front of the giant dragon. He didn't want to risk angering it, but his reflexes had betrayed him and he had done just that.

Seth still couldn't believe his actions had led to the death of his friend. Oh, sure, Glo was a pain in the ass sometimes, and Seth loved to tease him, but he was still his friend. Worse than that, the rest of his friends were about to join Glo.

As Glo stood there like a frozen popsicle, Lloyd completely lost it. After saving Andrella and Alys from a similar fate, he turned and lit his blades on fire while screaming at the dragon, "You bastard! You killed my friend!"

Seth could see that Lloyd was seconds away from launching himself at the dragon. He had to do something. What happened to Glo was his fault, and it was up to Seth to make it right. Thankfully, the dragon decided to talk instead of attacking again, buying Seth some much-needed time.

The dragon gazed down at Lloyd, responding in that cold, detached voice. "Well, now we are even. You killed my butler and your friend paid the price. Do you wish to join him?"

Seth wasted no time. He rushed toward the dragon, not even bothering to turn invisible. It probably wouldn't have helped anyway. Dragons had uncanny senses that made them nearly impossible to sneak past.

Andrella bought Seth a few more crucial seconds. She grabbed Lloyd by the arm and desperately tried to reason with him.

Still, the dragon chose to ignore Seth. He was certain it sensed him, but probably thought of him as no threat. *Well, it was about to find out it was wrong—dead wrong.*

Seth almost laughed at his own joke, but concentration was key at this moment. Finally reaching the dragon's foreleg, he did the one thing Glo had warned him against. He pulled out both portal bags and shoved the second one inside the first.

The results were nothing short of spectacular. The air around the bag in his hand stretched and distorted. It was all Seth could do to hold onto it. A moment later, the distortion erupted. A jagged rip spread through the air in all directions, engulfing him and the lower half of the dragon's leg.

Seth hung suspended in the center of that rift for a few seconds. He thought he heard someone call his name before the world imploded around him and everything went black.

Lloyd felt torn inside. Though relieved at having saved Andrella and Alys, he nonetheless felt as if a part of him had been ripped away.

Glo is dead.

The words passed through Lloyd's mind, but they still hadn't quite registered. He and Glo had been much alike. They both came from noble backgrounds. Each had concentrated solely on their craft, neglecting any worldly experience. Both had demanding fathers and left home to prove themselves.

Losing Glo was like losing a brother. Lloyd had been quite young when Thea died, too young to have made a difference. Yet now he was a spiritblade—warrior and protector. He should have been able to do something to save Glo.

Something abruptly burst inside Lloyd. He may have not been strong enough, nor fast enough, to save his friend, but he would avenge him. A cold fire spread inside of Lloyd as he spun about to face the dragon. He screamed up at it, "You bastard! You killed my friend!"

The cold flames traveled through Lloyd's arms and into his

blades, lighting them on fire. Something was different about the fire this time, though—traces of black flickered within the normal red and yellow flames.

Seemingly unfazed by his declaration, the dragon spoke once again in that cold voice. "Well, now we are even. You killed my butler and your friend has paid the price. Do you wish to join him?"

Infuriated even further by the dragon's apparent lack of caring, Lloyd invoked his cloak. He crouched to launch himself upward when he felt a hand on his arm. Andrella stood just behind him, her eyes filled with moisture and wet streaks running down to her chin. She gazed at him pleadingly, her voice choked with emotion.

"Please don't. I can't lose you, too."

Feeling as if he were going to explode, Lloyd clenched his fists and clamped his eyes shut. Desperate to avenge his fallen friend, inside he knew he had little chance of succeeding. Yet what good was he if he couldn't protect those he loved?

He opened his eyes as a gentle hand touched his face. "I know," Andrella choked out the words. "I miss him, too."

A sudden explosion made Lloyd whirl about. The air around the dragon's leg had ripped open. The strange phenomenon looked familiar, like the rift his mother had used to catch one of those stone dragons. Lloyd's eyes abruptly locked on a figure in the midst of the rift. *That's Seth!*

Aksel cried out their friend's name in anguish just before the rift imploded in upon itself. With a loud *whooshing* sound it was gone, along with Seth and the lower portion of the dragon's leg.

Feeling suddenly numb, Lloyd dropped to his knees, his blades falling from his hands. He stared at the air where Seth had just been, wondering to himself, *Did that really just happen?*

Andrella knelt by his side and wrapped her arms around his waist. More tears flowed from her eyes as she sobbed into his chest, "Oh, Lloyd. I am so sorry. So, very, very sorry."

The two of them knelt there together, everything around them feeling surreal. Lloyd watched unfeeling as the dragon peered with detached curiosity at the missing lower half of its leg. "Well, you are more clever than I imagined."

Without warning, the dragon's body began to glow. It turned almost white, then shrank and changed form. When the light faded, the dragon had shifted into a beautiful silver-haired woman. The woman wore a sleeveless silver gown that reached down to the floor. Upon her head she wore a silver crown laced with fine jewels. Her one arm ended in a stump at her elbow, but she ignored it as she approached them.

Stopping a few feet from them, the strange silver-haired woman peered down at them with no sign of emotion. "You may yet be of some use to me."

Lloyd still felt too numb to utter a word, but Andrella managed to speak for them. "Who are you?"

The woman peered down at her quizzically, a strange light in her eyes. "Why, it is as my butler said. I am Jinkolothos."

So the butler hadn't been lying after all. The dragon was the true mistress of the keep. Somehow, the realization did little to console Lloyd.

Andrella wiped the tears from her eyes, and rose to face the strange woman. "What do you mean, 'of use'?"

Jinkolothos peered off into the distance as if her mind had traveled far away. Her voice sounded hollow as she spoke. "Time has taken far too much from me—my love, my son, and now my castle."

She peered back at them, a cold intensity in her eyes that hadn't been there before. "You will go to the temple. Beneath it, you will find the artifact you seek. Remove the staff. It does not belong there."

Andrella stared back at the woman, her face contorted in a mask of confusion. "Do you mean the Staff of Law?"

Jinkolothos responded with a curt nod. "Yes. You will remove it—and soon. Once the Heart of Darkness fully appears in the material plane, the vampire lord will release his hordes." Her eyes grew hard and her voice took on a dangerous edge. "Yet, if you do not remove the staff before then, I will personally destroy your city."

Stunned by the deadly declaration, Lloyd shot to his feet. He fixed the woman with an incredulous stare. "Why would you do that?"

Jinkolothos turned to meet his gaze, her eyes still filled with that same cold intensity. "There is something buried there that I seek. Something that belongs to me."

Ever the diplomat, Andrella tried to reason with the cold-hearted dragon. "If we do this, can you stop the vampire lord? Surely you are far more powerful than he."

For the first time since they met Jinkolothos, Lloyd saw an emotion cross her face. In fact it was more than one, fear mixed with underlying anger.

"He was once my servant, but he betrayed me. He now serves another, one more powerful than I," Jinkolothos confided in them. The seeming chink in her armor abruptly disappeared, replaced again with that cold demeanor. "Enough. Remove the staff."

Lloyd tensed as Jinkolothos began to trace a symbol through the air. He swiftly picked up his blades, but Andrella placed a staying hand on his shoulder as he rose. "She's not attacking us," she explained with a wan smile. Still tense, Lloyd placed an arm around Andrella's waist as the spell released.

A spinning vortex of purple energy expanded out from Jinkolothos, engulfing them all. The world around them disappeared, replaced with that same black emptiness where Aksel had taken them previously. Lloyd held Andrella tight as they moved through that dark place, until they 'fell' once more.

They landed in the graveyard inside of Penwick. It was still nighttime outside, but more of the castle was now visible through the giant black sphere that hung over the graveyard.

Lloyd swept his eyes around the yard. Jinkolothos had brought all of them back, even Glo's frozen body. Alys lay on the ground, still out cold from her clash with the dragon's breath. Aksel knelt off to one side, a haunted look upon his face. Xellos stood off opposite Aksel, his head hung low and his face hidden beneath his cowl.

Jinkolothos swept her eyes around the night sky, a look of wonderment in her eyes. "It's been a while since I've been outside. It's beautiful out here." She paused a moment as if considering her next move. For a moment, Lloyd thought she had changed her mind about destroying Penwick, but then her voice turned cold again. "It's a shame it will all be gone soon."

Lloyd felt empty inside as the dragon woman cast another spell and disappeared from sight.

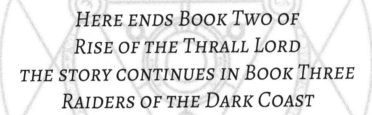

HERE ENDS BOOK TWO OF
RISE OF THE THRALL LORD
THE STORY CONTINUES IN BOOK THREE
RAIDERS OF THE DARK COAST

ABOUT THE AUTHOR

F.P. Spirit writes high fantasy fiction inspired by the likes of Tolkien, Eddings, Brooks, and Piers Anthony. An avid science fiction fan, he became hooked on fantasy the moment he cracked open the Lord of the Rings in high school. When he is not writing, F.P. is either spending time with his wife and sons, gaming, doing yoga, Tai Chi, or walking their dog.

A long-time lover of fantasy and the surreal, he hopes you enjoy his fun contributions to the world of fantasy and magic.

You can learn more about F.P. Spirit by visiting his website at:
Fpspirit.com